One Last Summer

One Last Summer

CATRIN COLLIER

First published in Great Britain in 2007 by Orion Books,
an imprint of The Orion Publishing Group Ltd
Orion House, 5 Upper Saint Martin's Lane
London, WC2H 9EA

1 3 5 7 9 10 8 6 4 2

A CIP catalogue record for this book
is available from the British Library.

ISBN: 978 0 75288 577 3 (HB)
978 0 75288 578 0 (TPB)

Typeset by Deltatype Ltd, Birkenhead, Merseyside

Printed in Great Britain by Mackays of Chatham plc, Chatham, Kent

The Orion Publishing Group's policy is to use papers that
are natural, renewable and recyclable products and made
from wood grown in sustainable forests. The logging and
manufacturing processes are expected to conform to the
environmental regulations of the country of origin.

www.orionbooks.co.uk

For my grandmother, Martha Gertrude Salewski, née
Plewe, who, during the Hitler years, lost husband,
daughter, mother, brother, two sisters, nieces, nephews,
friends, home, country, all her material possessions;
and who survived to teach me that money has no real
value and that I should spend every penny I earn lest the
Russians come and take it from me.

I am no longer afraid of the Russians — in fact, I love their
country and them — but, Liebe Omi, I learned the lesson
you taught me too well.

Also for my great-grandmother, Amalia Plewe, née
Mau, who disappeared, along with her daughter Gretel,
granddaughter Gisela and tens of thousands of other East
Prussian civilians and German soldiers in Königsberg in
January 1945. May they rest in peace wherever they lie.

Acknowledgements

My mother, Gerda Jones, née Salewski, for allowing me access to her own and my grandmother's diaries. I am indebted to her for the information they contain.

Helen Rodzina and her family in Oltszyn, at one time Allenstein, for their warmth and generous Polish hospitality, and for allowing my mother and me to stay in her apartment in the house that my grandfather, Albert Salewski, architect, master builder and a past burgomaster of Allenstein, designed and built for his family in 1936.

My agent Philip Patterson for picking out the manuscript of *One Last Summer* after it had lain for ten years in my 'unpublished' drawer. Philip, please take another look – there are several others there!

Absolutely everyone at Orion, but especially my editor Yvette Goulden, Juliet Ewers and Susan Lamb for reading the manuscript in the early stages and boldly daring to publish a book about the 'other side' of my family, and Rachel Leyshon for her incisive suggestions and meticulous copy-editing.

And the Polish people, who extended a warm welcome to a traveller who not only wanted to visit their country, but also the past.

Thank you.

Catrin Collier,
November 2006

Author's Note

I have changed the names of Grunwaldsee and Bergensee. Both houses
exist – Bergensee massive, imposing and regal even in dereliction;
Grunwaldsee restored to pristine condition – but neither are in the
locations I have placed them.

The Adolfs' house still stands in Olsztyn on the site I describe, in
the same street as the abandoned synagogue, next to the old Jewish
cemetery that, according to eyewitness testimony, was excavated by
the Polish Communist regime in the early 1970s. Several truck-loads
of valuables hidden in family graves by Jews prior to their war-time
deportation to concentration camps, were taken away, and the coffins
and corpses stripped of precious metals and jewellery. Even the bones
and coffins were removed. Today the site remains, a rough piece of
pockmarked wasteland between a street dominated by post-war, tower
block housing and a flea market.

The final death toll of conspirators involved in the von Stauffenberg
plot to assassinate Hitler may never be known. The army officers concerned had either witnessed the atrocities on the civilian populations
of Eastern Europe carried out by all branches of the German army,
including the Wehrmacht, or heard first-hand accounts. They felt they
had no option but to break their oath of loyalty to Hitler, just as Hitler
had broken his oath to the German people. Their intention was to sue
for peace.

Prior to the failed attempt, the conspirators contacted the Allies in
the hope of negotiating an end to the war. After the plot's failure, the
BBC broadcast lists of the conspirators, which proved useful to Hitler, as
not all were known to the Nazis. The failed plot was used as an excuse to
detain everyone who opposed Hitler. Over seven thousand people were
arrested and, by April 1945, five thousand had been executed. Over
two hundred army officers were sentenced to death in the infamous
'People's Court' between 20 July 1944 and 21 December 1944, before

the judge, Roland Friesler, was killed in an Allied air raid. Hitler initially intended to conduct 'show trials' modelled on the Soviet show trials of the 1930s with radio and film coverage. He later changed his mind and, on 17 August 1944, forbade any further reporting of the trials. From that date not even the executions were publicly announced.

Colonel Claus Schenk Graf von Stauffenberg, his aide, Lieutenant Werner von Haeften, General Friedrich Olbricht and General Staff Colonel Albrecht Ritter Mertz von Quirnheim were executed by firing squad on the night of 20 July 1944 in the courtyard of the headquarters of the reserve army in the Bendlerstrausse. Others weren't so fortunate. After their trials, civilians were guillotined, and military personnel stripped naked, hung and slowly strangled on piano wire, before being taken down, revived, and the process repeated, on occasions, several times before they died. Their ordeals were filmed on the personal orders of Hitler and the films shown to the staff in Hitler's HQ.

Thousands of relatives of the conspirators, principally women and the elderly, were separated from their children and one another, and incarcerated in 'VIP' blocks in prisons and concentration camps. The children of conspirators were taken to State-run camps and orphanages where attempts were made to make them forget their families and identities. Not all, but most – including Claus von Stauffenberg's wife, Nina, and his five children – survived the war.

The Gauleiter of East Prussia, Erich Koch, who insisted that East Prussia would not fall to the Russians, ordered the civilian population to stay in their towns and villages. He supervised the loading of two railway wagons with his own possessions and sent them into the Reich in December 1945 before flying to Libau where two ice-breakers were waiting to evacuate him and his staff. Although there was room in both vessels he refused to allow any refugees on board. He changed out of his Nazi uniform into field grey and evaded capture until 1949 when he was detained by the British. A brutal administrator in the Ukraine and Poland, he was handed over to the Polish authorities. The Soviets believed that Koch knew the location of the Amber Room that the Nazis had stripped from the palace of Tsarskoe Selo near Leningrad, and asked for Koch's extradition. The Polish authorities refused. If Koch knew the location of the Amber Room he never revealed it. His trial took place in Warsaw in October 1958. Found guilty of causing the deaths of 400,000 Poles (he wasn't tried for his crimes in the Ukraine) he was sentenced to death on 9 March 1959. This was later commuted to life imprisonment. Some believe he traded his life in exchange for details of the location of looted Nazi treasure. Erich Koch died in prison in Barczewo near Olsztyn (formerly Allenstein) in the heart of old East Prussia on 12 November 1986.

It is estimated that between forty and fifty million people died in the carnage of the Second World War, eleven million in concentration camps. More than half died after Colonel von Stauffenberg's failed attempt on Hitler's life on 20th July 1944.

Of five million Russian soldiers captured by the Germans, one million and fifty thousand survived the war to be executed or exiled to the Siberian gulag for periods of ten years or more by Stalin.

Eighteen per cent of the Polish population, over six million Poles, were killed in the Second World War, either by the invading German or Russian armies.

Between two and three million East Prussian civilians died during the invasion of East Prussia by the Soviet Army. Those who were not massacred died from starvation, cold and frostbite on their flight. (The Russian soldiers were told that East Prussia was the lair of the fascist beast, and they were as brutal in their treatment of the civilian population as the German death squads had been in Russia.)

Estimates vary as to how many German soldiers who surrendered to the Americans died in the American-run prisoner of war camps. Recently released documents suggest between 100,000 and 200,000, some as young as fourteen years of age. The camps were identical to those set up by the Germans for the Russian prisoners of war; open fields, with no water or latrines. The Americans fed the prisoners what is, in retrospect, recognized as below-subsistence level rations.

Some historians are undecided as to whether the atrocities at Nemmersdorf in East Prussia were committed by the invading Russian army in retaliation for atrocities committed by the German army in Russia, or the SS in a last-ditch attempt to galvanize the East Prussians into fighting for every inch of their country.

I wrote *One Last Summer* to put a human face on statistics I have difficulty in comprehending, even after seeing the memorials in Poland. I used archive material and private, family documents, principally the diaries of my grandmother and my mother, written between 1936 and 1948.

All the experiences and wartime events depicted in *One Last Summer* actually occurred. Charlotte von Datski and her family are typical of many Prussian Junker aristocrats of the period, but, aside from the well-known personalities, all the characters are creations of my imagination.

The inspiration for *One Last Summer* came in 1995, when I accompanied my mother to the home her family fled in 1945. The Polish Rodzina family, who now occupy part of the house (after it had been used as a Russian commander's HQ for several years it was divided into apartments), welcomed us as if we were lifelong friends. They not only allowed my mother and I to stay in the dream house that my grandfather had built for his family, but also to sleep in my mother's old bedroom.

I sat and listened while they and my mother exchanged wartime experiences. The farm the family had lived on for generations was taken from them at the end of the war by the Russians and given to a displaced Russian family. They were told to 'go north', search for an empty house or farm and occupy it, which they did.

In 1947, the Allies removed the name Prussia, which dated from 300 BC, from the map of Europe. With the exception of East Prussia, Prussia's lands were divided between the four Allied zones of occupation in Germany; French, British, American and the Union of Soviet Socialist Republics (USSR). Poland absorbed most of East Prussia, apart from the north-east, which was annexed by the USSR. The capital, Königsberg was renamed Kaliningrad after Mikhail Kalinin, the President of the Supreme Soviet. Russians came from all over the USSR, especially Siberia, to settle in the city. It remains part of Belorussia.

On 11 February 1945 at the Yalta Conference, Churchill, Roosevelt and Stalin resolved that German forced labour was legitimate war reparation. All the allies benefited from this declaration. Stalin ordered the deportation of the remaining ethnic Germans, both men and women, from Romania, Yugoslavia, Hungary, East Prussia, Pomerania and Silesia, and sent them into slave labour in the Soviet Union. The last 25,000 were transported in 1947–8. Of the one million Germans who entered the eastern provinces of the Soviet Union and the gulag prison system, only 55 per cent survived. Once East Prussia was ethnically cleansed of its German natives, the German place names were changed to Russian or Polish.

As the child and grandchild of 'refugees' I grew up aware that although my mother and grandmother had made every effort to adapt to their new post-war lives, they never recovered from their sense of loss, or the pain of being exiled from their beloved homeland where our family had lived and worked for centuries.

One Last Summer

Chapter 1

SATURDAY, 19 AUGUST 1939

My eighteenth birthday. No one can call me a child, or tell me that I'm too young for balls or parties ever again. Mama married Papa when she was eighteen, but she didn't have a career to think about, like me. I wonder why Greta didn't consider studying for a profession instead of becoming a BDM leader. All she ever does is organize group meetings for young girls and teach sewing and cookery — not that she is an expert chef or dressmaker.

No one is likely to propose to her now. She'll be twenty-seven this year, quite the old maid. She won't like having to make way for a sister who is every bit as eligible to receive the attentions of young men as herself.

Herr Schumacher mustered the entire orchestra to play the birthday song to me at six o'clock this morning. They blocked the corridor outside our carriage for twenty minutes. It was impossible to go up or down the train to the bathrooms or dining car, but no one seemed to mind, least of all the stewards. Afterwards I received birthday congratulations and presents from everyone, including roses and chocolates from Manfred and Georg, silly boys that they are, and I still have the most important ones waiting to be opened at home. I can't wait to see my birthday table set up next to Wilhelm and Paul's in the hall.

Hildegarde and Nina gave me this beautiful book, and Irena an elegant silver fountain pen embossed with roses. I've decided to use the book as a diary. When Greta discovered that I'd started one last year, she told me only important people keep diaries. Well, I consider myself important, and I know I'll be famous one day.

Herr Schumacher says I'm the most gifted member, not only of the musical section of the Allensteiner Hitler Youth but also of every other youth orchestra he's ever worked with. He insisted that I played a piano solo

1

as a finale to each concert as well as accompanying the Komsomol's star violinist. Now my mind is quite made up. When I complete my studies, I will become an international concert pianist.

My writing doesn't look as well as I'd like because the train shakes so. Hildegarde, Irena, Nina and I are sharing a carriage and, after the steward folded away the beds when my birthday concert finished this morning, everyone crammed in. They stayed for over an hour, even the boys. They're so juvenile compared with my brothers and their friends. Wilhelm and Paul would never have put violin resin in Herr Schumacher's tea, or crawled under the table in the dining car to paint his shoes with honey while he ate.

As Papa says, it was very clever of Mama to present him with me on the twins' birthday, so they can be twenty-one and I can be eighteen on the same day. Grown-up gentlemen and lady at last. What celebrations there will be tonight! And afterwards we'll have what's left of the summer together. I am _so_ looking forward to going to Königsberg with Wilhelm and Paul in October. I was very lucky to have gained a place at the conservatory, especially as the quota of further education places for girls has been cut to 10 per cent. I don't care what anyone says, I think it's unfair, and I don't believe our Führer did it. I think it was one of his ministers and our Führer doesn't even know about it.

Poor Irena did not get into Königsberg or any other conservatory, and will have to work in her father's office. It will be dreadful to leave her behind in Allenstein. We have been best friends ever since I can remember, just like our fathers before us, and I can't imagine what it will be like only to see her in the holidays.

Although the twins will be in their third year of studies and I'll only be in my first, they've promised to introduce me to all their friends. Paul says the music conservatory isn't far from the university. I do hope Papa's found us lodgings together. What fun we'll have without Greta to stop us.

We left Moscow early yesterday morning and I'm beginning to think we'll never reach Allenstein. Nina says she feels as though this is hell and we're doomed to clank around the countryside cooped up on this train like cursed souls for all eternity. (Nina has always had a morbid imagination; perhaps her fixation on the clanking is down to her father's job as a train driver.)

Irena has asked me three times in the last ten minutes if I think Wilhelm will meet me at the station. I wish she wouldn't make sheep's eyes at my brother every time she sees him. It's _so_ embarrassing for the rest of us to watch.

We crossed the border at dawn. I was glad to be in dear, familiar East Prussian countryside after a whole month away, even at that time in the morning. I hadn't realized how much I'd missed the forests and lakes until we saw them through the windows. Everything — the people, the architecture, the streets in the towns and villages — looks so much more orderly and prosperous than in Russia.

I was sorry to leave Masha. I enjoyed living with the Beletskys in their Moscow apartment for the final week of our tour. No one else liked their Russian family half as much but I think Herr Schumacher arranged for me to have the best available accommodation. Masha and her brother, Alexander, who is white-blond, blue-eyed and very good-looking for a Russian, as well as being an excellent musician, came to the station to see me off. They gave me an amber necklace of enormous, polished, solid nuggets — some with insects in — as a parting gift. It is longer and more beautiful than anything Greta has.

I promised to treasure it and think of them every time I wear it. How envious Greta will be when she sees it. Will she be at Allenstein station? I hope not. I do expect Wilhelm and Paul to be there to meet me, though, and, if I'm lucky, they'll bring at least one (hopefully the special one) of their friends.

It feels as though I've been away for ever. I can't wait to feast my eyes on the dear, dear house and hug Papa, Mama and the twins ...

'The doctor will see you now, Ms Datski.'

'Thank you.' Charlotte smiled at the nurse and closed the diary. The once-clean and pristine glossy pages had become fragile with age. She wrapped the book carefully in a silk scarf and gathered her shawl and handbag from the chair beside her. Ridiculous, really, to take a diary she hadn't opened in years into a doctor's waiting room. And strange how those few words had brought it all back: the rattling of the train; the smut-filled smoke from the funnel drifting past the window; the smell of cabbage and gravy wafting down the corridor from the dining car; her friends' faces, scrubbed, beaming, devoid of pain and experience; and herself, hopelessly naive, romantic and pompous with all the arrogant superiority of youth. Was there anything left of that young girl in the old woman she'd become?

'How are you, Charlotte?' Dr David Andrews left his chair and walked out from behind his desk to greet her.

'I came here in the hope that you could answer that question for me, David.'

'Well, you certainly look as elegant and beautiful as ever.'

'No one my age can possibly be regarded as beautiful. As for elegant, you make me sound like an expensively decorated salon.'

He shook her hand and returned to his chair. To avoid meeting her gaze, he studied the painting on the wall behind her. It had been hung by the New York interior designer who had remodelled his office suite a year ago, but this was the first time he had really looked at the bland, pastel-shaded, impressionist scene of fuzzy children playing on sands. He decided he didn't like it.

'Well, David?' she prompted.

He cleared his throat and began speaking, conscious that his voice was brisker and colder than he'd intended. 'I'd suggest a second opinion. I know a good man in Boston and another in New York. I can arrange a consult in either city. You could combine a visit with a little shopping, or visit a gallery.'

'And these "good men" of yours would find it easier to tell me what you can't bring yourself to say?'

He forced himself to look into her eyes. Startlingly blue and disconcertingly clear. He would have found it easier to cope with hysterics. He could have prescribed tranquillizers for hysteria.

'How long do I have?'

'Most people ask what can be done.'

'I am not most people, David.'

'You never were.' No one in their eighties had the right to look the way Charlotte Datski did. It wasn't as though she even tried to look younger. Her hair was unashamedly silver without a hint of artificial colour or blue-rinse, her skin wrinkled, untouched by cosmetic surgery or face lifts, yet it didn't seem to matter. Her beauty came from some mysterious, inner glow that manifested itself in those magnificent eyes. Her figure – tall, slender and straight-backed – still retained the elasticity of youth, and her long, flowing clothes were

4

accentuated by amber beads and multi-coloured scarves that would have looked tawdry on anyone else, yet so right on her.

When his father had introduced them thirty years ago, he had known instinctively that Charlotte was an artist. She simply couldn't have been anything else. And although she was the same age as his mother, he had joined his father and half the men of their acquaintance in falling a little in love with her. But unlike most widows, Charlotte Datski cherished her unmarried state, apparently relishing the independence it gave her. Even the rumours of affairs had remained just that – rumours. If Charlotte had taken lovers, she had chosen wisely. None of the men in their circle had ever spoken of a relationship, consummated or otherwise.

'The truth, David.' She fingered the beads around her neck, but there was no sign of nervousness in the gesture.

'It might be cancer of the pancreas,' he began cautiously, 'but, as I said, you should seek a second opinion.'

'You think you've made a mistake?'

'No doctor can be one hundred per cent certain of a diagnosis, especially one like this,' he hedged.

'David, you're the genius in a family of gifted academics. I'll take your word for it.'

'Even so, it's far from straightforward. There's no sign of a tumour, which means it's invasive. In simplified terms, the cancer can be likened to a spider's web of cells that has spread throughout the organ. Surgery is out of the question, but that doesn't mean we can't offer treatment. Initial tests suggest it's slow-growing and that chemotherapy—'

'Will there be much pain?' she interrupted.

'In my experience of similar conditions in other patients, very little. You might lose weight.'

'I can afford to,' she commented wryly. 'How long do I have?' she repeated.

'I hate that question. Twenty years ago I told a nurse at this hospital that she had six months. I still blush every time I see her.' Her silence brought the realization that his remarks were both patronizing and fatuous. 'If the treatment's successful, years.'

'And if it's not?'

'It will be successful, Charlotte.'

'But if it's not?' she repeated stubbornly.

'Difficult to say: six months, a year perhaps. But I'll arrange for you to be admitted this week and we'll start the injections right away. It won't be pleasant but—'

'I can't come in tomorrow.'

'I understand. A diagnosis like this is a shock; you have arrangements to make.' He flicked through his diary. 'Shall we say Thursday morning?'

'No.'

'Charlotte, nothing takes precedence over this. We're talking about your life.'

'I have to go home.'

'It's five miles up the road,' he pointed out in exasperation.

'I was born in Eastern Europe.'

'As your doctor, I strongly caution you against making any trips until you've completed the treatment.'

'I may have left it too late as it is.'

'You don't seem to understand. You could die.'

'We're all going to do that, David,' she smiled. 'I know you're thinking of me and you mean well, but this is not the first time I've faced death. The experience made me strangely unafraid of the inevitable.'

'Are you telling me you *want* to die?' He forced himself to meet her steady gaze.

'Far from it. I love life. Every wonderful, colour-filled moment. But I've discovered there are worse things than coming to an end. Like dehumanizing pain and loss of dignity. I watched my husband die of cancer. Forgive my cynicism, but I believe he suffered more from the treatment meted out to him by well-meaning doctors than the disease itself. If he'd still owned a gun he would have shot himself months before they allowed him to drift into a coma.'

It was the first time David had heard Charlotte mention her late husband in all the years he'd known her. She'd lived in the States for decades and he knew of no one who'd met him. 'Treatments have progressed enormously in the last thirty years.'

'I don't doubt it.'

'You can't expect me to stand by and do nothing,' he pleaded.

'At my age, quality of life is more important than quantity.'

'You could have both.'

'You guarantee it?'

'No physician can offer guarantees,' he said uneasily, 'but I believe you have a better chance than most of beating this. You've enjoyed excellent health until now. You've taken care of yourself and, as the cancer didn't show up on your last routine check-up, we can take this as an early diagnosis. Everything is on our side.'

'Would I remain much the same as I am now, without chemo-therapy?'

'You'd tire easily and sleep longer.'

'I wouldn't suffer pain?'

He gritted his teeth, not wanting to give her further excuse to avoid treatment. 'Nothing a few painkillers couldn't help you cope with,' he conceded reluctantly.

'I'll buy some. Thank you for your time and your honesty.' She picked up her shawl.

'My father would love to see you.' He followed her to the door. 'Please, dine with us this evening.'

'So your father can add his persuasive voice to yours? Thank you, but no, David.' She held out her hand and he took it. 'They say life is short, but from where I'm standing it seems long. Too long, when I think of all those I have loved and lost. I appreciate your understanding. A little more practice and you'll be able to add sympathetic to your other qualifications. Send your bill to my lawyer.'

'Isn't there anything that I can say to convince you to begin treatment?'

'Nothing. And as it's common knowledge that I'm a stubborn, impossible old woman, you've no reason to feel guilty. As soon as I can book a flight, I will leave for Europe. I've been planning this trip for years. You've just given me a reason not to delay any longer. You won't tell my grandson or anyone else about this?'

'Unfortunately, as you well know, I can't without your permission. We will see you again?' It was a plea more than a question.

She didn't answer. Kissing him lightly on the cheek, she murmured, 'That's for your father.'

He stood at his window and watched as she left the building, her long black skirt and autumn-coloured scarves blowing in the breeze.

'Doctor Andrews?'

He turned to see his nurse in the doorway behind him. 'Shall I contact Boston or New York to arrange an appointment for Ms Datski?'

'No,' he answered abruptly.

'Then I'll phone admissions to arrange a bed?'

'No.'

'But—'

'Send in the next patient.'

'And Ms Datski?'

'Keep her file to hand, and hope that we need it.'

Charlotte drove home slowly, observing the speed limit for the first time in years. When she realized the irony of what she was doing, she laughed out loud. After receiving the news David had just given her, she should be careering recklessly into whatever time she had left, instead of crawling cautiously along in the slow lane. But she was going home for the first time in over sixty years and it suddenly seemed very important that she get there in one piece.

She stopped her car at the head of the private drive that meandered through the woods towards her New England clapboard house. The leaves of the bulbs she had planted when she had bought the place thirty-six years before were withering into the mulch beneath the trees. Every spring a carpet of daffodils, crocuses and bluebells spread colour down to the banks of the lake. Their end marked the advent of summer.

Opening her window, she checked her mailbox, taking time to breathe in the scent of the pinewoods and the lake beyond the house. Was it her imagination or could she smell the last of the cherry and apple blossom? Fragrances that reminded her of a country which no longer existed. But then, everything she had created here had been built and planted to that end, resulting in a flickering reflection, no more substantial than that of an image caught on the surface of a pond, of a home she had loved and been forced to abandon sixty years before.

Closing her mind to her memories, she took her mail and drove on over the rough track towards the house. Leaving her car on the gravel driveway, she opened her front door and walked through to the kitchen. She filled the kettle before thinking better of the idea. There was a bottle of white wine in the fridge, and she carried it and her letters up the stairs to her studio.

It was her favourite room. Covering the whole of the first floor, one-third of the space had been given over to open deck; another third was glassed in like an English conservatory, leaving the wall in the remaining third to prop up her paintings. Glancing at the completed canvases she'd spread out that morning, she congratulated herself on a job well done, before opening the wine and curling into a wickerwork chair with her mail.

She dropped three unopened circulars into the bin before finding one she wanted to read – a large, fat envelope from her English granddaughter. After years of exchanging daily e-mails she was amazed Laura had consigned anything to the post. She cut it open with her thumbnail and extracted a file marked 'Grunwaldsee'. She opened it and a sheaf of photocopies dropped out. She unfolded them. There was no mistaking what they were: documents with passport-sized photographs overlaid with official stamps decorated with the eagle and swastika of the Third Reich. Images of her father, mother, her brothers Wilhelm and Paul, her sister Greta, and herself, impossibly young, stared up at her. All six locked into a past she had never entirely escaped.

> Dear Oma,
>
> This is the most difficult letter I've ever had to write. Please, don't ignore it, or the copies of the documents and the questions they raise, as I'm sure Aunt Greta and my father would do.
>
> I came across the original of this file in the Berlin Document Center when I was researching a documentary – it doesn't matter what. I don't have to ask if you and Aunt Greta were members of the Nazi Party; these papers prove you were. I would like to know why you joined and more about your life in Grunwaldsee ...

Charlotte shuddered and turned back to the photocopies. If she had suspected their existence she would have ... what? Told Laura and Claus about the past? Burdened them with secrets that haunted her?

... I am not asking just for myself but for the entire family, especially Claus's unborn child, because, in time, he or she will ask questions, just as I am doing now. No matter how father and Aunt Greta try to pretend that the war and Hitler are ancient history and of no consequence to generations born after the events, it simply isn't true. We deserve to know the truth and hear it first-hand, not stumble across it in a dusty file as I have done.

Please, Oma, I love you so much, and a part of that love is respect. I want to continue feeling that way about you and I won't until I hear your side of the story ...

Charlotte glanced across at the canvases she had taken such pleasure in a moment before. Could she offer Laura the truth as an explanation that would bring a degree of understanding from her granddaughter? Forgiveness was too much to hope for. She had never been able to forgive herself for joining the National Socialist Party. As a result she had never left the past behind her. But the blame, guilt and regrets were entirely hers – not her grandchildren's. There had to be some way of making Laura see that much.

I love you so much, and a part of that love is respect.

Dropping the letter and photocopies into her lap, she picked up the telephone and, without even checking the time difference, dialled Laura's mobile; it was answered on the sixth ring.

'Laura, can you talk?'

'Yes.' Her granddaughter's voice was thick with sleep.

'I woke you?'

'No ...'

'Please, don't lie to me, not even about small things. I received your letter. Are you still in Berlin?'

'Yes.'

'I'll be with you in a few days. I'll get a flight as soon as I can. I'm going home – to East Prussia,' she explained to the silence. 'And I'd like you to come with me, but I'll understand if you don't want to.'

'You'll tell me—'

'Everything,' Charlotte interrupted, 'but not on the telephone. Can you spare the time to accompany me?'

'Yes, of course.'

'I'll let you know when I'll be in Berlin. Before I see you, I need to talk to your father and to Uncle Erich.'

'When you see my parents, give them my love.'

'I will, but I intend to stay in England for only one day.'

'Oma ...' there was only the slightest hesitation, 'thank you.'

'I love you.'

Charlotte hung up, then flicked through the directory before dialling a second time. The bookings and arrangements with her agent's office proved more straightforward than she'd expected. Suddenly she realized she had very little time to pack, sort through her possessions and plan what she was going to say to Erich and Jeremy. But lost in the past, she continued to sit and stare blindly out over the lake.

'Oma, you upstairs?'

Shaking herself from her reverie, Charlotte pushed the photocopies and Laura's letter beneath the cushion of her chair and composed herself. Claus always had been far too sensitive to her moods for her peace of mind.

'Up here, Claus,' she called in a voice she'd intended to sound light, but came out brittle. Forcing a smile, she relegated all thoughts of Laura's letter into the 'think about later' compartment of her mind, which she had filled to capacity with painful memories and problems over the years. Hopefully, there would be enough time left for her to deal with all of them.

Her grandson climbed the stairs, his massive, raw-boned clumsiness making her tremble for the safety of her paintings.

'I saw the car ...' A frown furrowed his forehead as he lumbered towards her. 'Wine in the middle of the day? You celebrating, or drowning your sorrows?'

'Celebrating.'

'You don't have stomach ulcers?'

'Only very small ones,' she lied, clinging to the story she had woven around her symptoms.

'Are they going to operate?'

She shook her head. 'No operation, only a disgusting diet.'

'It can't be that disgusting if it includes wine.'

'You're clucking like an old hen.'

'I'll ring David and ask if wine's allowed,' he threatened.

'Today's the last day of my old diet, tomorrow the first of the new.'

'In that case, you'd better come to dinner tonight. Carolyn's cooking.'

'What time do you want me?'

He gave her a hard look. She had never agreed to dine with them so easily before. Usually an appointment had to be made two weeks in advance and then only after a certain amount of arguing and checking of diaries.

'Seven-thirty all right?'

'Fine.' She held up her glass. 'Want some wine?'

'I'll carve crooked chair legs all afternoon if I do.'

'Still making that dining set?'

'I enjoyed doing the table but twelve chairs are six too many. Who in their right mind wants to serve a dozen people a formal, sit-down meal in this day and age?'

'Someone who can afford a caterer and your hand-made furniture. There's coffee in the kitchen.'

'Beer?'

'In the fridge; help yourself.'

He returned with a can and no glass. Ripping open the top, he took the chair next to Charlotte's and propped his long legs on a table piled with magazines. 'This room is perfect. I feel so at home I have no qualms about making a mess, and the view is magnificent. Much better than ours. We're too close to the lake to get a wide perspective.'

'Move in while I'm away if you want. I've decided to pay a visit to East Prussia.'

'Poland,' he corrected.

'Part of it will always be East Prussia to me.'

'We'll go with you after Carolyn's had the baby.'

'The flight's booked. I'm leaving Boston tomorrow.'

'Tomorrow? But we were always going to make the trip together, and we can hardly take Carolyn when she's eight months pregnant,' he complained.

'It would be too risky, even if the airline allowed her to fly.' Reaching for the wine bottle, she replenished her glass.

'Are you telling the truth about the ulcers?' He narrowed his eyes.

'You doubt your grandmother's veracity?'

'Only when it comes to her health and the cost of the presents she hands out on birthdays and Christmas.'

'Undergoing all those tests made me realize I'm mortal. I've no intention of dying just yet, but I'm not going to get any younger or stronger than I am now, and I want to see my home again before I have to be wheeled around it in a chair. I rang Laura, she's coming with me.'

'Two women on their own in Poland. Haven't you heard what's happening in the Eastern bloc? There's a breakdown of law and order. The Mafia—'

'That's Russia,' she interrupted impatiently, 'and everyone knows the press exaggerate.'

'At least stop off in Germany. Perhaps my father or brother could go with you ...' His voice trailed off when he realized what he was suggesting.

'Do I need to remind you why you left Germany to come and live with me?'

'Perhaps not my father or brother,' he said ruefully, 'but there's Uncle Jeremy.'

'Claus, I may be old but I'm not senile. Both my sons would rather keep me at a three-thousand-mile distance, which suits me very well, as that is precisely where I prefer to keep them. And, of my four grandchildren, Erich is too strait-laced and Luke too young to put up with me. Which leaves you and Laura, and, as Carolyn's condition rules you out, Laura and I will have to manage as best we can without masculine protection. I'm sure we'll survive.'

'How is Laura?' he asked.

'Well,' she answered cautiously.

'Happy?'

'She sounded fine.'

'No sign of a man on the horizon?'

Charlotte shook her head. 'The curse of the happily married is wanting to match-make the world. Laura is a career woman.'

'Only until she finds the right man.'

'Perhaps.' Charlotte would never have admitted to Claus that the lack of one special person in Laura's life had also bothered her since Laura had turned thirty. She was inordinately proud of the cutting-edge, award-winning documentaries her granddaughter produced, which had been televised world-wide. But she couldn't help feeling that Laura's lifestyle of constant travelling and nights spent in hotel rooms had to be a lonely one.

'I wish there was some way that Carolyn and I could go with you.' Claus set his beer down beside his chair.

'You should have given the matter some thought eight months ago.'

'It was going to be our trip,' he protested, refusing to see any humour in the situation.

'But we never made it because I foolishly kept putting it off. I'll check out the country. If there's anything left worth seeing, you and Carolyn can go next year.'

'I suppose so.' He finished his beer and left his chair. 'Can I help?'

'All I have to do is cancel my appointments for the next month or so.'

'And pack,' he reminded her.

'A few clothes. I can manage. Take care of the house for me?'

'I will.' For an instant, he reminded her of his grandfather. Tall, blond, blue-eyed and impossibly good-looking, but then, a colonel in the Wehrmacht of the Third Reich would never have grown a beard and moustache, or dressed in sawdust-covered jeans and a tattered sweat-shirt, let alone loafers on bare feet. Physically alike, yet so different in character, temperament, attitude – and philosophy. 'Thank you.'

'For what?'

'Living with me in my dotage, and staying on after your marriage. Being here every day and caring.'

'And I suppose you've done nothing for us, like allowing us to build a house in your backyard and giving me the money to set up in business.'

'My motives were purely selfish. I needed someone to tend to me in cantankerous old age.'

'You'll never be old, Oma.'

'I'm growing older by the minute, and I need to make those calls and pack.'

'Seven-thirty,' he reminded. 'And don't go carrying any heavy suitcases downstairs.'

'The courier is coming tomorrow morning to pick up the paintings.'

'You've finished them?' Carolyn handed Charlotte a piece of cherry pie and a bowl of whipped cream.

'All forty-eight oils and twenty-four pen and ink sketches, and I never want to read or illustrate another of Hans Christian Andersen's fairy tales again.'

'I'd love to see them all hung next to one another.'

'That is in your hands. I've asked the publisher to send them to you, not the gallery, when he's done with them. You liked them so much, Carolyn, I thought they might make an acceptable christening gift.'

'Acceptable!' Carolyn reached across the table and grasped Charlotte's hand. 'I'm overwhelmed. They're going to look wonderful in the nursery. How can we ever thank you?'

'Great,' Claus broke in with mock indignation. 'Now my son will grow up surrounded by politically incorrect depictions of aristocratic castles and princesses, and scary, psychologically-damaging images of wicked witches and hobgoblins. Not to mention the heartless, icicle-firing Snow Queen.'

'Have I got news for you, sweetheart, the world is politically incorrect.' Carolyn rose from her chair and poured hot water on to herbal teabags.

'And the sooner he or she learns to cope with it, the better,' Charlotte agreed.

'She,' Carolyn divulged, savouring the effect her revelation had on her husband and Charlotte. 'I know I said I didn't want to know the baby's sex but I was looking at a baby catalogue and there were the sweetest little blue romper suits and pink dresses, and I couldn't make up my mind between them, so I telephoned the doctor.'

'Then we'll call her Charlotte.' Claus put his arm around his wife and dropped a kiss on her bump.

'Don't you think she deserves her own name?' Charlotte asked.

'Carolyn and I like Charlotte,' Claus smiled. 'We agreed on it months ago.'

'If you must use it, shorten it to Charlie,' Charlotte suggested. 'It's more suitable for an American girl.'

'Charlie,' Carolyn mused. 'Sounds like a tomboy's name.'

'I don't want a tomboy for a daughter,' Claus protested.

'Only a man could say that. Tomboys have much more fun than prim little girls in lace dresses. More tea?' Carolyn asked, as Charlotte left the table.

'No, thank you, dear. I need a good night's sleep before travelling.'

'Is Uncle Jeremy meeting you in London?' Claus fetched Charlotte's wrap.

'Samuel Goldberg. We have agent–client things to discuss and he offered to drive me to Jeremy's.'

'We'll take you to the airport,' Carolyn said decisively.

'Oh no you won't, I'll order a taxi,' Charlotte contradicted.

'I need to do some shopping. Baby things,' Carolyn protested gleefully, 'and it's not often I can persuade this one to leave his workshop to drive into the city.'

Charlotte looked at both of them. 'You really do need to shop?'

'You heard the boss.' Claus draped the wrap around his grandmother's shoulders. 'I'll walk you home.'

'You'd intrude on my thoughts, and your girls need you.' Charlotte kissed her grandson on the cheek and hugged Carolyn before leaving.

'Is she all right?' Carolyn asked, as Claus closed the door.

'I hope so. I think she's just preoccupied with the past now that she's finally decided to make this trip.'

'She must have loved your grandfather very much.'

'I'm not so sure. You've met my father and brother. They must have inherited their personalities from someone, and it sure as hell wasn't Charlotte.'

She patted her bulge. 'What will we do if this one turns out like them?'

'There's no chance of my daughter turning out anything other than perfect with you for a mother.' He pulled her down on to his lap and began to tickle her.

Charlotte heard Claus and Carolyn's laughter as she walked along the shore path that led from Claus's house to her own. Kicking off her shoes, she stepped into the lake and splashed through the sandy shallows, revelling in the feel of cold water on her stockinged feet.

The moon hung low, a huge, golden orb in an indigo night sky, the same moon that was shining down on her childhood home. A few more days and she'd be there. Everything was ready, the tickets waiting to be picked up at the departure desk, her cases packed, her papers stacked neatly in her safe. She'd redrafted her will when Claus had left Germany to join her six years before. The decisions she had made then still held. Would this trip make her feel any differently about the choices she had made in life? Why was she going? What was she hoping to find after all this time? And – most importantly of all – had she been right to ask Laura to accompany her?

She climbed the steps to her veranda and walked into her living room. Her diary was already packed in her hand luggage. She took it from the bag and unwrapped it. The words she'd written on the morning of her eighteenth birthday stared up at her from the page: *It feels as though I've been away for ever. I can't wait to feast my eyes on the dear, dear house and hug Papa, Mama and the twins …*

Greta didn't get a mention, even then. But what was the point of returning to Grunwaldsee now? There would be nothing left of the house but bricks and mortar, and, after decades of Communist neglect and misrule, decaying bricks and mortar at that. Or worse still, a burnt-out ruin, or a factory erected on the site. Wouldn't it be better to cling to her memories?

She delved into her bag again and brought out another book, a hardback, its jacket yellowing with age. She ran her hands over the title and illustration. *One Last Summer* by Peter Borodin. A picture of a substantial house, white, wooden, gleaming through a pine forest. Totally wrong, of course, but how could the American artist who'd designed the jackets of the Stateside copies know what an East Prussian country mansion looked like?

As she opened the book, two sketches fell out. One was of Grunwaldsee as she had last seen it: a long, low, classically designed, eighteenth-century manor, the simplicity of its façade broken by a short, central flight of steps that swept up to a front door flanked by Corinthian columns. The second was of a young man drawn from memory. She stared at it for a long time. When she finally laid it aside, she knew why she had to go back.

Chapter 2

'LAURA, IT'S Claus.'

Laura hesitated. Had her grandmother shown him the photocopies? It hadn't occurred to her that she might discuss them with Claus, but her grandmother and Claus were so close ...

'Laura, are you there?'

'Yes.' She mouthed an apology across the restaurant table to her librarian dinner date and headed for the Ladies. 'It's just a surprise to hear from you. I wasn't expecting you to call but it's great to hear your voice. How's Carolyn?'

'Burgeoning. It's going to be a girl.'

'Wonderful. Our family can do with all the women it can get. Does Oma know?'

'We told her last night. We took her to the airport this morning. She said you're taking time out to go to Poland with her.'

'Are you checking up on me or her?' she asked.

'Neither.'

'Pull the other one, Claus. As you're obviously dying to know, we're booked on a flight from Berlin to Warsaw on Friday.'

'You're in Berlin?' he said in surprise.

'Aren't mobiles great? No one ever knows where anyone is. But yes, I'm in Berlin. To be precise, in an extremely good Turkish restaurant. I've been working here for a month on a documentary about the Stasi for the History Channel, which I've just wrapped. So it's the perfect time for me to have a break. And I can't think of anything I'd rather do than take a trip with Oma.'

'Oma didn't tell me you were in Germany.'

'Possibly to keep the peace. Before you ask, I haven't called on your parents. It's so bloody between you and your father I'd rather

19

not get involved.'

'Also, you can't stand him,' he pointed out mildly.

'That, too,' she agreed.

'It's just as bloody between my father and Oma as it is between me and him,' he added defensively.

'Perhaps at her age she may want to bury the hatchet.'

'The only place to do that is in his head,' Claus said, not entirely humorously.

'I suggested she rest here for a few days before going on.' Laura deliberately changed the subject. Once Claus began to talk about his father he didn't know when to stop. 'A transatlantic flight is tiring for anyone, let alone someone her age, but you know Oma: now she's finally made up her mind to go, she won't be happy until she gets there.'

'Have you given a thought as to how you're going to get around Poland?'

'I passed my driving test when I was seventeen, dear cousin.'

'You've rented a car?'

'It will be waiting at the airport.'

'Be careful—'

'Claus, if you've rung to lecture, you can stop right now. I can look after Oma just as well as you.'

'I wasn't suggesting you couldn't.' He paused for a moment. 'But I don't think you should let her drive.'

'There's something wrong with Oma?' she asked in concern.

'Apart from the stomach ulcers – she has told you about her ulcers?'

'No.'

'According to her, they're minor and the only treatment is diet. She looks as though she's going to go on for ever—'

'Then why shouldn't I let her drive?' she interrupted.

'She seems a bit peculiar. Nothing I can put my finger on but ... preoccupied. It's difficult to explain but I have a feeling that something isn't right.'

As it was obvious that her grandmother hadn't told Claus about the existence of the documents, Laura made a swift decision not to mention them. She didn't take pleasure in withholding the knowledge from Claus but the secrets weren't hers to tell. 'Oma's finally decided to go home after sixty years in exile. Wouldn't you be feeling a bit peculiar if you were in her shoes?'

'I'd be running like hell in the other direction, and I only left Germany six years ago.'

'You do like to play hard done by.'

'If that means army discipline, cold showers and a father with the temperament of a Rottweiler, then yes, but to get back to Oma—'

'Are you genuinely worried about her, Claus, or simply peeved that it's me, not you, who is making this trip with her.'

'Bit of both,' he conceded frankly. 'I always assumed that the three of us would go together.'

'You were the one who got Carolyn pregnant.'

'Why do I have the feeling I'm being got at?'

'Because you are,' she said flatly.

'It's not just Oma. It's Poland and the Eastern bloc. According to the press, it's not the place to be right now.'

'Since when have you believed anything printed in the papers?'

'Since you took up journalism.'

'I work for television now.'

'That's even worse. Go for maximum audience impact and to hell with the truth.'

'Only in America.' She changed the subject again. 'Oma keeps telling me that you are blissfully happy. The full fairy story. Happily ever after.'

'She's right. I don't know what I've done to deserve Carolyn and the baby, but I'm afraid to think about it too much in case the spell breaks. You?'

'I have my moments and my work.'

'You're welcome to visit any time.'

'I know. I'll try to come after Carolyn's had the baby.'

'Come back with Oma. She'd love to have you, and you wouldn't have to see us unless you wanted to.'

'You live at the bottom of her garden.'

'Like English fairies.'

Remembering her abandoned dinner date, Laura said, 'This phone call must be costing a fortune.'

'It's only money,' he answered carelessly. 'Laura, you will take care of Oma, won't you?'

'As well as you would, Claus.'

'Carolyn sends her love.'

'Love back.'

'Stand godmother to our daughter?'

'Aren't you afraid a journalist might hex her?'

'I'm prepared to take the risk. Phone me from Poland?'

'As soon as we reach the hotel.'

'Check the time difference first. I like my sleep.'

The aircraft was swaddled in cloud. Inside, silence reigned and headsets were plugged in, as people prepared to listen to the programmes they'd chosen to be shown on their personal screens. Only Charlotte's remained abandoned as she adjusted the reading lamp until its light fell directly on to the page of the diary she'd opened on the tray in front of her.

Dawn, my bedroom, Grunwaldsee

SUNDAY, 20 AUGUST 1939

So much has happened since yesterday. I don't even feel like the same person I was then. I am the most fortunate and happiest girl in the world. Greta is furious, although she dare not let it show, especially to Mama and Papa. Her face was a most unbecoming shade of green when I came upstairs.

I am supposed to be sleeping, but I am far too excited, so I am writing this in order to have a complete record of my eighteenth birthday and the most important day of my life to date. Some day I will show this diary to my children and grandchildren. I know they will be beautiful but I wonder what they will be. Soldiers, musicians, academics? Will the boys look like their grandfather?

This is supposed to be a record so I must stop daydreaming and concentrate on exactly what happened.

Everyone was excited when the train finally reached Allenstein station. Herr Schumacher warned us during lunch not to tell our families about the accommodation we were offered in the smaller towns and country areas of Russia, especially the houses where we were expected to share a bed with our entire host family. I shudder even to think of it. Irena and I watched in horror as grandparents, parents, four sons and three daughters all undressed and climbed into the communal bed on top of the stove, but, as I told Herr Schumacher, no serious harm was done. The cells in the police stations, although not very clean and generally cold and draughty, were at least reasonably private. Irena and I promised not to carry any tales. Although we warned Herr Schumacher that we couldn't vouch for Hildegarde, Nina and the other girls.

Of course, the boys all thought it a huge joke, but the only one Herr Schumacher can rely on to keep quiet is Irena's brother, Manfred. The tour has made no difference. He is still a fanatical Communist. 'A lost cause', as Irena says. It was as much as Irena could do to persuade him to keep his opinions to himself for some of the time. She confided that their parents are terrified he will try to recruit someone into the Communist Party who won't make allowances for his youth and family.

If he does, he will end up in one of the dreadful camps people whisper about, like Dachau. Nothing he saw in Russia has affected his loyalty to the Communists, and he has sworn not to rest until Germany is a Communist state. Poor boy — he will never rest again.

Politics! It is all the boys talk and fight about when they are not huddled into corners sniggering over photographs of naked girls. Georg dropped his dirty pictures when Nina passed his seat on her way to the bathroom. He went bright red when she picked them up from the floor and handed them back to him.

She said they were more comical than disgusting, and the model looked stupid dressed only in beads and feathers. I don't know why the boys spend so much time drooling over such things. Irena and I discussed it and agreed we wouldn't want to spend hours studying photographs of naked men.

Paul was waiting for me at the station with <u>him</u>. They stood side by side, both of them tall and blond like the romantic knights of Aryan legend. <u>He</u> was wearing his uniform. Peter elbowed me aside and shouted for everyone to look at his brother because he had been promoted to major. I was angry that I hadn't noticed first. Peter was quite right. <u>He</u> is no longer a captain but a major. At only thirty years of age.

There was so much pushing, jostling and sheer bad manners that I returned to my seat and allowed everyone to leave the train before me, including Irena, who was irritable because Wilhelm wasn't there. Paul explained that they had brought a new horse back from Königsberg for Papa and, because it was half-wild, Wilhelm had stayed behind to lend the men a hand to get it into the stables.

Paul also said Greta had wanted to come to meet me, but <u>he</u> told her there wasn't room for her, Paul, <u>him</u>, Peter, me, and Peter's and my luggage in his car. I was glad. Greta wouldn't have come on my account, and I enjoyed having <u>him</u> and Paul all to myself. As Peter wanted to go straight home to Bergensee he left the station in Georg's father's car.

While I was talking to Paul, <u>he</u> sent a porter to fetch my luggage and take it to his car. It is an open-topped tourer, racier and more modern than Papa's big cars. Paul shook hands with everyone in the orchestra and reminded them of their invitations to our ball tonight. Herr Schumacher and his wife, who had come to the station to meet him, appeared quite overwhelmed that they'd been asked.

It was wonderful to drive through the town out into the countryside; past the lake, down the lane and into the courtyard of dear old Grunwaldsee. It never seems fair that life goes on here without me to see it.

Paul insisted I visited the stables before going into the house. Mama, Papa, Wilhelm and Greta were there, and I discovered that Paul had not been truthful about the horse. It is a grey mare, not a stallion, and the most beautiful riding horse a lady could want. He and Wilhelm had bought her for my birthday! They named her Elise after my favourite Beethoven piece. There was an elegant lady's saddle, too, and Wilhelm had tacked her up so I could ride her straight away. There was nothing for it; I had to go into the house and change into my riding clothes. Mama made me use the side entrance and servants' staircase so I wouldn't see the hall, ballroom or my presents until after dinner.

Paul and Wilhelm brought four horses around to the back of the house. Greta didn't want to ride, but the twins couldn't wait to see how Elise liked me, and <u>he</u> came with us. It was glorious. Elise canters and gallops like an angel. We flew around the lake. Paul and Wilhelm had difficulty keeping up with us, and to think all I had for them were first editions of Schiller and gold tiepins.

We were having such a good time Mama had to send Brunon to remind us to get dressed for the ball. <u>He</u> drove home to Bergensee, and the twins and I handed the horses over to the grooms and went into the house.

Papa ordered trestle tables to be set up in the yard so all our tenants, workers and servants who weren't helping at the ball could make merry and have a party of their own to celebrate our coming of age. He told Brunon to set aside twenty barrels of beer and eighty bottles of wine for them. Greta said it was too much. She's jealous because our party was bigger than the one Papa organized for her coming of age. She should remember ours are for three, hers for one.

Mama sent Minna to help me dress because Maria isn't fully trained. My evening gown had arrived from the dressmaker that morning. It is a sleeveless, textured silvery-blue silk. The bodice is fitted and the neck lower than anything I've ever worn before. Mama told me not to wear any jewellery, so I guessed what my present from Papa and her would be.

I insisted on wearing my hair up, and <u>not in a plait</u>. When Greta saw it she went wild. She ran to Mama, shrieking that no girl should wear her hair out of plaits until she is over twenty-one. Fortunately, Mama agreed with me. Eighteen is quite old enough to dress like a woman. Besides, it was my night, not Greta's.

Papa relented and allowed us to see our birthday tables before dinner. Mama had excelled herself. She had stitched red and cream roses around the edges of the tablecloths, and covered the spaces between the presents with French truffles, bon-bons, miniature champagne bottles and chocolate beetles. It looked wonderful, but we weren't allowed to open a single parcel until after dinner. One hundred of us sat down to the meal, and two hundred and fifty more came for the ball.

Mama and Papa gave me a gold watch and a pearl necklace and earrings. The twins came into the inheritances Opa and Opi had left them, and Papa and Mama gave them keys to cars — one each. Papa had hidden them in the barn, so we all trooped out to see them. They are open-topped Mercedes tourers. The twins were hoping for a car, although they thought they'd have to share. As Papa pointed out, they can't expect to go on doing everything together now they are men.

Everyone laughed because Irena followed Wilhelm the whole present-opening time like a little dog. When all the presents had been admired and the smaller ones carried upstairs, the dancing began. I tried to hide my disappointment at not getting a special present from <u>him</u>. His family gave me a jewellery casket carved from cedar wood and set with panels of amber. It is over three hundred years old and very valuable. <u>His</u> name was on the card as well as his parents and Peter's, but I had hoped for something just from <u>him</u>. Not anything expensive, but a single rose that I could have *pressed between the leaves of this diary and treasured for ever.*

Papa opened the ball with me, Mama danced with Wilhelm, and poor Paul was stuck with Greta, who was in a disgusting mood because she wasn't the star of the party. Mama had worked very hard to decorate the ballroom. Because we so seldom use it, I always think of it as a big, cold, empty space, but last night it looked enchanting. Mama had ordered the servants to drape the ceiling and walls with garlands of roses and evergreen, and the chandeliers had been washed, polished and filled with candles.

I'm glad Papa didn't have electricity put into that part of the house; it is so romantic to dine by candlelight in the formal dining room and dance under flickering flames in the ballroom. Papa had hired the orchestra from the Hotel, which was excellent, but not as good as the Allenstein Hitler Youth orchestra, although I would never tell Papa that in case he thought I was boasting.

Georg played the violin for us. He gave me another rose and a silver bracelet, and begged a dance. I don't want roses or bracelets from Georg, foolish boy that he is, but I did keep a dance for him. It would have been bad manners not to. The bracelet is pretty, with interlinked roses and musical notes.

Manfred gave me a book. I could tell what it was without unwrapping it, and I was afraid to remove the paper in front of other people in case it was by a banned author like Karl Marx. Manfred is always reading proscribed literature. Not even Irena knows where he gets his books from. I promised him that I would open his gift later when I was alone, and he had to be content with that.

Papa wouldn't allow me to hand anyone my dance card until the ball was formally opened. As it was, I had to fight to keep a polka free for Georg. I didn't have a single dance left two minutes after Papa and I had finished the opening waltz. It was full ten minutes before Greta's.

He booked the last waltz before supper and the final three of the evening, but before then I had to partner all sorts of boring boys ...

'Can I get you anything Ms Datski?'

Lost in the past, Charlotte gazed blankly at the stewardess.

'A drink, a newspaper?'

'Nothing, thank you.'

*

…When he finally walked across the room to claim the supper dance, I almost died of happiness. In his dress uniform he was the tallest and most handsome man in the room. He clicked his heels, bowed and said, 'The last waltz before supper is mine, I believe, Fräulein Charlotte.'

I felt as though everyone in the room was watching us as he led me into the centre of the ballroom. I tried to concentrate on my steps, to my shame; I think I even counted like they told us to in dance class. One, two, three — one, two, three — one, two, three … all the while trying to remember the refinements my dancing teacher had taught me. It would have been dreadful if he'd thought me clumsy.

When the music ended he suggested we walk out on to the terrace instead of going into supper. I hoped Greta would notice. I have never forgiven her for the time last summer when she caught me watching him from the balcony in the west wing. She said I was a stupid child to moon over a man who is far too old for me. I have longed to prove her wrong ever since. I may only be eighteen, but I will never, never love anyone as absolutely and completely as I do <u>him</u>. All the love I possess, my whole heart and soul are <u>his</u> and <u>his</u> alone. And a twelve-year age difference is not so great. After all, Papa is ten years older than Mama.

The garden looked enchanting in the moonlight, but because I didn't want to soil or damage the long skirt of my dress we stayed on the terrace. The lights from the house shone out behind us, gilding the trees and flowers. Although everyone was at supper, the orchestra was still playing a soft, gentle piece by Brahms. I'm not ashamed to say that I hoped I would get my first real kiss. The one Georg stole from me on the tour doesn't count because I moved my head and he ended up kissing my ear, which was all wet afterwards. Besides, I didn't want Georg to kiss me then, or ever.

We stood side by side, looking out over the garden, sipping the champagne he had taken from one of the waiters, happy in one another's company, not needing to say a word. A sign of true camaraderie and affinity of spirit.

<u>He</u> looked splendid in the moonlight, just the way I always hoped and imagined my own Prince Charming would. His blond hair shone like a halo, his blue eyes were deep, dark and mysterious. He asked my permission to smoke. I told him that I loved the smell of his cigars. Then he said I looked beautiful in my silk dress, like a goddess.

I wasn't sure how a lady should answer a compliment like that, so I said nothing, but I did step a little closer to him, still wishing for a kiss — I hope he didn't think me shameless, but considering what happened afterwards he couldn't have. The air was pleasantly cool after the heat of the ballroom and I could smell the roses. We could hear laughter and Brunon's accordion in the courtyard on the other side of the house. I murmured something about the servants taking father's directive that they should enjoy themselves to heart, and then he interrupted.

He told me he loves me. Me! <u>He loves me.</u> And all along I thought he came to Grunwaldsee to visit Greta. I can't remember saying much afterwards but then he finally kissed me. At last I know what it is to receive a proper kiss. He put his arms around me and held me very tight.

The sleeves of his uniform were itchy on my bare back. I know it's not in the least romantic to write that, but I have promised myself that this diary will be truthful in every possible way.

Close up he smelled of cologne, leather oil from his army belt, hair pomade and tooth powder. After the kiss I confessed I fell in love with him when I was twelve but I was convinced that he'd never noticed me, only Greta. I hadn't meant to say her name, but he made no mention of it. Instead he kissed me again. A wonderful kiss that quite took my breath away. Then he took a small box from his pocket and asked me to open it.

Inside was the most beautiful diamond ring I have ever seen. He told me that his great-grandmother wore it as her engagement ring and that it was given to one of his ancestors by Frederick the Great.

It is a little too big for my finger but he laughed and said that I will grow into it. Then he lifted my chin very gently with his fingertips and asked me to be his wife. It was the proposal every girl dreams of. Everything was perfect – my dress, the terrace, the ring and, above all, Claus von Letteberg. I am dizzy with happiness. I am to become <u>his</u> wife. Charlotte, the future Grafin von Letteberg. <u>His</u> wife.

The stewardess rolled the drinks trolley alongside Charlotte's seat. Charlotte asked for a mineral water, closed the diary, wrapped it in the silk scarf and replaced it in her handbag. It was strange how the passage of time enabled her to see events and revisit emotions with dispassionate clarity. Now she realized that Claus would never have been able to sweep her off her feet if Greta hadn't also been in love with him.

Greta's sneering that she should stop mooning over men who were

28

too old for her and stick to inexperienced boys like Manfred and Georg had hurt, and she knew her sister too well to suspect that they had been casual comments. Greta had intended to cause her pain, and she had been too naive and insecure to question her sister's motives.

She recalled all the nights she had cried herself to sleep before Claus's proposal because she suspected Greta was right. Why would a man of the world, like Claus Graf von Letteberg, with title, estates, money and the entire eligible, female population of aristocratic East Prussian society swooning at his feet, waste time on an unsophisticated girl like her? The question still remained. Why had he?

True, she had been younger than Greta and possibly, in view of his attitude towards her later, he had considered her a better breeding proposition. No prettier but more malleable perhaps, for all her spoiled, headstrong attitude. Or had Claus seen that, for all her youth and inexperience, she had never wanted anything in her short life as much as she'd wanted him, and her blatant adoration had simply flattered him into proposing.

Nurtured by the romances she read in bed every night instead of the philosophical works recommended by her tutors, before Claus's proposal she had tried to imagine her future without him. She had decided that if he married someone else, she would simply cease to exist. Fade away as Cathy had done in *Wuthering Heights*, or die coughing up her lungs and whispering her lover's name like Marguerite Gautier. She'd even consoled herself by picturing Claus, grief-stricken, returning to her after her death like Heathcliff and Armand, who had dug up their lovers from their graves.

Only reality was never as romantic as fiction.

Samuel Goldberg stood at the barrier and watched a stream of loud, excited American tourists push heavily laden trolleys out of the customs hall, towards the gates and waiting couriers. Behind them, looking more perfectly groomed and alert than anyone had a right to after a three-thousand-mile flight, was Charlotte.

'You look wonderful.' He kissed her cheek.

Charlotte returned his kiss and hugged him. 'Don't lie, Samuel. I'm a wreck. My hair always goes greasy on planes. It must be something to do with the air conditioning. But you look splendid, not a day older than when I last saw you.'

'Five years ago. Five long years since you paid a fleeting visit and left me alone with my broken heart,' he complained.

'A broken heart must suit you.'

'I see you're as cruel as ever.'

'Thank you for picking me up.' She leaned on his arm. 'Travelling is dreadful when you reach your destination and there is no friendly face to greet you.'

'It's part-payment for all the lunches I owe you; I've made excellent commission from the sales of your work. I hope this visit means you intend to spend more time in Europe in the future.' He signalled to the porter to follow them with Charlotte's luggage.

'This is a last visit, Samuel.'

'You can't say that.'

'Yes, I can,' she contradicted.

He looked into her eyes and took a deep breath. 'So, that's why you're intent on going back?'

'Yes. You ever thought of going back to Eastern Europe to visit your old home town, Samuel?'

'Sometimes in my dreams and nightmares, I do just that. It saves me the bother of booking an actual trip. I hate packing.' He patted the hand she'd hooked into the crook of his elbow. 'Now for the good news.'

'Jeremy invited you to dinner and you refused,' she speculated.

'I told him I had to dine with a client.'

'It might be good news for you, but it isn't for me. Is it the truth?'

'I arranged it five minutes after I spoke to him. I'll drop you off at Jeremy's and my chauffeur will pick you up anytime you choose. You will spend the night in my house and allow me to take you to the airport tomorrow?' he pressed.

'That would be putting you to too much trouble on my account.'

'Not for your first visit in five years. Besides, my housekeeper has put fresh sheets and flowers in my spare room, and bought melons and strawberries for breakfast. You wouldn't want to disappoint her, now would you?'

She laid her hand over his. 'You've been a good, faithful and loving friend for over sixty years, Samuel.'

'You gave me the sixty years.' He winked at her. 'Are you sure you want to dine with Jeremy and his family? My date is an old client who'd love to meet you. We could indulge in all sorts of debauchery after we've eaten.'

'Don't tempt me.'

'Is that a yes?'

'No. Jeremy disapproves of me, but his sense of filial duty demands he pay lip service to my existence, which means a dinner invitation every time I land in Britain. And my maternal duty demands that I accept.'

'A short meeting over coffee would be better. You wouldn't end up spitting food at one another,' he coaxed.

'I know, and *you* know, that Jeremy and I find it painfully embarrassing to be in one another's company because we have absolutely nothing in common. Sometimes I wonder if the fairies took my baby and left a changeling. But let's not talk about Jeremy. I'll see him soon enough.'

'Here's the car.' Samuel held up his hand when Charlotte opened her handbag. He thrust his hand into his pocket and tipped the porter for her. 'Charlotte, meet Hassan, my chauffeur. He's Kurdish.'

Charlotte shook the man's hand. 'You're a refugee?'

'I was until Mr Goldberg offered me a job and a home.' He returned her smile before wheeling her luggage around to the back of the car.

'People helped me when I needed it,' Samuel said, almost apologetically.

'And you've been helping everyone you can ever since.'

'I had a good teacher in you, Charlotte.' He opened the back door of the car. 'There's a fridge. Mineral water, wine or, given that the next stop is Jeremy's house, brandy and soda?'

'Mother, how nice to see you.' Jeremy Templeton extended his hand as he opened his front door. Charlotte shook it, and recalled the first time he had offered her his hand. He had been seven years old, and she had been forced to leave him outside the dormitory of his boarding school. The memory brought back the bitter tang of remorse, re-kindling her guilt over both the separation and the handshake. But would Jeremy's life have been any different if she had insisted on bringing him up herself? Could she have done anything to prevent his father from turning their son into a mirror image of himself, an embodiment of the 'English military gentleman'?

'Mother, how nice to see you,' her daughter-in-law, Marilyn, echoed. She stepped forward and pecked her cheek. 'Will this be a long visit?'

Charlotte smiled at the direct question. 'Not long enough to unpack more than my overnight case in Samuel Goldberg's. I've accepted his invitation to stay the night and he is driving me back to the airport tomorrow.'

'I didn't mean ...' Marilyn flushed with embarrassment. 'You would have been most welcome to have stayed here.'

'I know, Marilyn. Have you heard from Laura?'

'No,' Jeremy snapped irritably. 'She hardly ever rings. We don't even know where she is half the time.'

Charlotte almost reminded him that he had the number of Laura's mobile and it was just as easy to make an outgoing call as to receive an incoming one. Then she remembered the parsimonious attitude he had inherited from his father. And her reason for visiting him. Annoying him needlessly wouldn't achieve anything.

'Laura was very busy when I spoke to her. Wrapping up a documentary she's been filming in Berlin. She asked me to give you both her love.'

'We knew she was in Berlin. Let me take your coat, Mother.' Marilyn opened the hall cupboard and took out a hanger in readiness.

'I'm flying to Germany tomorrow.'

'You're staying with Erich and Ulrike for the summer?' There was an edge to Jeremy's voice. He didn't want his mother to stay in his house, but he had always disliked her spending time with Erich. Charlotte wondered if her sons would ever get over their childhood jealousy of one another. Then she recalled the rivalry between her and Greta which had been no different and, if anything, even more bitter.

32

'No, Jeremy, I am not spending the summer with your brother. But I intend to pay Erich a fleeting visit before going on to see Laura in Berlin. From there we're flying to Warsaw.'

'Poland? Whatever for?' Jeremy demanded.

'I still think of the north-east of the country as East Prussia, but then I'm a foolish old woman who occasionally prefers to live in the past than the present.'

'Please, go in, Mother.' Jeremy stood back to allow her to walk ahead, and she preceded him into the living room.

Jeremy had recently retired from the army, but the change from military to civilian life had made little impact. Thirty years of living in officers' married quarters had given him and Marilyn a taste for the bland, solid, functional furniture the army provided for the use of senior brass and their families. The room was a carbon copy of the ones they had occupied during Jeremy's postings and he had dutifully sent her photographs of every Christmas. Needing the luxury of her own space, Charlotte chose to sit on one of the easy chairs.

'Eastern Europe is a dangerous place, Mother.'

'You're usually the first to point out how the press sensationalize every situation, Jeremy. Besides, Laura is coming with me.'

'Laura can hardly look after herself, much less anyone else,' he snapped.

'She seems to have survived quite well on her own for the past few years, as well as make quite a name for herself as a producer of quality documentaries.'

'But you'll be two women alone. An obvious and easy target for criminals. And really, why go at all when there is no pressing need? Especially at your age, Mother.'

'You think I should be knitting socks in an old folks' home instead of visiting the country I grew up in?'

'I had forgotten how flippant you can be. I must protest—'

'Looks like your protests will have to wait, Jeremy. Isn't that your doorbell?'

Marilyn rose from the sofa. 'It's Aunt Greta. I thought, as you two hadn't seen one another for years, I'd organize a surprise reunion.'

'A surprise for me or Greta, or both of us?' Charlotte questioned.

'Marilyn told her that you were coming yesterday,' Jeremy revealed. 'We didn't want it to be too much of a shock. You know she has a weak heart.'

'She's always had one, Jeremy.'

'Pardon?'

'Hadn't you better let her in?' Charlotte steeled herself.

Her fragile relationship with her sister had passed breaking point shortly after the end of the war. The last occasion she had been in Greta's company she had found it extremely difficult to check her temper, and when she'd had time to mull over the things her sister had said and done then, she'd wondered why she had even bothered to try.

Chapter 3

'GOOD EVENING.' Greta sailed into Jeremy's hall, her husband John dutifully trailing in her wake, just as he had done all his married life.

Jeremy kissed his aunt's cheek. 'Please, allow me to take your coat, Aunt Greta.'

'Thank you, Jeremy; it is good to know that chivalry isn't quite dead.' She handed him her scarf and stood still, arms extended, so he could remove her quilted silk jacket. 'Marilyn, here are the baking tins I promised you. Now that I'm getting on I don't bake as much as I used to, and it's a waste to leave them in the cupboard gathering dust.' She handed over a bulging, disintegrating, stained Marks and Spencer carrier bag before turning to her husband. 'You left the trays of seedlings I promised Marilyn in the car.'

'I put them at the back door. It's what you told me to do,' he reminded her meekly.

'Good.' She glanced into the living room and finally acknowledged her sister. 'Don't get up, Charlotte.'

'I won't. I'm a little dizzy, probably from jet-lag.'

'Then you won't mind if I don't bend to kiss you,' Greta said tartly. 'I'm a martyr to arthritis these days.'

'I'm sorry to hear that.' A sufferer herself, Charlotte's commiserations were sincere, but Greta couldn't resist a snipe.

'I can't understand why anyone should find flying tiring when all they have to do is sit in a chair and be waited on by cabin staff.'

'Perhaps it's the five-hour time difference.' Charlotte gazed at Greta as she swanned into the living room. She would be ninety-five in a few months, but had retained the slim figure they had both inherited from their mother, and, with her grey hair rinsed pale-blonde, she looked twenty years younger. However, she still had the habit of pursing her mouth and looking disapprovingly at the world. It was an expression Charlotte remembered well.

'I'll call Luke. He'll want to say hello to you, Aunt Greta, Uncle John. And to you, of course, Mother.' Jeremy went to the stairs and bellowed his seventeen-year-old son's name, leaving Charlotte wondering why Jeremy hadn't called him when she'd arrived.

'Luke spends every minute he can in the attic playing computer games,' Marilyn explained when Jeremy yelled his son's name a second time.

Greta lowered herself on to the other easy chair and arranged herself comfortably, leaving her husband to sit between Jeremy and Marilyn on the sofa. 'I see you're looking well, Charlotte, but then, you have no excuse not to. Unlike us married ladies who have husbands to care for, you have nothing to do all day except pamper yourself.'

'You know me. I've always been a stickler for brushing my hair and cleaning my teeth,' Charlotte retorted.

Greta eyed Charlotte's long, large-beaded amber necklace, teardrop earrings and bracelets. 'I see you're wearing Mama's amber.'

Charlotte only just managed to quell her annoyance at the comment. 'You know full well all the family jewellery was lost in the war, Greta.'

'So you say.'

Greta's scepticism set Charlotte's teeth on edge. 'I bought the bracelets and earrings in the Dominican Republic in the seventies. They have fine amber there.'

'And the necklace?'

'Is the one I was given on the nineteen thirty-nine Allenstein orchestral tour of Russia.' Charlotte fingered her beads.

'Given?' Greta raised her finely pencilled eyebrows.

'By the host family I stayed with in Moscow.'

'Russians!' Greta exclaimed.

'It was a tour of Russia, arranged by the German and Russian authorities, Greta. The countries were allies at the time.'

'I don't remember you ever receiving a present as magnificent as that from strangers,' Greta commented.

'They weren't strangers to me, Greta.'

'Obviously, if they were that generous.' Greta placed her handbag on her lap and wrapped her hands around it as though it was in imminent danger of being stolen.

'Oma! How long have you been here? It's great to see you.' Luke ran in, sat on the arm of Charlotte's chair, flung his arms around her neck and kissed her cheek. 'Those are fantastic games you sent me for Christmas.'

Claus thought you'd like them.' Charlotte opened the airline bag she'd carried in with her and extracted a parcel. 'And he sent you these. He was going to post them to you for your birthday but he thought you wouldn't mind getting them early.'

Luke tore off the wrapping paper. 'Wow! Thanks, Oma.'

'Thank Claus, not me, and don't forget to e-mail him.'

'I won't.'

'Aunt Greta and Uncle John are here, Luke,' Jeremy prompted.

Luke climbed off the arm of Charlotte's chair and shook Greta and John's hands before returning to Charlotte. 'Last summer was super, Oma. Can Laura and I come and visit you and Claus again?'

'Of course you can.'

'I was glad to hear that Claus is about to become a father. I always say that the best things in life are the children and the flowers,' Greta declared.

Charlotte considered Greta's observation odd given that she had never wanted children of her own. 'That was one of Hitler's favourite sayings, Greta.'

'Was it? I never paid any attention to Hitler,' Greta lied. 'I was only saying the other day to John that we ought to pay you a visit, Charlotte. I'd like to see your house.'

'It's very modern,' Charlotte said pointedly. 'Even the furniture. I'm gradually replacing everything with Claus's designs. That is when he has time to execute my commissions. His work is very much in demand.'

'I'm surprised he set up business in America not Germany.'

'Claus did marry an American, Aunt Greta. Sherry?' Marilyn offered Greta a tray of drinks that Jeremy had poured.

'I trust Claus's wife is intelligent enough to learn German and teach it to the child,' Greta commented.

'She is,' Charlotte answered.

'Claus should return to his homeland. Things are so much more peaceful, prosperous and stable in Germany. Besides, Claus's family name is a well-known and respected one. His business would be more successful there.'

Charlotte shook her head when Marilyn offered her the tray. She had never liked sherry and sensed it wouldn't mix easily with Samuel's five-star brandy. 'Have you been following the news, Greta? The cost of reunification has been an enormous drain on Germany's economy. Unemployment is high and there's a resurgence of Fascism. Turks and other guest workers are being persecuted and attacked by neo-Nazis, and discriminated against by the government. They don't even have the right to vote in the country that taxes their wages.'

'Why should they, when it's not their country?'

'Not their country, Greta?' Charlotte questioned. 'Tens of thousands of Turkish guest workers' children have been born in Germany. Most of them have never even visited Turkey, and some don't even speak Turkish.'

'You can hardly blame the German government for the deficiencies of Turkish parents, Charlotte. Germany's problems have always stemmed from over-generosity to foreigners. If the government hadn't opened the doors of the Fatherland to an endless stream of ungrateful guest workers and refugees from every ailing Communist and Muslim country in the world, ordinary, hard-working German men and women wouldn't have to pay such high taxes to fund the welfare payments of idle immigrants who refuse to work.'

'Perhaps the German government could solve the problem by confiscating the foreigners' money and businesses as Hitler did with the Jews,' Luke chipped in.

'Luke! Have some regard for your grandmother and great-aunt's feelings,' his father intervened sharply.

'Please, Jeremy, don't stop the argument now. I'd be interested to hear Greta's reply.' Charlotte looked at her sister.

'Jeremy is right. Politics should not be discussed at a family gathering. They should be friendly, happy occasions.' Greta sipped her sherry.

'How can they be, if the younger generation are denied the right to air their opinions?' Charlotte asked.

'I see you're encouraging Luke to be as headstrong as you were as a child, Charlotte.'

'Seventeen isn't a child, Aunt Greta,' Luke countered. 'Although, given the way I'm treated in this house, you wouldn't think so.'

'Child or not, you appear to have inherited your grandmother's faults. Too many thoughtless words, and too much heedless action for your own and your family's good.'

'I'll second that, Aunt Greta,' Jeremy agreed. 'Have you heard the latest madness? Mother and Laura are going to Poland.'

'To Grunwaldsee?' Greta reddened in anger as she stared at Charlotte.

'I'd like to see our home again.'

'In God's name, why? Won't it grieve you to see Russians strutting about in our house, putting their feet on Mama's furniture, drinking in Papa's study?'

'The Russians have left Poland, Greta, and I doubt any of our family furniture has survived. Everyone I've talked to who has been back, has confirmed that the Russian army stripped every house of every moveable object at the end of the war and shipped the lot to Russia.'

'Then there'll be nothing left for you to see.' Greta sat back in her chair and cradled her sherry. 'And absolutely no point in you going back.'

'They won't have shipped back the countryside, and if a few bricks of the old house have been left standing, I'll be content.'

'Content!' Greta exclaimed indignantly. 'You have a harder heart than me, Charlotte. After all that we suffered as a family, all that we lost—'

'It was a long time ago, Greta,' Charlotte interposed, more exhausted by a quarter of an hour of her sister's company than eleven hours spent in flight and queuing at airports.

'Papa always said that you had a callous streak.'

'He never said it to me.' Charlotte had always known when her sister was lying.

'I remember it all as though it were yesterday,' Greta added.

'Principally the happy times, I hope, Greta. I was telling Samuel Goldberg in the car on the way here that I've just finished illustrating a new edition of classic European fairy tales. Painting all those castles, woods, lakes, wolves, wild boars, princesses and dragons made me think of our childhood. We were happy at Grunwaldsee.'

'Before the Russians took it from us,' Greta said bitterly. 'I simply cannot believe that you want to go back.'

'I hope to be there before the end of the week.'

'I'd rather die than see our old home destroyed. But then, you never were sensitive, Charlotte.'

Charlotte's temper finally broke. 'And you are even more reluctant to face up to facts now than you were at the end of the war, Greta.'

'Luke, I need help in the kitchen.' Taking her sherry, Marilyn went to the door.

Luke edged further up the arm of the chair, closer to Charlotte.

'Your mother needs your help, now, Luke,' Jeremy barked in his officer's voice.

'You only want me out of the way so Grandma and Aunt Greta can discuss politics and family history. Well, I'm entitled to know—'

'See what you've done with your insistence on going back to Poland, Charlotte? Upset the entire family. Even dear little Luke.' Removing a scrap of lace and silk from her pocket, Greta dabbed her eyes.

'I think "dear little Luke" will get over it.' Charlotte suppressed a smile at the wicked wink Luke gave her. 'And it's not as though I'm asking you to go back with me, Greta.'

'What good does it do to open old wounds? I suffered. Oh, how I suffered ...'

'There, there, Aunt Greta.' Jeremy went to her and patted her hand. Charlotte couldn't help wondering if her son would have been as eager to console his aunt if Greta had a more direct heir than her two nephews.

'The soup is ready,' Marilyn announced nervously through the dining-room hatch. 'It's your favourite, Aunt Greta.'

'Cream of asparagus?' Greta brightened at the thought.

'Carrot and coriander,' Marilyn said apologetically.

'Ah, a carton from the supermarket.'

*

Charlotte thought she saw even the normally implacable Jeremy heave a sigh of relief when Greta and her husband departed after dessert had been served and the coffee pot emptied.

'Aunt Greta is very good to us,' Marilyn said defensively as she gathered the cups on to a tray. 'She's very thoughtful, always bringing us plants for the garden, homemade jam, and bottled vegetables.'

Luke, who had disappeared upstairs at the coffee stage to try out the computer games Claus had sent him, returned in time to utter an 'Ugh'.

'I bottle vegetables and fruit, too,' Charlotte reminded him.

Luke made a wry face as he took the chair next to Charlotte's that John had occupied. 'I forgive you, Oma, because, unlike Aunt Greta, you don't try to make me eat them.'

'Luke! Have you been drinking?' Jeremy asked, somewhat superfluously given that his son was breathing lager and tobacco fumes across the table.

'Me?' Luke tried and failed to look innocent.

'I'll search that attic—'

'I'd appreciate a hand with the dishes, Luke,' Marilyn broke in.

Charlotte sensed that Marilyn was hoping to avert a full-blown row between father and son. 'Help your mother, Luke.' She surreptitiously slipped a roll of banknotes into Luke's hand when she rose to her feet. 'I have business to discuss with your father.'

'We can go to my study, Mother.' Jeremy was glad of an excuse that enabled him to overlook his son's behaviour. Luke was becoming increasingly belligerent and difficult to handle. In the last two months, even mild reprimands had turned into full-scale confrontations. Jeremy had made no secret of the fact that he couldn't wait for his son to go to university. His worst nightmare was that Luke wouldn't achieve the grades required and be forced to spend an extra year at home re-sitting his A-levels.

'Do you need help with your business affairs, Mother?' Jeremy asked hopefully. He ushered Charlotte into his study, closed the door and sat behind his desk, leaving her the only other chair in the room, an uncomfortable wooden upright. She felt like a petitioner facing a bank manager.

'No, thank you. I have everything under control, but as I'm here

I'd like to tell you about the arrangements I've made to dispose of my estate.'

'I trust you've made a will.'

She had always been able to rely on Jeremy to leave sentiment out of financial discussions. 'Naturally, and, as I'm hoping to avoid any argument or disagreement amongst the family after my death, if you don't like what I've done, I want to hear it from you now. As you know, I made bequests to my grandchildren, rather than you and Erich. You're both settled and have all the houses, cars and material goods you could possibly want.'

'Erich has a summer house on Lake Garda.'

'I always thought you and Marilyn made the better choice. By holidaying in different countries every year you've seen much more of the world.' After turning his grievance into a compliment, she continued. 'I'm proud of you and Erich, Jeremy. You've both built successful careers, taken care of your families and given your children every advantage of education and upbringing.'

'With very little help from anyone,' he observed caustically.

'You and Erich were lucky in one respect; the sixties and seventies were a kinder era to the young than the present, which is why I have set up a trust fund for Luke. It should be enough to help with his university education and buy him an apartment like Laura's.'

Jeremy frowned. Charlotte suspected that he was calculating how much of the money he had set aside for Luke's education could be diverted back into his own funds.

'I'm sure you've been very generous.'

'It's no more than I've done for my other grandchildren. You're aware that I've also set up a trust fund for young Erich.'

'You're paying for young Erich's education?' His voice rose an octave higher.

'As I did Laura's,' she reminded him. 'Claus, as you know, refused to go to university which was why I helped him with his business.'

'But Erich's reading law. A barrister needs to study for longer.'

'The trust funds are of equal size, Jeremy.'

'And my children are very grateful—'

'I've done no more than any grandparent would do in my position,' she cut him short. 'As for my remaining assets, I've disposed of them according to my wishes and no one else's, and I'd like an assurance from you that you won't contest my will. You accept that I am of sound mind?'

'Of course, Mother.'

'I have left the house and land in Connecticut to Claus.'

'Left, as in a gift?' he gasped incredulously.

'He has lived there for the past six years. It is his home as much as mine.'

'But there are two houses on the land.'

'One of which he built.'

'With money you gave him.'

'Laura has an apartment, Claus a house. They were both paid for by their trust funds.' She looked Jeremy coolly in the eye. 'And, given that Claus's house and mine are so close, it wouldn't be fair to inflict strange neighbours on him after my death.'

'Like me, for instance.'

'What would you do with a house in Connecticut, Jeremy, other than sell it?'

'Use it for holidays.'

'I'm sure Claus and Carolyn will accommodate you if you ask them. But the decision has to be theirs.'

'Claus has already had the same money as the others.'

'He has also put up with my presence for the last six years.'

'And your furniture, your jewellery – is he to inherit those as well?' Jeremy enquired acidly.

'The valuable furniture will be itemized in my will. With the exception of one or two pieces, my jewellery, such as it is, will go to Laura.'

'But you have two daughters-in law.'

'Who have amassed their own collections.' She opened her handbag and extracted a small leather case. 'Your father gave me these. He wouldn't take them back when I left. I thought you might like them for sentiment's sake.'

Jeremy opened the blue leather case. Nestling on a bed of faded, pale-grey velvet was a simple, narrow gold band, a second ring set with three tiny diamond chips, and a pair of earrings. 'The infamous utility wedding ring,' he mocked. 'I had no idea they produced austerity engagement rings as well.'

'Your father brought it back to me in Germany after one of his leaves.' She almost added, 'It would have been better if he'd found a more suitable girl to give it to,' but she bit her tongue. It had been over between her and Julian for a long time. There was no point in raking up old resentments.

'These, however, are quite lovely.' He lifted out the sapphire and gold earrings.

'Your father acquired them after the war.'

'Acquired?'

She didn't elaborate. How could she explain war-torn, defeated Germany to a man who hadn't seen it? The fever that had infected the victorious troops, the plundering and pillaging – not that Julian would have participated in anything that offended his very British, gentlemanly code of conduct. Knowing him, he'd probably bought the earrings for a few marks from some poor woman desperate enough to sell heirlooms for food. Was someone in Russia selling or bequeathing the von Datski family jewels now? Jewels that had been stolen from her on the flight from Grunwaldsee.

'This is very generous of you, Mother.'

She detected irony in his gratitude and knew he'd expected more. 'I've told my solicitor to forward you and Erich copies of my will. There's a clause I want both of you to sign, confirming that you won't challenge it.'

'If Claus is getting the house, and the children trust funds, who is going to inherit the bulk of your estate?'

'The trust funds took up a great deal of my money, Jeremy.'

'But surely not all?'

'Thank you for your concern. I have enough left to live on.' She deliberately chose to misunderstand him. 'The residue, such as it is, will be distributed in personal bequests.'

'May I enquire to whom?'

'Does it matter? I've already told you that it's not going to you or Erich. And now, if you don't mind, I'd like to leave. It's been a long day.'

'You want to call Samuel?'

'Please.'

He handed her the telephone. She dialled and spoke briefly to Samuel's housekeeper before returning the receiver to Jeremy.

'The car will be here in ten minutes.' She left the uncomfortable chair. 'You won't contest the will?'

'I'll have to read it first and discuss the implications with Marilyn.'

'If you take this to the courts, Jeremy, the lawyers will benefit at your expense, and your family won't get a penny more than I've already given you,' she warned.

'I didn't say that I wouldn't sign. Merely that I was going to discuss it with my wife.'

'How is your father?' Charlotte asked as he opened the door for her.

'Failing, but M ...' He faltered in embarrassment.

'You have every right to call Judith Mother, Jeremy. She's been more of one to you than I could be.'

'She looks after Father very well.'

Charlotte gripped the doorpost for support. 'Jeremy, I didn't want to leave you. You do know that?'

'I wouldn't have been happy in Germany.'

Like his father before him, he kept her at arm's length. How did he know he wouldn't have been happier living with her in Germany than in England with his father? But then, her relationship with her German son, Erich, was no closer or better. Perhaps it was a mother's fate to bear sons for men whose influence eventually superseded and eroded the maternal bond.

Now, when she looked at the two children she'd borne, she saw strangers she didn't like and could quite cheerfully ignore if it hadn't been for the cherished memories of their babyhoods.

'Will you be staying long with Erich?' he asked, when they stepped into the hall.

'No, I'm anxious to get home – to Poland.' Even as she offered the excuse she shivered at the thought of Erich's house, as cold and formally polite as this one, for all its luxurious furnishings.

'When do you have to go back to America?'

'Soon,' she replied vaguely.

45

'You will give Erich, Ulrike and young Erich our very good wishes.'

'I will.'

'I'm sorry we couldn't go to the States for Claus's wedding last year, but Marilyn's parents are elderly and Father—'

'Luke and Laura went to represent you.' She looked at him. 'It's all right, Jeremy. It really is.' She held out her hand and he shook it briefly, insensible to the warmth she'd intended.

'You'll call in on us on your return.' He lifted her wrap from the hall cupboard.

'I won't be travelling back this way.'

'You'll be taking a direct flight from Poland to America?'

'I have no firm plans.' She sat on the hall chair.

'You would have been able to negotiate a discount if you'd booked your return flight the same time as the outward one.'

'It's a little late to try to organize me at my time of life, Jeremy.'

'Probably,' he conceded. 'But I can't help wishing that the artistic temperament hadn't manifested itself quite so strongly in Laura.'

'She's grown into a fine woman, Jeremy. I'm very proud of her and everything she has achieved.'

'You are?' he said in astonishment.

'You're not?' She was even more shocked than him.

'When she took her degree I hoped she'd teach, not go in for all this journalism nonsense. The programmes she works on are positively left-wing – and she can't keep a boyfriend. Not that I'm surprised, given her personality. I keep telling her that men don't like forceful, strident women.'

'Perhaps "forceful, strident women", as you put it, don't need men.'

'Laura learned the lessons you taught her well. You sound exactly alike.'

'I can't take credit for teaching Laura anything, Jeremy. Even as a small child she was her own person.'

'And what kind of person would that be?' he demanded. 'She has no respect for anything, Marilyn and I value. Tradition, church, marriage, good, plain morality – the British way of life—'

'Which, thankfully, like the life in most of the countries in this world, is now multicultural,' she interrupted. Jeremy had inherited a streak of bigotry from his father, that given her own background, she categorically refused to condone or make allowances for.

'If that's your way of saying the English are now strangers in their own country, I agree.'

'That's not what I was saying at all, Jeremy. Laura makes films that are seen and appreciated world-wide by people of every colour and creed.'

'But where is her personal life?' Jeremy persisted.

'She'll settle down if and when she wants to.'

'That's what we're afraid of. She works with all sorts of unsuitable people. It's not their religion Marilyn and I object to, or their colour—'

'Then what, Jeremy?' she interrupted.

'The fact that she lived with one of them for two years without even telling us. He was a Somali. And we had to find out from strangers that they were together.'

'They could have simply been flatmates. Given rising costs, men and women do share houses on a friendship-only basis,' she commented.

'A likely story,' Jeremy snapped.

'Did you ever ask her about him?'

'No.' He looked closely at her. 'Did you know about him?'

'Laura talks to me about so many of her friends; I have no idea which one you are referring to. And, if she was living with someone, possibly she was merely being sensible. Marriage frequently leads to the trauma of a divorce these days. It must be easier – practically, if not emotionally – simply to walk away when things don't work out.'

'You approve of your granddaughter living with a man outside marriage?' Jeremy was clearly enraged by the thought.

'I wouldn't disapprove.'

'Claus is married.'

'That was his decision, Jeremy.' Charlotte took her wrap from her son. 'And he made it after he found the right girl.'

'But living so close, you must have influenced him.'

'I like to think that we are good friends despite the family connection and age difference. But influence?' She shook her head. 'I have absolutely none. Like Laura, Claus is his own person.'

Marilyn joined them from the kitchen. It was obvious she had been eavesdropping on their conversation. 'Perhaps you could have a word with Laura, Charlotte,' she suggested diffidently. 'Remind her that time is moving on and if she doesn't settle down soon she will run the risk of ending up alone.'

'Like me?'

Embarrassed, Marilyn shrank back.

'I intend to have several words with Laura in the coming weeks, Marilyn.' Charlotte heard a car pull up outside the house and rose to her feet. 'Thank you for the lovely dinner and for going to all that trouble on my behalf. Oh, I almost forgot.' She took a large box of Belgium chocolates from her bag and handed it to Marilyn, before giving Jeremy a bottle of brandy. 'Duty Free.'

'Thank you, Mother.' The bell rang, and Jeremy motioned his wife to open the door. Marilyn went outside and waved to Samuel's chauffeur.

Jeremy took Charlotte's bag from her. 'Do warn Laura not to broach the subject of your old home with Aunt Greta if she visits her and Uncle John when she returns to England. Or talk at length about it, even if they ask. Aunt Greta's an old woman, quite frail despite her robust appearance, and unequal to dealing with unpleasant memories.'

'You're not curious, Jeremy?'

'Not about a country that no longer exists, or a war that was over before I was born.'

'Or the small part of both that was your family's history?'

'Like Aunt Greta, I think the past best forgotten.'

'You're going, Oma?' Luke looked crestfallen when he walked out of the kitchen and saw she was ready to leave.

'I am.' She hugged him.

'You'll be back soon?'

'I don't think so.' Reluctant to let him go she clung to him.

'But Laura and I can visit you again. What about this summer?' he asked hopefully.

'Come any time you want. And if I'm not there, Claus, Carolyn and the new baby would love to have you.'

'Why wouldn't you be there, Oma?'

'Art,' she replied. 'There are always new places to see and paint.' She kissed him for the last time, then the telephone rang and he went to answer it.

'Have a good trip, Mother.' Jeremy escorted her to the car. 'Do telephone to let us know that you have arrived safely, and remind Laura that her parents would like to hear from her once in a while.'

'Marilyn.' Charlotte hugged her daughter-in-law, shook her son's hand again and climbed into the car.

Hassan loaded her bag into the front. 'Mr Samuel told me to tell you that you're most welcome to join him for brandy and coffee in his dining room, but if you'd like to go straight to your room, there's a bottle of white wine on ice and brandy on the drinks tray in the kitchen.'

'Tell Mr Samuel he's a very special man.'

'I will, madam.'

As they drove slowly down the street, Charlotte turned to catch a last glimpse of Jeremy. He was standing in the doorway of his house, Luke waving to her on one side of him, Marilyn waving less enthusiastically on the other. Charlotte brushed away a single tear and took consolation in the thought that, with Laura and Claus to watch out for him, Luke would be all right.

However, the tear wasn't for her grandson. She suspected that she had just seen Jeremy for the last time, but the sadness came from her indifference. She felt nothing. Absolutely no emotion – no pain, no joy, no sorrow – only relief that she wouldn't have to make small-talk in Jeremy's presence or enter his cold, unwelcoming house ever again.

Chapter 4

'YOU HAVE everything you need, Ms Datski?'

'More than everything. Thank you, Mrs Green. I am not used to such pampering.'

Charlotte placed her diary on the bedside table, untied the belt on her robe, hung it in the wardrobe and slipped into bed.

'Mr Goldberg thinks a lot of you, Ms Datski.'

'As I do him,' Charlotte smiled.

Mrs Green, who had been born Melerski, had succeeded to her mother's post as Samuel's housekeeper after her mother's death. Samuel had found her teenage mother and uncle in a displaced persons' camp at the end of the Second World War, while searching for his wife and children. He'd never found his own family so, in typical Samuel fashion, he'd adopted someone else's.

'Sleep well. Shall I turn off the lights?'

'The main light, please, Mrs Green,' Charlotte asked. 'Leave the bedside light. I intend to read for a little while.'

Late afternoon, my bedroom, Grunwaldsee
SUNDAY, 20 AUGUST 1939 (continued)
After Claus slipped the ring on to my finger he left me to look for Papa to ask his consent. I stayed on the terrace in an agony of suspense until Claus returned, bringing not only Papa but also Mama and his own parents. I could see at once how happy Papa was. The von Lettebergs are an even older family than ours. Mama was overcome with happiness, and she and Grafin von Letteberg couldn't stop hugging and kissing one another and me. Claus had asked his parents for their blessing that afternoon, and his father told me they couldn't be more delighted with their son's choice of a bride. After

they embraced me and welcomed me into the von Letteberg family, all that remained was formally to announce the engagement.

Papa wanted to go to the dining room and tell everyone there and then, but Mama insisted on waiting until supper was over and the dancing had resumed. She then left to find Greta. I think she wanted to tell her before anyone else did, because she knew that Greta had hoped Claus would ask <u>her</u> to marry him. Claus and I looked for Wilhelm, Paul and Peter. We found them drinking champagne with Irena, Nina and Hildegarde. Claus invited the boys to join him on the terrace for a cigarette and, although they were reluctant to leave the girls, I think they suspected something because they went without argument. When I followed outside a few minutes later, they were all shaking hands.

Wilhelm and Paul congratulated me on bringing a good fellow into the family. They have respected and admired Claus as a friend for a long time and it pleases me immensely that everyone I love approves so wholeheartedly of my future husband.

When the music started, Claus led me back into the ballroom. His ring felt strange and heavy on my finger. I was sure everyone was looking at it. I know I would have noticed if one of my girlfriends was wearing an engagement ring but no one said a word. All I could think of as we danced, all the while waiting for the music to stop so Papa could make the announcement, was how wonderful it is to love someone and to be loved in return. To want to spend your entire life with one special person. To be theirs completely and utterly as Claus and I will be to one another.

I was so excited I barely heard a word of Papa's speech. I could tell that all my girlfriends were surprised at the suddenness of the news and envious of my good fortune in securing such a wonderful, aristocratic, handsome and well-respected man. I looked for Greta when Papa was speaking, but I couldn't see her anywhere.

I was so proud and happy when Claus claimed a fiancé's right to kiss me for the first time in public that I resolved to be extra kind to Greta in future. I know how heartbroken I would have been if he had chosen her instead of me. I would have wanted to <u>die</u>.

Papa had barely finished speaking before congratulations flooded in from all sides. Everyone asked questions. Did I still intend to go to Königsberg to study at the conservatory? (Herr Schumacher.) How soon we will be married? (Irena.) Are we were going to have an engagement party? (Peter and

Nina.) Papa caused a lot of laughter when he invited everyone to stay for breakfast. He said it would be less trouble to hold a breakfast engagement party than organize another ball.

We could have done so because no one left before dawn. While the servants were serving soup to our departing guests Papa switched on the radio. The orchestra was packing up and I think he was hoping for some light music to send everyone on their way, but there was only news. Bad news. Polish troops are massing on our borders. Georg said Germany will not stand by and watch foreign aggressors point their weapons into the heartland of Germany. It can mean only one thing. War.

Papa upset everyone when he said, 'No good can come from war.' It sounded unpatriotic and disrespectful to the Führer. Everyone knows that although Papa was one of the first to join the National Socialist Party he was also a Freemason for a few months when he was a young man. The Party officials said they forgave him and would make an exception in his case, but even I can see it would be better if Papa didn't question the Führer's policies quite so much.

Mama tried to smooth things over by explaining that Papa lost many close friends during the last war, and there were a few murmurs of sympathy, including one from Grafin von Letteberg. I like her very much already.

While everyone discussed the inevitability of war, Claus locked himself in Papa's study to telephone his commanding officer, and I realized I will no longer be able to ignore politics. Not when my future husband is an army officer. When Claus returned he confided that his superiors believe the army will soon be ordered into Poland to put an end to the aggression. Georg overheard him and repeated the Führer's assertion that it is unfair that we Germans have to battle for the land and living space that is our birthright. Unfortunately, Manfred heard Georg and started a long, boring political discussion about land and common good and each taking according to his need not his wants, which ended in a fist-fight between Georg and Manfred.

Why do stupid boys think they can change someone's views by beating them senseless? Thankfully Claus broke it up before it became too serious – or noticeable. I am glad Claus never discusses politics. I think he believes, that as an army officer, he should keep his opinions to himself.

After the guests left, Papa, Mama, Claus, his parents and I breakfasted in the small dining room. Greta went to bed. She said she was tired but I know she couldn't bear to see me so happy with Claus. I felt sorry for her when she went upstairs alone.

In view of the worsening situation between Germany and Poland, Claus asked Papa's permission to marry me right away. He has three weeks of his month-long summer leave left, and he wants to spend as much of it as possible as a married man. Of course I agreed, but Papa was very reluctant to give his consent. He was hoping for a long engagement and suggested we wait at least a year. It was very forward of me, but I reminded him that Mama was married at my age. He argued no more after that.

I love Claus so much I cannot bear the thought of life without him. If we are truly man and wife, it may be a little easier for me to endure the weeks, perhaps even months of separation that will come if war does break out. I wish he was anything but an army officer. I cannot bear to think of him being hurt or killed in battle.

Claus was so persuasive that, in the end, Papa and Mama agreed to hold the wedding as soon it can be arranged. Papa sent for the pastor. He came at once, thinking that there had been a tragedy. How we laughed at the expression on his face when he realized it was a wedding not a funeral that we wanted him to conduct. So, next Saturday morning in Grunwaldsee chapel, I will become Claus's wife.

As soon as the date was fixed, Mama and Grafin von Letteberg began panicking about clothes, guests and arrangements, but Claus said he wanted the wedding to be a simple and small one. Just family and a few close friends. I agreed with him. Our future life together is what is important, not wedding dresses, flowers and cold meats for the guests. But I doubt we'll get our way. Grafin von Letteberg and Mama have already compiled a list of over two hundred people they say it is essential to invite.

Afterwards Mama wanted me to rest, but I told her I wasn't tired. Claus invited me to go riding with him. I knew Mama thought it wasn't right for me to be alone with Claus, although we will be married in less than a week, but Papa knows Claus is an officer and a gentleman. He gave his permission and, while Brunon saddled the horses, I changed into my riding clothes.

We rode down to the lake. There were many things Claus wanted to discuss with me. Like where we will honeymoon. He suggested the Grand Hotel in Sopot, my favourite hotel in all the world. I love the way the dining room opens on to the beach. I told him that if I could design a perfect *place for a honeymoon, the Grand Hotel and Sopot, with its fashionable crowds and gardens, would be it.*

Claus said he will telephone and try to book a suite overlooking the sea, but it will be difficult because it is the height of the summer season. Afterwards, if there is time, we will return to his family's home, Bergensee. A home, he reminded me, that will be mine this time next week.

I didn't want to consider what I will do after he leaves to rejoin his regiment, but he insisted that I make plans. We agreed there is no point in my continuing my studies at the conservatory in Königsberg. I can practise the piano just as well at home, and Claus believes that when war breaks out the universities will have to close because so many young men will be enlisted into the army. As reservists Wilhelm and Paul will be among the first to be called up. They told us so after the news broadcast.

It was eventually decided that after our honeymoon I will return to live at Grunwaldsee. If war does break out, some of our workers will have to join the army, so Papa will need my help to exercise the horses and manage the farm. I will be busy, but, as I told Claus, not happy. Not without him.

I had hoped that he would kiss me again, but all he did was hold my hand and run his thumb over my ring finger. When I dared to kiss his cheek, he smiled and said there would be plenty of time for that sort of thing after we were married. Until then he feels honour-bound to respect Papa's wishes and my reputation, and I love him all the more for it.

He began to talk about children and said he hoped we would have a large family, but Brunon interrupted us. Although it was a Sunday, Mama had sent the car to fetch the dressmaker. I have only just finished the fitting. Mama's wedding dress is to be cut down for me. Greta was furious, because she is taller than me, it means that she won't be able to wear it when she gets married, but, as Mama said, Greta will have more time for planning than me, so she will be able to have one made to fit her.

I am tired now. It is late afternoon. Claus is coming in two hours to take me to the church to talk to the pastor about the wedding and what marriage means. Before then I must try to sleep a little, but, exhausted as I am, all I can think of is my beloved Claus, and how wonderful it will be to be his wife.

I am excited, happy and just a little, a very little, afraid. Mama came to my room to talk to me. She told me it is a wife's duty to submit to her husband's every wish, and that means in the bedroom as well as the drawing room. *I know what she means, because Nina is always talking about sex. Hildegarde says no nice girl likes the horrible things men want to do, only bad girls who go with men for money. When I think of Claus, all I know is that I want to please him in every way I can. I do so hope and pray that I will never disappoint him, or make him unhappy, and that if there is a war, God will keep him safe for me.*

Samuel waited until Charlotte had checked her luggage into the Lufthansa desk before giving her a bear hug. 'Glad to be leaving the London suburbs?'

'Yes,' she agreed, 'but I'm not glad to be leaving you, Samuel.'

'I hope you find what you're looking for in Poland.'

'Thank you.' Charlotte kissed him on the lips for the first time.

He lifted his fingers to his mouth. 'If you had done that sixty years ago our lives might have been very different.'

'Fate meant us to be good friends, Samuel.'

'Take this.' He thrust an envelope at her.

'What is it?' She turned it over.

'My top secret telephone numbers, including my mobile.'

'I have them.'

'I know, but I thought you should keep them in your passport together with instructions to contact me in case of an emergency. Your sons are busy people. Claus will have his wife and new baby to care for. You and Laura may need help.' He shrugged. 'I know people.'

'I don't doubt you do, even in Poland,' she replied.

'There too, I can smooth things over and get things done.'

'Samuel.' She embraced him again. 'What would I have done if I'd never met you?'

'I know what I would have done.' He lifted her hand luggage from the trolley and handed it to her. 'I will see you again, Charlotte, either in this world or the next. Oh, and if you should get to the next before me, look for my wife. Her name is Taube. She should have the boys, Shlomo and Simcha, with her, and baby Lola. I don't know if children grow up there but Lola was a real stunner; only one year old but such black eyes and a mop of hair.' He fell silent. Charlotte recognized that stillness. She indulged in it herself when she allowed herself to remember.

He glanced at her and returned her smile. 'Tell Taube I'm on my way and warn whoever's in charge of the catering up there that I like my brandy strong and my coffee weak with lashings of whipped cream.'

'Mutti, it is good to see you looking so well.' Erich sat at the head of the dinner table and raised his glass to his mother. 'To your continued good health.'

'Thank you, Erich.' Charlotte touched her glass to his. 'And thank you, Ulrike. This is a splendid table and I'm sure the dinner will be very good.'

'Our new Indonesian cook is excellent.' Ulrike patted her immaculate hair nervously before fiddling with her plate and cutlery. 'How was Claus when you left America?'

'Happy with Carolyn, looking forward to the arrival of the new baby. They intended to give me a letter,' she lied diplomatically, 'but I left so suddenly they didn't have time to write.'

'Pregnancy and birth is such a strain on a woman. I do hope Carolyn is looking after herself. I was never the same after Claus and young Erich were born—'

'Carolyn is a fit young woman. Pass the salad,' Erich broke in impatiently.

Charlotte saw Ulrike's bottom lip tremble and, although she had little patience for her daughter-in-law's hypochondria, she gave her a sympathetic smile. Erich's brusqueness had brought an unwelcome reminder of life with his father.

'Claus is taking care of Carolyn beautifully.' Charlotte clasped Ulrike's hand briefly before unfolding her napkin.

'I can't imagine that young layabout taking care of anything. The hamster we bought him when he was six starved to death,' Erich growled. 'I went into his room every morning to check on it. There was never any food and he hardly ever changed the bedding or water.'

'Claus never stops working, Erich,' Charlotte protested. 'His business is thriving.'

'If he had worked when he should have – in school – he wouldn't have to do manual labour now.'

'Claus is a craftsman, Erich, not a labourer. I think he inherited his love of working with wood from my father.'

'Venison, Mutti?' Ulrike gave a fragile smile as she offered the dish.

'Thank you, Ulrike.' Charlotte took the smallest steak from the plate, and looked across at her grandson, who had been given the same name as his father and was universally known to family and friends as 'young Erich'. Three years younger than Claus, he had also inherited his father and grandfather's tall, blond good looks, but there was a downward, disapproving turn to his mouth that was entirely his own. 'Are you looking forward to going to university this autumn, Erich?' she asked.

'Yes, although it is a lot of responsibility knowing that it is up to me to carry the family's good name into the future.'

'University isn't for everyone, Erich.' Charlotte took a potato from the tureen Ulrike handed her.

'No, Oma. It is only for those who work hard,' he replied pompously.

'Sauce, Mutti?' Ulrike held out the jug.

'For pity's sake, Ulrike,' Erich senior snapped, 'there's no need to offer food that's on the table for everyone to help themselves to.'

'How is business, Erich?' Charlotte asked, in an attempt to defuse the escalating tension.

'We're surviving. It's not easy in the present economic climate. All the large companies are shedding staff. Their cutbacks have affected Germany's economy.'

'I thought your firm specialized in corporation law.'

'It does. But all the multi-national as well as the national companies are scaling down.'

'That is a lovely suit, Mutti; may I ask where you bought it?'

Charlotte knew what it had cost Ulrike to ask her a direct question in Erich's presence. She racked her brains in an attempt to recall all she could about clothes and designers, although she had given up following the vagaries of fashion when she had escaped England and Jeremy in the 1950s, ostensibly to save money, but really so she could create her own style. She embarked on a conversation to which Ulrike struggled to contribute, and only after looking at her husband to check his reaction to every opinion she dared voice.

Ulrike had suffered three nervous breakdowns since her marriage; illnesses Charlotte attributed as much to Erich's lack of sensitivity as Ulrike's disposition, and judging by her present jittery state, she seemed to be on the brink of a fourth.

'Mutti?'

'Sorry, Erich, you said something?' Charlotte waited until Ulrike finished speaking before turning to her son.

'I asked what prompted you to decide to visit Poland now.'

'No specific reason, apart from the fact that I'm not getting any younger and I'd like to see the old country one more time.'

'Everyone I've spoken to who has been there has said it's changed beyond all recognition.'

'So I've heard, but I would like to see those changes for myself. Do you remember anything of Grunwaldsee or the countryside?'

'Very little, but as I was only four when we left, and given what happened to me afterwards, it's probably just as well my early memories are sketchy.'

'Thank you.' Charlotte handed her plate to the Filipino maid who had entered the room to clear the table.

'Perhaps we could have coffee and dessert in the conservatory,' Ulrike ventured, glancing apprehensively at her husband again.

'That would be lovely, Ulrike,' Charlotte agreed, 'but if you don't mind, I'd like to see Erich alone for a few minutes first. I need to discuss some business with him.'

'Jeremy telephoned me last night,' Erich informed her as they walked into his library, which was six times the size of Jeremy's study and more austerely and expensively furnished. The custom-made desk and glassed-in bookshelves were solid, dark-stained oak, the chairs upholstered in rich, burgundy leather.

'I didn't know you two kept in contact.'

'We don't generally, apart from the Christmas and birthday cards our wives send. He wanted to warn me that you'd cut us out of your will.'

'I see.' Charlotte sank down on to a chair, grateful that, unlike Jeremy's house, all the chairs were comfortable and exactly the same, placing host and guest on equal footing.

'Is he mistaken?' Erich reached for the brandy bottle on a side table and poured out two measures without asking if she wanted one. He looked her in the eye as he handed her a glass.

'I have set up trust funds for the children. Young Erich's is of equal size to Claus's, Laura's and Luke's.'

'That is very generous of you and much appreciated.' He sat opposite her.

'Thank you.'

'Jeremy told me that you have left your house and land in America to Claus.'

'As his house and mine are within a stone's throw and we have never separated the plots, it seems only fair.'

'Jeremy thinks that it is anything but fair.'

'And you?' She met his steady gaze.

'I am of the opinion that you have the right to dispose of your possessions in any way you see fit.'

'That is precisely what your father would have said.' Charlotte hadn't expected Erich to say anything else. He was a past master when it came to concealing his emotions and doing and saying the correct thing. Excellent qualities, but there had been occasions when she had wished that both father and son had been a little more spontaneous, human and tolerant of the failings of others.

'Jeremy also said that you want both of us to sign a clause stating that we won't contest your will after your death.'

'I do.'

'I have no problem with that. If you have nothing else to discuss we can rejoin the others.' He finished his brandy.

'Erich, before we do,' she looked up earnestly at him, 'I want you to know that I do love you very much.'

'Mutti—' he broke in impatiently, embarrassed, as he always was, by any display of emotion.

'Your life didn't quite work out the way your father and I intended.'

'Yes, well, it's all water under the bridge now,' he responded, switching from German to perfect, clipped English.

'But I want you to know how proud I am of you.'

'Thank you,' he replied awkwardly, leaving his chair.

'Just one more thing, Erich. Please, try to be a little more patient with Ulrike.'

'Highly strung women need a firm hand.'

'She needs help, Erich.'

'She has the best medical help available.'

Charlotte knew when she was beaten. They might have been speaking in different languages. She took the arm he offered her.

'I know young Erich would like to thank you for the trust fund. May I tell him about it?'

'Yes, Erich, you can tell him. And, after coffee, if you don't mind, I'll go to bed. I have a lot of travelling to do. Berlin to meet Laura, then on to Warsaw and Allenstein – I mean, Olsztyn.'

'I have to leave the house at five-thirty. Business meeting in Brussels,' he explained briefly, 'but Ulrike will be here to supervise breakfast, and young Erich will drive you back to Frankfurt airport.'

'I could take a taxi.'

'No need. Let's find Erich and have coffee before we say our goodbyes, Mutti.'

Dessert, coffee, more meaningless kisses from Ulrike, two more cold, firm handshakes from her son and grandson. Her sons' houses and their languages were different, but the sterile atmosphere that stifled all emotion was identical.

Guilt smothered Charlotte like a winter quilt when she closed the door of Erich and Ulrike's principal guest bedroom half an hour later. Then she remembered Claus, Carolyn, Luke and Laura, and the close, affectionate relationship she had with all four of them. Somewhere, sometime, she must have done something right to have deserved grandchildren as warm and loving as them.

The Grand Hotel, Sopot
SUNDAY, 27 AUGUST 1939

After today I will have to find somewhere secret and secure to hide this diary, a place where no one will find it, especially Claus, but for now I have to tell someone what has happened, if only myself, so I can see it written down. Perhaps it will not seem so terrible then.

Yesterday, I was married. Already it seems as though the ceremony was held years ago and involved someone else. Despite all the rush it was the wedding of my dreams. But now … what am I to make of it and the rest of my life? How am I to bear it?

In a few weeks Claus will go back to his regiment and I will return to Grunwaldsee and Papa and Mama, and, if I am lucky, I won't have to see Claus very often. But I cannot, dare not, ever tell anyone how I feel, outside of this book.

But for now, I will write of what happened before my life changed for ever.

I was so happy when Wilhelm and Paul drove us to the station after our wedding feast. Everyone followed. Mama, Papa, Mama and Papa von Letteberg, Irena, all my friends and Claus's fellow officers. The stationmaster joked that he would run out of platform tickets. I threw my bouquet and Irena caught it. The last Claus and I saw was Irena holding it up to Wilhelm and laughing. Claus had booked an entire carriage so we could be alone. The steward served us dinner in our private car. Caviar canapés, smoked salmon, wild boar steaks with potatoes and asparagus, French lettuce salad, and fresh strawberries and whipped cream. Claus had arranged for the dinner to be prepared at Bergensee by his father's French chef and delivered to the kitchen on the train together with two bottles of champagne and ice for the bucket.

We ate, we toasted our future, we drank and, by the time the train reached Sopot, I thought I would die from joy, perhaps because the platform seemed to wobble beneath my feet. The hotel had sent a limousine for us and for the first time I signed my name Frau Claus von Letteberg.

I love everything about the Grand Hotel: the reception area with Tiffany lamps in jewelled colours that reflect in the massive mirrors behind them; the curved twin staircases in wrought ironwork that sweep down from the upper floors; the murals in the dining room; the doors that open into the gardens that adjoin the beach.

Claus had booked a suite on the third floor: a bedroom, sitting room, bathroom and balcony overlooking the sea. There was more champagne waiting for us together with a basket of fruit, and all the rooms were filled with flowers.

Mama had insisted that I should have a proper trousseau in spite of the lack of time. It meant buying some clothes and lingerie ready-made, but the dressmaker had managed to finish a white silk nightdress and négligé, which she had trimmed with the Bruges lace Oma had left me in her will. While the maid unpacked and Claus opened the champagne, I went into the bathroom, perfumed the bath water and myself, let down my hair, brushed it out, dressed in my bridal nightwear and tried to make myself look as beautiful as possible.

Why!

Charlotte stared at the last tear-splotched word on the page, and the past returned so vividly she could smell the perfume that hadn't been manufactured in over forty years. She was that naive, apprehensive eighteen-year-old girl again, studying herself critically in the mirror in the bathroom of the honeymoon suite in the Grand Hotel in Sopot, terrified that her bridegroom would find her ugly, repulsive or wanting in some way.

My heart pounded erratically because I was so eager to experience, yet so frightened of what was about to happen. I loved (already I speak of my feelings for him in the past tense) Claus so fervently I was terrified of disappointing him. I delayed as long as I could; brushing my hair until it clung to the brush with static, haloing my face. And, for the first time in my life, I didn't plait it before going to bed. I knew it would be horribly tangled in the morning but I was so desperate for Claus to think of me as a woman, not the schoolgirl I had been a few short weeks ago.

Everything I had chosen for my honeymoon had been selected to make me look older. My perfume was French, 'the most sophisticated in stock', or so the girl in the Parfumerie had assured me. It was certainly expensive, as was the scented cream I had rubbed into my face to tone and pale my skin. I studied myself in the mirror as I hung the towels back on the rail. My silk nightdress and négligé clung to my figure, but I was shocked when I saw how much of my body the delicate panels of lace revealed.

Claus called to me and asked if I was all right. I said I was fine and, unable to delay any longer, turned the key and stepped outside.

The door to the balcony was open and Claus was standing outside. He told me that I looked lovely. Then he offered me champagne. He had carried a bottle and glasses on to the balcony. I joined him, took the glass he filled for me, and saw that the bedroom door was open and the maid had turned down the bed before leaving.

Claus made a toast: 'To a long and happy life together and many, many children.'

He touched his glass to mine, wrapped his arm around my waist and drew me close. The warmth of his body and the weight of his arm made me realize how strong he was – and how weak I am in comparison. Suddenly afraid, I tried to concentrate on the scenery, the poetry I'd studied, anything but him and what was about to happen.

The night air on my face and bare arms tingled, full of salt. The sands below stretched, indigo-blue in the moonlight. The lights on the pier gleamed in twin rows on out right, silver diamonds above the navy sea, the furthest blending with the stars glittering in the night sky.

The scene was so beautiful I intended to say something profound and poetic but instead blurted, 'The moonlight looks like a silver road.' It sounded childish.

Claus didn't seem to mind, he told me that it was the road to our future, then he set his glass on the parapet and gazed into my eyes. Embarrassed, I turned away. It was easier to look at the pier than at him, but the silence between us was so uncomfortable I begged him to take me there.

He asked if I meant the pier or our future. When I said both, he said, 'We'll start with the pier, the longest in the Baltic.' Then he said he'd get ready for bed. I shivered but not from the cold.

He went inside and hung his uniform tunic in the wardrobe. I looked back at the pier and the flocks of swans sleeping beneath it – their heads tucked under their wings, their curled bodies bobbing up and down with the movement of the waves – and I wanted to be closer to them on the beach. Running and laughing in the moonlight, as I had done so many times with Wilhelm and Paul after we had sneaked out late at night when we had holidayed here with Papa and Mama.

Claus returned and asked if I was happy. Of course, I said yes. Then he kissed me on the lips, such a gentle kiss I wasn't afraid any more. In that instant I truly felt that I was experiencing the happiest moment on the happiest day of my life. He told me not to stay out on the balcony too long, then he went into the bathroom.

I returned to the bedroom when I heard the bathroom door close. The linen sheets were cool, crisp with the kind of starch only hotels seem to use. I lay there wondering what it would be like to sleep with Claus not only that night, but every night for the rest of my life.

The bathroom door opened and he walked out naked. I couldn't look at him. I hadn't seen a naked man or boy since the twins were ten years old and had swum nude in the lake. (A practice Greta had put a stop to.)

He threw back the bedclothes and climbed in beside me. His legs touched mine: they were long, cold and hairy. I began to shake and couldn't stop. He pulled me towards him and said, 'There's no need to be nervous, Charlotte. It's a perfectly natural function, and a necessary one to have children.'

He flung back the sheet and lifted my nightdress. I tried to cover myself but he gripped both my hands in one of his and said, 'It's all right, it's allowed, we're married. How about you undress so I can see you properly? Here, if you sit up, I'll help you.'

I recalled what Mama had said, and remembered that I had promised to obey Claus before God only that morning. I allowed him to undress me. When I was naked he went to the bathroom for a towel and laid it beneath me.

I begged him to turn out the light but he said he needed to see what he was doing. He gripped my breasts painfully. I tensed myself and he rolled on top of me, forcing my legs apart with his.

I cried out as he lunged into me. I had never felt such pain. He put one hand over my mouth, so I couldn't make any more noise, then he pinned me down and thrust himself into me again and again and again …

There was no love or tenderness in what he did, there couldn't possibly have been. It was brutal. It killed every hope and expectation I had of married life. I was hurt, humiliated and wounded, and not only in my body.

I couldn't believe that the horrible, degrading, bestial act could be the culmination of all the poetry and romance of love – and my dreams.

I did what I always do when I am faced with something unpleasant and painful like a visit to the dentist or doctor – I closed my eyes and tried to pretend that I was somewhere else and it wasn't really happening. But I couldn't. He continued to force himself on me until I lost count of the number of times. No sooner did I think he was finished than he started again. It went on and on until I wished I were dead.

Grey light was filtering through the curtains when he finally rolled away from me. He actually smiled and said, 'That wasn't so bad, was it?'

I couldn't answer him.

He looked down at the bed and told me to clean myself up.

The towel he had placed beneath me was soaked with blood, as were my nightdress and the négligé which I had left on the sheet. I rolled them into a bundle, crawled off the bed and went into the bathroom.

I turned on the taps, sat on the bath and cried. When the tub was full I lowered myself in and tried to scrub away the blood. Afterwards, I wrapped myself in the hotel's bathrobe, and crept out into the bedroom. He was lying on his back on the bed snoring. I tiptoed into the sitting room, fetched this diary, returned to the bathroom and locked myself in. At least here I can be alone.

The pain is so severe I can hardly move, and walking is agony. How am I going to face him when he wakes? I only hope he won't want to do anything so disgusting ever again. If he does, how will I endure it?

How do other women cope? Mama? Grafin von Letteberg? Why did I marry?

It would have been far better to have died an old maid.

Chapter 5

LAURA WAS waiting at Berlin airport. She was so well-organized that less than twenty minutes after Charlotte's plane had landed, a porter was loading her luggage into the car Laura had hired. After the initial greetings and euphoria at their reunion was over, Charlotte noticed Laura looked tired and that she'd lost weight. She wondered if her granddaughter had been working too hard, or if the change was down to the documents she'd found in the archives.

Charlotte sat in the passenger seat and closed the car door. Laura climbed into the driver's seat and slotted the key into the ignition.

'I've booked a room for you in my hotel for tonight and I have flight tickets for Warsaw for tomorrow. But they can be changed if you'd like to rest for a day or two before going on to Poland.'

'I'd like to leave as soon as possible.'

'Tomorrow soon enough for you?' Laura looked sideways at her grandmother.

'It is. Your time really is your own for the next couple of weeks?' Charlotte glanced out of the window but saw nothing familiar. Berlin had changed so much from the city she had once known.

'I have absolutely nothing lined up for the next three months. I've been promising myself a break for some time.' Now that she was actually with her grandmother Laura realized how difficult it would be to raise all the questions about the past that she'd listed in her mind.

'And you're well?' Charlotte tried to sound tactful.

'Perfectly. How long do you intend to stay in Poland?' Laura edged the car out into the stream of traffic exiting the airport.

'As long as it takes me to see everything I want.'

'I wish I could ignore clocks and calendars the way you do.'

'I've been an absolute slave to the clock these past six months but,' Charlotte revealed, 'I've finished illustrating the fairy tales.'

'All of them?'

'All of them. And, although I say it myself, it's my best work to date.'

'You must have worked non-stop.'

'It felt like it.'

'Claus sounded happy on the telephone when I last spoke to him'

'He is euphoric, but with Carolyn for a wife, a new baby to look forward to and a business he loves that's going well, he has every right to be smug.'

'Lucky Claus.' Laura stopped at traffic lights.

Charlotte laid her hand over Laura's on the steering wheel. 'How are you really, Laura?'

'Tired. The last documentary was emotionally draining. I interviewed dozens of people who didn't realize that their family and close friends were spying on them. The Stasi may be history but it will take years for the bitter legacy that the organization has left in Germany to be forgotten.'

'I suspect that, like the evils of the Second World War, the bitterness won't end until the generation who lived through it are all buried,' Charlotte said sadly. 'Laura, you can call me an interfering old busy-body if you want, but you don't look at all well. Is it because of the Nazi documents you found? If it is, I promise I will answer all your questions, but, if you don't mind, not until we're in Poland.'

'You can't answer them now?'

'I'd prefer not to. Not because I want to make you wait, but – and I know this must sound strange – there are things that I am not sure about even now. Not events. I remember those clearly enough. But how I felt about them at the time and how differently I feel about them now.'

'I think I can understand that.' The lights changed and Laura drove off.

'Is anything else worrying you?' Charlotte probed.

'What makes you ask?'

'Something your father said about a Somali boy.'

'If he was worried about my marrying an African national he

doesn't have to any more. It didn't work out. Ahmed has moved on.'
She looked across at Charlotte. 'Back to his wife and daughter.'

'I'm sorry, Laura.'

'You're not shocked about him being married?'

'I know you, and you would never have embarked on an affair with a married man unless you loved him.'

'I did,' Laura concurred.

'I hope he was worthy of you and that you have been left with some happy memories of your time together.'

'I wish everyone was as tolerant and understanding as you, Oma,' Laura said feelingly. 'We were very much in love, and yes, we did make a few happy memories.'

'Then I'm glad.'

'How are my parents and Luke?' Laura changed the subject.

'Your parents are your parents. Luke, on the other hand, is driving your father to exasperation.'

'Good old Luke. I feel better just for seeing you. I'm glad we're able to spend some time together, Oma. I'm in sore need of good companionship and advice.'

'The companionship is easy. The advice I'm not too sure about. Is it personal or career you're looking for?'

'Both.'

'Then you won't get either from me. I'd prefer to take the coward's way out and sit on the fence, because I can't stand people coming back to me and saying, "I did what you suggested and look at the result. It's all your fault."'

Laura managed a smile. 'Has anyone ever dared do that to you?'

'Only family.' Charlotte brushed her hand against Laura's cheek. 'In my experience, worrying never achieves anything, darling. Most of us make choices only when we are forced to, and if we make the wrong ones, time will tell soon enough. In the end, life works out the way it's supposed to.'

'I wish I could believe that.'

'Try to keep what you want in mind, and look ahead, not back.'

'I do, but the only thought that consoles me these days is that, a hundred years from now, no one will care about anything I did or didn't do.'

'You need to stop worrying about other people, Laura, and consider yourself more. I'm sorry that you've lost your love; let's hope that somewhere out there, another knight in shining armour is waiting for you.'

'At the moment I wouldn't recognize him if he turned up riding a white charger and wearing silver battle armour. As for my career, I've been offered a job, a permanent one, that pays an obscene amount of money, working for an American television station.'

'Are you going to take it?'

'Despite the advantage of being closer to you and Claus, I'm not sure I want to live in the States, or make the kind of films they want me to produce. Twee stories about underdogs who become cheer-leaders or quarterbacks.'

'Then don't take it,' Charlotte said decisively.

Laura laughed as she drove into the hotel car park. 'Why is it that a few words from you always puts everything into perspective? You're absolutely right. The last thing I want to do is take it. And I've just this minute decided I won't.'

Laura followed her grandmother into her room after they'd dined in the hotel restaurant. She picked up the copy of *One Last Summer*, which Charlotte had taken out of her hand luggage and placed together with her diary on the bedside table.

'You still carry this everywhere?'

'Yes,' Charlotte confirmed.

'You must have read it a hundred times.'

'Probably two hundred,' Charlotte replied. 'Did you read the copy I gave you?'

'The beginning.' Laura took the book and sat in the chair closest to the window.

'You didn't finish it?'

'I couldn't bear to. All that Russian gloom and suffering was too much for me. That poor man imprisoned in a Siberian gulag, waking every morning to inhuman brutality and starvation rations. Forced by the freezing misery of his surroundings to live out every day in his head; having to resort to imagining himself in another time, another place, with the only woman he had ever loved.'

'Couldn't you see that his reality was his dream world?' Charlotte argued. 'His life in the camp held no more significance than a fleeting nightmare.'

'I couldn't bear the thought of him only having his past. No future, no bearable present beyond that conjured by his imagination. Nothing to look forward to except death.'

'It would have been far worse for him if he hadn't had that past. It gave him a reason to live, to keep fighting for survival. As for a future, when you live within the world of your imagination, anything is possible.'

'No amount of imagination could make up for the filth, degradation and inhuman conditions in that camp.' Laura turned the book over in her hands. 'I wanted more for him.'

'Perhaps you'll appreciate the book better when you're my age.' Charlotte sat on the dressing-table stool, unpinned her hair and brushed it out with fifty strokes, just as she'd done every night of her adult life. 'Your mother is hoping that I'll have a word with you.'

'Did she stipulate what kind of word?'

'Something about settling down. I told her that I intended to have several words with you.'

'You're incorrigible and I love you.' Laura kissed her grandmother on the cheek.

'Even though I was once a card-carrying Nazi?' Charlotte said softly.

'Then it wasn't a mistake.' Laura fell serious, and Charlotte knew that her granddaughter had been hoping she could provide proof it was just that – a mistake.

'No, it wasn't.'

'If you tell me about it, I'll try to understand.'

'In the nineteen thirties most of the people I knew were card-carrying "good Nazis". It was what everyone aspired to be. A good citizen, a good Nazi, a loyal follower of the Führer, who had given the German people everything they wanted and more. We really believed the slogan: "One people, one country, one leader." A law was passed in nineteen thirty-six making it compulsory for every German boy and girl to join the Hitler Youth, but we didn't need to be coerced. We loved the Hitler Youth. It meant trips away from home and our parents' watchful eyes. Instruction in sailing, riding, shooting, fencing, skiing, gymnastics – and flying. Even after the war, when everyone knew exactly what the Nazis had done, some of my school friends still insisted that the Hitler years were the best years of their life.'

'I know about Hitler's economic miracle,' Laura said uneasily. 'But the horrors – the camps, the Jews; people must have known what was going on.'

'I was a child but I can just about remember what it was like in East Prussia in the nineteen twenties. There was a breakdown of law and order. Raging inflation devalued wages before they were earned. Rival gangs fought in the streets. Allenstein was full of beggars – crippled ex-servicemen, the unemployed and their children. My father was inundated with offers from people prepared to work just for bread. I'm not saying conditions were worse in Germany than America and Britain during the world slump, but Germany was a defeated and humiliated nation that had been forced to hand over large slices of territory when the peace treaties were signed after the First World War. Hitler gave everyone hope. He restored national pride and he gave people scapegoats to blame for the Depression. So, in answer to your question, yes, everyone knew the Nazis were anti-Semitic. It was impossible not to know given the amount of anti-Jewish and anti-Communist propaganda on the radio, in the newspapers, on posters, in films, not to mention spoon-fed to us in the Hitler Youth. But we Germans were told so often we were members of a superior race that most young people, and I'm ashamed to say that includes me, really believed we *were* special. Yes, we saw Jews being persecuted in the streets. My Jewish friends were expelled from school. We knew they'd lost the right to work, vote and own property. The official line was they were going to be resettled. There were rumours of Madagascar and the East. But most people argued, my father among them, that Hitler's anti-Jewish laws were a small price to pay for full stomachs and full employment.'

'And it ended in the Holocaust.'

'Yes, it did.' Charlotte's eyes creased in pain. 'And all I and every German who lived through that time can do is acknowledge that, to Germany's eternal shame, it happened and we must beg forgiveness. Not that I think for one moment we deserve to receive it.'

'I can't imagine being indifferent to the persecution of a minority,' Laura said quietly.

'You and Claus wouldn't have been, because, unlike me when I was young, both of you are special and sensitive people. My father was not easily taken in but he joined the Nazi Party the same night he heard Hitler speak for the first time. Then, when Hitler became Chancellor, everything changed.'

'Overnight?' Laura set *One Last Summer* aside.

'It seemed like it. My father's closest friend was a master builder and architect. His family could barely scrape by on what he made from doing odd jobs. Every time we visited them before Hitler came to power we took them a basket of food. As we did most of my parents' friends.'

'You were rich?' Laura asked in surprise.

'My father owned a few farms; the tenants paid their rent in produce. We had more food than we needed for our personal use, and my father couldn't bring himself to sell the surplus while his friends and their children were starving. As a result the farms made no money and became run-down. When Hitler came to power he started building – roads, schools, youth hostels, factories. Within four years my father's friend had made enough money to build an enormous house for his family and buy acres of land on which he erected houses and workshops.'

'All your family were Nazis?'

'Before the war, yes,' Charlotte confirmed. 'My father arranged for me, my brothers, and sister to become full Party members on our eighteenth birthdays, so we wouldn't have to wait until we were twenty-one – the usual age for joining. Your Great-Aunt Greta was an area organizer for the BDM, the Hitler Youth group for girls. I performed in the musical section of the Allenstein Hitler Youth group, and both my brothers were in the Hitler Youth before they became officers in the Wehrmacht. My father had been Burgomaster of the town and my mother organized fundraising events. After the war not many Germans were willing to admit that their family had been Party members. But I can't deny it, and you have every right to be horrified.' Charlotte picked up her diary. 'I know you can read modern German; can you read old-fashioned handwritten Gothic script?'

'After a month spent delving into the Document Center here, I can.'

'This is a diary I began on my eighteenth birthday and kept during the war and for a short while afterwards. Would you like to read it?'

'If you don't mind.'

'It will give us somewhere to begin. But not tonight. We have a long journey ahead of us tomorrow. Not just in miles, but into the past.'

'We do.' Laura rose from the bed. 'Oma, you didn't do anything ... I mean, in the camps ...'

'I can't speak for Greta, but my father, mother and I did the worst possible thing.' Charlotte looked Laura in the eye and saw that her granddaughter was too afraid to ask. 'We did nothing to help the people who were sent to them,' she said. 'Nothing at all.'

SUNDAY, 27 AUGUST 1939 (Continued)

We are returning to Bergensee. Yesterday, while Claus and I were married, the Führer made a speech demanding the return of Danzig and the Polish corridor that separates Prussia from the rest of Germany, and an end to the Anglo–French pledge to support Poland in its aggression towards Germany. Everyone in the hotel was talking of it this morning. When Claus and I came down after breakfasting in our room we found the reception area crowded with holidaymakers anxious to get away because they were expecting war to break out at any moment. But that didn't stop them from staring at me and nodding knowingly to one another.

There were no maids free, so I returned to our room to do our packing. Claus joined me later. He had secured the only tickets available back to Allenstein. Third-class on a late-evening train. It will be a very different journey from the one we took last night. Claus is disappointed but I am not. This afternoon he is taking me for a walk on the beach and the pier. A visit to the medieval quarter is out of the question now.

A band is playing military tunes in the gardens; children are danc-ing and singing, the boys parading and marching with straight legs like soldiers. It all seems so normal. I can't believe that war will actually break out in a few hours. Surely the Poles will accede to the Führer's demands? All the newspapers insist they are perfectly reasonable, and that we have every right to ask for the restoration of territory that was stolen from us at the end of the Great War, territory that will unite Prussia with the rest of Germany again.

Claus managed to telephone his commanding officer, although it took the hotel switchboard four hours to reach his regimental headquarters. His leave has been curtailed. He will have to return to his command on 30 August. Ours will be a very short honeymoon, only three days. I tried to look disappointed when he told me, but I am sure he suspects that I hate the things he does to me. This morning was even worse than last night. As soon as he woke he undressed me again, and afterwards, at breakfast, he kept trying to touch me, making vulgar jokes the whole time.

Tonight we will be at Bergensee. He has telegraphed his father to send a car to the station to meet us.

Grunwaldsee

TUESDAY, 29 AUGUST 1939

Claus has gone and I am alone again — thank God — in my bedroom in Grunwaldsee, although Mama has taken away my small bed and replaced it with a huge monstrosity of a four-poster big enough to hold a regiment. Mama and Papa von Letteberg left for their house in Berlin before Claus and I returned from Sopot so we could continue our honeymoon at Bergensee. They were afraid of encroaching on our privacy, but I wish they had stayed. If they had, we would at least have had to leave our bedroom to eat in the dining room.

I had been to Bergensee many times, but I never realized how much grander and more formal the house is compared to Grunwaldsee. Probably because I only had eyes for Claus when I was there. I knew it was vast, but I had no idea it had 465 rooms. The staff are dignified (dare I say pompous) and the housekeeper terrifies me. She is so prim and proper, and is always looking down her long nose. When she showed me the family portraits in the gallery I felt she considered me nowhere near beautiful or noble enough to be a von Letteberg bride.

The tour she gave me was a short one. Claus said I would have plenty of time to become acquainted with the house after he had left. He ordered all our meals to be served in his suite. He insisted that although we had such a short time together, we should try to produce an heir for his father and his family.

I hate sex — I refuse to call it lovemaking. What Claus does to me is nothing to do with love. There were times when I couldn't stop myself from crying, no matter how hard I tried to remember Mama's advice that it is a wife's duty to submit.

Mama telephoned to invite us to lunch at Grunwaldsee today. I was pleased, because it meant that I could keep my clothes on and say goodbye to Claus at home surrounded by my family. Despite all its magnificence, I find it difficult to think of Bergensee as my new home. I wonder if I ever will.

Although it was warm, I had to wear a dress with long sleeves so Mama and Papa wouldn't see the bruises on my arms, but I think Mama suspects something is wrong because she kept asking me if I was feeling well. I tried to smile and reassure her. Claus was the same as ever. He never changes, never seems happy or sad with anything or anyone. Now I realize that before we were married I saw no further than his handsome face, uniform and aristocratic refinement.

The twins were in their new lieutenants' uniforms, as was Peter. They were all called up into their regiments on Monday. Papa is devastated. He kept telling the boys that they have no idea what war is really like. He went on and on about the killing, the maiming, the blood until I felt sick. I don't understand why he was so angry with the twins and Peter. It isn't as if they were given any choice about being reservists or going into the army.

As they have all already completed their military training all three have been given commissions. So my brothers and brother-in-law as well as my husband are now officers in the Wehrmacht.

It seems strange to think of Peter as my brother-in-law. He was always playing the fool in the orchestra; there we were contemporaries. Now I am married I feel years older than him and that carefree girl who travelled out of Russia only a few short days ago.

The boys couldn't talk about anything other than the coming war. Greta joined us. As Peter is too young for her to flirt with and there were no other young men around except Claus, she was determined to be catty. I scarcely know what I said to her. I felt so ill and wretched after my 'honeymoon' I couldn't eat any of the lunch Mama had taken such pains over, and I could see that Papa as well as Mama was concerned for me. They thought it was because Claus was leaving. Little do they know. I couldn't wait for him to be gone.

Mama and Papa had invited Mama and Papa von Letteberg to lunch. They drove all the way from Berlin just to spend the day with us and Claus.

Although Papa von Letteberg had recently retired, he has been recalled to the army, given his old rank of General and appointed to an important position at army headquarters. He and Mama von Letteberg are making arrangements to move to Berlin for the duration of the war — however long that will be. Grafin von Letteberg is so kind. She asked me to visit them there as often as I can. I think she guessed that things are not so wonderful between Claus and me.

But for now I have a breathing space. No Claus or horrid 'married life' for weeks or, if I'm lucky, months. But although being married is not all I expected or hoped it would be, it is bearable while Claus is away. Is it so wrong of me to pray for his safety — and his continued absence?

Grunwaldsee

WEDNESDAY, 7 SEPTEMBER 1939

War! German troops marched into Poland one week ago tomorrow. We cannot be sure but we are almost certain that Claus, Paul and Wilhelm were among them. I pray to God that he will keep them all safe from harm. But Papa has warned me that it may be a long war. Britain and France demanded that we withdraw from Poland. The government couldn't do that, so both countries declared war on us on 3 September. We will soon have troops in the West as well as the East. Will Claus and the twins be sent there?

Grunwaldsee

TUESDAY, 12 DECEMBER 1939

I have not written a word in over three months because I am hardly ever well. First the honeymoon and now this baby. Mama keeps telling me I will be my old self again after the baby is born, but I don't believe her. I don't think I'll ever feel well again after my wedding night.

Claus has not been granted leave since he left me in Grunwaldsee at the end of August. It is a dreadful thing to say, but here, alone with my thoughts, I can be truthful. I am not sorry. We know he is stationed in Poland, as are Wilhelm and Paul. Wilhelm and Paul's letters are full of stories of how quickly Poland fell before our victorious army, and of their drinking and singing parties. Claus's letters speak only of what we will do in Bergensee after the war and how he intends to bring up his son. I wonder what he will do if I dare to present him with a daughter.

I stay in bed most mornings. I feel so sick and weak; I can barely lift my head from the pillows. In the afternoons I sit with Mama in the drawing room. I haven't touched the piano since I married. Papa dropped some hints that he would be glad of my help with running the estate, if only with the book-keeping and the ordering of supplies for the horses and the sale of produce to the war department, so last night I brought the estate account books up to date. Something is bothering Papa. I'm not sure what and, whenever I ask him, he says the only cares he has in this world are the war and my health.

Papa is leaving soon to represent East Prussian businessmen at a conference in Bavaria. I asked him about it but all he would say is what he always says whenever Mama or I question him about business, that it is nothing for us to bother our pretty little heads about, which probably means it is something to do with the war or the Party. He has had so many responsibilities since he was appointed burgomaster.

Fortunately for Grunwaldsee, Brunon is too old at fifty to be called up, so he, at least, will remain with us for the duration, but all the young men have been conscripted, except the idiot, Wilfie. Most of the maids have gone to the factories. The labour shortage is so bad that Brunon's wife, Martha, now has to help in the house.

Wood and coal are in short supply, so Mama has decided to shut off the ballroom, eight of the guest bedrooms and the formal dining room. I can't imagine how we will all squash into the small dining room when the boys come home on leave at Christmas. Claus will not be coming. He doesn't think it right for officers to take leave when so many ordinary soldiers have to remain at their posts. He wrote to tell me that he will probably be home for the New Year. If the angels smile on me, he'll change his mind about that, too.

Greta is also in Poland, supervising her BDM girls. They are preparing houses to receive ethnic Germans from Estonia and other eastern countries under Soviet rule. She writes to Mama and Papa nearly every day, telling them how the Poles didn't deserve decent houses because they are such dirty people, and it is very hard work getting the Polish women to scrub out their old homes to make them fit for occupation by the incoming ethnic German families.

Nina and Hildegard have both gone to Berlin to work in the War Office. Hildegard wrote to me and made her work sound very grand and important, but Nina, who is in the same office, says all they do is push models of planes, tanks and troop deployments around on a big board, in between answering the telephone and typing letters.

I wish I didn't feel so ill. Yesterday afternoon Mama ordered the car, and insisted I accompany her on a drive into town, but Brunon had to stop three times for me to be sick.

Wilhelm wrote to ask Papa's permission to marry Irena at Christmas in Grunwaldsee church. They are very young, but, as Papa says, it is not easy for boys who are about to go into battle to think of their whole life. Not when so many of them face an early death. Now the twins are finally serving officers, Papa has had to accept that they are adults as well as soldiers.

I can't imagine kind, gentle Wilhelm wanting to do the dreadful things to Irena that Claus does to me. And the more I think about Nina's assertion that some women like it, the less I believe her. I find it incredible that some poor women are desperate enough to do it for money! I would rather hang myself or starve to death.

Irena is so excited. She asked me what married life is like. I think she wanted to talk about sex, but I couldn't tell her the truth. She looked so happy. As happy as I did before my wedding night, and, as she has already accepted Wilhelm, there is no going back on her promise. Besides, it is the duty of every German girl to marry and produce sons for the Fatherland, so if Irena didn't marry Wilhelm, she would have to marry someone else.

Mama and Irena's mother, Frau Adolf, discuss the wedding over endless coffee afternoons. It will be held at Grunwaldsee, not only because we have more room, but because it is the only place for a von Datski to marry. Unfortunately, the constraints of war and rationing will limit the food and the number of guests, so poor Irena and Wilhelm's wedding will not be as lavish as mine.

The twins will be home on Christmas Eve, and the wedding will take place on the evening of Christmas Day. Wilhelm and Irena will have to honeymoon at Grunwaldsee because Wilhelm has only one week's leave and the railway warrant system is so uncertain. Papa has ordered the lakeside summerhouse to be cleaned and painted inside and out, and they will stay there. Martha will go down to cook for them.

In some ways I envy Irena. It was horrible in the Grand Hotel in Sopot the morning after our wedding night, knowing that all those people realized we were honeymooners, and were thinking about what Claus had done to me.

I will try to write more regularly, but now I am going to the station with Mama and Papa to say goodbye to Papa. Afterwards, Mama and I will call on Irena and her mother. I must make more of an effort to welcome Irena into the family, and try to warn her, tactfully, that married life is not everything the storybooks say it is.

'Wrong side of the road, Laura,' Charlotte said.

'Oh, hell, so I am! It's Britain's fault for driving opposite to every-one else.'

'If you're tired I can take over.'

'No, I feel fine; that is, unless you'd rather be at the wheel,' Laura replied, before remembering Claus's warning about letting their grandmother drive.

'Not at all.' Charlotte folded the map spread out on her knee. She had studied the route. North from Warsaw, then follow the Elblag road until they saw the sign for Olsztyn. To her surprise, it had proved as easy as it looked. 'Another hour or so and we should be at the hotel.'

'Provided I don't tempt providence by driving on the wrong side of the road again,' Laura qualified. 'After a month in Berlin you'd think I'd be used to it. I hope we reach Olsztyn in time to have a shower and unpack before dinner.'

'I'll never get used to calling Allenstein Olsztyn. It's such an ugly word,' Charlotte said feelingly.

'Perhaps not to the Poles.'

'Why are all these Trabis and Fiats at the side of the road? Surely they can't all have broken down?'

'Apparently spare parts for cars are still a major problem in Eastern Europe,' Laura answered. 'That's probably why there are so many horses and carts plodding in the middle of the road.'

'Not to mention bicycles that come from all directions,' Charlotte commented, as a young man swerved precariously in front of them.

'Do you recognize anything?'

'Not yet, but the countryside is just as I remembered. I was afraid it would be polluted, but the forests are as green and the lakes as clear as when I was a girl.'

'I'm not sure what I was expecting, but it certainly wasn't all this new building and freshly painted houses.' Laura slowed the car to read a signpost. 'Olsztyn eight kilometres. Do you want to stop off anywhere on the way?'

'That depends what road we go in on.'

'We must be on the main road now.'

Charlotte looked around. 'I don't see anything I know.'

'What about that lake?' Laura pointed to a small lake on their left.

Charlotte paled. 'Two, maybe three kilometres ahead there'll be a turn to the right.' She had thought she'd have more time to prepare. Some things had changed, after all. The trees had grown taller and altered the landscape. 'It will be little more than a lane. There used to be gates with stone wolves' heads capping the pillars.'

Laura noticed that Charlotte was trembling when she slowed to look for the landmark. She had never seen her grandmother upset, and stopped the car when Charlotte's hands tightened into gnarled fists.

There were no gates, no pillars, no stone wolves' heads; only two ivy-shrouded mounds of rubble.

'Is this the lane you'd like me to go down, Oma?'

Charlotte nodded.

Laura drove slowly over the track. Piles of leaves and pine needles were trapped between broken cobblestones. She swerved to avoid potholes, some large and deep enough to trap a wheel. The lane veered sharply to the right, she turned, and they entered a vast courtyard. In front of them and on their left towered an L-shaped, six-storey baroque mansion.

'You lived here?' Laura gasped.

Unable to answer, Charlotte fumbled with the door handle. Shivering in spite of the sunshine, she stepped outside. The breeze carried the distinct pine-resin smell of the forest. She looked around and took in everything; the fountain in the centre of the courtyard; the features on the stone cherubs that decorated it, disfigured and crumbling; the water spouts choked with weeds and caked slime that had dried to a rusty brown; the curved roofs, more gaping hole than red tiles; the windows boarded over with planks that had been prised away in places in the lower storeys; the decay in the once-decorative stonework, the cement veneer crumbling at the corners, so weather-stained and filthy its original cream could only be guessed at in one or two of the more sheltered nooks and crannies.

'Is this Grunwaldsee?' Laura's voice fell unnaturally loud into the silence.

'Bergensee.' Charlotte's voice was clotted with tears. 'The home of your Uncle Erich's father.'

'And you lived here, too?'

'For a little while after I married him.'

'I had absolutely no idea you lived somewhere so splendid, and I'm sure Claus doesn't. Why didn't you tell us?'

'So you'd never be dissatisfied with what you have.'

As Charlotte spoke, dark-skinned, ebony-haired women, with babies in their arms and small children clinging to their skirts, left the stables and walked across the courtyard towards them.

'Why are you here?'

The question was put to her in Polish. Charlotte understood it, but only just. Her command of the language had never progressed beyond the rudimentary, even when her father had employed Poles before the war. She pointed to herself and said, 'Von Letteberg.'

The reply came in German. 'You've returned to claim the house?'

Charlotte looked back at the ruins of the mansion. She shook her head. 'I couldn't even if I wanted to, and I don't.' She turned to Laura. 'Let's go.'

'You don't want to see any more, Oma?'

'I've seen enough.'

Realizing that her grandmother was too upset to make a rational decision, Laura suggested, 'Perhaps we could return later?'

Charlotte climbed into the passenger seat and closed the door. 'There's nothing to come back for.'

'Is this what Grunwaldsee will be like?'

'I don't know.' Charlotte looked at Bergensee for what she hoped would be the last time. Sad, broken, with gypsies in the courtyard where carriages and motor cars had once waited for princes and presidents. 'Grunwaldsee was never as grand as Bergensee. My only hope is it's not as derelict now. Greta was right. I should never have come back.'

Laura gripped her hand. 'The sooner we get you to a hotel, a good meal and a soft bed, the better.'

'You sound like my mother.' Charlotte tried to smile through her tears.

Laura switched on the ignition, slammed the rented Fiat into gear and drove back out on to the main road.

Chapter 6

LAURA KNOCKED on the door of Charlotte's room an hour after they had checked into the hotel. When Charlotte opened it, she stepped inside and looked around. 'Your room is identical to mine.'

'Bland, soulless, comfortable and easy to clean.' Charlotte walked through the French doors on to a small balcony that overlooked the lake.

'Our balconies adjoin. All you have to do is knock on the wall and I can climb over.'

'You make me sound like a sick old martinet who needs constant attention. Next thing you'll be giving me a cane to rap and a code. One knock for "urgent", two for "you have time to put your shoes on".'

'I am concerned about you. I can't make up my mind whether you're ill or just worn out.'

Charlotte smiled. 'Physically exhausted from all the travelling, and emotionally spent after seeing Bergensee. I thought I was strong enough to face anything. It's come as an unpleasant surprise to realize I'm not.'

'You've had a shock. Bergensee must have been some house in its heyday.'

'My mother-in-law's housekeeper would have delighted in telling you that it had four hundred and sixty-five rooms, acres of marble from Italy, original artwork by Bartlomiej Pens and Piotr Kolberg on the walls of the principal reception rooms, the same artists who decorated the baroque church at Swieta Lipke in the seventeenth century. There was even a painting attributed to Leonardo da Vinci in the dining room.'

'It could still be there?'

'The Russians looted and stripped every house in East Prussia. I promise you, there's nothing left behind those broken walls except empty rooms.'

'And ghosts?' Laura ventured.

'Perhaps. But not mine.' Charlotte walked back into the room and sank down into a chair.

'You should have told us what it was like.'

'Too many people looked back instead of forward at the end of the war, Laura. That was the last thing I wanted for my sons and grandchildren.'

'Claus would have dragged you here years ago if he'd known he had an ancestral home like that.'

'Like what?' Charlotte asked. 'It has no roof, no windows, gypsies living in the outbuildings. Another few years of freezing winters and warm summers will destroy the fabric even more, making it so unstable it will have to be pulled down before it collapses.'

'It could still be saved.'

'Not by me, and not by Erich or Claus,' Charlotte said decisively. 'When Germany was reunified, the West German government agreed that no reparation could be given or claims recognized for land, buildings or possessions lost in what is now Polish territory.'

'But it could be for sale,' Laura persisted. 'Few people would want a house in that condition. We might be able to pick it up for a song.'

'Even if we did, no one in our family has the kind of money needed to renovate Bergensee, let alone restore it to what it was. Besides,' Charlotte reminded her, 'none of us speaks Polish, so why would we want to live here?'

'You've never said much about Grunwaldsee.'

'You'll see it for yourself,' Charlotte replied evasively.

'Would you like to dine here, alone in your room?' Laura asked tactfully.

'I know it's dreadfully anti-social of me, but would you mind?'

'Not at all. I have to unpack and get my bearings. I love exploring new places on my own. You never know who you're going to meet.'

'Thank you for being understanding and for being here with me.'

Laura went to the door. 'They serve breakfast until ten; shall I call you at nine?'

'I promise you, I'll be more human then.'

'You're always human, Oma.' Laura kissed her grandmother before leaving her in the shades of a country long gone and the ghosts she sensed were crowding her out of the room.

WEDNESDAY, 20 DECEMBER 1939

*Papa is **dead**. Even now, when I have written the words, I can't believe it. The telegram came at midday. He died last night of a heart attack in a hotel in Munich. They are sending his body home for burial. Mama is hysterical with grief. I sent for the doctor and he sedated her. He telephoned the authorities, who told him that the coffin will be sealed and cannot on any account be opened. He explained to me that the features sometimes contort during a heart attack and we should remember Papa as he was, not as he will look now.*

I am trying to be strong and do what Papa would have wished, simply because there is no one else to organize Papa's funeral, although, like Mama, I would like to take to my bed, pull the blankets over my head and shut out the world.

The doctor promised me that Mama wouldn't wake for at least six hours, so I asked Minna to sit with her. Then I telephoned the pastor and Papa and Mama von Letteberg. Because Papa von Letteberg is in the War Office, I hoped he would be able to contact Paul and Wilhelm and arrange leave so they would be able to come home for the funeral. I also telephoned Greta in Poland. It was hateful having to tell her about Papa on the telephone. She sounded so odd that afterwards I telephoned her lodgings again and told one of the BDM girls about Papa. She promised that she would look after Greta until her travel warrant comes through.

Brunon was in the hall when the telegram came, so I asked him to gather all the workers together. It should have been Mama, Wilhelm or Paul telling them that Papa had died, but because Mama was in no condition to face anyone and the boys were away, the responsibility fell to me. I have never felt so unequal to a task. But now Papa has gone, someone has to manage Grunwaldsee until the war ends and the twins return. It is only right that I should shoulder as much of the burden as I can to spare Mama some of the work and worry. If only I didn't feel so ill with this pregnancy.

Papa and Mama von Letteberg drove all the way from Berlin and arrived late this evening. They are wonderful. Papa von Letteberg had already telephoned Wilhelm and Paul's commanders, and sent a telegram to Claus, who is away from his headquarters. He helped me to arrange the order of service for Papa's funeral, which will be held on Christmas Eve, and promised that they would stay with me at Grunwaldsee until New Year's Day.

They think I am resting but the last thing I want to do is go to bed. I know I won't be able to sleep, and the doctor can't give me any sedatives because of the baby. So I went into Mama's room, sent Minna to bed, and now I am sitting with Mama, writing this.

It is hard to believe that we will never see Papa again. The door to his dressing room is open. I can see his dresser and, resting on top of it, the amber panelled box he keeps his shirt studs and tiepins in. Next to it are his silver hairbrushes. He never would take them away from Grunwaldsee because he thought them too ostentatious for travelling. Will they send his clothes and plain wooden brushes back with him when he comes home?

He will be arriving in Allenstein on Saturday afternoon on the three o'clock train. I am going to meet it. Papa von Letteberg didn't want me to, but I insisted. Papa von Letteberg ordered a hearse to meet the train. I would probably have sent Brunon with a cart. I have so much to learn. I am lucky to have Brunon. Whatever else, I must make more of an effort to fight my weakness and sickness. I have to be strong, for Mama and Wilhelm and Paul's sake, because, when this war is over, the boys will return, and it is my responsibility to see that the estate of Grunwaldsee is run properly until such time as they can take over.

Our home is so precious and it is the duty of my brothers and me to care for it, to keep it safe and in good condition until we can pass it on to the generation who will come after us, and I must look after Mama, too. It is what Papa would have expected of me. I must be strong. I simply must.

'Well, now we're finally here, what would you like to do first?' Laura asked, as she and Charlotte queued at the breakfast buffet.

'Eat, if there's any food left.' Charlotte stepped back to avoid being elbowed by a large German, who was intent on piling half the cold meats from the buffet on to his plate.

Laura picked up a bread basket. 'What rolls would you like? Sesame, poppy seed, wholemeal, milk?'

'You choose.'

'I've been thinking; if you don't want to go to Grunwaldsee today,

86

we could wander around the town. From what I saw on the way in, some of the buildings look old and interesting, and there is bound to be a craft shop or art gallery.'

'There's an art exhibition in the castle,' the waitress informed them shyly in English when she set the coffee they had asked for on their table. 'It's French poster art from the nineteenth century.'

'What do you think, Oma?' Laura looked at Charlotte.

'Are you that sensitive, or am I being that obvious?' Charlotte picked up the cafetière and poured herself a cup.

'You don't have to be overly sensitive to realize that the sight of Bergensee upset you. It was dreadful. I was in tears and I didn't know the house before it was derelict.'

'I couldn't bear to see Grunwaldsee in the same condition.'

'We could ask around to find out if the house is still standing.'

'No,' Charlotte broke in quickly. 'I know it's irrational but I don't want to discuss Grunwaldsee with anyone until I have been there and seen it for myself.'

'But there can't possibly be anyone left in the town who knows you,' Laura said.

'No, there won't be, but you saw those gypsies yesterday. They knew the name von Letteberg, yet they couldn't have moved into Bergensee until after the war. Their families have probably been living in those outbuildings for decades. Wouldn't you resent someone turning up and saying it was theirs?'

'You didn't and you'd lived there,' Laura pointed out. 'And, if I were them, I'd like to find out something about the history of the house.'

'Unlike you, I don't think they are the slightest bit interested.'

'They can't blame you for wanting to visit your old home.'

'From the stories I've heard from friends who have already come back, some of the present owners are more amenable than others when it comes to showing the old owners over their property.' Charlotte buttered a roll and placed a slice of smoked cheese on top.

'Perhaps they realize no compensation was paid, and are afraid of people making claims against their homes.' Laura poured milk into her coffee.

'Legally no claims can be recognized; the new owners know that.

And quite a few of the present owners bought their homes from the Communist regime.'

'I thought that wasn't allowed.'

'It happened, particularly with government workers like policemen.' Charlotte sat back and looked around the room. Aside from a sprinkling of young people in business suits, most of their fellow hotel guests were elderly and, she suspected, visiting the town for the same reason she was.

'I still think you ought to show Bergensee to Claus.'

'I agree he should see it – if he wants to. But even if we could lay claim to Bergensee or Grunwaldsee – and we can't – what would I or your Uncle Erich do with the houses? Erich told me that he barely remembers living here. He was only four years old when we had to leave.' Charlotte closed her eyes against images of her flight from her homeland that had been seared indelibly into her mind.

'Even derelict, Bergensee is still quite something,' Laura mused.

'I hope the new owner, whoever he or she is, or will be, is rich. You saw the state of the place. What do you think? A million dollars to demolish it? Six million to put it right?'

'You're probably right,' Laura conceded. 'But after seeing the house, I envy Claus. His father's history is so much more interesting than mine, and I can't imagine having an ancestral home like Bergensee and not wanting to live in it.'

'Then it's just as well you're a Templeton and not a von Letteberg. What on earth would you do for work in the middle of Poland, bearing in mind that you can't speak a word of the language?'

'Sorry, my romantic streak doesn't run as far as accommodating mundane, everyday things like paying bills and work.'

'A romantic streak is not a bad thing, provided you temper it with a little realism. Without it, I would never have become an artist.' Charlotte topped up her coffee cup. 'And although Claus's family history may be grander than yours, I don't know about more interesting. Your father told me a few years back that your grandfather traced the Templeton family tree to the fifteenth century after he retired and took up genealogy.'

Laura made a face. 'They were cloth merchants in Cheapside who didn't have the vision or drive to build a Bergensee.'

'Bergensee was just a house. Rich or poor, a person can only live in half a dozen rooms at most, and that includes the bathroom and kitchen. The servants and guests filled the rest of Bergensee, which meant none of us had a moment's privacy or peace when we were there.' Charlotte pushed her coffee cup and plate away. 'Shall we look around the town?'

'I'd like that.' Laura left the table.

'In an hour.' Charlotte wanted to read more of her diary so she could move on from the tragedy of her father's death. 'Since I reached eighty, I like a short rest after breakfast.'

'An hour will be fine, Oma. That will give me time to check my e-mails.'

'Still working?'

'Anxious to know what the station thinks of my last documentary. They should have had the discs by now.'

SUNDAY, 24 DECEMBER 1939

Brunon and the workers did not want to put the Christmas tree up in the hall as usual but I insisted. Papa would not have wanted to disappoint the workers' children, particularly in wartime when there is so little to look forward to. I am trying to do everything just as Papa would have if he were here. Mama is still too ill to leave her bed.

Papa von Letteberg and I went to the station yesterday, and found Greta there trying to get a taxi. I don't know why she hadn't telephoned home to let us know when she was arriving. I would have sent Brunon to fetch her. She waited with us for the Munich train that brought Papa. I wanted to talk to her but the station wasn't the right place, and when we reached home we found Frau Gersdoff, the florist, waiting to see us. After we'd chosen and ordered wreaths and flowers for Papa, Greta locked herself in her room. I could hear her crying but, as I felt like doing the same, I couldn't think of anything that I could say to her that might make her stop.

She had the most dreadful argument with Frau Gersdoff. Apparently there is a shortage of red roses, which isn't surprising at this time of year. Greta wanted a wreath made up of two hundred buds, but she has had to content herself with a dozen roses and a few lilies. I told her that Papa would have hated an ostentatious display, particularly during wartime, but she wouldn't listen and refused to discuss the funeral service Papa von

*Letteberg and I had arranged. I asked Mama if she approved of the hymns
we had chosen but she couldn't even speak, which was no help at all.*

*Wilhelm and Paul came home at lunchtime today, and now we are all
dressing for the service. Irena and her parents, and Manfred, who is home
on leave, are coming, and Papa and Mama von Letteberg, of course, as well
as all our tenants and the workers from the estate. I don't know who else
will be there, but ever since I came upstairs I have heard cars pulling up in
the courtyard and the sound of footsteps plodding through the ice and snow
down the lane towards the church.*

*I went there this morning to look at the flowers. It was horrible to see
the crypt open to receive Papa. I simply can't bear the thought of his coffin
being laid in there beside Opa and Oma's and all the other von Datskis. I
haven't heard a word from Claus, which everyone except me finds strange. I
feel cold and empty. I thought marriage would mark the end of my childhood but it didn't. Papa was always there to love, protect and guide me.
Now I am without him, I feel so burdened and so alone.*

Charlotte insisted on driving the rental car into the centre of
Allenstein. She headed for the old quarter of the town and parked in
a quiet, wide, tree-lined street.

Laura gazed at the solidly built buildings. 'These apartment blocks
look pre-war.'

'They are. It's most peculiar; this street hasn't changed in over sixty
years. People and governments have come and gone, yet domestic life
is still being carried on here regardless. The Mullers lived on the first
floor.' Charlotte pointed to an Art Deco block that wouldn't have
looked out of place in New York. 'Above them were the Heines, and
that one on the end above the shop was the home of the Freibergs;
their father was my father's second cousin.'

'Did they all get out when the Russians invaded at the end of the
war?' Laura asked.

'No. Frau Muller and her husband were never very bright, bless
them. They married late and had one daughter, Nina. She was a great
friend of mine. She was working in Berlin when the Russians came. I
heard later that she survived the war. Her father worked for the rail-
ways. His train was scheduled to go east, and although what was left
of the German army was flooding back from the advancing Russians,

he insisted on sticking to the timetable he'd been issued with and drove straight towards them. His wife wouldn't leave without him, although the neighbours begged her to. She insisted on waiting for his return.'

'What happened?'

'No one ever discovered Herr Muller's fate, although we guessed it. Frau Muller was gang-raped and murdered by Russian soldiers, who threw her body into the street. A German soldier from the town who had been captured by the Russians wrote about what he'd witnessed here years later. Apparently she lay there for days.'

Laura stared at the window Charlotte had pointed to. It was difficult to imagine horrific scenes being played out in such a quiet area. 'And your relatives the Freibergs?'

'Herr Freiberg was a pharmacist. He poisoned himself, his wife and four children. The oldest was twelve and considered something of a child prodigy by the tutors in the music school.'

'I had no idea things like that happened in East Prussia at the end of the war.' Tears started into Laura's eyes.

'It is so strange to be here again.' Charlotte studied the old convent in front of the apartment block. It was exactly as she remembered; painted cream and brown with black and white garbed nuns walking up and down the steps and into the Catholic church opposite. 'This is my home town. I knew every street, families in almost every block. Classmates, relatives, business acquaintances of my father's; people so much a part of my everyday life I took them for granted. I feel as though I've woken in a nightmare where the buildings have aged and the people disappeared, yet I am still young.' She gave Laura a rueful smile. 'That's the most appalling thing about old age. Inside I feel no different from when I was eighteen. And just being here makes me think that if I walk around this corner, the aches and pains in my joints will disappear and my brothers will be waiting for me in one of their new cars.'

Laura took her arm. 'I can't imagine enduring what you have. Seeing your home town emptied. Having to run for your life, and now coming back to find everyone gone and everything changed.'

'Not everything.' Charlotte glanced at the convent.

'Time to visit the art exhibition in the castle?'

'The chambermaid told me there is an excellent ice cream parlour close by. What's that saying? "Eat as much ice cream as you can, before the doctor forbids it!" Let's go there when we've seen all we want to in the castle, and order the largest sundaes they have on the menu.'

'And afterwards?' Laura asked.

'Afterwards we'll return to the hotel, have lunch and a short rest before taking one of those pony and trap rides around the lake that are advertised in reception.' Charlotte hooked her hand into her granddaughter's arm, and they walked up the hill towards the fourteenth-century, red-brick castle. She omitted to mention that the lake was the same one that bordered Grunwaldsee.

The main house was some distance from the lake, but it could be seen from a few vantage points on the bank, and she hoped to find out if the walls were still standing. She also longed to know if the small wooden summerhouse that her father had so lovingly restored for Wilhelm and Irena's honeymoon in December 1939, and which had later served as her retreat and sanctuary during the happiest summer of her life, had survived into the new millennium.

MONDAY, 25 DECEMBER 1939

We laid Papa to rest in the crypt at four o'clock yesterday afternoon. The pastor was forced to restrict entrance to the church to family and close friends. Crowds stood outside in the snow, the men bare-headed to pay their respects. There were hundreds and hundreds. I think everyone in the town was there. I had no idea Papa knew so many people.

Although Mama had not left her bed since we received the telegram, she insisted on going to the church. She said that if we prevented her, she would regret not saying goodbye to Papa for the rest of her life.

The doctor allowed her to attend the service on condition she returned to bed immediately afterwards. Greta and I helped her dress and, because we were worried that she might collapse, Paul and Wilhelm walked either side of her and sat with her throughout the service. It was dreadful, following the coffin out of the house and down the lane to the church.

Brunon and five of our oldest workers carried Papa on their shoulders for his last journey. Paul and Wilhelm followed next with Mama. Greta walked with me. I felt a hand on my shoulder as we reached the church. I turned and saw Claus behind me. He looked ill. Afterwards, he told me that he had travelled non-stop for three days and nights. He was on manoeuvres when he heard the news of Papa's death, and although his commanding officer gave him immediate permission to leave, there were problems with the trains because of the Christmas holidays.

I never thought I would write this, but it was good to have him standing beside me in church. He came into the crypt with us when Papa's coffin was placed in it, and escorted me back to the house after the service. So many people came to pay their respects. I was grateful that Brunon's wife, Martha, had taken it upon herself to organize the food. I have no idea where she found it, but there was tea and real coffee, and wine and brandy enough for everyone. The cakes, preserves and sandwiches the mourners ate probably took all our food ration for the next month, but it doesn't matter. What is important is that Papa was buried with respect and the correct ceremonies.

After most of the people from the town had left, Greta and I helped Mama undress, and the doctor gave her another sedative. As Greta insisted on sitting with Mama, I went to look for Claus. He was in the dining room with Wilhelm, Paul, the Adolfs, his parents and a few relatives and close friends. He told me that he has to leave the day after Christmas. Neither he nor the twins would say very much about what is happening in Poland, but when Herr Adolf and some of the other men asked when the Wehrmacht intends to push the English out of France, they clammed up, so I suppose there will be fighting in France soon.

I knew Claus wanted to be alone with me but that was the last thing I wished for, so I went into the hall to superintend the decorating of the Christmas tree. Minna had ordered tables to be set up for the family's Christmas presents. Mine were upstairs in my room but somehow it didn't seem right to bring them down and lay them out in the hall on the same day we buried Papa, especially as out of respect for Papa, Brunon and I had decided to break with tradition.

Not wanting to celebrate Christmas Eve on the same day as Papa's funeral, we arranged for the workers' children to come in to see the tree this morning and we also opened our presents then. It was strange to have the small ceremonies – such as they were – a day late and after breakfast. Christmas will never be the same for me again.

Before she went to bed, Mama insisted that Wilhelm and Irena's wedding should go ahead as planned, because Papa would not have wanted them to postpone it on his account.

All the time, everyone, including me, says, 'That is what Papa would have wanted.' We say it without thinking. I have even written it here, but when Mama began talking about the wedding, I realized that none of us could possibly know what Papa would want when he is no longer here to tell us.

I sent Minna upstairs to get my presents for everyone, but told her to hide them in the sewing room until Christmas morning. And I asked Brunon to bring down another trestle from the attic for Wilhelm and Irena's wedding gifts. It was then that Mama von Letteberg noticed how impatient Claus was to be alone with me, so she insisted on taking over the organizing so Claus and I could go upstairs.

I had no idea how much I would resent his presence in the room that has been mine since I was a baby. Although the four-poster bed Mama had ordered placed in the room during our honeymoon is huge, I couldn't endure the idea of sharing it with Claus. And there he was, lying on the embroidered linen cover in his uniform, his dirty boots outside the door for Brunon to take down and clean.

Claus kissed me and complimented me on my figure. I told him I have been too busy vomiting to put on any weight. He said he is very glad about the baby and he knew from his mother's letters that I was far from well and missing him. I tried to smile but found it very difficult. All I could think about was Papa lying in that freezing cold vault. Papa, who had always hated the cold.

Claus suggested that we should have some wine and go to bed. It was only nine o'clock but he said I looked as exhausted as him. There was no point in arguing because I knew that everyone expected us to remain there until morning.

I wonder if I am getting used to the things he does to me, or if he really was gentler. It didn't hurt as much as I remembered although it was still disgusting, and afterwards I was horribly sick, but by then Claus was asleep so it didn't matter. I sat up and wrote because I couldn't stand lying next to him listening to his snoring. Then, at three o'clock I felt terribly thirsty and hungry, and realized that I had eaten hardly anything since Papa had died, so I put on my robe and left the room.

The house was quiet. I looked in on Mama. Greta had stayed with her, probably to let everyone know what a martyr she was being, although she needn't have bothered because she was sleeping on the chaise longue, so if Mama had wanted anything Greta wouldn't have been any use. And she was sleeping very soundly because she didn't stir when I tiptoed in and switched off all the lights except the small light next to Mama's bed.

Even Putzi barely lifted her head out of her basket when I walked down the stairs; so much for her being a guard dog. Someone had filled all the tables with presents. There were several with Claus's handwriting, so I knew that he must have given his case to his mother to empty.

While I was making my way to the kitchen I heard a noise in Papa's study and froze, half-expecting him to be there. I was terrified when I pushed open the door. It wasn't Papa, but Wilhelm and Irena. They had locked the door from the hall, but Wilhelm hadn't bothered with the small door that connects with the servants' part of the house. They were standing in front of the fire whispering so low I couldn't hear what they were saying. Irena was unbuttoning Wilhelm's trousers, something I could never imagine doing for Claus, then she helped him undress while he undressed her.

I stood there, worried that if I moved they would see my reflection in the mirror over the fireplace, and also, although I am ashamed to admit it, I wanted to see if Wilhelm would hurt Irena as much as Claus hurts me.

But when they were both naked, they lay, side by side on the rug in front of the fire. Irena kissed Wilhelm all over. Every part of him. I was shocked. Just the thought of kissing Claus's lips makes me sick. Then he began stroking and kissing her. I should have moved away but I simply couldn't believe Irena. She didn't stop him from doing whatever he wanted, and she smiled and laughed the whole time as though she liked him touching her. If she was in any pain she didn't show any sign of it.

Can Nina be right? Do some women actually want men to do those things to them? It was obvious from what Irena was doing to Wilhelm, and he to her, that it wasn't the first time they had been alone and naked together.

I crept back up the staircase to the bedroom where I am writing this. Claus is still sleeping. I feel tired and sick, and I am still hungry because I didn't get anything to eat in case I made a noise that would disturb Wilhelm or Irena.

I can't understand Irena lying naked and unashamed in Wilhelm's arms. Is she a better actress than me? Or can it be that she really likes making love?

Is my disgust with the things Claus does to me all my fault? Should I try harder to be a wife to him? I wish I had someone to talk to. I have always been closer to Irena than Greta. We can and do talk to one another about everything. Perhaps after she marries Wilhelm I will be able to discuss the private side of married life with her. I do hope so.

Laura leaned out of the open carriage to check that the coachman was only pretending to whip the pair of greys pulling their carriage. Reassured she sat back and said, 'This countryside reminds me of some of the more isolated areas in Maine. That stretch of woodland looks as though it hasn't changed in centuries.'

'It probably hasn't,' Charlotte agreed absently. She scanned the shoreline for a sign of the lakeside summerhouse below Grunwaldsee. If it was there she couldn't see it, or the walls of the outbuildings. But where she remembered young saplings, tall trees now towered, and bushy undergrowth that would have hidden any surviving walls from view.

Laura watched a pair of dinghies race towards a jetty. 'Did you ever sail on this lake when you lived here, Oma?'

'Yes, but our boats were not as dashing or colourful as those.'

'You used to live here?' A brash, elderly woman with dyed blonde hair and an American accent interrupted their conversation.

'A long time ago,' Charlotte conceded, wishing she hadn't given in to the coachman's plea that they share the carriage with two other hotel guests. He'd offered a discount which hadn't swayed her. But the hour's wait for the next carriage had.

'So did I,' the women said eagerly. 'My family used to live in Lake Street. Perhaps you remember them, the Schulers?'

Charlotte shook her head. 'The only family I knew in that street were the Adolfs.'

'I remember them. They had a Communist son, who was always in trouble with the police, and a beautiful daughter, Irena. She married well, one of the aristocrats, a von Datski. But then everyone knows what happened to them; it was such a disgrace at the time ...'

'A disgrace?' Laura looked at the woman questioningly, then at Charlotte.

Charlotte interrupted. The last thing she wanted was this stranger telling Laura a gossip-laden version of the family history. 'Have you come back to look at your old home?'

'I wanted to show my daughter where I was born.' She nodded to the younger version of herself sitting next to her. 'Mrs Charles Grant the third.'

'Pleased to meet you.' Charlotte offered her hand. 'This is my granddaughter, Laura Templeton.'

'You're English.'

'I am,' Laura answered.

'We're turning.' Charlotte took Laura's arm. 'If you'll excuse us, I would like to concentrate on the view.'

'So would I. Of course, none of this was developed in our day, and now look at it. All the woods on this side of the lake cut down to make way for those small huts, summerhouses and vegetable gardens. They've completely ruined the scenery.'

'Probably not for the people who live off those vegetables,' Charlotte observed. 'Food prices have rocketed since the Communists fell from power.'

'And a good riddance, too. Did your family own property in Allenstein?'

'Some,' Charlotte answered guardedly.

'Of course, the Germans who fled in nineteen forty-five can't claim it back, although Poles who fled the Russian army can. I'm here because I heard that my father's old house was up for sale.'

'You're going to buy it?'

'I already have. It was a snip. Only forty-five thousand dollars.'

'What will you do with it?'

'Renovate it for a start. It hasn't been touched by so much as a paintbrush since we left. Once it's modernized, I'll rent it out to tourists. A rented house is cheaper for families than a hotel, and this is a good base from which to tour the Masurian lakes. There you are, Ranolf,' the woman greeted an elderly man, who walked towards the carriage as it slowed to negotiate the drive to the hotel. 'I've just met this charming woman and her granddaughter. She's another refugee come home to show her kinsfolk the old country. We must bring our grandchildren here next year.' She turned to Charlotte. 'My husband, Ranolf Hedley the fourth. I'm sorry, I didn't catch your name?'

'Charlotte Templeton. If you'll excuse us, we must go. We're expecting a telephone call.'

'Templeton?' Laura repeated when they walked towards the outdoor café area. 'I've never heard you use grandfather's name before. Why didn't you tell that woman who you were?'

'Because she's a snob. You heard her talk about the aristocratic von Datskis and their disgrace.'

Laura braced herself. 'What was the disgrace?'

'It was only a disgrace to Nazis old enough to remember the Hitler years.' Charlotte avoided answering the question. 'And to those who aren't, a mystique has grown up around the Prussian Junker families. Who's to say now how rich, splendid and powerful any of them were? There is nothing like loss, time and distance to lend distinction to any background, not to mention a vast increase in numbers. I have heard people who lived in the slums of the town claim that their family owned large estates.'

'You never corrected them?'

Charlotte smiled. 'What was the point? Nothing could be proved either way for years, and why upset them?'

'You've never spoken to me about your childhood.'

Charlotte took Laura's hand. 'That ruin over there was a fourteenth-century watchtower. My brothers and I used to take a boat, row over the lake and picnic there as children.' She hesitated. 'I will tell you more, Laura, after we have visited Grunwaldsee. Until then I want to hold on to my memories, because while they remained imprisoned here,' she tapped her forehead, 'they remain entirely mine. Once I have told you about them they will become the past – history. For the moment, apart from Bergensee, my dead are alive again, and I would like to live with them for a little while longer.'

Chapter 7

It has been a long time since I have had the leisure to write in this diary, but, as we are constantly told on the wireless, everyone must work hard in a country at war, women as well as men. With Mama ill, and the twins in France, just as I anticipated, the management of Grunwaldsee has fallen to me. Wilhelm suggested to Greta that she give up her BDM work to help, but she said her job implementing the Reich's resettlement programme was far too important, as it didn't only concern the war effort but the entire future of the Third Reich.

I pleaded with Wilhelm not to argue with her. I am happy to assume sole responsibility for our home, because I would hate to live with Greta again. Running the estate is a burden, but a welcome one, as it leaves me little time to think about how much I miss Papa or my marriage to Claus.

I have discovered just how much hard work it takes to make everything run smoothly at Grunwaldsee. So many things I always took for granted need a great deal of organizing. I was used to reaching for cleaned and polished tack; ordering the stable boys to saddle my horse; walk into the animal feed store and see the bins full. Now, just writing the weekly work sheets takes a full day; and that's without keeping the accounts up to date, filling out invoices, war department forms and paying the bills. The office work takes two, sometimes three, full days a week; time I would prefer to spend helping Brunon supervise the workers. There is so much that I need to learn.

I wish I had taken the trouble to listen more to Papa when he was alive, but I thought we had all the time in the world. And in those days I couldn't imagine Grunwaldsee without him or the boys.

I work in Papa's study, and frequently look at the framed document that hangs on the wall opposite his desk. It is a copy of the charter that granted the lake of Grunwaldsee and the surrounding lands to the first Wilhelm von Datski to live here. It was signed by the Grand Master of the Order of Teutonic Knights in 1286. Sometimes I feel weighed down by the long line of von Datskis who have lived here before me, sensing their disapproval at the decisions that I, a woman, and a young one at that, am forced to make on the family's behalf.

Before going to bed, I often stand on the balcony outside my bedroom, looking down at the lake and imagining not only all those dead von Datskis stretching back through the centuries, but all the von Datskis who will live here after me. I hope I won't earn their disapproval as well. It would be frightful to go down in family history as the Charlotte von Letteberg, née von Datski, who ruined the estate, or ran it into bankruptcy, but hopefully, with Brunon's help, I will avoid making any serious mistakes.

God willing, one day my grandchildren will play here with Wilhelm and Paul's. Irena is expecting a baby in September. She and Wilhelm are ecstatic but no one could be happier than Mama. She says she knows that Irena will have a boy who will ensure continuity of the von Datski line into the Führer's thousand-year Reich. I cannot begin to imagine what Grunwaldsee will look like a thousand years from now. With luck, unchanged and as perfect as it does now.

I rely completely on Brunon. Papa always said that he is the best steward Grunwaldsee has ever had. He knows more than anyone about the estate. I am glad that he is too old to serve in the army because in place of the able-bodied men who have been conscripted, we have been given girls from the land army and Polish civilians.

The land army girls have been billeted with the families of the men who are away fighting. At first it was difficult, but once the wives realized that they would get paid for lodging them they agreed to take them. We housed the Poles in some of the older cottages Papa always meant to renovate but for various reasons never did. Their food allowance is less than ours, but I have supplemented their rations. They were nowhere near enough for farm workers.

Brunon told them to make the cottages as comfortable as they could, and gave them wood to repair the doors and windows as well as some of the old furniture we had in the attic. They have done a good job; the cottages now look better than they have done in years.

It took a while but now, at last, everything seems to be going smoothly, although we have to keep the groups entirely separate because the German girls look down on the Poles and never miss a chance to belittle them. We received a directive from the Gauleiter's office stating: 'All Germans must treat the Polish workers in the Reich with an attitude which corresponds to our national dignity and the aims of German policy.' I was confused when I read it but Brunon says it is a warning that we must not get too friendly with the Poles. They needn't have bothered to send us the paper. I barely have time to see my own family.

The harvest this year will be a good one, but we will not make much money because three-quarters of it has been requisitioned by the army and we have to sell it to them at the prices they have fixed. But it will be a small sacrifice if it means a swifter end to the war.

So many have been killed in France during the last two weeks, including four boys from my orchestra; Peter was one of them. Dear Peter who was so much fun, if a torment and a tease at times. Mama and Papa von Letteberg received the telegram three days ago, but he died on 30 May. It was a great blow to both of them, as it will be for Claus. My poor brother-in-law; we were related for such a short time.

I haven't yet come to the reason why I have picked up my pen after all this time.

My son, Erich Peter Claus von Letteberg, was born at two o'clock this morning, two days after our flag flew from the Arc de Triomphe and our soldiers paraded up the Champs-Elysées.

The birth was agonizing. The doctor gave me as much morphine as he dared, and if it hadn't been for Minna and Mama von Letteberg I think I would have died, but when it was over and I saw my darling son for the first time, I couldn't believe it. A beautiful, blond, blue-eyed boy, so alive, angry and perfect, and exactly like his father, or so Mama and Papa von Letteberg assured me.

They drove down from Berlin to see me as soon as they received the news of Peter's death because they wanted to tell me themselves. It was thoughtful of them and truly made me feel like their daughter. And they stayed when I went into labour soon after they arrived.

They dote on little Erich. Poor Peter was killed before he became an uncle. Claus had already written agreeing that if we had a son he was to bear my father's name but I also called him Peter after his brother.

I know Claus tried to get leave but I was glad he didn't, because he would have come home to hear my screams filling the house for two days and nights. Papa von Letteberg told me that no German soldier could be spared from the big push into France, but he used his influence to telephone Claus to tell him that he has a son. Claus said that now the English and French armies have surrendered and Germany has freed Europe from the presence of the Allied forces, he wants me and his parents to visit him in Paris. Papa von Letteberg said it is out of the question for him, but not for me and Mama von Letteberg. Poor Mama von Letteberg; all she wants to do at the moment is nurse Erich and talk about Peter. He has been buried in France so there won't be a funeral, only a memorial service for him.

As for me, Claus will have to wait until I am well again. The doctor warned me that as Erich's birth was such a difficult one it will take me at least two years to recover; besides, Erich is far too young to travel. I am glad that I have an excuse. Perhaps I will feel differently about seeing Claus again in a month or two. Although I don't think so.

As I look at my son sleeping beside my bed in the cot that was used for Greta, my brothers and me, I pray the war will end soon and that there will never be another one. The thought that eighteen years from now Erich could be conscripted and killed like Peter makes me want to gather him into my arms and hide him from the world, so he will never know hurt or pain.

A train travelling from Paris to East Prussia via Berlin
FRIDAY, 23 AUGUST 1940

I am returning to Grunwaldsee after spending two weeks with Claus in Paris. Since he has been promoted to colonel it is impossible for him to get leave. I wasn't sorry until Greta arrived in Grunwaldsee at the beginning of the month with Helmut Kleinert, a distant relative of Papa's second cousin. She announced that they were staying for two weeks because they needed a holiday, although why she thinks that they deserve one more than the boys at the front escapes me.

Greta was as irritating and catty as ever, and wherever I went in the house or on the estate, she followed, so I finally accepted Claus's invitation. I told Mama I could go because Greta was there to look after her.

Greta met Helmut in Berlin. She was transferred to the BDM head-quarters there at Easter. She and Helmet celebrated their engagement with their fellow workers, which is just as well, given the food situation at Grunwaldsee. Papa would have approved of Helmut — he is a quiet and pleasant enough boy — but he would have hated Greta's vulgar engagement ring. Greta told me she had chosen it herself. I would have been ashamed to admit it. I wouldn't have the courage to wear such an ostentatious diamond, especially in these days of wartime austerity.

Helmut's father manufactures armaments and has used his influence to secure a staff post in Berlin for his son, which means that Helmut will never have to fight at the Front. Greta always did look after her own interests to the exclusion of all else, even the welfare of the Fatherland.

When I left Grunwaldsee I was worried about taking Erich to a city that might be bombed, but there was only one air raid warning the whole time we were in Paris and that was a false alarm. I remained with Claus for fourteen days — and nights. It was such a long way to travel he insisted it would be ridiculous of me to make the effort for less time. I only agreed because I didn't want to return to Grunwaldsee until Greta had left. That way I could go back to running the estate without worrying about organizing formal dinners and entertainments for her.

If Greta's attitude is an example of what's going on in Berlin, it's time everyone there took notice of what's happening in the rest of the country. Everything is in short supply — food, clothing, petrol. Sometimes it is impossible to find your allocated ration of food, and heaven only knows it is small enough. Yet Greta and Helmut carry on as though there isn't a war. They assume that we have limitless supplies of meat, butter and eggs just because we live in the country.

Irena said her father is so short of labour to run his building business that he has asked the authorities for prisoners of war. I wouldn't like to have English and French prisoners at Grunwaldsee. I would be too afraid that they would sabotage our efforts to increase production.

I have written about everyone except Claus. The best reason for our marriage is sleeping in his pram beside me. Claus used his rank to get us a carriage to ourselves, in case Erich came into contact with someone with a contagious disease. It couldn't have been easy, even for a colonel. All the trains are crowded and travel warrants scarce, but Claus, like his parents, adores our son and would do anything to protect him, even use his rank to gain privileges, something he would never do on his own or my account.

For the first time I saw a touch of tenderness on his face when he kissed Erich goodbye. I think we have a strange marriage. It is nothing like Irena and Wilhelm's. Wilhelm has only managed two leaves since his wedding at

Christmas but Irena will travel miles, beg rides and sit on trucks with all sorts of strange men just to spend an hour or two with him. When they are together they can barely keep their hands off one another, and Irena is as bad as Wilhelm.

Claus is always formal and polite. But then he is a colonel, and always has to be seen to be behaving correctly, unlike Wilhelm, who is only a lieutenant and allowed to be outrageous.

Claus wasn't at the station to meet me when I arrived in Paris, but he sent his driver. The sergeant apologized and said there was a problem with the English bombing the guns we had pointed at their coast. I was too polite to say anything to him or Claus, but I knew it was an excuse.

Claus has a suite in a beautiful hotel overlooking the Seine. It has a sitting room, private dining room, two bedrooms and two bathrooms. For the first time Erich didn't sleep next to me. Claus had asked the hotel to place the cot in the maid's room. I took Brunon's daughter, Maria, with me. She has helped me care for Erich since the day he was born and she promised faithfully to call me if he woke, but she didn't. I think Claus warned her not to, and she, like all our servants, is terrified of him.

Claus, or more likely his aide, had been most thoughtful. There were fruit and flowers in all the rooms, perfume and cosmetics in the bathroom, iced champagne and brandy in the sitting room, and his driver was at my disposal to take me to the couturier where Claus had opened an account for me. Claus had left a note to tell me that he had booked opera tickets to celebrate my first evening in Paris and afterwards there would be a formal dinner in my honour.

I was glad Claus had made the arrangements; it is easier to be his wife in public than private. I bathed and changed out of my travelling clothes, went to the couturier and chose a selection of day frocks and three evening gowns, one of which they altered immediately, so I could wear it that night. Then I visited the hotel beautician and had my hair washed and set and a manicure. When Claus arrived at the suite at six o'clock I was dressed and waiting for him.

I was almost as nervous as I had been on our honeymoon. We have been married a year but until this holiday had spent only seven days and nights together. Before he arrived I took his photograph from my suitcase and set it on the dressing table to remind myself what he looked like. Terribly handsome, a little remote, and every inch the Wehrmacht colonel. I was taken aback when I saw how deferential everyone was to us. Doors opened and people bowed — not only German military personnel but also French civilians.

The first thing Claus did was ask to see his son. Although Erich was sleeping he insisted on waking him. I thought men weren't supposed to like babies. Claus held him in his arms and was so proud when Erich pushed his feet down as though he were trying to stand. He insisted he was a prodigy.

It was no use my telling him the doctor and Minna maintain all babies do the same. After he played with the baby, he asked me to accompany him to the bedroom to talk to him while he bathed and changed into his dress uniform. I knew what he wanted. It made no difference that I was already dressed. He simply bent me, face down over the bed, lifted my skirt and pulled down my underclothes.

Perhaps I really am becoming a woman, because the thought of what was about to happen was worse than the reality. It was still painful and humiliating, a bit like the doctor's examinations when I was pregnant, but I have learned to concentrate on other things, and nothing lasts for ever. Not even that.

The rest of the evening was wonderful. The opera was superb; it made me realize how much I have missed good music. Claus's fellow officers were charming, the meal at the restaurant excellent; the sauces were made with real cream and butter, and the meat and gateaux were perfect. I don't think I have ever danced so much. Every single one of Claus's fellow officers asked me to honour them. But as the evening drew to a close I began to dread going back to the hotel.

I scarcely slept during the two weeks; Claus wouldn't leave me alone. He wants me to have another child as soon as possible. I told him that the doctor warned me against another pregnancy until I have fully recovered from the last, but Claus insisted childbirth and pregnancy is the natural state for a woman, and if my doctor can't look after me, I should move to Paris where he will find me a better one.

He wanted to rent a villa outside the city, somewhere not too far away, where he could visit Erich and me, and occasionally stay overnight. If I hadn't had Grunwaldsee to manage I think he would have ordered me to remain with him.

I am glad to be on my way home. I have no idea when I will see Claus again, but I do hope it won't be before Christmas. Someday the war will *be over and we will have to live together. I am looking forward to the end of the war but I am not looking forward to living every day with Claus. Married life is just about bearable for two weeks. It will be insufferable when it is for ever.*

'That was a good dinner.' Laura pushed her coffee cup aside and picked up her brandy. 'What would you like to do tomorrow?'

'I've already said that I want to go to Grunwaldsee,' Charlotte answered.

'We don't have to. I've been looking at the guide books. There are a lot of sights within easy driving distance of Olsztyn. The castle at Malbork, Hitler's Wolfschanze, or we could tour the Masurian lakes.'

'I came here to see my old home. Don't you think I've put it off quite long enough?' Charlotte asked.

'We'll go then, but only if you're absolutely sure that it won't be too much for you.'

'I'll try not to cry this time.'

'I didn't mean it that way,' Laura said quickly.

'I know you didn't, darling.'

'I hate to see you upset.'

'I was a fool to ask you to stop off at Bergensee on the way here and a bigger fool to expect it to be unchanged. Communist Poland had higher priorities than the upkeep of old mansions.'

'We could ask someone about Grunwaldsee before we go there,' Laura suggested again.

Charlotte shook her head. 'All I need before I see it is a good night's sleep. Do you mind if I leave you to your own devices again?'

'To be honest, at the moment there's nothing I'd like better than to curl up in bed with a good book and half the contents of the mini-bar.'

'A bottle of brandy would be better. Mixing leads to headaches.'

'Are you advising me to get drunk?' Laura smiled.

'A little merry maybe. You deserve a celebration after finishing your film.' Charlotte left her seat. 'See you in the morning.'

Laura finished her brandy and walked into the foyer. Sandwiched between the inevitable amber jewellery shop and an over-priced ladies' fashion outlet was a small booth that sold Polish and foreign news-papers, and a few books. The English language selection was limited to the half a dozen top bestsellers of the last ten years. Recognizing the jacket of *One Last Summer*, and deciding it was as good a time as any to pick up the book again, she took it to the cash register. She was only sorry the next morning when she realized she'd fallen asleep over the first page.

MONDAY, 30 JUNE 1941

Now I understand why Claus, Paul and Wilhelm were given three weeks' leave at the beginning of the month. Eight days ago our troops invaded Russia, and we believe all three were among the advance guard.

It has been a hard year. The War Office plagues us constantly, wanting more and more produce that we cannot give them. Last time their officials paid us a visit they took a dozen horses. They insisted they were for transport, but Brunon and I are convinced they went for horse meat. I saw one of the officers looking at Elise. I told him he would take her over my dead body.

I have no idea how they think we are going to replace the cattle and pigs they have taken. Our breeding stock has been halved since the beginning of the war, food rations have been cut to the bare minimum and there is talk of reducing them again. Our 'friends' in Allenstein don't help. People we hardly know visit us, offering money and goods for food we don't have. When I try to explain that we don't have enough left to feed ourselves after supplying the army quota, they accuse us of living off the fat of the land while everyone else starves.

It is the same with Mama von Letteberg at Bergensee. Because the farms pay rent to the Bergensee estate, everyone assumes they pay in food. Even Irena's father gives away most of the eggs the chickens lay in his back yard. As he says, everywhere you look there are children with big eyes and empty stomachs.

Irena and Wilhelm spent his leave in the summerhouse by the lake with their little girl, Marianna, who was born last September. They named her after Mama in the hope it would please her, but poor Mama is worse than ever. Most of the time she doesn't even remember that Papa is dead. Martha, Minna, Irena and I do what we can, but she often refuses to leave her room for days at a time. When we managed to persuade her to come down to dine with Paul, Wilhelm and Claus the evening they arrived, she began crying, then picked up a knife and pointed it at herself. We are terrified she will injure herself.

Having Claus home for three weeks was a terrible strain. He spent most of the time working on the farm and playing with Erich. I have come to the conclusion that marriage is simply a question of getting through the nights as best I can. In the day it is not so bad when there are other people around.

We spent three nights at Bergensee. His mother gave a dinner party in his honour, and his father also managed to get a few days' leave.

Greta came back to see Paul and Wilhelm. I think there is something going on between Paul and Brunon's daughter, Maria. I saw them coming out of the barn together late at night and both were covered with straw. He spends most of his days riding with her. I do hope it isn't serious. It wouldn't do for a von Datski to marry a steward's daughter.

Since Wilhelm, Paul and Claus have left, we live day by day, putting all our strength into running Grunwaldsee, waiting and praying for the war to end. And when it does? Claus has already said he will continue with his army career. Wilhelm has decided to finish his studies and set up law practice in Königsberg. Irena would be happy anywhere as long as it's with him. She moved into Grunwaldsee after they married, stayed for Marianna's birth and hasn't left since. I think she finds it comforting to sleep in Wilhelm's bed even when he isn't in it, and I am very glad of her company.

I can talk to her about anything except my married life because she assumes that I am as happy with Claus as she is with Wilhelm. I cannot disillusion her. It would make her unhappy and I can't bear the thought of upsetting her, especially when she is so kind to me and more of a sister than Greta ever was or could be.

Only Paul hasn't made up his mind what he will do after the war. I do hope he will take over the management of Grunwaldsee. I am so tired, yet at the moment I cannot imagine living any other life. If Claus does remain in the army he could be stationed in Paris, or Russia. He didn't say whether he would want me to join him, and I didn't ask. Sometimes I think he only married me to bear his sons. He is disappointed that Erich is still an only child. I wish it were possible to get babies some other way.

After Paris I thought I would become accustomed to married life; after three weeks with Claus I know I never will. Even Paul noticed the contrast between me and Irena. She cannot bear to be parted from Wilhelm for a moment. I am always looking for excuses to get away from Claus.

I have just read the beginning of this diary again. So much has happened since then. Herr Schumacher visited this morning. High Command has asked him to organize a concert party to entertain the troops in Poland. He wants me to join them for two weeks. The troops have so few pleasures. Should I go?

It would be difficult to leave Erich and Mama, although Irena, Minna, Martha and Brunon insist they can manage without me. Perhaps I should. I will think about it.

THURSDAY, 13 NOVEMBER 1941.

I am so angry and ashamed. Yesterday Irena and I drove into town to do some Christmas shopping, although we knew there would be very little in the stores. We went to the confectioner's. It is rare to see sweets of any kind these days. The army takes so much food. Sugar, butter, cream and almonds are almost impossible to find unless you know a farmer who dares risk prison by hoarding extra. In the end, my pleadings touched Herr Meyer's conscience; after all, we were among his best customers before the war. He gave us a small box of truffles, but he warned us that they weren't up to his usual standard because of the poor quality of the ingredients.

After we left his shop, Brunon drove us to Irena's parents' house. Herr Adolf bought a huge plot of land from the Jews in 1934 on which he built his house and the workshops he needed for his building business. The Jewish cemetery and synagogue adjoin his yard. I can't remember when I last saw the synagogue open. Like most people, I avoid thinking and talking about the Jews. The slightest mention of them seems to bring out the worse in some people, especially young boys.

Papa insisted they weren't all bad; although he wouldn't go as far as old Uncle Ernst, who used to invite every Jew he could find to stay in his house to annoy the authorities. It was a blessing Uncle Ernst died in 1938. If he hadn't, he would have succeeded in getting the entire family into serious trouble.

Papa told me that he was as sorry as I was when Ruth and Emilia and my Jewish friends were expelled from school in 1935 along with all the other Jews who were no longer allowed to study. They were good friends, and Papa never minded me visiting them or inviting them to Grunwaldsee, but I hadn't heard from either of them since my seventeenth birthday and Papa warned me that it wouldn't be wise to invite them to the ball for my eighteenth birthday.

Since all the Jewish businesses in the town have been taken over by Germans I haven't seen any Jews on the streets. I assumed that they were trying to keep out of trouble. There has been talk of resettling them in Africa or Madagascar, or giving them their own homeland in the East. I wasn't sure if Ruth and Emilia's families had already left, but today I saw them for the first time in over three years.

Brunon had to stop the car when we turned into Irena's street because the road was blocked by a convoy of trucks parked outside the synagogue. SS officers and soldiers were milling about, Georg amongst them. Trust Georg to join a new regiment with such an awful reputation. He was strutting about in his boots and field grey uniform like a bantam cock pretending to be a rooster.

The soldiers were driving crowds of young children and girls out of the synagogue. There were so many I couldn't imagine how they had all crammed in there. It isn't a large building. Most were beautiful with blond hair and blue eyes, nothing like the ugly, horrible old Jews on the posters. Some of the older girls were carrying babies, and then I saw that Georg was pointing a gun at Ruth and Emilia.

I couldn't believe it. He was in the same class as us in kindergarten; he had played in the orchestra with Ruth and Emilia until they had to leave. Despite the cold I wound down the car window. I know Ruth saw me because she called my name and began to run towards the car, but Irena caught hold of my sleeve and whispered, 'In God's name, close the window. Think of the children if you won't think of yourself.'

Georg hit Ruth on the side of her head with his gun. She stumbled, obviously hurt, but he forced her back into line. We sat there watching the soldiers beat and kick the young girls and children, and herd them on to the trucks for what seemed like hours, although when I looked at my watch afterwards it was only ten minutes. And the whole time Marianna slept and Irena held her hands over Erich's eyes so he wouldn't see what was going on. He thought we were playing a game of hide and seek.

After Irena wound up the window we sat in silence. Neither Irena nor Brunon said a word, although I'm sure Irena recognized Ruth and Emilia as I did.

The first truck moved off, and the Rabbi and some old men were brought out of the building. At that point the SS waved Brunon on. When I looked back I saw the Rabbi lying on the ground and the soldiers kicking him. He was covered in blood.

I suppose the SS were angry because he'd hidden so many children in the synagogue. Was he trying to save them from deportation? Why bother, if they can have their own country? And why beat him? He was old; he couldn't fight back or hurt any of them. The soldiers were laughing as though they were enjoying what they were doing, Georg loudest of all.

I tried to talk to Irena about it but she wouldn't say a word, and when I saw that she was as upset as I was, I didn't press her. My life has been nothing but secrets ever since Herr Schumacher said we weren't to tell anyone about our accommodation in Russia. I can't confide my feelings about Claus or our marriage to anyone, and now this.

How could Georg hit Ruth? How could he and the other soldiers be so cruel? How can anyone beat a helpless old man until the blood runs from him?

Irena's mother was waiting for us with coffee and little cakes, but I couldn't eat a thing. I felt sick. Some of her windows overlook the synagogue. How could she ignore what was going on?

I hate the war. I hate not being allowed to be friends with Ruth and Emilia. I hated seeing them being driven away at gunpoint by an idiot like Georg, and I hate living all these lies and not being able to say whatever I want to; and having to tell everyone that I miss Claus all the time when I don't.

Perhaps I am following Uncle Ernst. He never cared what people said about him or his opinions. For the first time I understand why he argued against the Führer's policy of racial purity. It is one thing to be proud of being a German, quite another to see Jews being kicked and marched off at gunpoint. Especially when they are your friends.

But will Ruth and Emilia ever think of me as their friend again when I ignored them and allowed Irena to wind up the car window, shutting them out?

Although I tried to join in the conversation at the coffee afternoon, I couldn't pretend to be happy. I was glad when it was time to go home. While the maid was helping us on with our coats, Herr Adolf returned. He winkled Brunon out of the office kitchen downstairs, where he had been drinking tea with Herr Adolf's secretary, then, with Frau Adolf, walked us to the car. The cold air felt good after the heat of the house. Herr Adolf began to tell us about the peculiar noises they'd heard in the Jewish cemetery behind the house late at night and in the early hours of the morning.

Only a low wall separates part of the Adolfs' garden from the Jewish cemetery. It really isn't a good area, but Irena told me it was the only place her father could buy enough land to build a house, offices, all his workshops and garages, and everything else he needed for his business. I had wondered how Herr Adolf could afford to buy such a large plot of land and open a business, when only seven years ago they were living in a rented house and he was working for someone else. Now I think he bought it below market price from Jews who were forced to sell because of the racial laws forbidding them to own land and businesses.

Herr Adolf opened the car door for me, but I insisted on hearing more about the peculiar noises. I imagined the SS coming back late at night and burying Ruth and Emilia. Herr Adolf lowered his voice and told me that the noises were people opening graves, not to hide bodies or rob them but to conceal valuables. Frau Adolf thinks it is because of the law that doesn't allow anyone to take more than ten marks out of the Reich. The Jews who are going to be resettled want to hide their property in the hope that they may be allowed to return at the end of the war to reclaim it. But will they be allowed to return?

I remember one of the Führer's speeches before the war. I didn't take much notice of it at the time, but Wilhelm did. And I heard him and Paul talking about it with Uncle Ernst afterwards: 'In the event of war the result will not be the bolshevization of this earth, and thus the victory of Jewry, but the annihilation of the Jewish race in Europe.'

Does 'annihilation' mean the imprisonment and deportation of all those children and young girls like Ruth and Emilia? Or, after what I saw the SS do to the Rabbi, perhaps even worse? Why doesn't anyone ask questions or try to stop it?

No matter what the Jews have done, surely young girls like Ruth and Emilia don't deserve to be beaten and forced on to trucks by boys like Georg, who then go on to beat up old men. Very brave of them to pick on people who are too weak to fight back. I will talk to Paul and Wilhelm about it when they next come home on leave.

Chapter 8

'YOU ARE absolutely sure?'

'Absolutely,' Charlotte echoed emphatically, as they walked into the hotel's secure car park.

'We can put it off.'

'Until when? Next year?' Charlotte asked. 'I gave myself a stern talking-to this morning. We've been here two whole days—'

'A day and a half,' Laura corrected.

'Either way, it's time we visited the place I flew halfway around the world to see.'

Laura unlocked the car. 'Do we go back on the road we came in on?'

'No, you turn right at the gates.'

'Then Grunwaldsee isn't near Bergensee?'

'They're built on different lakes at opposite ends of the town. It's not far. About two miles down the road there'll be a lane to the right.'

Laura drove in silence. Occasionally she glanced across at her grandmother, who was sitting, poised, in the passenger seat, ostensibly studying the view.

'Has anything changed?' she ventured when they left the grim tower blocks of the Communist-built suburbs behind them.

'Too much. That pile of rubble was a flourishing farm. It belonged to a family called Zalewski. They had a son the same age as my brothers; they used to go riding together. Turn just up ahead.'

Laura reached over and covered her grandmother's hand with her own. 'It will be all right.'

'I'm not sure what I dread the most. To find Grunwaldsee neglected and decaying like Bergensee, reduced to rubble, or vanished.'

'Is this the drive to the house?' Laura asked, as the car bumped from pothole to pothole.

'No. This leads down to a summerhouse. My father renovated it for my brother Wilhelm when he married in nineteen thirty-nine.'

'I can see the lake ahead.'

Charlotte felt as though her heart had lurched into her mouth as they drew closer to it. 'The summerhouse is on the left,' she whispered.

'It's beautiful. A fairy tale cottage!' Laura exclaimed as she drew up in front of a *dacha* set in a small orchard that bordered the lake. Ripening miniature apples, pears and full-size cherries hung from the branches that framed the baroque roof.

Charlotte opened the door before Laura stopped the car. Rummaging in her handbag, she pulled out an enormous bunch of keys that Laura had never seen before.

'You still have the *keys* to the house?'

'Silly, isn't it?' Charlotte was embarrassed at being caught out. 'I didn't lock anything against the Russians. I saw no point. I knew they'd only smash down the doors, and I couldn't bear the thought of the damage.' Pushing the gate open, she walked up a paved path towards the front door.

'It looks well maintained and cared for,' Laura observed.

'The old locks are still here.' Charlotte pointed to an enormous keyhole, but above it gleamed a bright new lock. She knocked on the door; the sound echoed hollowly back at her. After waiting fruitlessly for an answer, she stepped into the garden of the cottage, sinking down on to a wooden bench set against the wall. She blinked against the strong sunlight, and Laura saw a tear roll down her cheek.

Charlotte realized Laura was watching her. 'This place looks exactly as it did during the war. New cement between the stones, everything clean and tidy. It reminds me of the work Papa had done when my brother Wilhelm became engaged to Irena.'

'Did they live here after they married?'

'Not really. Irena stayed in the house with us when Wilhelm was away. But they did spend Wilhelm's leaves here. I doubt they had more than two or three weeks together in the whole war.'

'But they must have been happy. There is a wonderful atmosphere about this place.'

'Yes, there is.' Charlotte turned aside. If people's happiness contributed to the atmosphere of a place and a house, it wasn't only Irena and Wilhelm's happiness that had been captured. 'I wish we could go inside and see what it is like now.'

'Perhaps some of the furniture has survived.'

'For sixty years?' Charlotte shook her head. 'Papa had it furnished with old pieces from the house. They weren't the best, even then.'

'We could go round the back and look in through the windows,' Laura suggested.

'And if anyone is inside?'

'They would have answered the door.' Laura offered Charlotte her arm. Before they had taken half a dozen steps, a young man walked up from a path that bordered the lake. He addressed them in Polish.

Charlotte, who was still tearful, was unequal to replying. Laura tried German. He shook his head.

'Oma, can you try to explain why we're here?'

'English?' The young man beamed at them.

Before Charlotte could stop her, Laura plunged headlong into conversation. 'This is my grandmother; she used to live here.'

'In this house?'

'No, not this house, in Grunwaldsee.'

The young man frowned. 'The big house?'

'Oma?' Laura prompted, looking for help.

'My grandfather lives there. Come, I will take you to him.' Suddenly, remembering his manners, he checked his hand for cleanliness, wiping it on the back of his trousers before holding it out. 'Pleased to meet you. I am Brunon Niklas.'

Charlotte stared at him. He was dark-haired and dark-eyed, of medium height and stocky.

'We have a car.' Laura closed the gate as they left the garden.

'I saw it. I'll show you the road. Follow me.' Picking up a pair of shears and a scythe, Brunon tossed them into the back of a battered old truck parked at the back of the summerhouse, and climbed into the driving seat.

'You shouldn't have told him I lived in Grunwaldsee,' Charlotte remonstrated when they were alone in the car.

'Why not? You want to see the house, don't you? And he said his grandfather lives there, so it can't be in as bad a state as Bergensee. Do you remember this road?'

'The road, yes, but it has been widened. We never brought cars down here, but in my day carts were used for everything around the farm.' Charlotte's knuckles whitened and she gripped the seat hard when the stables came into view.

Brunon swung his truck sharply to the left and left again. Not wanting to see Grunwaldsee crumbling and neglected, Charlotte closed her eyes.

'Is this it, Oma?'

There was a catch in Laura's voice, and Charlotte dared to look. Where there had been tall, silver-painted gates, there were rusting posts. The farm workers' cottages that formed the right-hand side of the quadrangle that enclosed the courtyard were framed by scaffolding, and men were busy working on the buildings, ripping out broken windows and rotting wooden casements. She was glad they were being renovated. There had never been enough money to keep the cottages in good repair, not even in her father's day.

The yard itself was full of rusting farm machinery. But behind the tangle of abandoned iron stood the house, exactly as it had looked when she had driven out of the yard on a farm cart on a snow-filled January afternoon in 1945.

The walls were painted the same shade of rich cream, the stonework around the door and windows picked out in the deep tint of burgundy that her father had chosen before the war. The lawn between the front of the house and the cobblestone yard had been trimmed and mown. The wooden crossbars on the sash windows had been freshly painted in white and the slate roof was in good repair. The pillars either side of the front door were white, banded with fresh burgundy paint. The steps that rose above the half-windows of the basement had been newly tiled in marble, and the ironwork balustrades and railings on the balconies looked as good as the day they had been forged, even on the small balcony that opened out of her father's dressing room.

'Is this Grunwaldsee?' Laura repeated.

Charlotte continued to stare, mesmerized. After all her nightmares of dereliction, to see it looking as though it had been trapped in a time warp was traumatic.

She half-expected Laura to fade and Wilhelm and Paul to come running down the steps, riding jackets slung over their shoulders, crops in hand, shouting and play-fighting as they made their way to the stables. Her mother walking out on to the small balcony over the front door, calling down, warning them not to be late as guests were expected for dinner. Her younger self standing on the path that led around the back of the house, squabbling with Greta. Her father emerging from the side door that led to his study in the west wing, pleading with them not to quarrel.

'Fräulein Charlotte?' An old man walked up to the car. She opened the door, recognizing the voice but not the man.

'You've come back, Fräulein Charlotte. After all these years, you've come back.'

Chapter 9

'MARIUS?' CHARLOTTE left the car and moved tentatively towards him. 'You stayed? All these years, you stayed?'

'Did you think for one moment that I would leave Grunwaldsee to the mercies of the Russians, Fräulein Charlotte? Of course I stayed. Who else but a Niklas would know how to care for Grunwaldsee?' Marius's German was halting, fractured from disuse. Charlotte recalled someone telling her that the language had been banned during the Communist years in the old Prussian states and had only just been reinstated.

They continued to stand staring at one another, and, for a moment, Laura thought her grandmother might embrace the old man. But something – propriety, or a class structure that had died in the aftermath of a world war over sixty years before – kept them apart.

It was Marius who broke the silence. 'Come inside, Fräulein Charlotte. Drink a vodka and coffee with us.'

An old woman stood behind Marius obviously his wife. She clearly hadn't understood a word her husband had said, who Charlotte was, or why she was there, but Marius's gestures indicated that he had extended an invitation, and speaking Polish, she added her appeal to his.

Sensing they were neither needed nor wanted, Laura and Brunon stepped back. Charlotte looked to her granddaughter.

'Go on, Oma,' Laura urged. 'Talk to your friend. I'll be fine here.'

'I'll show her the stables,' Brunon said in English before speaking Polish to the old couple.

Laura watched Marius and his wife escort Charlotte into one of the twin lodges built either side of the main entrance to the courtyard.

One was in the same pristine condition as the main house. Scaffolding had been erected around the crumbling walls of the other, presumably in preparation for a similar renovation.

'Would you like to see the horses?' Brunon asked after his grandfather had closed the door of his house and they were alone in the yard.

'I'd love to.'

'My grandfather called your grandmother Charlotte,' he commented. 'She was Charlotte von Datski?'

'Still is, but she never uses the von.' Laura followed him to a series of buildings that enclosed the left-hand side of the yard.

'It's strange she uses her maiden name.'

'She has done since her husband died almost forty years ago.'

'She must have told you all about this place.'

'Very little, and I can understand why.' Laura turned and looked back at the main house. 'It must have been a tremendous wrench to leave it.'

'The Germans had no choice, at the end of the war,' he said flatly. 'If the Russians found them they were killed, or put on a rail transport to Siberia. There they were dumped in open countryside. Most froze and starved to death.'

'I'm amazed your grandfather still lives here.'

'The Niklas family were stewards to the von Datski estate for over three hundred years. It's not easy to abandon that kind of history.'

'Didn't he have to leave when the Russians came?' Laura asked.

'Generally the Russians left the Poles alone, which was fortunate for me. If they hadn't, I would never have been born. My great-grandmother absolutely refused to leave Grunwaldsee. She believed that my great-grandfather, Brunon, I'm named after him, who'd been conscripted into the Wehrmacht home guard in December nineteen forty-four, would return, and that if she left they would never find one another again. Although my grandfather was only thirteen at the time, he wouldn't abandon her. When the Russian army made Grunwaldsee their local headquarters, they gave her the job of cook, and made my grandfather a stable boy, paying them in food, which was worth more than gold at the end of the war.'

'Yet they worked for my grandmother's family.'

'You find it surprising that they could work for the Russians after working for the von Datskis?'

'Not at all, just incredible that someone my grandmother knew is still here.'

'There's something else that's still here.' He opened a wooden door and led the way into the stables.

Laura followed and saw that although the exterior of the building was crumbling and awaiting renovation, the inside was pristine. The stalls had been freshly concreted and the wooden partitions so new they smelled of sawdust and pine. 'What a beautiful horse,' she cried out when a mare with an almost pure white coat came forward. It bent its head and nuzzled Brunon's pockets for food. Even to Laura's untutored eye it looked a magnificent specimen.

'Surely your grandmother told you about the Datski greys?'

'No.' Laura realized that he was shocked by her ignorance.

'Can you ride?'

'My grandmother paid for lessons, but I'm not brilliant.'

'If you like, we could tour the estate on horseback.' He looked at her flimsy summer dress and sandals. 'You have riding clothes with you?'

'I have slacks.'

'Then we'll go, perhaps tomorrow, or the day after. And don't worry, I'll find you a quiet horse and a hard hat.' He closed the stable door and they walked back across the yard.

'It's wonderful to see my grandmother's old home looking like this.' Laura almost mentioned Bergensee and how upset her grandmother had been by its dereliction, but something held her back. 'Your family has looked after it well. It must have cost you a fortune to restore the main house.'

Brunon threw back his head and laughed. 'My family didn't renovate this place. My grandfather couldn't have afforded to buy the paint, let alone employ workmen to repair the roof and the walls.'

'Don't you own Grunwaldsee now?' she asked in surprise.

He headed for the lodge. 'I told you, the Niklas family have always been stewards, not owners.'

'But it's in such marvellous condition.'

'Even the Communists knew a good thing when they saw it. When the army abandoned the house in the fifties, someone in authority remembered the Datski greys. Most had ended up in the stew pot or been shipped back to Russia, but my grandfather had hidden a few on neighbouring farms. There were enough left to establish a breeding programme. He offered to oversee it. The government were keen to sponsor sports that would enable them to compete in international competitions, especially the Olympics. They took him up on his offer, and when they opened this place as a riding school and stud farm they made him manager. Datski greys have been ridden in every Olympic show-jumping and dressage competition for the last forty years.'

'If my grandmother knew, she never said anything.'

'Oh, she would have known. There is no mistaking a Datski grey,' he said authoritatively. 'Once seen, never forgotten. Did your grand-mother never ride after she left East Prussia?'

'Not that I know about. But she still works; she's an artist.'

'An artist, not a musician. That's surprising. My grandfather says no one could play the piano or violin like Fräulein Charlotte von Datski. Before the war she was studying to become a concert pianist.'

'My grandmother musical? I had no idea.' Laura stared at him in amazement, then remembered Charlotte mentioning that she'd been a member of a Hitler Youth orchestra. She'd assumed that her grand-mother had played third violin or the flute along with several others – not been a potential concert pianist. 'She has a vast collection of recorded classical music, but I've never heard her play a piano or any other instrument.'

'The artist Charlotte Datski,' Brunon Niklas mused. 'It's strange we haven't heard of her in Poland.'

'She illustrates children's books. She's very talented but not well known outside of literary circles.'

'I suppose it only goes to show that we don't know all there is to know about our families, especially our grandparents. What do you do?'

'Make television documentaries.'

'On what subjects?' he enquired directly.

'Mainly historical and current affairs. I have just finished one on the Stasi.' She sat on the steps that led up to the veranda of the main house and looked around, trying to imagine what it must have been like to grow up in Grunwaldsee.

'I'm studying agriculture in the local technical college. My mother and brother live in Warsaw but I've always spent a lot of time here. I love this place. Even when it was full of Party officials, there was something special about it. You're going to stay, of course?'

'In Poland, for a week or two perhaps.'

'I don't mean Poland, I mean here. Your grandmother must have a lot to show you, and my grandparents will insist that you stay with them.'

'This trip was my grandmother's idea. She's wanted to return for a long time. I'm only here to keep her company and because I was curious to see where she grew up and what she left behind. She is the one making the decisions as to what we will do.'

He nodded. 'Then let's go and see what she has decided.'

They found Charlotte and the old couple sitting in a small, dark, congested living room. An enormous stove took up a third of the floor space, and massive pieces of dark wood furniture which looked as though they had been made for a giant's kitchen, took care of what was left. In the centre was a round table covered with a hand-worked lace cloth. On it stood a bottle of vodka, a plate of home-made marzipan and a pot of coffee.

'I'm sorry.' Charlotte rose to greet her granddaughter and Brunon. 'I didn't introduce you. This is Marius Niklas, the son of my father's last steward, also called Brunon. And this is Marius's wife, Jadwiga. Marius, Jadwiga, this is my English granddaughter, Laura Templeton.' She repeated the introduction in German for Marius's benefit and wished she could do the same in Polish for Jadwiga, but her Polish had never been fluent, not even when the estate had employed Polish workers before and during the war.

'Pleased to meet you.' Laura intended to shake the old man's hand but he lifted it to his lips and kissed it.

'Brunon was named after his great-grandfather?' Charlotte asked Marius.

'He was born the year my mother died. It pleased her to think that my father's name would live on.'

'You have something of the look of him about you.' Charlotte said in English, before shaking young Brunon's hand.

'I am pleased to make your acquaintance at last, madam. My grandfather talks about you and the old days incessantly.' Brunon translated his comment for the old man.

'Only the good things,' Marius qualified in German before speaking to his wife.

'We've missed out on a party here, Laura.' Brunon glanced at the vodka.

'Please sit down, Fräulein Laura,' Marius invited in German, rightly assuming that Laura was fluent in the language. 'Jadwiga will get more cups and glasses.'

Laura looked at the floor space and doubted that another chair could be squeezed into the room.

'I thought this might be a good time to take our guests around the main house,' Brunon suggested.

'I have the key, but the owner might not like it,' Marius cautioned.

'He won't mind,' Brunon replied confidently.

'He may prefer to show Fräulein Charlotte and her granddaughter the house himself,' Marius warned.

'And he might not return for days.'

'The owner is away?' Charlotte asked, only just following the gist of their Polish conversation.

'He could be back at any moment,' Marius answered briefly.

'He's Polish?'

'Russian.' Marius turned aside, unable to look Charlotte in the eye. He thought he knew how a von Datski would feel about a Russian owning Grunwaldsee. Before he'd met him, he'd had mixed feelings about staying on in the lodge that had been the Niklas's family home for over three hundred years. 'He's not a bad sort,' he added in an attempt to temper the news.

'How long has he lived here?' Charlotte asked.

'A year. The authorities put Grunwaldsee on the market after the revolution in nineteen eighty-nine, but between red tape and legal hold-ups it wasn't sold until early last year.'

'And so far he has spent fifty times more than he paid for the estate in renovating the main house,' Brunon interrupted.

'These days the Russians are the only ones with money,' Marius commented.

'Does he have a family?' Charlotte had difficulty keeping her voice even. Finding Grunwaldsee unchanged was miraculous. But facing the harsh reality of anyone other than a von Datski making the house their home hurt more than she would have believed possible.

'He's not married.' Marius stared down into his glass. 'And he hasn't moved into the main house. He lives in the summerhouse down by the lake. That was the first building on the estate that he restored, not that it needed anything more doing to it than your father did in nineteen thirty-nine. But it didn't look good before he put in new windows and repaired the roof.'

'I saw it,' Charlotte said softly.

'It would have broken your heart to see the estate before he started work on it, especially the main house.' Marius finished his vodka. 'Like every other building in the country under Communist rule, Grunwaldsee was used, abused and neglected.'

'The first thing the Russian did after he bought the place was call in a builder who specializes in restoration work. He had very definite ideas about what needed to be done. Brickwork and external repairs first, new roof timbers as well as tiles, new internal woodwork, plumbing, electrical wiring, all the inside walls replastered, the ceilings restored, everything re-painted. But why are we sitting here talking about it when we can look at it?' Brunon opened the door.

'How did he know which colours to choose?' Charlotte followed Brunon outside.

'I helped,' Marius confessed, wondering if Charlotte would take his collaboration as defection to the enemy.

Charlotte's voice wavered. 'Is any of our furniture left?'

'The Russians took everything,' Marius said shortly. 'They made big piles. All the electrical equipment, the sewing machines, the lamps, radios, stoves, hotplates, everything with a plug on it was taken from the town and villages and heaped in a clearing in the forest, and there they stayed for two years. Two whole winters before they were loaded on to trucks and sent to Russia.' He shook his head dolefully. 'You can imagine how useful they were after that.'

'What a waste,' Charlotte murmured.

'The furniture was piled in another clearing.' Marius led the way across the yard. 'Jewellery, toys, everything small and valuable was slipped into haversacks and kit bags. They were like locusts. The entire countryside was stripped bare, of people, valuables, food. All that was left was empty houses. Which displaced Polish families from the south were resettled in.' Marius took his wife's hand. 'And thankfully for me, one of those Polish families was Jadwiga's.'

Brunon walked up the steps to the front door of the house. He held out his hand to his grandfather for the key. But Marius held back.

'Are you sure you want to go inside, Fräulein Charlotte?'

'It's a long time since I've been Fräulein Charlotte, Marius. I'm plain Charlotte now. And yes, I am sure. I would like to see it again, just one more time.'

Brunon opened the front door. Charlotte was conscious of everyone standing back, waiting for her to make the first move, and she stepped inside.

Charlotte almost reeled back, overwhelmed by the smell of paint and varnish. Looking down, she saw that she was standing on new parquet flooring.

'All the floors had to be replaced,' Marius explained. 'The winters of forty-six and forty-seven were cold ones. The Russian soldiers ripped up the blocks to feed the boiler; afterwards, the authorities put down cheap linoleum. It didn't last long.'

Charlotte felt she was expected to say something. 'This is good quality wood.'

'Not as good as the old flooring, but at least it's free from the scuff marks your mother used to chide the maids for never being able to remove.' There was a huskiness in Marius's voice that Charlotte found difficult to ignore.

'Is this new, too?' She touched the staircase, unsure whether the stairs and balustrade had been stripped of varnish and restored, or entirely replaced.

'Like the floor, the rails were used to feed the boiler.'

'Whoever did this had a good eye for the original. You said that you helped?'

'As much as I could,' he admitted diffidently.

'You did well, Marius. It would have been dreadful if Grunwaldsee had crumbled into rubble.' She glanced up at the ceilings. They were obviously new, but the ornate coving and ceiling roses were identical to the old.

'These were cast from moulds of the original. There were just enough pieces left for the plasterer to recreate the patterns.' He sank down on the bottom step of the stairs and looked around. 'The hall suffered the most at the end of the war because it's where the soldiers used to wait for their orders. But if you go into the drawing room you'll see it still has the old fireplace.'

Charlotte opened a door on her right. Unfurnished, the size of the room was breathtaking. The long casement windows overlooked the woods, framing the lane that led down to the lake. She walked to the hearth and ran her hands over the smooth marble. 'Not just the fireplace,' she whispered. 'Even the tiled surround has survived.'

'And two of the chandeliers in the ballroom.' Marius rose to his feet and opened the double doors to the largest room in the house. 'They broke the third one when they tried to take it down, so they decided to leave the other two and clean them where they hung.'

It was the same wherever they went. A ghost of an old house that lived on in new, shining, beautifully proportioned rooms with walls, ceilings and floors devoid of ornament and furniture. The colours were the same as they had been in 1945: green and gold in the drawing room; blue, white and silver in the ballroom and formal dining room; red in the billiard room, although the table had been ripped out. Charlotte felt as though she had stepped back to the eighteenth century when Wilhelm von Datski had brought his Hanoverian bride to Schloss Grunwaldsee and, deciding that the old red-brick castle was no longer to his liking, torn it down and employed an architect to erect the classical family home of Grunwaldsee on the foundations.

Only the kitchen made no concession to the history of the house. Modern, stainless-steel work surfaces, black and white units and gleaming tiles hid the scars that had been inflicted during the Communist era, when it had been a riding school and hotel that catered for the elite.

'I've kept the best until last.' Marius walked through the kitchen and servants' corridor back to the main hall and the library. Dark wood shelves lined the walls but Charlotte saw that, although similar to the original, they too were new.

'The shelves as well as the books were fed into the boiler?'

'All of them, as were the ones in your father's study.' Marius opened a door that led into a smaller, cosier room. At the opposite end of the house to the ballroom it overlooked the lake.

'How many rooms are there?' Laura was bewildered and amazed by the size of the house.

'I never counted,' Charlotte answered. 'Do you know, Marius?'

'For a house that served an estate the size of Grunwaldsee, not that many. On this floor, apart from the kitchen, store rooms and servants' quarters, there are two drawing rooms, the informal and formal dining rooms, the ballroom, library, study, billiard room, your father's study, separate estate office, the conservatory and four general purpose rooms.'

'General purpose?' Laura looked quizzically at her grandmother.

'My mother used one as her morning room, one as her study, and another as a sewing room for the housekeeper. My brothers commandeered the fourth and refused to allow anyone, even the maids, inside. I dread to think what they did in there.'

'Serious smoking and drinking,' Marius disclosed. 'I climbed in through the window when I was six years old and got horribly ill on the beer and cigarettes they fed me. Do you remember this?' He ushered them into the room that had been Charlotte's father's study.

'Papa's cupboard,' Charlotte cried out. 'So something is left after all.' She walked over to an immense, carved, ebony cabinet that filled a generous-sized alcove from floor to ceiling. 'All the estate records going back to the thirteenth century were kept in here.' She opened the door and looked inside. It was empty. 'Why wasn't it burnt?'

'The wood's hard. The Russians were too lazy to take an axe to it when there was easier kindling to be had.'

'After everything that's happened, Papa's cupboard is still here. I can scarcely believe it.'

'Try moving it, Fräulein Charlotte. Ten men failed. The builder couldn't even replaster the wall behind it. I'm sorry we can't go upstairs,' Marius continued, as they returned to the hall. 'Furniture was moved in there yesterday. In fact, if you had been a week later I think all the rooms would have been furnished.'

'Then the new owner intends to make Grunwaldsee his home?' Charlotte grabbed the door post for support.

'I don't know, he hasn't confided in me.' Marius saw Charlotte sway and offered her his arm. 'It's almost time for supper. You will stay and eat with us?'

'Please,' Jadwiga coaxed in Polish, guessing that Marius had extended another invitation.

Charlotte looked to Laura, who was walking ahead of them down the steps with Brunon. 'Only if it's not too much trouble for you.'

'Trouble? In your family home?' Marius commented indignantly, as though Charlotte had never left the place. 'This evening you must move out of the hotel and in with us. Brunon will help you with your cases.'

'Thank you, but no, Marius. A visit is one thing but I could never sleep at Grunwaldsee again.' Charlotte glanced across the courtyard at the tiny two-roomed lodge. She was touched by Marius's invitation. It had obviously been extended from the heart, without thought to practical arrangements. 'The hotel is very comfortable, and, if we may, we'd like to come back again.'

'Tomorrow?' Marius brightened at the thought. 'I'll harness one of the carriages, and we will drive over the estate and visit the church.'

'You still have the original carriages?' Charlotte asked, as they drew close to the stables.

'Two of the old ones, and this beauty.' He went into the stable, opened a stall and led out the mare Brunon had shown Laura earlier. 'Here is our pride and joy, soon to be a mother, which is why she is in here.'

A lump rose in Charlotte's throat. 'She looks like Elise.'

'And so she should, she's descended from her. We hid her foal on Zalewski's farm. At the end of the war we brought her back and bred from her. What do you think? Not as good as her grandam but something of the spirit?'

'Something.' Charlotte buried her face in the horse's neck in the hope that no one would see her tears.

'Laura said earlier that she can ride,' Brunon said to his grandfather. 'Can I take her riding around the lake tomorrow?'

'You can ride?' Marius asked Laura in German.

'Of course she can ride,' Charlotte said proudly. 'She has von Datski blood.'

TUESDAY, 23 DECEMBER 1941

I have written so little this year. Running Grunwaldsee takes every waking minute. Brunon and I have been working sixteen hours a day just to keep the farms going, but however much we produce, there never seems to be enough left to feed the workers after the War Office quota has been filled.

At Irena's and Brunon's insistence, I visited Warsaw to entertain the troops. I knew Irena would look after Erich and Grunwaldsee as well as I could. She kept repeating that the troops have so few pleasures. She hopes that someone in authority will think of organizing entertainments for the soldiers in Russia. Wilhelm is always in her thoughts.

We played in a concert hall outside the walls of the Jewish ghetto in Warsaw. I asked about the people inside. Herr Schumacher took me aside and said the area inside the walls was one of several that the Reich has set aside to contain Jews and it is wiser not to ask questions about what goes on within them. Nina, who had special leave from Berlin to join the concert party, had travelled through the ghetto on a tram. She told me conditions inside are dreadful. The streets and houses are filthy and unkempt; the people dirty, unwashed, dressed in rags and clearly incapable of looking after themselves or their children properly.

I remembered the scenes outside Irena's parents' house. Are Ruth and Emilia in the Warsaw ghetto or one like it? And if so, how are they supporting themselves? It is hard enough to find food and clothes for everyone at Grunwaldsee, and we have the small profits of the estate and, when necessary, our savings to live on. I recalled Georg then, and asked Nina if she had seen any soldiers inside the ghetto, but she said no one is supposed to talk about it. I wanted to go on the tram ride myself, but there was no time. After two days I had a telegram from Irena telling me that Mama had taken a turn for the worse.

I returned to find Mama frail, weak and agitated. Irena said she began to look for Papa the moment I left. Irena tried to soothe her and keep her quiet, but she left her bed and the house in the middle of the night and walked down to the lake. One of the land army girls saw her wading into the water at three a.m. I was so pleased that someone had stopped Mama before she drowned that I didn't ask the girl what she was doing down by the lake at that time in the morning. Brunon confided that she is over-friendly with the son of one of the tenants who was home on leave.

Irena was dreadfully upset. I had trouble convincing her that it wasn't her fault and that Mama would have left her bed in the middle of the night even if I had been home. Mama is getting more and more confused, and there is nothing that any of us can do to help her. Her shell is with us but for most of the time her mind is out of our reach.

Last week two of the land army girls left to get married. The estate has never been so short-handed. Worst of all are the people who persist in thinking that we are sitting on mountains of butter, cream, milk and meat. Even people who should know better, like the Adolfs, expect us to provide a little extra for them at this time of year.

The war news is not good. Since America has joined the Allies it feels as though we are fighting the whole world. But tonight was truly special. I invited the Adolfs and Papa and Mama von Letteberg to join us for the holiday. Frau and Herr Adolf and Mama von Letteberg came today and will stay until the New Year. Irena and I played the piano while the others sang carols and decorated the drawing room and the tree. For a few hours I think we all managed to forget the war, but not the people we have lost. I know Claus's brother Peter was in all our thoughts.

Secretly we are all hoping that the twins and Manfred Adolf will come home for Christmas, although no one dares say so, in case our hopes are raised only to be dashed. Irena cries every time she thinks that she and little Marianna might not see Wilhelm over the holiday. She is seven months pregnant, although Marianna is only sixteen months old.

Claus wrote and warned me that he won't be home. He doesn't think it right for the commanding officer to take holiday leave when the men can't. But there's no reason why his father shouldn't come here to be with Mama von Letteberg. I'm sure he will make the effort. She simply hasn't been the same since she had the telegram about Peter.

I have managed to keep back a goose for our Christmas dinner. After the War Office took their requisition there were only two left fit for killing, and I insisted Brunon take one. We owe him everything. I could never keep Grunwaldsee going without his loyalty, common sense and help.

We cut down a tree as usual, but as sugar is in such short supply, there are some very odd sweets for the children on its branches this year. Brunon and the other old men have been busy carving, and Irena, Minna, Martha and I did some sewing, so every boy will have an animal of sorts and all the girls a rag doll, although we had to cut up old dresses to finish them. I dread to think what it will be like next year if we haven't won the war.

At least there are plenty of vegetables, and we pooled our fat rations to make stollens. Almonds are rarer than bananas, but we made walnut marzipan and it does not taste at all bad. Presents were a problem. I packed Claus a parcel of all the tinned food I could find, including the last of our liver sausage. I only hope he gets it. I put his rank on the outside in large red letters, so if anyone dares to thieve from a colonel I hope they get caught and punished.

The twins have both been promoted to captain, but I cannot believe that it is essential they remain at the Front. I pleaded with Claus and Papa von Letteberg to do all they could to help them get Christmas leave. Mama is now so ill she hardly recognizes anyone, and Irena grows thinner and paler every day. I am worried about her and the new baby.

FRIDAY, 26 DECEMBER 1941

They all came on Christmas Eve: Wilhelm, Paul, Manfred, Papa von Letteberg, Greta and Helmut Kleinert — and even Claus; apparently, his General insisted he take leave. After we opened our presents we had a wonderful evening with music and singing. I think Claus must have another woman. He came in with the boys at suppertime and didn't suggest going to our room. Instead he joined us for a meal, then sat up talking to his father, the twins, Manfred and Herr Adolf half the night. When he finally came to bed I pretended to be asleep but I needn't have bothered. He didn't try to touch me. I was so relieved I almost cried. He couldn't have given me a better Christmas present.

When he woke on Christmas morning, I carried Erich into our bedroom to wish him Merry Christmas and forestall any attempt at 'married life'. He was delighted and amazed to see Erich both walking and talking. I had been up for hours, helping Martha with our Christmas dinner, because I thought it only fair that she, Brunon, Marius and Maria have dinner in the lodge and not serve us for once. When I went back upstairs to change before dinner, Claus and Erich were playing in the bath, and I managed to sneak in and out of the bedroom without him seeing me.

We had a busy Christmas Day. Claus became acquainted with Erich, and Mama seemed to recognize the boys and Greta. She ate dinner with us, although she asked to return to her room straight afterwards.

The house was warm thanks to Brunon, who spent most of the autumn chopping logs. He had lit fires in every downstairs room except the ballroom, even the formal dining room, and I was pleased to see that, due to Martha's and my efforts, we had enough food. The girls did very well without Martha to direct them, and after they had laid out the cheese, cold sausages and winter salads I had helped make for supper, I told them to take the rest of the evening off.

The twins, Herr Adolf, Papa von Letteberg, Manfred and Claus had brought plenty to drink. So we all became a little merry. Was that such a bad thing?

Things must be easier in Berlin than they are here. Helmut and Greta turned up with Belgium chocolates, French truffles, liqueurs and lavish presents for everyone — gold cufflinks for the boys and Claus, a gold brooch for me — and Helmut gave Greta a sapphire necklace, tiara, bracelet and earrings that must have cost a fortune.

Claus gave me a set of diamonds that had belonged to his grandmother. Because I put so much in the parcel of food I sent him I had very little left to give him. Just three warm shirts. When I apologized, he looked at little Erich and asked for another son. I suggested a daughter. I really wouldn't mind. Erich makes everything worthwhile, but I do know I would be a better mother if I wasn't so worried about the war, and whether or not I can keep the estate going next year.

There was a terrible scene on Christmas night. Manfred had spent most of the day drinking and, after supper, he decided to tell us a joke. As he has made it clear that he has never abandoned his Communist beliefs, his parents and Irena gave him warning looks, but to no avail.

He began innocuously enough. Just like at Sleeping Beauty's christening, he said, three good fairies presided over Hitler's, and each gave the Führer a very special gift. The first promised Hitler that every German would be honest, the second that every German would be intelligent and the third that every German would be an ardent National Socialist. Then the bad fairy appeared. Furious because she hadn't been invited to the festivities, she stipulated that every German would be possessed of only two of those qualities. So she left Germany with intelligent, dishonest Nazis, honest Nazis with no intelligence, and intelligent, honest Germans who were not Nazis. When he finished there wasn't a sound in the room, although I swear I saw Papa von Letteberg smile.

Claus and Paul were angry, but Wilhelm was furious. He told Manfred he was an absolute blockhead to make the rest of us, especially Irena and I, witness to his treasonous schoolboy jokes, and we could all be shot or sent to camps because of his stupidity.

I think he would have hit Manfred if Irena hadn't dragged him off to the summerhouse. Afterwards, Paul insisted that Manfred join the men in the billiard room. They shut themselves away and, although I heard them arguing, they all seemed calm enough when they left the room at midnight.

So I ended up spending Christmas evening in the company of Greta, Frau Adolf and Mama von Letteberg. All Greta could talk about was herself, how much money Helmut's father is making, the latest fads and fashions in Berlin, the parties she goes to, and the wedding she and Helmut will have at the end of the war.

Mama von Letteberg warned us never to repeat Manfred's stupid joke to anyone lest they think that we too are disloyal to the Party. She and Wilhelm are right. All it would take is one word of Manfred's joke to reach the wrong ears for all of us to be put under suspicion.

Claus, Manfred and the twins left very early this morning. There was no time to talk to Wilhelm and Paul about Ruth and Emilia because there were too many people around, and, after Manfred's foolishness, I was wary of upsetting Wilhelm again, but we all noticed that they were unusually quiet.

Claus and I were together only two nights; the first he was so tired he slept, and the next so drunk he didn't even kiss me in the privacy of our room. The 'married life' was very short and confined to this morning. So perhaps I will be able to give him another child. I have no idea when I'll see him again, but when he held me and kissed little Erich goodbye I could almost believe that he really does miss us.

All evening we heard the tramp of marching feet along the road at the top of the lane. I thought it was our armies moving west on leave, but when Brunon went to investigate he told us that the columns were Russian prisoners of war being marched into Germany. Irena and I went up to see them. Some were wounded and they all looked cold, miserable and hungry, but when we tried to give them bread and old blankets the guards shouted at us. They told us we were stupid, disloyal and traitorous Germans.

Shortly afterwards, a captain knocked on the door and told us that because we were young girls who didn't know better, he would let us off this once, but the next time we offered subhuman enemy military personnel food or clothing that was needed for the people of the Reich, we would be imprisoned.

This war gets stupider by the day. I can't see how putting Irena and I in prison, or being cruel to prisoners who haven't done anything except fight for their country when they were ordered to, will help the Third Reich in any way.

Chapter 10

CHARLOTTE LAID down her diary, her mind transfused by images of the bloodied, pathetic, hollow-eyed men of over sixty years ago, their gaunt figures bowed by blows and defeat as they trudged westwards in broken boots.

She looked around her hotel room. It was only half past eight in the evening, but she felt as though it were midnight. She wondered if her exhaustion had been caused by the cancer, or the emotional strain of seeing Marius and Grunwaldsee again. There were so many questions that remained unanswered. Questions she would have asked if she and Marius had been alone.

Laura knocked on the door.

'How pretty you look,' she complimented, when her granddaughter walked in wearing a calf-length, blue silk dress.

'You're not changing for dinner?'

'I ate so much in Marius's house, I couldn't face a meal.'

'Are you ill?' Laura asked in concern. 'Or just tired after today?'

'Tired,' Charlotte conceded. 'Returning to Grunwaldsee has brought back so many memories. But although I don't want to eat, if you give me five minutes, I'll change and come to the dining room with you.'

'There's no need. I met two American Jewish girls in the lobby. They're here with their mother. Their great-grandparents left East Prussia in nineteen twenty and they're searching for their old home. You never know, a dinner with them might lead to a documentary. Not many filmmakers have explored post First World War migration from Eastern Europe.'

'So many people coming back, looking for a country that has gone,' Charlotte murmured absently. 'I mean the past, not East Prussia.'

'"The past is a foreign country, they do things differently there",' Laura said quoting the first line of Hartley's *The Go-Between*.

'Are you sure you don't mind if I stay here?'

'Not at all. But you will order yourself something later, if only a drink?' Laura pressed.

'Perhaps some brandy and ice cream,' Charlotte said mischievously.

'We don't have to return to Grunwaldsee tomorrow, Oma.'

'Aren't you forgetting Marius and Brunon have offered to show us around the estate?'

'We could put them off and go somewhere else.'

'No,' Charlotte answered decisively. 'If I can bear to see the house, I can bear to see the fields.' She reached for her diary.

Laura tiptoed from the room, closing the door softly behind her, as her grandmother returned once more to her past.

WEDNESDAY, 22 JULY 1942

Sometimes it seems as though I only turn to this diary to record tragedy. I can barely see this page for tears. Paul was killed in Sevastopol on 1 July. Three weeks ago, yet the telegram only came this morning. Brunon was with me when the boy walked into the yard. He offered to tell the maids and warn them not to say anything to Mama, but I couldn't risk her finding out accidentally, so I went to her room.

Her screams were appalling but mercifully short-lived. Five minutes later she was smiling, unwilling or unable to remember what I'd told her. Irena had left before the telegram arrived, to visit her parents with her new baby, Karoline, and Marianna. I'm glad. I don't want to see anyone, not even Brunon or Martha. I think they understand, because when I left Mama's room I fetched this diary and locked myself into Paul's bedroom. They must know I'm here, but they haven't knocked on the door.

The twins shared this room from the day they were born. After Wilhelm married, Paul continued to sleep here whenever he came home on leave. Now I can only look at what he left behind. His books, his chess set, his collar studs, cufflinks, tiepins and cologne. It's like Papa's death all over again. A moment ago I opened Paul's wardrobe and touched his clothes. Clothes he will never wear again. It's so unfair. He hadn't even begun to live the life he wanted to.

I can hear a woman sobbing in the yard. I know it's Maria and I feel that I should go to her, but even the thought seems hypocritical. Paul never spoke to me about her, and we all pretended that nothing was going on between them.

I don't know whether I should order the carriage. We have no petrol for the car. Should I go and see Irena, or wait for her to return this evening? I hope and pray that Wilhelm is safe. I cannot bear the thought of losing him too ...

SUNDAY, 27 DECEMBER 1942

This Christmas was much more dismal than last. Every year there are fewer of us – first Papa, then Peter, now Paul and Maria. She killed herself a week after the news came about Paul. She tied a sack full of stones to her ankles and jumped off the pier into the lake. We think she may have been carrying Paul's child. I couldn't write about it then because I blame myself. If I had talked to her, treated her like a sister, spoken to her about Paul, accepted and welcomed her into the family, she might still be alive, and we would have had her and Paul's child to love.

Instead, all we have is her grave, and it is my fault for ignoring her grief.

Brunon and Martha have been very brave. The doctor helped by writing 'accidental drowning' on the death certificate so we could bury Maria in Grunwaldsee churchyard and not outside it with the other suicides.

Sometimes I feel as though I am surrounded by death, although I try very hard not to think about it, with Wilhelm and Claus returning to the Russian Front and Manfred already there. They must survive this war. They must! Must! Must! Must!

Charlotte recalled breaking the nib on her pen when she wrote the exclamation marks. It was as though she had tried to keep Wilhelm, Claus and Manfred alive by sheer force of will.

There were no geese left for us to slaughter this Christmas, so we made do with the old chickens that were no longer laying. Everyone except Manfred managed to come home, even Greta and Helmut, unfortunately. Their engagement must be one of the longest on record. I asked her when she intended to marry, and she replied, 'Not until the war is over.' I told her to prepare to die an old maid. She insisted her war work is far too important to interrupt for marriage, as though running Grunwaldsee is inconsequential.

Wilhelm, Claus, Papa and Mama von Letteberg, and the Adolfs were here for Christmas Day, and I managed to organize a good Christmas dinner, but if it hadn't been for the hams and food Mama and Papa von Letteberg brought, we would have had a very bare supper table. I tried to get Mama to eat Christmas dinner with us, but she kept looking around and asking for Papa and Paul, until it seemed better for everyone, and kinder to her, to allow her to return to her room.

Claus and Wilhelm were with us for only two days. They had twelve days' leave and spent five days travelling to get here and faced a five-day journey back. Irena and Wilhelm disappeared to the summerhouse as usual. Claus was more remote than ever. He was furious when he discovered that I allowed Erich a nightlight. He accused me of wanting to keep him a baby when he should be preparing for manhood. I reminded him that Erich is only two years old, but Claus shouted that he wanted a man for a son not a sissy, with the result that I had to get up in the night when Erich woke screaming because he is terrified of the dark. I am glad Claus was only home for two days; any longer would have been intolerable.

Irena cried and clung to Wilhelm when they left. I simply waved to Claus. Someone who expects his two-year-old son to behave like a man would undoubtedly be embarrassed by a show of affection from his wife.

The one thing that hurts is Mama von Letteberg's gentle questioning as to whether everything is all right between me and Claus. How can it be when I quarrel with Claus every time we meet and I hate him to touch me?

SUNDAY, 7 FEBRUARY 1943

It has been announced that the Sixth Army fought to the last man at Stalingrad. Just like at Thermopylae there are no survivors. Although Wilhelm and Claus were not with the Sixth Army they are in Russia, and we know that officers frequently carry messages to other units. Dear God, there were a quarter of a million German soldiers at Stalingrad. So many German boys I know were stationed there. I can't bear to think about it. I am desperately worried about Wilhelm, Manfred and Claus. It was stupid of me to think last Christmas that things couldn't possibly get any worse.

I am only glad that the demands of running the estate leave me little time to sleep and no time to think. We have hardly any breeding stock left after the army requisitions. Even dumb Wilfie has been taken, to do what we can't imagine. All the men have gone except the very young like Marius, who, for all his ten years, works like a slave outside school hours, and the old like Brunon, who is labouring when he should be in retirement.

There isn't enough food; we go without just to feed the children. Officials from the War Office came with a list of produce they expect us to supply to fulfil next year's quota. Whether it was worry over Wilhelm and Claus, realizing the impossibility of meeting the quota, or the way Claus behaved when he was home, I don't know, but I broke down. I told the officers that there was no way I could supply another thing until I had more labour.

I was heartily ashamed of myself afterwards, but Brunon said it was the best possible thing that I could have done, because two days later I received an official letter to say that we have been allocated extra labour in the form of twelve Russian prisoners of war.

I had to sign what seemed like a thousand documents to state that I would pay the Reich not the men, and that neither I nor my family nor my employees would feed them, or collaborate with them in any way.

An officer came from the prisoner of war camp to warn us to expect sub-humans in appearance and behaviour. I told him that I had toured Russia in 1939 with the Allenstein Hitler Youth orchestra, and there was nothing he could tell me about the way Russians lived in the country areas.

They came tramping down the lane at dawn this morning. We assembled to watch as they entered the yard. Brunon and Marius had armed themselves with pitchforks. They needn't have bothered. Three soldiers with rifles were guarding them, not that the prisoners looked as though they had strength enough to create trouble or run away. The wrists, hands and faces poking out of their rags were encrusted with dirt and painfully thin. Their eyes are dark, ringed by black, which could be grime or exhaustion. And they have lice. I saw some crawling in their beards, and they were scratching at their armpits.

Brunon put them to work right away, clearing snow from the courtyard, forking manure and cleaning out the stables. The ground is too hard to begin ploughing. They are not good workers. They are slow, and won't do anything until the guards shout and threaten them.

I watched them from Mama's bedroom window when I took Erich up for his daily visit. Every afternoon I try to organize a small treat for Mama. I visit, and Minna brings us acorn coffee, all that we can get now. Real coffee and cakes are something we see only in our dreams. Mama and I sit and drink the ghastly coffee while I desperately try to pretend that everything is normal.

For the first time in months Mama sat next to me. She watched the men working for a while, then she turned and, almost like her old self, said, 'You must feed our workers, Charlotte. Your papa says that a man must eat well to labour well.'

When I returned to the kitchen, one of the land army girls was complaining that she had picked up a louse in the stables. That is something I cannot possibly have. If the Russian prisoners are carrying typhus lice, we could end up with an epidemic.

I telephoned the camp right away and demanded to speak to the commandant. He said there was nothing he could do. The Russians live like animals and refuse to wash or obey the basic rules of hygiene. I spoke to Brunon and he said the only solution was for the Russians to live here at Grunwaldsee where we could ensure that they keep themselves clean. That is impossible. I cannot have twelve enemy prisoners of war sleeping here in a household of women, babies, old men and young children.

I put a call through to Papa von Letteberg to ask his advice. I can't possibly fulfil the army quotas without extra labour, but neither can I risk a typhus epidemic which could kill the children and the rest of us. Hopefully he will telephone tonight and advise me what to do.

TUESDAY, 9 FEBRUARY 1943

Papa von Letteberg telephoned with the news that Wilhelm and Claus are alive, safe and well, but Manfred was at Stalingrad. The Adolfs and Irena are broken-hearted. Poor, idealistic, stupid Manfred. I can't believe that he will never create trouble at a family gathering again. If anything, the tragedy has brought Irena and I even closer together. My beloved sister by marriage. Even if the war ended tomorrow we will have lost too much for the world ever to be the same again. Both of us spent most of the day crying for Manfred, Paul, Peter ... It is so hard when there isn't even a body to bury or a grave to mourn over, only a memorial service to arrange.

Papa von Letteberg couldn't say where Claus and Wilhelm are, or what is happening on the Russian Front, but he has solved the problem with the Russian prisoners of war. He telephoned the camp commandant personally and insisted that the men who work at Grunwaldsee be kept clean. The commandant then telephoned me to give his assurance that would be the case in future, but I could tell he was furious with me for daring to contact one of his superior officers about the matter when he had assumed that he had already dealt with it.

I asked Brunon to visit me in Papa's office so we could be alone, and told him what Mama had said about feeding the prisoners. He advised me that the soldiers had already repeated the instructions that the Russians were not to be fed, although one or the other of the guards are always scrounging in the kitchen.

Almost as though he knew what I was thinking, the camp commandant telephoned again later to make it plain that if anyone at Grunwaldsee gives the prisoners food, he would make it his business to see that person severely punished, whoever it was.

I had no choice but to agree that the prisoners will be left alone. That means setting them tasks that won't bring them into contact with us, the land army girls or the Poles. Brunon and I looked at the work sheets and decided that as soon as the weather breaks, the Russians will be put to ploughing and planting the potato fields. No one need go near them, provided we keep them on that side of the farm and, if they are locked in the barn while their guards are fed at midday and then taken directly from the fields back to the camp at the end of the day, we will see very little of them.

I only hope that these prisoners will make things easier. I am so tired of struggling. So very, very tired.

SUNDAY, 30 MAY 1943

Today Wilhelm and Claus returned to the Russian Front after a four-day leave. It wasn't long enough. I forgot all our differences when I saw him and Wilhelm drive into the courtyard in a staff car. They looked so pale, ill and exhausted that my heart went out to both of them. There were many questions from the land army girls and women whose men are at the Front, but all they would say is that the German army is doing the best it can.

Wilhelm looked so weak that Irena and I wanted to call the doctor, but Claus, who'd been driving, insisted it wasn't necessary and what they both needed was rest and food. I ran to the kitchens to see what we had, while Irena went upstairs to draw baths.

Neither Claus nor Wilhelm would come near us until they had been deloused. As soon as they had bathed, and Martha had wrapped their uniforms in rubber sheeting to be taken to the laundry to be steam-cleaned, they dressed in the civilian clothes they had left behind and came to eat.

Because of the shortage of fuel and maids, we have closed off even more rooms in the house. I laid the table in Mama's morning room. If either of them found it strange that we were eating in there they didn't say anything.

While they were bathing, I asked Marius to kill one of the chickens. We couldn't spare it, but it was all I could think of giving them. The first of the new potatoes had been lifted and there was a cabbage, so I made sauerkraut.

Martha, who has been teaching me to cook says I am almost as good as her now.

I gave Wilhelm and Claus a bowlful of the ham bone and dried pea soup Martha had made for everyone on the farm. It was dreadfully thin, but Irena and I gave up our bread ration and, by the time they'd eaten that, the chicken and potatoes, which I had fried in the chicken fat, were ready and, together with the sauerkraut, made a fairly presentable meal.

There was one bottle of cherries left from last summer, and we gave it to them with a glass of Papa's brandy. I couldn't bear to serve them acorn coffee, so Irena made rose-hip tea. They both declared it to be the best dinner ever. How different from the five- and six-course meals we used to eat in the old days.

Afterwards, all they wanted to do was sleep. Irena went to bed with Wilhelm but I went back out into the fields. Yet another cat has disappeared. This time it is Martha's favourite. Brunon and I are certain that the Russians are killing and eating them, but I don't want to say anything, as the guards don't need any more excuses to treat them badly.

Yesterday, when Martha took Brunon and Marius their lunch in the fields, she saw one of the soldiers beat the youngest Russian prisoner. He looks far too young to be a soldier, yet the guards are always hitting and kicking him. She said blood ran from his head and there was a loud cracking noise that sounded as though the guard had broken the poor boy's skull.

Yesterday evening, after we ate a supper of herb omelette, black bread and one of the last few bottles of Papa's wine, we heard the prisoners tramping up the lane. Claus went to the window. He said the Russians were the lowest of the low, and if we had seen what they had done to the German soldiers they captured, we would not have them on the farm.

I tried to explain about having no labour, and the Reich needing our harvests. Wilhelm sat very still. He said nothing for a while, just allowed Claus to rant and rave, then he spoke very softly and quietly, insisting that if we hadn't treated the Russians so badly when we had invaded their country maybe they wouldn't be so hard on us now.

I have never seen Claus so angry.

'They are subhuman! Ask her!' He pointed to me. 'She toured Russia before the war. They are medieval in outlook and behaviour. They have set new standards in barbarism.'

Wilhelm exclaimed, 'Have you been walking around with your eyes shut?'

I begged them not to quarrel for the children's and Mama's sake. Irena interceded and succeeded in calming Wilhelm. I think he would walk into hell if she asked him to, but I also knew there was nothing I could do to soften Claus's attitude. If I truly loved him, or was close to him as Irena is to Wilhelm, I might have been able to talk him out of his anger. But it was useless for me even to try. Claus's final comment to Wilhelm was: 'Mutiny and revolution are words not in a German officer's vocabulary, and you are close to both.'

If this is the way captains and colonels behave towards one another, what chance do we have of winning the war?

Wilhelm put an end to the quarrel by asking if he could see Mama. I told him there wasn't much point, but Irena, he and I went anyway. She was sitting at the window. The Russians were still walking up the lane. We could see them dragging their feet, their guards laughing and joking behind them.

Without turning her head, Mama said, 'You really must feed them more, Charlotte. They cannot put one foot in front of the other.'

Wilhelm looked at me and I shook my head. He took her hand and said, 'Mama.' She turned to him and, for an instant, a small instant, I swear she recognized him. Then she said, 'Papa will be in shortly; you must go and put your toys away.'

We sat with her for a while. But it was useless. I don't know what has happened to me. I used to cry so easily, now I hardly cry at all. Sometimes I think that with Paul and Papa dead, Mama the way she is, and Claus so remote and distant, so totally unlike the man I thought I was marrying, my heart has turned to stone. Then I saw Claus carrying Erich across the courtyard to stroke the horses and I felt an overwhelming wave of love for my son.

Whatever happens, as long as I have Erich, life is worth living. I will survive and fight for both of us, no matter what. He deserves the very best that I can give him.

SATURDAY, 10 JULY 1943

We heard on the radio this morning that our armies launched an offensive along a 170-mile front at Kursk in Russia five days ago. Now I understand why Claus and Wilhelm were given leave at the end of May, and why Wilhelm was so odd, depressed and anxious for Irena and his children. I can only presume that both of them are in the thick of the battle.

It has rained ever since they left, and I feel as miserable as the weather. I am sorry now that I pressed Wilhelm to tell me how Paul died. It was after lunch on the last day of their leave. We had ordered the pony cart to take the children for a ride, but, pleading a headache Wilhelm retreated into Papa's study. Making my excuses to Claus and Irena, I followed and insisted he tell me everything he knew about what had happened to Paul.

Paul's commanding officer had written to Mama and me. He told us that Paul had died instantly from a head wound. At the time Brunon tried to console me by saying that Paul hadn't suffered, but I didn't entirely believe the letter. I remembered something Claus had said at the beginning of the war about commanding officers always comforting the relatives of the men who'd been killed by telling them that they had died quickly and without pain.

Wilhelm insisted that in Paul's case it was true. He was commanding a battery that was firing on the Russian front line, until the enemy blew both guns and men sky-high with howitzer fire. When I asked about Paul's grave, he said there wasn't enough left to bury. I don't think he meant to tell me that, but once he began to talk about Paul he couldn't stop.

The thought of Paul's perfect young body being blown to pieces horrifies me. All I have done since Wilhelm told me is picture Paul's death.

Wilhelm insisted that, as we all have to die, to be killed quickly in battle is not such a bad way. I reminded him that Paul wasn't even twenty-five.

144

Wilhelm said youth, along with truth, was one of the first casualties of war, and that by being blown up, Paul had escaped a long, drawn-out death in a field hospital.

But I still don't see why Paul had to die at all. This war seems so senseless, although I felt that I couldn't tell Wilhelm that, not when he was on his way back to the Front.

And that means keeping even more of my thoughts secret. Claus would be furious if he ever saw this diary or heard me express half the ideas I believe. I know they are unpatriotic, but am I really betraying my country by wanting to keep what is left of my family alive?

Wilhelm went on to say that there was nothing worse than standing by helplessly and watching a comrade die slowly of cold, gangrene and frostbite. He spoke so seriously and sincerely that I am sure he has had to do just that, many times.

He then spoke about the Russian winters and, when I asked, admitted that they are every bit as dreadful as the returning soldiers say they are, and the only reason he and Claus haven't suffered frostbite is because both of them are attached to command posts.

All I could do once he began to talk was sit and hold his hand. I desperately wanted to comfort him but I couldn't think of anything to say, and all the time he spoke, Papa's declaration that 'no good can come from war' echoed through my mind.

Wilhelm insisted that we are fighting the entire Soviet population because the SS, Gestapo and even the Wehrmacht units have alienated every man, woman and child in Russia with their inhuman brutality. He told me that when our troops first crossed the border, people rushed out of their homes to finger and kiss the crosses on our tanks because they saw the Wehrmacht as Christian saviours sent to free them from the ungodly world of Communism, but now they spit on the bodies of our dead. He fell silent for a long time after he had spoken, then he said, 'I have seen behind the curtain of lies, Charlotte. So help me God, I know what is going on, but I dare not tell anyone, not even you, because in this magnificent Third Reich of ours, the truth kills more surely than bullets.'

The silence in Papa's study was worse than Wilhelm's words. I couldn't understand what he was trying to tell me. I know I haven't seen all the brutality of war but after what he told me about the way Paul died, I tried to imagine it. As for knowledge being dangerous, in wartime we all have to be careful what we say. Wilhelm's reaction to Manfred's stupid joke taught me that much.

Wilhelm buried his head in his hands. I sat uselessly beside him, not knowing how to offer him comfort. Irena would have known, but she and Claus were still out with the children. When there was a sound on the staircase outside, Wilhelm jumped as though he'd been shot. I went to the door. It was only Minna taking up Mama's herbal tea. I tried to reassure Wilhelm, but he wouldn't listen to anything I tried to tell him.

He began to cry, tears that he didn't even try to wipe away. I hadn't seen him cry since we were small children. He grabbed my hand and held on to it, crushing my fingers.

'I have seen things that you and decent, normal people couldn't begin to imagine, Lotte; horrible, vile things that have destroyed my peace of mind, and poisoned my life, even my love for Irena and the children. Sometimes I think I am living in a mad house. I worry for Irena, Marianna, Karoline, for you and Erich, and for the future of every German child in this glorious country of ours, because we are building a legacy of suffering that they will inherit for our sins. An inheritance of brutality, savagery and hatred that will be aimed at Germany as a country, and the Germans as a race.'

Outside in the courtyard I could hear the children laughing as Claus and Irena returned. Wilhelm took my hand and begged me to look after his wife and daughters. That, no matter what, I would never desert them. I promised, but my promise was not enough for him; he pressed my hand down on Papa's Bible and made me swear.

I shivered, wondering what he could be so terrified of. I tried to tell him that the men at the Front like him and Claus are the ones who are taking the risks, not the women and children who stay at home. And although towns like Dortmund and Berlin have been bombed, not even the English would think it worthwhile to send a plane to blow up the countryside outside Allenstein.

He smiled at my attempts to calm his fears, warned me to take care of myself and Erich, but then said, 'You will be all right, Lotte, because you have General von Letteberg to look out for you.'

Troubled by his dark mood I pleaded with him to take care of himself, not just for his own and my sake, but for Irena and his daughters, telling him that I couldn't bear to lose him the way I had Paul. I even mentioned Mama, and he smiled, saying, 'Mama, God bless her, is well out of it. There is only you now, Lotte.' He kissed my forehead, such a gentle kiss. 'Poor little Lotte who never did have her fair share of balls and parties. One day a child and the next having to carry the load of ten men.'

I reminded him that I have Brunon, Marius, Martha, Minna and all the women and land army girls to help me, but he would not be persuaded.

'One old man, a few women, a child not out of school, cripples, conscripted land army girls and enslaved Poles and Russians, all who'd rather be somewhere else.'

There was so much bitterness in his voice I felt there was no way that I could help him. But later I made a resolution.

I know my brother and my husband. Both would prefer to die in battle than beg for favours, but rather than see Wilhelm get blown to pieces like Paul, or Claus die a lingering death on the Russian Front and my son grow up without his father, I will write to Papa von Letteberg and pray that my letter will not be opened by the authorities. Papa von Letteberg has already lost one son in Peter. I have lost a brother in Paul. Irena has lost Manfred. Surely we have paid enough? It cannot be unpatriotic of me to want to keep Wilhelm safe? Papa von Letteberg must still think of and remember Peter. If he considers what Claus, his one remaining son, means to Mama von Letteberg, perhaps he will arrange for both Claus and Wilhelm to be posted to Headquarters in Berlin. Somewhere where they will have to work hard — but survive.

THURSDAY, 26 AUGUST 1943

Allenstein is rife with rumours that things are not going well on the Russian Front, but there is nothing in the papers except the usual reproductions of speeches, descriptions of parades and 'we are winning the war on all fronts' articles. Are they lies?

Claus and Wilhelm have not returned, but others have come back on leave after being wounded and, although they say very little, they are grim-faced and serious. It does not take a genius to work out that the situation in the East is precarious and East Prussia will be first in the firing line if the Russians push our troops back.

The conversation I had with Wilhelm has been worrying me. What did he mean by 'behind the curtain of lies'? Are things as dreadful in Russia as he says? Why was Claus so angry when Wilhelm started talking about the way the Russians are being treated by our troops?

Papa von Letteberg telephoned me after I wrote to him asking him to help arrange transfers for Claus and Wilhelm. He insisted that he cannot give preferential treatment to anyone, least of all his own son and members of my family. That it would not be fair on all the soldiers who have no influential friends to speak for them.

I told him I didn't care about what was fair, only about keeping my brother and my son's father alive until the end of the war. He didn't answer me, but Wilhelm and Claus are still stationed on the Russian Front.

The standard of prison labour they are sending to Grunwaldsee has deteriorated. In the beginning the men did at least try to work. Now they have to be beaten to complete even the smallest task.

Mama still watches them from her window and she keeps telling me to feed them. Yesterday two more cats disappeared. I have decided to speak to Brunon about the state of the prisoners. The twelve men they send us can barely accomplish as much in a day between them as dumb Wilfie used to. Is it because they're lazy, or, as Mama says, because they are starving? One thing is certain: if things go on as they are, we won't be able to get the harvest in before it spoils, and then the War Office can stamp its feet all it likes. It won't get its quota.

THURSDAY, 2 SEPTEMBER 1943

Yesterday Brunon and I agreed that it was worth trying to feed the Russians in the hope of getting some work out of them. Whatever they are being given in the camp is clearly not enough.

I asked Martha to make a stew from some of the vegetables in the store and two of the hares Brunon had caught in his traps. There are still five fields of carrots and cabbages to be lifted, four of swedes and six of parsnips besides the last of the wheat, corn, hay, barley and potatoes. That's a lot of work to be done before the frost sets in.

As the stew for everyone in the house and another for the land army girls and guards were already simmering, Martha must have guessed who we wanted the extra food for, but she didn't say anything, just set about making it.

She boiled it up in one of the coppers in the wash kitchen so as not to alert the soldiers. When the guards were safely in the kitchen eating dinner with the land army girls, and the Poles had returned to their cottages where they cook their own rations, so the guards and land army girls can't see that we give them extra, Brunon, Marius and I carried the pot out to the barn. The prisoners are always locked in there at lunchtime so the guards can eat together.

Brunon opened the side door − he has never given the guards the key to that entrance. The men were lying on the few remaining bales of last years' straw. They stank horribly and looked even more wild, filthy and fierce than they do from a distance. I was petrified, but Brunon spoke to them, first in German, then Polish, telling them they had nothing to fear. We laid the copper on the floor and lifted the lid. Before Marius could open the sack that held the spoons, bowls and bread, they fell on the pot, knocking Brunon to the floor.

They ate with their hands, plunging their filthy fingers into the boiling stock, scooping what they could to their mouths just like animals at a watering hole. I helped Brunon to his feet.

Marius stood back, round-eyed in wonder. He murmured, 'They really are subhuman beasts, aren't they, Papa?'

I am ashamed to say that I had been thinking the same thing, but Brunon said, 'No son, they aren't beasts, just starving.'

It was then that I noticed how thin their hands and wrists are beneath the layers of rags. They are little more than skeletons. For the first time I understood why the cats had been disappearing, why they risked beatings from the guards by rummaging in the pigswill bins, and even a little of what Wilhelm had been trying to tell me.

I turned away sickened, not by the way they were eating, but the fact that I was not only a witness to, but responsible for their state. How could I be so blind and indifferent to the plight of fellow human beings I see every day?

The Russians have been working at Grunwaldsee for months. Even Mama's sickness hadn't prevented her from noticing their state, but I, who was supposed to be in charge, had ignored their desperate condition. Watching them cram the food into their mouths made me feel as though I was peering through a keyhole at an intimate scene. I looked at Brunon, then someone called my name.

One of the men left the food and the others and walked towards me. He repeated my name. Brunon took my arm to protect me and Marius ran to the door ready to open it.

The man turned back, apologized in German for bothering me, and said he could understand why I didn't want to know him. It was then that I *recognized him. The filthy skeleton in rags was Masha's brother Alexander, who together with Masha had given me the amber necklace on Moscow station. The one I had thought was good looking for a Russian.*

Charlotte set aside the diary, opened the mini-bar and poured herself a brandy. She lifted the glass and murmured, 'To you, Sascha, wherever you are.'

Chapter 11

DAWN, FRIDAY, 3 SEPTEMBER 1943

After Alexander spoke to me, Brunon sent Marius outside to keep watch on the guards in the kitchen and told him to warn us when he saw them preparing to leave. Brunon stayed with the prisoners while I filled a bowl with stew for Alexander. We sat to one side, talking while he ate. I tried very hard not to let him see just how much the sight and smell of him and the others sickened me.

I apologized for not recognizing him sooner, but he said he doubted that his mother, sister or the girl he had married when war broke out would recognize him as he is now.

I asked what it was like in the prison camp. He said no prisoner had lived there for longer than two months, and the lucky ones died sooner. Sitting close to him and the others, I couldn't believe that I had ignored their condition for so long. They are not only thin, but their bodies and faces are covered with masses of open, running sores.

I asked what I could do to help them, and Alexander said the most important thing was food, because they weren't given any rations. When they were marched out of Russia, they were turned into pasture fields every night and told to graze like animals.

They thought things would get better once they reached a camp, but even there, all they had was the grass in the open field they sleep in and, with so many men penned together, the last of it went months ago. They only get one barrel of water a day and it is not enough for drinking, so there is none left for washing themselves or their clothes. There are no latrines and the guards refuse to give them spades to dig one. So much for the camp commandant telling me that Russians won't keep themselves clean.

I promised to do what I could for them. Alexander begged me not to risk my life or the lives of anyone at Grunwaldsee on his or his men's behalf.

He said that so many Russians die every day in the camp; they regard themselves as already dead.

I offered him my hand, but he refused to shake it because he was filthy and crawling with vermin. As if to prove his words, he pinched a louse from his sleeve and killed it. I picked it up from the floor and tucked it into my handkerchief.

I left the barn and went into the kitchen where the guards were eating one of Martha's apple cakes and drinking acorn coffee. Alexander told me that the fattest of the three guards, an invalided veteran, wasn't a bad man, and often turned a blind eye when he saw him or one of the other prisoners stealing pigswill from the bins or raw vegetables from the fields. So, as the guards are all of the same rank – corporals – I decided to approach him.

After pouring myself a cup of acorn coffee, I sat opposite him. He was arguing with the other two about which was the best nightclub in Berlin. I took my handkerchief, unfolded it and placed the louse in front of his plate. The land army girls were leaving, but one of them looked back, saw it and screamed.

I told them that I had found the louse on my clothes when I went into the stable after the prisoners had cleaned it that morning. The second guard, the thin one that Alexander had told me was a sadist, said the solution was simple. The Russians would have to be kept outside at all times and the land army girls would have to take over the inside work.

I pointed out that we couldn't bring in this year's harvest or plant the next without the help of the prisoners of war, and the easiest solution would be to wash them and their clothes. He replied that would be a useless exercise because even if the Russians wanted to wash themselves and their clothes – which, according to him, they most certainly didn't – the camp was full of lice and the rest of the prisoners filthy. So, as soon as our prisoners returned there in the evening they would pick up fresh lice again.

Then I suggested that we should clean up our twelve prisoners and allow them to live at Grunwaldsee.

I knew the guards didn't have the authority to allow me to do that, but they are men first and soldiers second, and all three, even the fat married corporal, are chasing the land army girls. I hear them laughing together and see them going off to the woodsheds in pairs when they think no one is watching.

I reminded them that if the Russian prisoners were barracked at

Grunwaldsee, they too would have to stay with us. I didn't have to say any more. In between guarding the prisoners and enjoying their playtimes with the land army girls, they eat in our kitchen and are always complimenting Martha on her cooking and saying how much better her food is than the rations that are served at the camp.

I proposed that I telephone my father-in-law, General von Letteberg, in Berlin, and, while he made the necessary arrangements, Minna, Martha and I would wash the men's clothes; as they were drying, the men could wash themselves. When the guards hesitated, I picked up the louse and reminded them that typhus is not fussy whether it kills Aryans or subhumans.

As I was leaving the kitchen to go to Papa's study to telephone, I saw the guards check their own clothes. After what had happened the last time I spoke to the camp commandant, I did not even try to reach him but telephoned Papa von Letteberg's office. His aide promised to get a message to him. I stressed the urgency of the situation, and said that Papa von Letteberg's grandson, along with everyone else in the household, was at risk of contracting typhus. Also it was vital we bring in the harvest to supply the troops, and we couldn't do that without the assistance of prisoner labour.

I then went to the wash-house to help Minna and Martha with the Russian uniforms. Martha wanted to burn them, but I knew the guards would never stand for that, so we threw them into the wash boilers. In the meantime they had to wear something, so I went to Papa's and Paul's rooms and raided their wardrobes. Fortunately, they had a great many clothes. There were warm trousers, underclothes, shirts and pullovers, enough for all twelve prisoners and more. I sent disinfectant soap, combs, brushes and scissors into the barn with Marius and Brunon. (They hid the scissors; the last thing I wanted was an argument with the guards over whether or not the prisoners could use them as weapons.)

It was hard to believe that the men who emerged an hour later were the same ones who'd entered the barn at lunchtime. Alexander saw me watching them from Papa's study window, but gave me no nod of recognition.

I understood. It would not do for the daughter-in-law of General von Letteberg, the wife of a Wehrmacht colonel and mistress of Grunwaldsee, to admit to knowing a prisoner of war, a subhuman and enemy of the Reich. Why does life have to be so complicated? Alexander's family were kind to me when I lived with them in Moscow. If there hadn't been a war, Papa would

153

have insisted that I reciprocate their hospitality and invite him and Masha to visit Grunwaldsee as our guests.

By late afternoon, Papa von Letteberg had gained permission for both guards and prisoners to be billeted at Grunwaldsee. Then we had to decide where to put them. Brunon and Martha offered to give up their house so the guards could move into it. It was generous of them. They knew I hated the thought of having the men living in the house with Mama, Irena, the children and me.

I helped Brunon, Marius and Martha to empty the lodge of their personal belongings and carry them into the main house. I gave them the rooms at the end of the corridor on the second floor of the east side. There are four rooms and a bathroom there, and a door separates that part of the house from the rest, so they almost have their own front door.

Brunon said that it was far better that he, Martha and Marius move in with us than the guards, but he repeated it so often that I knew it was a wrench for him and Martha to leave their home.

Minna and I sorted through the linen closets. We found a dozen clean blankets. They were coarse and of poor quality, but warm enough for this time of year. There is enough straw in the barn for the men to sleep there tonight, and tomorrow we will make better arrangements. Martha boiled up another stew, and cooked all the windfall apples, so the Russians could have an evening meal.

The guards locked the prisoners in the barn before returning to the camp to pick up their things. I warned them that the prisoners couldn't remain in the barn indefinitely because we needed it to store hay and straw, and the chickens nested there. They wouldn't hear of my billeting them in the ballroom, so Brunon and I decided that tomorrow the Russians will have to clean out the loft above the stables and move in there.

The guards were happy with that because they think there is only one outside staircase that leads up to it, which makes their job easier. They don't realize there is a door in Papa's study that opens directly into the tack room adjoining the stables, and a hatch in the tack room ceiling that opens into the loft. My great-grandfather had it put in so sacks of feed could be lifted up or dropped down to save the bother of hauling them up and down the outside stairs.

It will be useful for passing up forbidden items. The guards have already berated us for giving the prisoners soap and disinfectant, which are in short

154

supply at the Front. I pointed out that Grunwaldsee isn't the Front, and that if it will help I will send parcels of both to my husband and brother in Russia so they can distribute them there. That shut the guards up. They have a very cosy billet at Grunwaldsee while Claus and Wilhelm ... I can't bear to think what they will suffer during a second winter on the Russian Front.

I don't feel good about what Brunon and I are doing. We haven't made the Russians' lives any safer or easier, only ensured that they will be in better health to work, which means that we can produce more food for the war effort. A war the Russians are praying that we Germans will lose. And I wouldn't have lifted a finger to help them if Alexander hadn't been one of the prisoners. Why is it so easy so ignore people you don't know, even when they are starving to death, and so difficult to walk away from someone who has once shown you kindness?

'Why indeed?'

Charlotte set the diary aside, walked to the window, opened the balcony door and stepped outside. Above her the vast dome of the night sky stretched infinite, immeasurable, over the shimmering lake. Moonlight shone on the water that lapped below her. Fire and candlelight flickered on the bank to her right, and the melancholy strains of a Brahms violin concerto echoed in the cool night air. She could smell meat roasting and hear the high-pitched voices of young people raised in song wavering in snatches on the breeze.

It was a scene that had been played out on the banks of the lake time and time again during her youth, and, she didn't doubt, in the decades since and the centuries before. If she left the hotel and went in search of the party, would she see boys who'd remind her of Paul and Wilhelm, and girls like she and Irena had been?

A shadow of a yacht moved into view. Its ghost-white sail flapped and picked up the wind, and the boat sliced through the surface of the lake, scattering the reflected images of the moon and stars. On the opposite bank, darkness encroached with the woods at the water's edge. She looked for and found the light that marked the lakeside end of Grunwaldsee's jetty. Was it her imagination or could she really see the glimmer of white that was the little summerhouse?

'I knew you wouldn't be sleeping.' Laura was standing on the balcony of her room next door. She turned on the outside light, and mosquitoes danced in a cloud around it.

'I trust you are wearing insect repellent,' Charlotte warned. 'The Grunwaldsee species can be particularly vicious when offered fresh meat.'

'Why do you think they are all up there, well away from me?' Laura leaned on the railing and looked out. 'It's beautiful. I hope it never changes.'

'It's bound to in some ways, but, with luck, not drastically, so something will be saved for future generations. There are many more buildings around the lake than there were in nineteen forty-five, but the waters are not polluted and, judging by the singing and barbecue smells, young people still come here to have fun.'

'Did you ring room service?' Laura asked.

'I forgot, but I helped myself to a brandy from the mini-bar, which was very extravagant, knowing the prices they charge,' Charlotte confessed.

'I knew you wouldn't send down for something, so I asked the waiter for take-out.' Laura went into her room and returned with a plate, napkin-wrapped cutlery and two boxes. 'A *kielbasa* on rye sandwich and a slice of poppy-seed cake.'

Charlotte took them. 'Who's the grandmother and who's the granddaughter?'

'If you're not hungry, dump them.'

'What was your dinner like?'

'Good. Polish pork with cabbage rolls, or rather *golabki* – you see, I'm learning Polish. Washed down by *krupnik*.'

'I'd forgotten about fire vodka.'

'Two was my limit. Three and I'd have forgotten my name,' Laura joked.

'And is there a documentary?' Charlotte set the boxes on her balcony table.

'With the Jewish girls, no.' Laura shook her head. 'The area where the family farm once stood is covered by Communist tower blocks, and the cemetery where their great-great-grandparents were buried is now a hospital car park.' She looked at her grandmother. 'I'm sorry, I didn't think. Your parents—'

156

'Were buried in the family vault in the church at Grunwaldsee. I must ask Marius if their memorial is still there.'

'There's a church at Grunwaldsee as well?'

'There is. You still look tired, Laura.'

'I am. When I'm making a film I work such long hours, I don't even realize I'm tired. Then, when I stop, I'm ready to sleep around the clock.'

'Why don't we breakfast in my room tomorrow morning on the balcony? Then we can eat whatever time we like,' Charlotte suggested.

'Is ten o'clock too late, Oma?' Laura knew her grandmother was an habitual early riser.

'Ten o'clock sounds perfect.'

Charlotte watched her granddaughter close the balcony door and the curtains of her room. Then she took the boxes and returned to her own room, closing the door behind her. The mosquitoes around Grunwaldsee had never bitten her before. But as Greta used maliciously to say when she dabbed lotion on her bright-red swellings, 'If there's any justice, one day there will be a first time for you, Charlotte.'

SUNDAY, 5 SEPTEMBER 1943

We hadn't used the loft for anything, not even feed storage, for years – probably, as Brunon said, for a century or more – so it was very dirty. But the Russians had it scrubbed out before eight o'clock in the morning after spending their first night at Grunwaldsee. They worked hard, especially after Brunon whispered to Alexander's lieutenant, Leon, who can speak Polish, that it was going to be their new living quarters. Brunon made sure they were given plenty of fresh straw to make beds with, and, when I went to see it, it really didn't look too bad.

The guards are careful to keep all civilians away from the prisoners. Thinking that I had forgotten about the hatch, Brunon reminded me about the trap-door that leads from the tack room into the stable loft. He said it will be comparatively easy for us to smuggle extra food to them. Not that we will have that much to give them other than vegetables, oats, and the rabbits and hares Brunon traps.

Martha has been given the guards' rations to cook. They are good. I know because their first full week's allowance was delivered this morning, but all we were given to feed the twelve prisoners for a week was one small bag of worm-infested swedes. They're not even fit to feed the pigs.

I would like to tell Alexander what Wilhelm said about events in Russia, but it is too dangerous. Perhaps in another week or two, when the guards and prisoners are used to a routine, it will become easier to find a time and a place where we won't be overheard.

SUNDAY, 26 DECEMBER 1943

There was some Christmas joy this year, but only because everyone at Grunwaldsee has learned to be happy with the small things that we would have taken for granted before the war. Fortunately, Erich, Marianna and Karoline are too young to know any different. It was Papa von Letteberg who gave me my best present. Wilhelm and Claus have both been transferred to staff posts in Berlin, effective as of four weeks before Christmas.

I suspected he used his influence, although he denied it when I tried to thank him after following him into the library on Christmas Eve. He had gone in there to borrow a book. I would never have dared to mention it if we hadn't been alone. And I am always very careful whenever I telephone his office in Berlin.

Wilhelm has been posted to the General Army Office, which is based at the Headquarters of the Reserve Army in the Bendlerstrasse, so I really have grounds to hope that he will never have to see Russia or active service again.

There were no toys in the shops, so I cut up some old clothes and a rabbit-skin coat, and made three toy rabbits, but I doubt they will replace the real rabbits on the farm in the children's affections. We grown-ups were prepared to settle for good wishes and whatever Christmas dinner we could organize. But Claus and Wilhelm changed everything by coming home laden with presents.

Claus brought a carved, wooden farmyard and a little cart for Erich, one that he can fill with toys and pull along. He also brought a perfect little Wehrmacht uniform in Erich's exact size. As we have both lost brothers to this war, and with so many of our friends and neighbours killed, it seemed a peculiar present. But I didn't say anything when I laid it on Erich's table along with his rabbit, the suit I had made him out of a pair of Paul's trousers and the rest of Claus's gifts; although I must admit I was delighted after church on Christmas Eve to see that the presents Erich liked best were the pencils and papers Papa and Mama von Letteberg gave him, Claus's truck and my stuffed rabbit.

Mama von Letteberg is to stay with us the whole of Christmas week; Claus, Wilhelm and Papa von Letteberg could only spare us two days. They left at dawn this morning. I know that all the problems between Claus and me are my fault, but that does not bring me any nearer to resolving them.

However hard I try, I simply cannot love him as a wife should. It is as much as I can do to stop myself from screaming whenever he touches me. He must sense how much I dread being alone with him. I have to force myself to lie still and allow him to do what he wants, because I know how much he and Mama and Papa von Letteberg want me to have another son. And not only them. I love Erich so much I too would also like another child.

It is obvious that the Berlin shops, especially for staff officers, are nowhere near as empty as those in Allenstein. Wilhelm and Claus not only brought presents and sweets for the children but a whole carload of food and gifts for the entire family. I had an emerald and gold necklace, earring and bracelet set from Claus.Wilhelm brought jewellery and lingerie for Irena. Claus gave me lingerie, too — in private. It is too big, and not at all the kind of thing a wife would wear. I couldn't help wondering if Claus had asked his mistress to choose it for me. I know he has one from the hints Greta took such delight in dropping when she helped Irena and I make supper on Christmas Day while the men sat and talked over their brandy and cigars. Irena was horrified by the thought, but I have no reason not to believe Greta.

Greta and Irena don't understand that I really don't mind the thought of Claus sleeping with other women. The more often he does those disgusting things to someone else, the less he will want to do them to me. It is only when I see Wilhelm and Irena in perfect harmony, each thinking the other's thoughts before they are voiced, that I become jealous. Not of Claus's mistress, but what my brother and his wife share. It is very hard knowing that I will never experience that perfect love.

I want this war to end. I want to be able to go into Allenstein and walk the streets without seeing more and more women and children wearing black. I want to be able to switch on the radio without hearing Wagner's bombastic chords preceding 'special war announcements'. But the end of the war will mean living with Claus.

If Claus does stay in the army when peace comes, I hope he will allow me and Erich either to live here or at Bergensee. Then he can visit us on his leaves and spend as much time as he likes with his mistress.

I wish I could stop comparing us to Wilhelm and Irena. They live for the moments they spend together. It was as much as they could do to leave the cottage to bring the children to eat Christmas dinner with us. While we were all sitting at the table, Papa von Letteberg suggested that, as I can run Grunwaldsee this well in wartime, with the help of only a few prisoners of war and conscript women and Poles, fulfil all the military quotas, and lay on hospitality and a fine meal like the one we were enjoying, then Claus could retire at the end of the war, put Bergensee in my hands and concentrate on writing his memoirs.

Unfortunately, that comment turned the conversation on to what is happening at Bergensee now. The army medical department has commandeered the house and turned it into a convalescent hospital for severely wounded and mutilated soldiers. Mama von Letteberg can't even bring herself to visit.

I go once a week with whatever little we can spare, which isn't much, mainly a few apples and vegetables, and to play the piano for the patients. I started calling there after Paul was killed. It is terrible to see so many young boys with eyes, hands or limbs missing. I told Mama and Papa von Letteberg how grateful they are for the loan of their beautiful home.

Wilhelm said I shouldn't feel sorry for them. They are alive, and they can learn to adapt. His new commanding officer was badly wounded in the retreat from North Africa. He lost an eye, his right hand and two fingers from his left, and has severe shrapnel wounds in his legs and back, yet all his junior officers regard him as the best soldier they have ever served under. They all admire and respect him, and are ready to follow him to the ends of the earth. It is obvious Wilhelm adores him. I am glad. His talk of injustice and the futility of the war after the defeats in Russia were close to treason, but his new commanding officer, Lieutenant-Colonel Graf von Stauffenberg, seems to have given him a renewed interest in his work. I am so pleased for him and Irena. She cannot bear to see him unhappy.

As always, whenever Claus, Wilhelm and Papa von Letteberg leave after one of their short visits, the house seems unnaturally quiet. Brunon has set the Russian POWs the tasks of cleaning tack, mucking out the stables and pigsties, and chopping down the dead trees in the woods for firewood. It means that during these winter months the land army girls have an extended holiday, but we are terrified that if we don't give the Russians enough work they will be sent back to the camp.

I see Alexander often, but as he is the senior Russian officer, the guards watch him all the time. We are careful not to smile or show any outward sign of recognition lest one of them or a land army girl notices and realizes that we know one another. The guards allow Brunon to tell Leon, Alexander's second-in-command, what work needs doing. As none of the Russians have admitted that they speak German, the guards permit Brunon and Leon to converse in Polish, which fortunately, for Alexander and his men, none of the guards understand.

Martha killed three of the oldest chickens for the Russians' Christmas dinner. She should have boiled them but she said that didn't seem right at Christmas, so she roasted them, although they were undoubtedly tough.

Brunon smuggled them and a huge pan of fried potatoes, gravy and steamed vegetables into the tack room and passed them up through the trap-door into the stable loft. He found an old stove in the rubbish at the back of the barn at the beginning of the winter and gave it to the prisoners. Thankfully, the guards had no objection. They don't seem to care what the Russians do now, so long as they don't make any trouble for them.

The prisoners soon had the stove re-assembled and working. They connected it to the kitchen flue that runs at the back of the stables, so if the camp commandant visits he won't realize the prisoners have heating unless he goes into the loft, and he isn't likely to do that. They burn the little wood the guards allow them to carry up, alongside the logs Brunon and Marius pass through the trap-door. Brunon says it is warmer there than the drawing room.

Brunon sees that the straw in the loft is changed regularly, and I found some more blankets in Mama's linen cupboards. They were old but still quite good. Without the hatch, the Russians wouldn't have enough clothes, food, wood or any soap or blankets.

Fortunately, the trap-door can be opened from both sides, so the prisoners can push anything they know the guards will confiscate down into the tack room when the soldiers carry out their regular searches and inspections. Marius or Brunon pass everything back up when the guards have finished. I laughed when Brunon told me that the prisoners have erected a make-shift latrine in front of the hatch so the guards can't see it from a distance, and avoid going near it to take a closer look.

One night, when I went into the tack room, I found a folded piece of sacking with my name in charcoal on the outside. Inside was a piece of feed wrapper with music written on it and one word 'Danke'. It wasn't signed, but I knew it was from Alexander.

I played the music when the prisoners were working in the yard and could hear me. It is very beautiful, probably the most beautiful piece of music I have ever heard, and must have taken hours to write out, but I dare not write back. Any communication with POWs is severely punished.

If only this war would end so everything could go back to what it was before – but then it never will. I will never see Papa, Paul, Peter or Manfred again in this life. There are too many people dead and too many empty places that cannot be filled. When will winter end and spring begin?

MONDAY, 7 FEBRUARY 1944

The drifts are six feet high, and, as fast as the prisoners clear the yard, the snow blows in or starts falling again. Irena is pregnant. If she isn't having a child when Wilhelm comes home on leave, we can be sure that she will be by the time he goes. This one will be born sometime around Marianna's fourth birthday. Irena is a wonderful mother, much more devoted and less distracted than me. Both she and Wilhelm (who telephoned from Berlin after she wrote to him with the news, just to tell her how delighted he was as the thought of becoming a father again) say they would love three girls. I think that they wouldn't mind a boy, either.

Just like her last pregnancy, and the one before, Irena cannot keep any food down. She is generally exhausted by the end of the day, so when the children go to bed, we make her go, too. When Wilhelm is home she will stay up all night with him if that's what he wants, but once he returns to Berlin it is as though the spark has gone from her life, and there is nothing that I, Martha or Brunon can do to cheer her.

After I put Erich to bed tonight I left the kitchen and went to the tack room to see what kind of a job the prisoners had made of repairing the saddles and bridles. When I lit the lamp I heard a noise. Alexander whispered through the trap-door that he had been watching the kitchen door from the skylight. He had seen me leave the house and wanted to talk.

I bolted both doors – the one to the yard, and the one to Papa's study – then he climbed through from the stable loft into the tack room. He replaced the trap-door in seconds and, as Brunon has screwed hooks into

162

the back of it and hung horse blankets on it, unless you look very carefully, you'd think that the ceiling was solid.

Alexander promised me that although he and his men can climb through the trap-door whenever they want, they have no thought of escape. They know that if they even try, everyone at Grunwaldsee will suffer.

Also they realize they have virtually no chance of getting across East Prussia and back through the German lines to their own without getting caught and shot. But knowing that they can get out whenever they want makes them feel a little less like caged animals. I pointed out that they can only break into the tack room, and the only door out of that, apart from the one that leads into Papa's study and the house, opens into the yard and is in plain view of the guards in the lodge.

We sat on bales of hay and talked while Alexander helped me inspect the saddles and bridles. It didn't take long. One of the Russians was a cobbler before the war and he had made sure that all the prisoners did a workmanlike job. I have never seen the tack in such good repair, and I asked Alexander to thank the man.

He said they took pride in their work at Grunwaldsee because they wanted to repay my kindness for saving their lives by giving them food and allowing them to live on the estate. But he also added that none of them could see how mending my bridles and saddles could possibly help the Reich's war effort, reminding me that the prisoners are Russians and enemy soldiers first, and workers second.

He told me that they had heard me playing the music he had written out for me, and it brought them great pleasure as well terrible homesickness. I thought that he had composed the music, but he laughed and said he wasn't that talented. It was written by a Russian called Shostakovich.

Long after we finished looking at the tack, we continued to sit and talk about music, art, literature, the concerts we had heard and played in together in Moscow. I am amazed by how many Russian composers I haven't heard of besides Shostakovich. But then we were only allowed to study German composers in school and play German pieces in the Hitler Youth orchestra.

Alexander misses his violin and cello. I wish I could loan him ours, but the guards would hear him play and then there would be trouble.

The second drawing room that we used as a music room is rarely visited now. The piano is shrouded for most of the time, the instruments packed away in their cases. I have little time to play the piano other than on my weekly visits to Bergensee and at Christmas. All that studying and time Alexander and I spent practising come to nothing. It seems a terrible waste.

We talked about our families. Alexander married a girl called Zoya, who was in the orchestra with us in 1939. I can only just remember the name; I cannot picture her at all. Alexander said it was a typical war wedding; they barely knew one another but felt they had to make the gesture in case one or both of them were killed. A bit like Claus and me. They only had one week together before his unit was ordered into Poland.

Zoya wrote to tell him she was going to have his child, but, as he hasn't heard from her or seen her since Christmas 1939, he doesn't know whether it was a boy or a girl. He confided that sometimes he even forgets that he is married. I can understand that. I find it easy not to think about Claus in between his leaves.

Alexander has seen Erich in the yard and thinks his child must be about the same age. I do so hope that he finds his family after the war. He was so easy to talk to that, for a short while, I managed to forget my problems with the estate, Claus and even the war. Alexander asked me to call him Sascha. I remember his parents and Masha calling him that when I stayed with them in their Moscow apartment.

Whenever I think of Papa and Paul, and recall Wilhelm telling me how Paul died, I feel as though my heart is breaking. How much worse it must be for Sascha not knowing whether his wife, child, parents or sister are alive. Not hearing one word, one single word, in over four years. He said his unit had received very little mail even before they were captured.

I tried to hearten him by telling him that it looks as though the Russians are driving us out of the Soviet Union. I felt dreadfully disloyal for saying it, especially as Paul and Manfred died there. But when I talked to Sascha I couldn't help wondering what we are doing in his country, for all the Führer's insistence that we Germans need Lebensraum. Why ship ethnic Germans out of the East after they have lived there for generations and move them into Poland? And what right have we Germans to appropriate Polish and Russian territory, houses, land and crops that were never ours in the first place?

Neither of us is naive enough to think that there will be a quick or easy end to this war. Alexander said that, as he was captured, he could think of no better prison than Grunwaldsee and no kinder warden than myself.

He is a captain, the same rank as Wilhelm — and Paul when he was killed. He has only told his lieutenant that he knows me and, as they are old school friends, he assured me that Leon Trepov can be trusted, so if I can't speak to him directly, I can always pass on a message.

I couldn't believe it when I looked at my watch and saw that it was midnight. I can't remember another evening that passed so quickly.

I promised to meet Sascha again tomorrow evening. I will take some leather oil with me in case the guards get suspicious, although in this cold weather they lock the prisoners into the stable loft early and watch the outside steps and door from the comfort of the lodge window.

It is crazy. Here we are in the middle of a war and I cannot sleep for thinking about a meeting that I have arranged with one of the enemy. The enemy! It is easy to think of foreigners as such when you don't know them. Even when we invaded Russia, I only spared a quick thought for Masha, Sascha and their parents. Now I cannot bear the thought that one day he and Wilhelm might face one another in battle.

Chapter 12

The papers and the radio are full of photographs and stories of our troops marching into Hungary, but the casualties continue to pour through on the trains and it is obvious that there is heavy fighting in Russia. Every day I thank God that Wilhelm isn't there – and Claus, too.

The spring thaw has finally come. There is very little snow left, and every tree and bush is full of buds. We, or rather the Russians, have begun ploughing the fields. I still go to the tack room nearly every evening, but now I always use the door that leads into it from Papa's study.

I keep the door locked except when I actually use it. The fat guard looked into the tack room one day when I was fetching Elise's saddle and noticed the door. He asked me what was behind it. I told him it was an old entrance to the servants' quarters but the key had been lost years ago. Fortunately, he believed me. Thank God for a stupid man.

Although I cannot be seen from the lodge or the yard, I go to the tack room just after nine o'clock when the guards switch on the radio and get out their schnapps bottles. Mama, the children and Irena are always in bed by then. Martha, Brunon and Marius are upstairs in their rooms, and Minna stays in Mama's room. She sleeps there now in case Mama wakes in the night and goes wandering again. They are all too busy to notice what I'm doing, and no one except me and the Russians know that Sascha and I spend our evenings together.

Once the lamp is lit, the hatch shut and the doors locked, I feel as though Sascha and I are closed into our own private world. We wrap up in horse blankets and sit and talk about anything and everything – except the war.

It is strange how many things we have in common: music; a love of literature; art; horses; and the countryside. Although Sascha was brought up in Moscow, his father had a country house and he learned to ride there.

He has described the woods and fields around his father's dacha so well, I feel as though I have visited them. A few weeks ago I smuggled a couple of sketch pads, some pencils and charcoal into the tack room. Sascha is a brilliant artist. He drew a portrait of me and a sketch of Grunwaldsee. I was reasonable at art at school but I gave it up to concentrate on music. Sascha said it was a mistake and he is teaching me basic drawing techniques. He says I am improving, but I think he is only being kind.

Yesterday, after I had drawn a passable portrait of Elise, he kissed me — only on the cheek but I shuddered. He apologized. I didn't mean to, but I began to tell him about my marriage to Claus and how much I hate married life, and once I started talking I couldn't stop. Afterwards I felt very foolish, but Sascha was not at all embarrassed, only kind and understanding. He said it is easy for a man to frighten his bride and that love, like everything else that is worth having in life, has to be worked for.

Sascha is sensitive, gentle and sympathetic; the exact opposite of Claus, who is always stern, impatient and exacting. When I lay in bed last night I began to wonder what it would be like to be married to him; to live and work beside him; to sit and talk to him every evening in the drawing room about art and poetry and music; to eat all my meals with him; and to sleep with him. Perhaps even make love with him the way Irena does with Wilhelm.

I have always been careful with this diary, now I am doubly careful. Should anyone read it, I would be in such trouble. Quite apart from some of the things I have written that border on treason, Sascha and I would certainly be shot.

Charlotte looked up from the page. Dawn had broken, and she hadn't noticed. The light had grown in the room until it outshone the bedside light. She hadn't meant to read through the night, but there was so much that she had forgotten. Not events, but sights, sounds; the texture of Sascha's skin beneath her fingertips; how he had smelled of rain, pine woods, the clean outdoors and wood smoke from the stove in the loft.

She recalled the bitter struggle she'd had with her conscience from the earliest days of their friendship. She couldn't forget the sacred vows she had exchanged with Claus in Grunwaldsee church on their wedding day. But the sense of guilt that had tormented her hadn't prevented her from stealing away as often as she could to spend time with Sascha.

That evening, when Sascha had kissed her, lightly and chastely on the cheek, had marked a turning point in their relationship. She believed that Sascha had meant it as a teacher–pupil kiss, a recognition and reward for work well done. But from that moment, things happened between them she had never dared commit to her diary. Yet every second they had shared remained etched indelibly into her memory. Secret treasures she had clung to, dwelt on and relived during the most wretched times in her life.

Those memories had both sustained her and caused her anguish for over sixty years. They had given her the strength to go on when she had nothing and no one to live for. And they had given rise to her bleakest despair when she had doubted Sascha's motives for befriending her. Had he sought simply to gain food and warmth from her that would enable him and his men to survive? Had he ever truly loved her as she had him? Were her memories of Sascha and their love real, or was she, like so many elderly people, remembering what had never been?

Had the most momentous evening of her life meant anything to Sascha? Had he clung to it, cherished it and relived it time and again afterwards, as she had – and still did?

The day had been cold and fresh, but it had lost its harsh winter bite. She had smuggled a wooden box stuffed with hay into her father's study. Inside was unimaginable luxury: a small pot of real coffee, made with beans Mama von Letteberg had sent from Berlin along with a few other delicacies. She had stolen a few spoonfuls of the coffee and two truffle chocolates from the parcel before sharing out the rest of the contents between her own and Brunon's family.

Sascha had been waiting for her. As soon as she'd pushed the bolts home in the tack room doors, he'd dropped down through the hatch, closing it behind him. He'd landed lightly on the balls of his feet, sniffed and said, 'I don't believe it.'

She proudly opened the box, showed him the contents and said, 'Believe it.'

She laid a lace tablecloth over a wooden crate, set out two porcelain cups and a silver jug of cream. Not knowing if he took sugar, she'd brought the honey pot and a porcelain dish for the truffles. When she'd finished setting out the feast she'd felt embarrassed, as if she were a child playing house.

He caught her hand, lifted it to his lips and said, 'Thank you. I feel almost human again.'

Even now she didn't know why she'd said it, but she repeated automatically without thinking, 'As opposed to subhuman.'

He gazed into her eyes, and she'd felt as though he were looking into her soul. 'Is that how you think of me and Russians, Charlotte?'

'Never,' she had protested. 'You, Masha, your family – you are no different from us.'

'We were – are,' he contradicted. 'But we didn't realize it. It takes a special kind of sadist to turn prisoners of war into a field and tell them to graze like cattle. And an even greater one to point a flame-thrower at a wooden house and shoot children when they run out.'

Her blood had run cold. Then from somewhere she had summoned the courage to tell him what Wilhelm had said, and ask if he knew what her brother had meant by 'behind the curtain of lies'.

It was just as well that coffee had been almost impossible to get hold of for another five or six years, because, for a long time after-wards, the smell had catapulted her back into the tack room. And brought with it all the paralyzing horror she'd felt while listening to Sascha recite lists of atrocities that the German military had carried out on the defenceless civilians in his homeland.

He told her about Reich soldiers who had shot children while they sat at their school desks. The platoons of Wehrmacht, as well as SS, that had hung and shot civilians, women as well as men, for no fathomable reason; the organized 'actions' that had wiped out entire towns and villages. He had talked to survivors who had hidden and watched the German death squads that roamed the countryside behind German lines, rounding up men, women and children – Russians, Jews, par-tisans – before taking them to the forest, making them dig their own graves and shooting them.

She began to cry long before he finished. Silent tears that had run cold down her face. A shame had been born in her that night, shame that German soldiers could do such things, and she had finally understood what Wilhelm had been unable to tell her. It was one thing for a soldier to fight in battle – quite another to kill unarmed civilians and children no older than Erich, Marianna and Karoline.

When Sascha finished talking he had kissed away her tears. She had locked her arms tightly around his neck and kissed him back. She had wanted to prove that she considered him her equal, that she wasn't like those among her countrymen who murdered indiscriminately. But most of all, she wanted to thank him for telling her the truth. A truth not even her brother had been able to confide. Only she hadn't stopped at kissing.

And afterwards, when she had lain naked in Sascha's arms, rejoicing that at last she knew – really knew – what love between a man and a woman could be like, she wouldn't have cared if the guards had dragged her out into the yard and shot her like a dog. Because, for the first time in her life, she had found and known perfect love – and happiness.

WEDNESDAY, 7 JUNE 1944

Spring has given way to warm summer. The most beautiful I have ever known. For the last few months we have been ploughing, planting and hoeing from dawn to dusk, and afterwards … afterwards I have been too happy to write. But now it is one o'clock in the morning. Everyone and everything at Grunwaldsee is asleep, my window is open to the still, warm night air, and I feel more alive than I ever thought possible. At one with the stars, the moon, the trees, the perfumed flowers – all of the natural life around me.

The darkness is so quiet, so peaceful, I feel I have only to hold my breath and listen hard to hear Sascha's heart beating. Which is foolish, considering the distance between the stable loft and my bedroom.

If only Sascha could move freely about the house and grounds, sit with me at the table, be with me every minute of every day, sleep with me, here, in this room, watch as I write this, but, as Papa used to say every time Greta asked him for something that was not in his power to give her, 'Don't cry for the moon.'

Like every child, I have to learn to be content with the blessings I have, instead of longing for the impossible.

I suspect that the war is going badly for Germany, but, along with everyone else, I dare not voice my fears lest someone accuse me of being unpatriotic. We know there is fierce fighting in Russia and Italy, because Marius has been conscripted for postal duty and he told us that hundreds of telegrams are being delivered to the families of the boys and men who are serving there. I never knew there was so much black cloth to be bought in Allenstein.

Irena and I went to have coffee and cakes – acorn coffee and honey cakes – with her mother this afternoon. It was a fundraiser for the Red Cross. Because we have no petrol for the cars, I asked Brunon to harness the cart. The children thought it quite an adventure to drive into town in it. We passed the shuttered and barred synagogue, and I remembered the day we saw Georg and the SS driving Ruth, Emilia and the Jewish children out of the building and kicking the old Rabbi until he bled.

Is there a chance that Ruth or Emilia will be able to return some day? I do hope so, perhaps then I may have a chance to tell them how sorry I am for being such a coward and doing nothing to help them.

Georg's mother was at the coffee afternoon. Georg is safe, posted somewhere in Poland, on 'special duties' where he has access to all kinds of goods that are in short supply. I wondered what Georg's 'special duties' could be, beating more old men and mistreating defenceless children and girls? Or running one of the dreadful camps like Dachau that people whisper about? Whatever those duties are, I dared not ask Georg's mother about them. It wouldn't have been polite to start an argument in Frau Adolf's house.

Frau Adolf had invited twenty women to help her raise funds, and, of the twenty, sixteen of us had lost a son, husband or brother.

It was meant to be a pleasant occasion, but inevitably the talk turned to the war, and although no one actually asked the question, I knew that everyone was wondering how many more sacrifices will be required of us before we can live in peace again. Irena was very quiet on the journey back. She held her two little girls close to her and had the faraway look in her eyes that told me she was thinking of Wilhelm, Manfred and Paul. But when we reached home, there was the greatest happiness waiting for her. Wilhelm was there!

His colonel had urgent business in East Prussia. He flew into a secret destination from Berlin this morning and brought Wilhelm along as his aide. He will pick Wilhelm up at Grunwaldsee in two days. I am already making plans to give Wilhelm's colonel an excellent thank you dinner when he arrives.

While Wilhelm and Irena played with the children and put them to bed, Martha and I went down to the summerhouse and prepared it for them. I took some food, two of Martha's bottles of homemade strawberry wine and what was left of a bottle of brandy Claus had brought at Christmas. The wine cellar has been empty for months, and even the cupboard is depleted, as we have not been able to lay down any wine since the start of the war. I promised Irena that I would look after the girls if they woke in the night, although she knows full well they never do, and Martha and I will take care of them in the morning and give them breakfast, so she and Wilhelm can make the most of their unexpected holiday.

Before they walked down to the summerhouse, Wilhelm handed me a duty letter from Claus. I could tell from the way he looked at me that he knows something is very wrong between us.

After they left, I checked on Mama and the children. Sascha and I have to be much more careful now that the evenings are light. The guards and the land army girls often go for walks together and cross the yard at all hours. I am terrified that they will hear Sascha and me talking. But tonight was easy. I went to the barn to check where the guards were, and I saw three of the land army girls drinking schnapps in the lodge with them. They were singing the 'Horst Wessel Song', so I knew they were well away. I went straight to Papa's study and from there to the tack room.

Sascha was listening for me. He waited only as long as it took me to fasten the bolts and whistle our signal before dropping down through the hatch. He had that special smile, the one he reserves for when we are alone.

Before him, I knew about happiness because of Wilhelm and Irena, but I never dreamed that one day it would be mine, or how it would make me feel.

I now know why Wilhelm and Irena touch one another all the time. There is no pain, no shame, no humiliation in what Sascha and I do. Only love. A deep and abiding love that grows more profound, passionate and perfect every day whether we are together or apart. I cannot imagine how I lived through my days and nights before he came into my life. I adore him, I exist only for him. For the first time I feel as though there really is a higher purpose. That this life cannot possibly be all that is.

I also understand why Maria drowned herself after Paul died. True love cannot end on this earth, and I fervently believe that somewhere, despite committing what her church believes to be a mortal sin, Maria is reunited with Paul. Like Maria, I have lost my fear of death because I have experienced this one perfect relationship, this great unselfish love. Sascha is, and always will be, my true husband. My husband of the heart.

I drift through days, doing what has to be done, living only for the evenings when we can be alone. It is enough to catch a glimpse of Sascha during the hours we are apart. We don't have to look one another in the eye. I see his tall, blond figure stripped to the waist working in the fields, hoeing or planting, or walking across the yard with the others, and I remember how it feels to hold his naked body against mine, to hear his voice whispering in my ear, his heart beating above my own.

I can tell Sascha anything – every secret desire, every burning ambition, every petty, shameful, spiteful thing I have ever done – knowing that he will accept me for who and what I am. But there is one thing we never dare speak of: the future.

When the war is over, it is anyone's guess what will happen to the prisoners after the peace treaties have been signed. I try to concentrate on now; the warm days and love-filled nights and the beauties of summer. Sascha is calling it 'our summer'. I hope and pray that it will not be our only one.

I am so greedy. I want more for us than just one summer. I want us to have a lifetime together. I want to know that he will always be with me. I cannot bear the thought of living a single day without him. I love him totally; his mind, his thoughts, his heart, his body. Even as I write this I am warm from his touch. I have only to close my eyes to feel his fingers brush across my breasts. My lips burn from his kisses. I can smell his clean scent on my skin.

But now it is time to return this book to its hiding place in the hole in the wall beneath the window sill. I have to tell someone about my love for Sascha or I will burst, and better that I write my thoughts and consign them to secrecy than risk Sascha's death as well as my own.

German women have been shot for less than I have done, and I know just how little value the Reich places on Russian lives. But I will do everything in my power to keep him at Grunwaldsee, where I can protect him and help him and his men survive the war.

*

The Allies invaded France on 6 June. Now we are fighting in Italy, Russia and France. It seems that Germany is surrounded by enemies and struggling for survival on all fronts. Claus is in France again; he sent me a postcard from Paris. If it was meant to reassure me, it didn't, because Allenstein is rife with rumour, and more and more wounded pour into Bergensee every day.

Wilhelm, thank God, is not at any of the Fronts. We know because his Colonel has to visit East Prussia quite often. Wilhelm says very little about their work, but there are rumours that Hitler's headquarters are somewhere near the von Lehndorff estate in Steinort, and I think that is why Colonel Graf von Stauffenberg has to make so many trips from Berlin into East Prussia. Every time he comes he allows Wilhelm to snatch a few hours with Irena. The last time was only four days ago.

The only good thing at the moment is the weather. It is so hot the guards allow the Russians to bathe in the lake at midday, while they sit in the shade and eat the picnic lunch Martha prepares for them. Afterwards, the guards laze around for an hour, and Sascha slips away to the summerhouse. I wait for him there. It is dangerous, although his fellow prisoners are always ready to cover for him and I am careful to leave a few carpenter's tools in the living room, so if the guards do walk in and catch us together, I can say that I asked him to help me hang a picture.

We pretend we are married and the summerhouse is ours. We discuss the improvements we will make when we have time, like where we will put my piano and his art materials, and where he will build a bookcase and a cupboard to hold our music. His favourite piece is the Shostakovich he wrote out for me but he also likes Beethoven's 'Moonlight Sonata' and Schumann's 'Dreaming'.

I have opened up the small drawing room again, and early in the evening, just after supper, I throw the windows wide and play as loud as I can, so Sascha and his men can hear me in the stable loft. The guards frequently come to the window to listen. They have complimented me on my playing. One asked me who composed the Shostakovich piece. I was so afraid that they would find out it had been given to me by Sascha and written by a Russian, I told them I had, and now they think I am a genius.

Sascha and I never dare steal more than half an hour in the summerhouse during the day, but we both know how to make every second count. Most of the time we just sit side by side on the old sofa, holding hands and staring at the clock on the mantelpiece, willing time to stop.

I have been happier during my few snatched moments with Sascha than I have been during all the days and nights that I have spent with Claus. But I must be careful. I have caught Irena, Brunon and Wilhelm looking at me rather oddly of late.

I know I am different — quieter, calmer, more content. My happiness shows. But if anyone should ever suspect the truth about me and Sascha it would mean death for both of us. I don't care about myself but I cannot bear the idea of Sascha being shot.

FRIDAY, 20 JULY 1944

Martha came running out into the fields this afternoon to tell us that an announcement had been made on the radio. Hitler has survived an assassination attempt. Brunon and I immediately rode back to the house in the hope of hearing more, but we only heard the same announcement repeated several times. In between they played very solemn funereal music that suggested the Führer was dead, which we thought peculiar given the initial declaration that he had survived.

I was uneasy about Irena. She was in the kitchen when Brunon and I ran into the house, and I thought she was going to faint. She looked very white and was shaking like a dog just lifted from a cold bath. Wilhelm has been very outspoken when Irena and I have been alone with him lately, criticizing Hitler's leadership, citing the unnecessary losses in Stalingrad because the Führer would not countenance a German retreat or surrender. I wondered if Irena knew something about the attempt on the Führer's life. It was then that the horrible thought occurred to me that Wilhelm could be involved.

Despite her advanced pregnancy and exhaustion, which has worsened in the hot weather, Irena insisted on sitting up to hear Hitler make his promised broadcast to the people.

At nine o'clock I made some excuse about checking the horses and went to the tack room. I only stayed long enough to speak to Sascha through the hatch and tell him what had happened. I promised to bring him more news as soon as I could, then I returned to the house and sat with Irena. We had a long wait. The broadcast wasn't made until one o'clock in the morning, by which time Irena looked so pale and ill I thought she was going to collapse.

When I heard Hitler speak I froze and felt as though my heart had stopped beating. I remember every word he said:

'A small clique of ambitious, irresponsible, senseless and criminally stupid officers have formed a plot to eliminate me and the German Wehrmacht command. The bomb was placed by Colonel Graf von Stauffenberg ...'

When Hitler uttered the name, I knew for certain that Wilhelm was involved. I looked at Irena but I was too shocked to say anything for a few minutes. She lowered her head. All I could think of was Wilhelm. What will they do to him and his brave, charming and courteous colonel? How many others are implicated?

When I could speak, I asked Irena about Claus and his father, but Wilhelm had been careful not to tell her any details that could incriminate her. She said all he had asked for was her permission to risk his neck and their happiness. He said no sacrifice would be too great if the end result was to rid Germany of Hitler. That the man we call Führer is leading us along a path of death and destruction.

Irena told me that far from forgetting the horrors he saw on the Russian Front, Wilhelm told his colonel and everyone else who would listen about the atrocities he witnessed. Like Sascha, Wilhelm said that Hitler is not only waging war, but inflicting mass murder on the defenceless populations of the countries in the East that we have added to our empire. Not just soldiers, but women and children.

Like Irena and me, he had seen Jews and other civilians being herded, but not in small groups. He had seen hundreds and thousands force-marched into the countryside, where our soldiers massacred them. Sometimes it took the execution squads days to finish their task. And Wilhelm told Irena that afterwards he had seen blood gushing from the earth and heard cries coming from the ground, even when the graves had been filled in.

Irena only confirmed what Sascha had told me and what I had secretly feared ever since I saw Georg point a gun at Ruth and Emilia.

I fetched the remains of the bottle of brandy. Neither Irena nor I went to bed. I don't know why. There was nothing we could do except sit, hold one another and pray. And, after what Sascha had told me about what was happening in the East, and Papa, Paul, Peter and Manfred's deaths and Mama's illness, I'm not sure I believe in a God any more. There, I've finally written it. Has Sascha turned me into an atheist, too?

*

176

Wilhelm arrived at dawn. He looked at me with the eyes of an old, old man. Neither of us spoke. I knew that if I tried I would break down and cry. I hugged him and sent him to Irena, because I knew he had come to see his wife, not me. After he had kissed his daughters, he and Irena went down to the summerhouse. I went to the tack room. I could only risk staying for a moment because the guards were already moving around the lodge and would soon roust the prisoners from the loft.

I climbed the ladder, knocked at the hatch in such a way that it could have been accidental and whistled our signal. When Sascha came I told him what had happened. He offered to write a letter to the Russians telling them what Wilhelm had done. The letter might protect Wilhelm, but I doubt that he will get through the German lines and even if, by some miracle, he did reach the Russian Front unharmed, there is no guarantee that the Russians wouldn't shoot him first and read Sascha's letter afterwards. But I saddled Elise and left her standing in the yard, in case Wilhelm was prepared to chance an escape.

I had just finished giving the children their breakfast when eight armed SS officers arrived in two Mercedes staff cars. I went out to meet them. Trying to look braver than I felt, I told them that I objected to anyone bringing guns into the house because they frightened the children.

Ignoring my request, they asked for Wilhelm. I replied quite truthfully that he wasn't in the house. They didn't believe me and began to search. Before they went upstairs I saw Wilhelm cross the courtyard with Irena at his side. Either he or Irena had brushed and cleaned his uniform, and they were holding hands as though they had been out for a morning stroll.

I ran outside and begged Wilhelm to take Elise and hide in the woods. I insisted that a battalion of troops could search for a year and not find all the places we played in as children. He listened to me, smiled gravely and shook his head, as though I were a silly child again.

Then he looked up and saw the major in charge of the SS detachment standing outside the kitchen door watching us. He asked if he was looking for him. When the major replied that he was, Wilhelm offered up his gun.

I have never been angrier or more proud of my brother. Only the set of his jaw betrayed his nervousness. He and Paul always used to clench their teeth whenever Papa reprimanded them for their pranks. The major ordered one of his men to pin Wilhelm's arms behind his back. Wilhelm assured them that

177

there was no need for restraint. He told them that he was prepared to go with them wherever they wanted, so long as they spared his wife, daughters, mother and sister.

I think he shamed the major, because he ordered Wilhelm released, and gave him permission to go upstairs and say goodbye to Mama.

I went with him. It was awful. Mama didn't recognize him. He embraced and kissed me before we left the room, and reminded me of my promise to look after Irena and the girls. As if I needed reminding.

Irena, Marianna and little Karoline stood waiting for him in the hall. The SS watched while Wilhelm hugged and kissed them. He told Irena that he loved her and was sorry that he had loved his country more, but he was sure that he had done the right thing. He smiled and looked at the soldiers as he said, 'As God told Abraham that He would spare Sodom if he could show him ten just men in the city, so I hope that God will be merciful now and not destroy Germany because we stood firm for our country. None of us can complain that we have to die.'

Then he looked at me over Irena's shoulder. I knew what he wanted me to do. I took Irena from him. Wilhelm turned on his heel and walked out of the house for the last time.

Irena was in the most dreadful state. She broke free from my grasp and, shouting Wilhelm's name, ran outside after the cars. I thought she would never stop screaming. Minna took the children into the kitchen, Martha brought the brandy, and between us we tried to get Irena to bed, but she didn't calm down until I promised to telephone Papa von Letteberg and ask him to help Wilhelm.

I couldn't get through to Papa's office, or the one Claus works out of. I only succeeded in speaking to a series of officious clerks, who kept repeating that a state of martial law had been declared in the wake of the assassination attempt. I telephoned Irena's parents, and they came at once with the doctor, who sedated Irena despite her pregnancy. He warned that if he didn't she'd undoubtedly miscarry.

At four o'clock, another two cars arrived with another six SS officers, three in each car. I knew who they had come for when I saw that two of the officers were women.

They asked for Irena, Marianna and Karoline. I told them Irena was ill and pregnant, and we feared for her life as well as the child's. But they pushed me aside and quoted the doctrine of Sippenhaft, 'blood guilt', as though the two babies or Irena could be tainted because of something Wilhelm had done.

They went upstairs, thrust Irena's mother out of the room and dragged Irena out of bed. Frau Adolf was hysterical. I insisted on seeing Irena, and one of the SS women officers allowed me to help Irena dress, but she removed her gun from its holster, pointed it at us and stayed with us the whole time. I asked her just where she thought a heavily pregnant woman could run to with SS officers all over the house, but she didn't answer me.

When we went downstairs, the woman handed Irena to the captain in charge, then she and another officer went to the kitchen and took the children. They knew exactly who they were looking for. They didn't even glance at Erich, just took Marianna by the hand, picked up Karoline and dragged them into the hall.

I tried to take the girls from them, pleading that I was their aunt. That it was my duty, not theirs, to care for my brother's wife and children, but they ignored me. I used my father-in-law's and Claus's name, all to no avail.

In the end, one of the officers hit me across the face, sending me spinning back into the staircase, warning that if I didn't stop making such a fuss they would take me and Erich, too, but only after shooting everyone else in the house.

It was then that Irena behaved as bravely as Wilhelm. She kissed her father, mother and me, thanked me for being a good sister, and asked me to take care of her parents as well as Mama and Erich, and, if there was a future for Germany, and they lived, her daughters.

Her father and Brunon stood tight-lipped, while Irena's mother, Erich, Martha and Minna began to cry. Mama came out of her room to see what all the commotion was about. I asked Minna to take her back. The SS women took charge of Marianna and Karoline. They placed the two little girls side by side in front of Irena and ordered them to say goodbye. I could tell from the confused expression on their faces that neither Marianna nor Karoline understood a single word that was being said to them.

One of the women then said, 'You will have to change your names so no one from your family will ever be able to find you again. Hitler will educate you and you will never see your mother, father or one another from this moment on.'

We all knew the warning was directed at us not the children. Less than five minutes later they were gone. Nothing I could do or say would change the minds or melt the hearts of the officers. I begged that Marianna and Karoline be allowed to take their favourite dolls, but they didn't permit them to take anything except the clothes they stood up in. Irena told her parents she was sorry that she had brought them grief, but she could not and would not condemn what Wilhelm had done. Then she said to me, 'Do what you can for the girls.'

She walked out of the house upright, dry-eyed, staring straight ahead, just like Wilhelm. I thought her pregnancy would evoke some sympathy, but the children were wrenched from her and bundled into one car, she into another. Her last words to her daughters were: 'Remember who you are and who your father was.'

The doctor tried to give me a sedative after the cars had gone, but I wouldn't take it. He drove Herr and Frau Adolf back to town. Irena's baby will be born in two months. Surely they won't kill a pregnant woman? What will they do to her? Will they really separate the children? Will they kill them?

I sat in the kitchen nursing Erich on my lap for what seemed like a long time, not knowing what to do or think, wishing I could stop crying, wishing it were dusk so I could go to Sascha and ask his advice. All I can think of is my broken promise to Wilhelm. How could I stand by and allow the SS to take his family away?

Chapter 13

I have been so wretched and miserable I haven't spared a thought for Grunwaldsee, and I have left Brunon to do all the work by himself. On Sunday I couldn't bear to face anyone, so I stayed in my bedroom most of the day, reading stories to Erich. He keeps asking for his Auntie Irena and Marianna and Karoline. He cannot understand why the nasty soldiers came and took them away and repeats endlessly that they hadn't been naughty.

I can't find the words to reassure him or the strength to visit Mama. I am sure that the guards are watching me, so I stayed away from Papa's study and the tack room.

In the early hours of this morning Sascha took a terrible risk. He left the loft, went into the tack room, crossed the courtyard and climbed the wall on to my balcony. I heard him whispering my name outside the French doors. It was crazy of him. If one of the guards had caught sight of him, he would have been shot.

He stayed with me, just holding me and letting me cry, not saying a word, until an hour before dawn when I led him back through the house to the study and unlocked the door to the tack room. Even then I went in first to check that no one was there. It was dangerous to walk through the house, but it was a safer route than across the courtyard.

I left him there and went foraging in the kitchen. I brought back some milk and bread, which would have been breakfast for Irena and the girls. He passed most of it up to his men but stayed with me while he ate and drank his share. He told me that the guards have been talking about nothing else but Wilhelm, Irena and the children. Even they are ashamed of the treatment meted out to a pregnant girl and two babies.

Mama von Letteberg arrived unannounced as I was in the tack room with Sascha. Brunon somehow knew where I was and banged on the door.

Sascha returned to his loft before I opened it. My face was swollen and red-eyed, so I hoped that Brunon and Mama von Letteberg had assumed that I'd locked myself in there to have a good cry away from Mama, Erich and the servants.

I didn't have to tell Mama von Letteberg anything; she knew it all. She sat with me while I continued to cry. Then she closed the door and said that no matter how hard it was, I had to pull myself together and be brave. That if I made a fuss, Erich, Mama and I would be taken away, just like Irena and the children. She told me that Colonel Graf von Stauffenberg had already been executed, and that the evidence against Wilhelm was overwhelming.

She said that Papa von Letteberg was doing what he could to help Wilhelm but it was very little, as every officer connected to von Stauffenberg and his department, and thousands more, have been rounded up, and it can only be a matter of time before Claus and his father are questioned because of their relationship to von Stauffenberg through Wilhelm and me.

When I looked at her, I realized that she is as upset as I am; only she is far more adept at concealing her feelings. I wanted to ask her if Papa von Letteberg knew of the plot to kill Hitler beforehand, and if he and Claus were party to the conspiracy. But I didn't have the courage to question her. I can see that the less anyone knows about who exactly was involved the better.

Mama von Letteberg doesn't think Hitler will dare kill a pregnant woman and children, especially ones who bear the old and respected name of von Datski. I do so hope that she is right and not just saying it to give me hope where there is none. Papa von Letteberg has discovered that Irena is being held in a women's prison not far from Berlin but it is forbidden to send anything to her or to write any letters. He hasn't, as yet, found out where the children have been taken, but he doubts that we'll be able to see them or send them anything.

Mama von Letteberg knew some of the details. Colonel Graf von Stauffenberg and three other officers were executed by firing squad shortly after midnight on 31 July in an inner courtyard of the War Office. I knew Wilhelm would be executed the moment Mama von Letteberg said that the colonel was fortunate to have such a quick and merciful soldier's death.

Wilhelm, along with many others, will stand trial. The Führer has ordered the arrest of all the men involved and also their families, so Irena, Marianna and Karoline aren't the only women and children to be imprisoned. Colonel

Graf von Stauffenberg, or someone close to him, had contacted England in an attempt to try to end the war. After the failure of the plot to kill Hitler was announced by the Reich, the BBC broadcasted a list of the conspirators, so the Führer knew exactly who had plotted against him. Didn't the British understand that although all the officers were Germans they were Hitler's enemies, too?

After a while Mama von Letteberg persuaded me to leave the tack room and return to the house. The doctor was waiting to see us. Herr and Frau Adolf are dead. They wrote a note saying that they could not bear to live with the knowledge of what had happened, and then took poison. The doctor suggested that they found it impossible to live with the disgrace of having a son-in-law who tried to overthrow and kill our beloved Führer, but I think it was the loss of Manfred and the cruelty meted out to Irena and their grandchildren that drove Herr and Frau Adolf to take their lives.

Claus telephoned at midnight to tell me that he is returning to the Russian Front and will call in Grunwaldsee on his way through. That was all he said. I was too afraid to ask him any questions because I suspected that someone was listening in. Mama von Letteberg knew about his posting. I asked her if it was Hitler's way of punishing Claus because he is related to a member of the conspiracy. She insisted that it wasn't. That things are so uncertain and dangerous in Berlin, Papa von Letteberg had arranged for Claus to be sent back to the Front because it is safer than the War Office right now.

For the first time I am glad that Claus is coming to see me. In all this mess of death and cruelty there is one secret that I am glad about. I have been carrying Sascha's baby for over a month. No one knows except me, not even Sascha, but I will tell him before Claus arrives.

If I can make Claus believe that he is the father, I may be allowed to keep the child – at least for a little while.

Charlotte closed her eyes and, once again, Sascha's blue eyes gazed into hers, glittering in the flickering light from the lamp she had hung on the tack room ceiling. From the moment they had first made love she had never kept anything from him. But she had found it so hard to tell him what should have been such happy news.

'I have something to tell you,' she had finally whispered.

'I know what it is,' he had replied soberly.

His sudden change of mood made her afraid. 'How do you know?'

The warmth and intimacy engendered by their lovemaking had shattered. He drew away from her, sat up and reached for the shirt she had torn from his back; an old linen one of Paul's that she had darned many times. 'Does it matter?'

'Yes.' Refusing to allow him to move from her side, she rose to her knees and wrapped her hands around his chest.

'I overheard Brunon tell Marius to make sure the grey stallion's tack was clean because your husband is expected tomorrow.'

She had felt his pain as if it were her own. 'You have no reason to be jealous of Claus.'

He had hung his head, and she knew he was ashamed of his anger. 'I cannot bear the thought of you lying in his arms, of him kissing you, caressing you, loving you ...'

'I don't lie in Claus's arms!' She tightened her hold on him. 'I don't love him, can never love him the way I love you. But—'

'While I remain here, I am a prisoner, a slave, a nothing and no one,' he interrupted harshly. 'And Claus von Letteberg is an aristocrat, you are his wife—'

'I am having your child.' She had intended to choose a better time to break the news to him. And had planned to do it gently. She had even rehearsed what she would say.

He turned and stared at her. She saw shock, fear and something else reflected in his eyes.

'I'm having a baby, your baby,' she repeated quietly, aware of his men in the loft above them, separated only by a layer of wooden planks.

'When ... when will it be born?'

She hadn't needed to calculate, she had done nothing else for the past month, ever since her suspicions had hardened into certainty. 'The spring. Late March or early April.'

He had dropped the shirt, sank back on the hay and looked up at her. 'You will tell Claus it is his?'

'Not now, but in a month or two, yes. What choice do I have?' she begged, willing Sascha to offer her hope that it could be otherwise. That they could escape, make a new life for themselves somewhere far from Germany and Russia, but even as the thoughts formed in her mind, she knew they were futile.

'There is no choice for either of us while the war still rages. But if it ends ...'

She knew why he had left the rest of the sentence unspoken. It was the reason neither of them had ever broached the subject before.

'The war will end. If only because there will soon be no soldiers left alive to fight it,' she said sadly.

'If Russia wins, I will go home, and take you and Erich with me,' he promised rashly.

'To your wife?' She forced a smile to take the sting from her words, although she wanted to remind him that he wasn't free, either.

'And if Germany wins?' he had asked.

'The men will return.'

'There won't be enough survivors to do all the work. If I'm lucky I will remain here, a prisoner and a slave, and you and my child will live with Claus von Letteberg. And if I'm not lucky ...'

'Sascha, don't!' She buried her head in his chest, unable to bear the thought of separation. 'I love you.'

'And our child?'

'The child will be born of our love. I will cherish, adore and protect it with all my strength. Please, Sascha, can't you be glad? This war has brought so much death – Papa, Paul and, it seems certain, Wilhelm. So many people I loved, and so many friends, gone for ever. And, in some ways, not knowing what has happened to Irena and the girls is even worse. Every night I imagine them being tortured, crying, screaming for me to help them ...'

He pulled her down on top of him. She laid her head on his chest and he stroked her hair. 'This child won't take their place, Charlotte.'

'I know.' It was as though an iron fist had closed over her heart. 'No one can.'

He turned, faced her and smiled; the slow smile she had come to love so much. 'The child won't take their place. But it will bring hope for the future – our future.'

She was almost too afraid to ask the question. 'And in the meantime?'

'We will make every second of every minute count. We will love one another as no man and woman have ever loved before, and,' he trailed his fingers over her naked body, 'I will be grateful for every day that I am able to watch our little one grow within you. And hope that fate will allow us to be together when it is born.'

Charlotte laid the diary on the bedside table, left the bed and opened the balcony doors. The sun had risen above the lake, shining through the morning mist that clouded the waters and hazed the woods, just as it had done on so many other summer mornings.

She returned to the bedroom, picked up her wrap and diary, and sat at the table outside, cherishing a beauty she had never quite forgotten. The trees, the grass, the flowers, even the swans gliding across the waters at the head of trains of ripples — all looked just as they had done when she had lived at Grunwaldsee. If Paul and Wilhelm were standing beside her now, she knew that they would recognize their beloved country.

Had she ever ceased mourning her brothers? Poor Paul and Wilhelm ... the passage of years couldn't stop her from shuddering. She hadn't known the full story until after the war.

She had wanted to go to Berlin to support Wilhelm at his trial, but Papa von Letteberg had persuaded her that the ordeal would be humiliating and difficult enough for Wilhelm without her there to witness it. She gave him a letter in the hope that he would be able to smuggle it to Wilhelm, who had been stripped of his rank and expelled from the army before undergoing what the Gestapo called 'heightened interrogation', which had turned out to be another term for torture.

Along with the other conspirators, he suffered for three weeks without divulging any names, other than those of the men he knew had been already executed. Then he had been tried in the People's Court. The judge had handed down the inevitable death sentence. Wilhelm wasn't granted the military death accorded to his superior. He had been hanged, naked, from piano wire suspended from a meat hook in a cell in the Ploetzensee prison.

An eyewitness recorded that it had taken Wilhelm a full twenty-five minutes to die because, like his colonel's brother, he had been taken down and revived twice before being replaced on the hook.

On the morning of his execution Wilhelm had been shown papers Greta had signed; papers that renounced all ties between them and denounced him as a traitor who had defiled the name of von Datski. But, Charlotte reflected, Wilhelm would not have expected anything else of Greta.

She had her father-in-law's word that her last message had been given to him. It had been short and simple: '*I love you, and I am and always will be proud of you, my beloved brother.*'

She opened her diary and turned to the back cover. Wilhelm's last letter to her was tucked inside. She unfolded it, tears starting in her eyes as they always did whenever she saw his familiar handwriting: '*My only regret is that we did not succeed, and that Irena, the children, and you and Mama will suffer. I hope that one day you will forgive me and understand why I had to sacrifice even my family in the cause of Germany. Your loving brother, Wilhelm.*'

She wished that she could have told him that seven months later she had understood, and had longed with all her heart and soul that Colonel Graf von Stauffenberg and his conspiracy had succeeded.

Charlotte flicked through the next few pages of her diary. The entries were sparse, gradually growing fewer and fewer with weeks rather days between them. She had been busy running Grunwaldsee but she had busy before and that hadn't stopped her from consigning her thoughts to paper. But fear had. An all-consuming, blood-chilling, paralysing fear that had dogged her waking moments and turned her dreams into nightmares; a fear not for herself, but, after what had happened to Wilhelm, Irena and their children, for her son, her mother, Sascha – and Sascha's baby.

Where she had been open and friendly she became suspicious of everyone who called at Grunwaldsee, old friend or stranger, it made no difference. Spies were everywhere, and her brother's actions had marked the entire family as traitors.

The commandant of the prisoner of war camp telephoned her. He told her it was necessary to replace the guards because every experienced soldier was needed at the Front. She knew it was useless to argue with him and didn't even try. It wasn't as if she had liked the old guards, but they had lived at Grunwaldsee for so long she had become accustomed to them. When their replacements arrived she had looked back fondly on the three corporals and thought of them almost as friends.

Two of their new guards were vicious, bitter amputees, with artificial legs. Both enjoyed whipping and humiliating the prisoners. One was a boy too young to shave, but deemed old enough by the authorities to carry a gun. And there was a fourth. A painfully thin consumptive who never stopped coughing and spent most of his days standing looking out of the window of the lodge kitchen, watching every move she, Brunon, Marius, Minna and Martha made. And whenever they looked back at him, he made a point of writing in a notebook.

It was obvious he had been sent to spy on them. But in those dark days of the dying summer, there was one consolation – Sascha. Even after everything that had happened afterwards to cause her to doubt Sascha's motives, that summer she had truly believed that Sascha had cared for her and their coming child.

Taking the diary, she left the balcony, walked back to the bed and kicked off her shoes. She lay back on the pillows and remembered.

Blue skies, long hot days working in the fields, followed by warm summer evenings spent closeted behind bales of new-mown hay in the tack room. If Brunon had wondered why she had ordered so much hay to be stored there instead of the barn, he had never questioned her orders.

And Sascha – Sascha who had worked like the slave he was during the days, held her close through every stolen evening; burdening himself with her grief for her lost father, brothers and friends, sharing it, and promising to help her search for Irena and the girls after the war.

She had only to smell new-mown hay to be transported back to that time, which, for all its sorrow, anguish and uncertainty, had been the most passionate and intensely lived of her life.

TUESDAY, 17 OCTOBER 1944
Germany is in mourning. Field Marshal Rommel is dead. The radio and newspapers reported that he was killed three days ago when his car was strafed by RAF planes, but Brunon heard rumours in Allenstein that he too was involved in the von Stauffenberg plot.

The matron in charge of the hospital in Bergensee asked me to stop visiting after Wilhelm was executed. She had obviously been ordered to do so by a higher authority. She was embarrassed the whole time she spoke to me, and even said that if it was up to her she would still allow me inside. But the corporal in charge of admissions overheard her and told me bluntly that the authorities didn't think it appropriate for the sister of a traitor to be allowed to visit a military institution.

I don't go into town often, there is little point when the shops have virtually nothing to sell, but when I do, people cross the street so they won't have to greet me. Girls who were in school with me, the mothers of boys who were in Paul and Wilhelm's Hitler Youth group, even the doctor and his wife, who have been good friends of Papa and Mama's ever since I can remember, are afraid to speak to me in public.

So many have been arrested and executed – generals, colonels, officials – all respected, aristocratic, clever, able men Germany can ill afford to lose. Now I wonder if Papa really died of a heart attack. The Führer hates Freemasons, and so many people knew of Papa's youthful indiscretion as well as his criticism of the war.

When Papa died, I believed that losing him was the worst thing that would ever happen to me, and now, not even four years later, I am mourning not only Papa, but Wilhelm and Paul. Only Mama, Greta and I are left, and although Mama's body may be here, her mind is with Papa and the boys. And Greta … a year ago I thought I couldn't dislike her any more than I already did. Now I hate her with every fibre of my being.

It is seven weeks since Wilhelm was executed. There is still no official word about Irena. I know Papa von Letteberg has had to work very hard to keep Erich, Mama and I from being taken away. He drove to Grunwaldsee from Berlin to tell me that Wilhelm was dead because he did not want me to hear the news from a stranger. My brother wasn't even accorded an officer's death by firing squad. They hanged him like a common criminal.

I begged Papa von Letteberg to tell me everything he knew about Wilhelm's death. He had talked to a soldier who'd witnessed Wilhelm's execution, and everyone who was present agreed my brother died bravely. I never doubted he would, although the thought of any strong, healthy young man, let alone my darling, beloved brother, being deliberately killed in the prime of life sickens me. One minute alive – the next, nothing.

Wilhelm refused to name his fellow conspirators, and insisted until the *last that no one other than those men who had already been executed knew of the plot to kill Hitler, and no women, not even his wife, mother and sisters, had an inkling of what he and the others were planning.*

Shortly afterwards, Greta wrote to me, a letter that had been opened in the mail, as are all the letters that are delivered to Grunwaldsee now. In it she enclosed a copy of the letter she had sent to the High Command, denouncing not only everything Wilhelm had done, but also Wilhelm himself.

As no one has demanded that I should write such a letter I can only assume she wrote it of her own volition in an attempt to distance herself from what she called 'Wilhelm von Datski's treasonous crimes'. But Greta always has had an over-developed sense of self-preservation. As Paul used to say, Greta places Greta first, second, third and so on, right down to last.

In her personal letter to me she said that, as Paul and Wilhelm are both dead and have left no legitimate non-criminal heirs — as if poor little Marianna and Karoline can possibly be criminals — Grunwaldsee is now hers by right, as Papa's eldest surviving daughter, and she and Helmut will move in and live here after their marriage.

I was so angry I burnt both letters. I hope Greta has the sense to stay away from me and Grunwaldsee. I will not be responsible for what I do or say to her if she tries to set foot in the house. If the estate belongs to anyone it is Marianna, Karoline and — if the child Irena is carrying is a boy — Wilhelm's son, and I intend to see that his heirs inherit the estate, not Greta and her lapdog of a fiancé.

I didn't need Papa von Letteberg to warn me that all the roads around Grunwaldsee are under surveillance. If I could send Erich away I would, but to where? Mama von Letteberg is the obvious choice, but I know from her last visit that she worries more and more with every rumour of further arrests. She is terrified that Papa von Letteberg will be detained next, and if he is, neither she nor anyone living with her will be safe, and I can't bear the thought of losing Erich as I have lost Marianna and Karoline.

I try not to think about what the girls will be like after months or years in a camp or State orphanage — that's supposing they survive and I find them after the war. After seeing Claus briefly for a day — and a very necessary night for the child I am carrying — before he went to the Russian Front, I am convinced that he wasn't involved in the conspiracy, even if his father was.

Papa von Letteberg insisted the Russian Front was safer than Berlin when he arranged Claus's transfer immediately after Count von Stauffenberg's execution. But I know from hints in Mama von Letteberg's guarded letters that he is now having second thoughts. I am not surprised. From what Brunon has heard, there is no more Russian Front, only a Polish one, and the Russians are actually massed on the borders of East Prussia and Belorussia.

I wrote to Claus at the end of September to inform him that he is going to be a father again. At the same time I telephoned Mama von Letteberg to tell her that I am carrying her second grandchild. She pretended to be glad, but I sensed my news only gave her one more reason to worry. Pregnancy makes me more vulnerable, another pawn that could be used against Papa von Letteberg should they find evidence to implicate him in the July plot.

Brunon told me it is rumoured that thousands of relatives of the conspirators, including old people, children and babies, have been taken to prisons and camps. I only hope that Irena, Marianna and Karoline are alive, and that conditions are not too harsh for the women and children. But with food scarce for civilians, I dread to think what the prisoners are being given. The guards' rations have been cut in half, although there are four not three of them now, and it is months since we have been given anything at all for the Russians.

Little wonder that the commandant of the Russian POW camp telephones me every week to ask if we need replacement prisoners. Brunon says it is official policy to starve the Russian POWs to death. The new guards insist the Russians can survive on only one bowl of watery soup a day. Every day I am grateful for the trap-door, although we have to be very careful. It is obvious from the appearance of Sascha's men that we are feeding them extra and the guards search the stable loft at all hours of the day and night to try and catch them with food. So far we have been lucky.

If she is alive, Irena will have had her baby by now. I do so hope it is a boy, then there will never be any question as to who should inherit Grunwaldsee — that is, if there will be anything left to inherit. Nearly all the animals have been taken by the army. Brunon has hidden a few horses around the neighbouring farms, including Elise, because we are convinced that they are being taken for meat.

Brunon, Marius and I killed three pigs secretly, at night down by the river, so the guards wouldn't see us doing it, and we could wash away the blood. We salted the quarters and hid them behind Papa's wine racks in the cellar. If we hadn't, we would have nothing to eat. The weekly bread ration was cut by another 200 grams yesterday. It is bad enough for us, but even worse for Sascha and the prisoners. We have so little for ourselves and the children on the estate, it is getting harder and harder to find anything to smuggle into the loft.

I could not have survived the last few months without Sascha to love and comfort me. Night after night he has held me in his arms while I have cried my heart out — for Papa and Mama, for Paul and Wilhelm, for Irena and her babies, and for us.

I have never known an August to be so hot. At the height of the heat-wave, Sascha and I sneaked out of the tack room in the early hours of the morning. We stole through the house and went through the woods to the summerhouse to bathe in the lake.

It was insane to take such a risk, but after what has happened to Wilhelm and Irena, our time together is all the more precious. Who knows how much longer we have left? And the danger didn't seem to matter as much as spending every possible moment together while we can.

Now I have memories of swimming under the stars with Sascha, of lying naked in his arms on the bank, and watching the moon sink slowly in the skies. I will never forget that night, nor, I think, will Sascha. It was almost as though we actually succeeded in freezing time. For a long while nothing moved. There wasn't even a breeze. Everything was so still, so silent, I could almost believe that we were the only living creatures in a paste and cardboard world.

Nothing existed outside of us until a bird began to sing and a current of air ruffled the surface of the lake. The bird broke the spell but even then I wanted to stay until dawn, although Sascha was concerned, not for himself — never for himself — always for me.

We climbed back into the house through the ballroom window, and I led him down the passage to the tack room. All the while I couldn't help thinking what would happen if one of the guards should see us — these new ones insisted on being given keys to the house. They use them any time they choose, day or night, and they always carry their guns. I think that they would shoot Sascha first and then me.

My childhood terror of death seems odd now. Plagued by nightmares, I woke screaming night after night in the weeks following Oma's death when I was five years old. Papa and Greta lost patience; even Mama didn't understand my fears — or did she? Perhaps everyone secretly feels the same way. Terrified by the thought of your body being eaten by worms and insects, of falling into a black nothingness where you can no longer even think.

I believe Wilhelm and Paul understood what I was going through. Now, after everything that has happened since the war started, I think of death far too much for my own or Erich's good.

I do hope there is something after death. A life of sorts, even if it is not as we know it here on this earth. And that the twins have been reunited with Papa and Maria, and Peter and Manfred, and that someday I will see them again. But I do not believe for one minute that if there is such a life it has anything to do with an all-seeing, all-knowing, all-forgiving God. No God would allow the terrible things to happen that are happening to innocent people and children all over Europe.

If a guard should shoot Sascha and me, would death be quick? Is a bullet in the head as painless as soldiers insist it is? Supposing it doesn't kill right away and that, after you've been shot, you feel immense pain. Are you aware of death coming minutes before the end?

I don't want it to happen, but I wouldn't want to live without Sascha. He insists that, if the worst happens, I must carry on because so many people rely on me. That I have responsibilities to Erich, the child I'm carrying, Irena and Wilhelm's children, Mama, Minna, Brunon's family – and to him. The more the baby grows within me, the more Sascha insists that we have a future together. But I am not so sure, and I am too afraid to ask Sascha where he thinks it will be.

THURSDAY, 19 OCTOBER 1944

Yesterday, all the able-bodied men between sixteen and sixty were called up to form a Home Guard. The Führer himself made the announcement, at the same time condemning all our allies for defecting. He made it clear that Germany now stands alone against our international Jewish enemies.

I was devastated, not at the confirmation that the war is going badly – I have suspected that for months – but at losing Brunon. I cannot imagine running the estate without him. He has already received his orders and a travel warrant for Königsberg. Martha is distraught. I promised Brunon that I will take care of her and Marius; I only hope that I will be able to keep this promise, unlike the one I made to Wilhelm. Thank God Marius is only thirteen.

I had a letter from Claus this morning. It was headed 'somewhere in Poland'. He is pleased that I am pregnant, and suggested that if the child is a boy he should be named Peter after his brother. I wondered if he remembered that Erich's second name is Peter. If it is a boy, I would like to christen him Wilhelm Paul, but I know Claus wouldn't allow it because it could be seen as condoning Wilhelm's complicity in the July plot.

But what does Claus have to do with this baby? One of the hardest things that I have ever done was to allow him to touch me again on his last leave. The feel of his naked body against mine was sickening after Sascha's lovemaking. With Claus away it is so easy for me to pretend that Sascha is my husband, but pretend is all it is and perhaps all it ever will be. No, I cannot believe that. I won't!

The nights are growing colder. Sascha and I spend as much time as we dare in the tack room. We desperately try to forget the war, but both of us know that things are about to change. With the Russians continuing to mass on our eastern borders there is talk of moving the Russian prisoners west. I hope they won't. I can't imagine having to live without Sascha.

WEDNESDAY, 8 NOVEMBER 1944

The Russians crossed into East Prussia last month and massacred German women and children at Nemmersdorf, a village outside Königsberg. The papers were full of dreadful photographs of crucifixions and people being disemboweled and burned alive. I wished I hadn't looked at them because ever since all I can think about is Erich, Marianna and little Karoline being butchered as those poor children were.

Sascha said the photographs might be propaganda, but he warned that, whether they are or not, Russian troops who invade East Prussia will not be kind to German soldiers or civilians after the atrocities our army perpetrated in the East.

People from the east of the country have tried to book hotel rooms in Allenstein, but the police have ordered the hoteliers to turn them away. Our Gauleiter, Erich Koch, insists that the Russians have been driven back. We have all been ordered to remain in our homes, even the people who live close to the Polish and Russian borders, and the civilian population in Königsberg, which is bound to be the first city the Russians attack as it is our capital.

Is it true that the Russians have been driven back? Is Brunon safe? Martha has had only one letter from him since he left Grunwaldsee last month. Will the Russians invade East Prussia? What will happen to us if they do? I shudder to think.

Chapter 14

This has been the most dismal Christmas I have known. Martha, Minna and I tried to make it special for Erich, Marius and the estate children, but none of us felt like celebrating. Papa von Letteberg couldn't get away from Berlin and Mama von Letteberg refused to leave him.

I know from the rumours Marius brings back from the town that the Gestapo are still arresting people connected to the von Stauffenberg plot. Mama von Letteberg must fear that Papa von Letteberg will still be implicated. The Allies are bombing German cities and advancing on the Italian and French Fronts; some people are saying that the German border towns in the west are already in Allied hands. It is insane. Allied troops are closing in on Germany from every side and the authorities are arresting, imprisoning and killing our own officers, when we need all the men we have to fight our enemies.

I went to church this morning and pretended to pray for Papa, Wilhelm, Paul, Peter, Manfred and Herr and Frau Adolf's souls, Irena and her children's safety, and Mama's peace of mind. I did it because everyone expected me to, but I resent every wasted minute I spend in the cold, draughty building. Attending services seems such a mechanical, futile exercise, when I no longer believe in God.

However, I did think of my family, living and dead, and wished that somehow they could all know that my thoughts were with them. As a Communist, Sascha jokes a great deal about God. He says that if a God exists he went on holiday in 1939 and hasn't come back.

My only consolation is that Mama knows nothing of what is happening. When I took up her Christmas Eve supper and the gift of handkerchiefs that I had cut from old sheets and embroidered, she asked me to remind Papa and the boys to wrap up warm, as the frost is getting harder and the snow thicker. Sometimes I wish I could ignore everything that is happening and live in the past like her.

Greta didn't send any presents, not even for Mama, but she wrote to tell us that all leave has been cancelled and Helmut has been assigned to a front-line regiment. About time! Why should old men like Brunon fight while young men like Helmut have safe, cushy jobs? She scolded me for not answering her last letter, but I cannot trust myself to write a single word to her after her denouncement of Wilhelm and her threat to take over Grunwaldsee, so I didn't even send her Christmas greetings.

I wanted to send Christmas messages and food parcels to Irena and the children, but Mama von Letteberg warned me against even trying, as any attempt at communication could make things worse for Irena and the girls — wherever they are.

So, only Martha, Minna, Marius, Erich and I sat down to a Christmas dinner of salted bacon and boiled potatoes. The food stuck in my throat. I remembered other years when the house was full of people, laughter, joy and Christmas spirit. Even the tree Marius — who tries so hard so take his father's place both as steward and head of his family — had cut down and carried into the hall, and the few sweets we had concocted for the estate children from syrup and mashed potatoes looked sad in comparison to the decorations we made last Christmas, let alone the Christmases before the war.

I feel as though the house is full of ghosts. A door only has to bang in a draught and I hear the twins running and whooping downstairs on their way to a party. Or I walk past the study and open the door, expecting to see Papa smoking and reading the paper instead of doing the accounts, as he pretended to do every morning. Even Mama's sewing room looks forlorn.

Just after dark on Christmas afternoon a truck drove into the yard. The snow was thick on the windscreen, and the sides and top of the canvas awning were encrusted in ice. Remembering the SS who had taken Irena and the children away, I ordered Martha and Minna to hide Erich and Marius upstairs, before walking out to meet it. I was terrified, even before I heard the moans coming from the back.

The driver and an officer climbed out. I looked inside. It was packed with wounded soldiers. The men were in a terrible state, with bloodstained bandages wrapped around their frozen heads, hands and feet. Even in the cold, the stench was awful.

While the driver checked the men, the officer, a ridiculously young lieutenant, clicked his heels, bowed and handed me a parcel and a letter. He said they were a special delivery from Standartenführer Graf von Letteberg.

I suggested that the men might like to come inside in the warm, and have something hot to drink. Martha always has a soup of sorts simmering on the stove, although these days it is more vegetables and water than anything else.

The lieutenant refused. Some of the men were badly injured, and most had lost fingers and toes to frostbite. He said that if he didn't get them to the doctors at Bergensee soon, gangrene would set in. I asked if I could do anything to help, but he shook his head.

I watched them drive away, then returned to the kitchen and called Martha, Minna and the children. I hoped the parcel would contain something to cheer Erich. He is old enough to know that Christmas should be special, and this one has been lonely for him. He still constantly asks for Marianna and Karoline — they used to play so well together — and he misses Irena, who spent hours telling the children stories. Not even Marius has been able to stop him from moping.

There was no Wehrmacht uniform this year, but a small, wooden train, which Erich loved, a box of candied fruits, which I shared between Martha, Minna and the children, and a set of hand-knitted and embroidered baby clothes for me. I dread to think how much Claus had paid for them.

Claus's letter was guarded, but he suggested that I pay his parents a visit in Berlin as soon as I could. So I know that the Russians are on the point of invading East Prussia again. But there is no way that I can leave Grunwaldsee, with Brunon gone.

After I put Erich to bed I sat in the kitchen for half an hour with Martha and Minna. They were so depressed they went to bed before nine o'clock, or perhaps they suspect that something is going on between me and one of the prisoners. As soon as I was alone I took what food I could find and two bottles of Martha's homemade cherry wine, and went into the tack room.

Mama is right; the frost is hard this year. The old stove in the loft still works well but even so, Sascha told me that his men spend most of their time huddled under as many layers of clothes as they can find. The tack room was freezing. It is almost as cold in there as it is outside.

I offered to sneak Sascha up to my room and bed, but he insisted that with the new guards having keys to the house it was too dangerous, so we nestled together under the horse blankets after he had passed most of the food and wine through the trap-door to the others.

His unselfishness gives me one more reason to love him, but I wish he'd eat more of the food I bring and not hand everything over to his men. No one knows what lies ahead, but one thing is certain. We are all going to need every gram of strength we possess.

For the second time we dared to discuss the future. Sascha suggested that if the Russians break through the German lines and invade East Prussia, I give him and his men horses and a cart so they can make a run for the Russian Front, taking me and Erich with them. I reminded him that, apart from Erich, I had Mama, Minna, Martha, and Marius to care for, and the Russian army wouldn't feel well-disposed towards a party of German women and two boys, especially if they knew that one of the women was the daughter-in-law of General von Letteberg and the smallest boy his grandson.

Then Sascha began to weave even crazier daydreams and, wrapped in his arms, warm and cosy under the blankets, with a glass of cherry wine inside me, I allowed myself to believe they were possible.

He talked of heading for the coast, stealing a boat, sailing to neutral Sweden and finding a house there, something small and cosy, like the summerhouse by the lake. We would live there with Erich and the baby, seeing no one and living off the land. He would use the boat to fish in the sea and in winter he would hunt for deer. We would keep a few chickens and a milk cow or two, and grow our own vegetables.

It was an enchanting fantasy and a wonderful Christmas present, but I am more afraid than ever. I try to hide my fears from Sascha, but he knows me too well. It is impossible for me to keep any secrets from him. Soon it will be another year, 1945. It should be a happy one with a new baby to look forward to, but I am frightened for Erich, Irena and the children, Mama, Germany, and Sascha and his men. What will it bring?

Charlotte made a wry face as she fingered the following pages. They were of a coarser, thinner paper with a crêpe-like surface. Torn from a notebook she had been given when she had been conscripted, she had sewn them into the diary the day after Germany had surrendered. She pictured herself as she had been, sitting in a corner of the strange farmhouse kitchen, stabbing holes with a needle she had borrowed from the farmer's wife, and tying the loose papers together with a thread torn from the hem of the uniform she no longer needed.

Closing the book, she lay back on the pillows. She looked at the clock. Eight o'clock. Laura didn't want to breakfast until ten. She could sleep for an hour. She even closed her eyes but her diary had evoked memories too vivid and real to ignore.

Once again she was in Grunwaldsee. Saturday, 13 January 1945. She had been helping Martha peel vegetables in the kitchen. It was snowing so heavily there had been no point in trying to do any outdoor work. The Russians were cleaning the stables, and both she and Martha flinched at the intermittent swish of riding crops interspersed with shouts from the guards. The new guards beat and humiliated the prisoners continually and mercilessly, but they never touched Sascha or Leon. Sascha had told her that it was an old trick; give the officers 'soft' treatment and in time the men under their command will turn on them. But in this case it had backfired. Sascha's platoon had followed him and Leon into the hell of the prison camp, entrusted them with their lives, and that trust had been rewarded with survival. The respect Sascha's men bore for him and Leon couldn't be so easily eroded.

After everyone in the house went to bed that night, she had smuggled gauze and iodine into the loft. The brandy bottle had been emptied months before but she had taken a bottle of rough, homemade vodka that one of the estate's Polish workers had given Martha in gratitude when she had taken a pan of chicken broth to his sick wife. Sascha had pulled the cork with his teeth and taken a draft, before passing it, the bandages and the bottle of iodine through the hatch. After he closed it they had curled up together, shivering under the horse blankets.

'I'm sorry.' She hadn't had to explain why. 'Are your men badly hurt?'

'Battered, bruised and bleeding, but they'll live. I wish the beasts wouldn't always pick on the youngest. The skin on their backs is in shreds.' He had clenched his fists. 'I want to kill those bastards ...' He looked at her and his anger died. '"A word of kindness is better than a fat pie" – you will give me many kind words, won't you, my love?'

'Yes. And thank you for another of your Russian proverbs. There is a lot of truth in them.' She kissed the tip of his nose, because his mouth was covered by the blankets.

'Especially in "All ages are submissive to love". I will still love you fifty years from now.'

She had clung tightly to him, too afraid to look so far into the future. 'If we're still alive, we'll be old, gnarled, bent and grey.'

'And living in peace, if only because Stalin and Hitler will have run out of soldiers to do their fighting for them.'

'"Eternal peace lasts only until the next war,"' she said, quoting another of the sayings he had taught her. 'My father fought in the last war to end all wars. Twenty years after they signed the peace treaties, Hitler started this one. How long before the next?'

He sensed her despair and tried to comfort her. 'We will survive, Charlotte.'

'How can you be so sure, Sascha?'

'Because of this little girl.' He moved his hands beneath the blanket, closed them over her stomach and smiled when he felt the baby kick.

'It's a boy.'

'A girl,' he corrected, 'who will carry our love into the new world, which will be built on the rubble of the old. Want to dream?'

'Of our house,' she agreed.

He pulled her head down on to his chest. He knew it was the position she liked best because she could hear his heart beating beneath her. 'I think we should paint all the inside walls white as well as the outside ones.'

'And the furniture?'

'We'll paint it red and green. Red in the children's rooms, and green in the living and dining rooms. And we'll fill the children's bookcase with all the fairy stories we can find – Russian, German ...'

'And you'll paint pictures on the wall of the nursery.'

'Of hobgoblins and fierce bears.' He made a ferocious face.

Forgetting caution, she had laughed. 'I won't let you, they'll frighten the children.'

'Our house will be so quiet, so peaceful and so full of love that we will have to invent danger to teach them that there are some things they should be afraid of.'

'If only that could be true.'

'You doubt our dream world?'

'Never,' she had lied.

'Good, because it's time we discussed what fruit bushes to plant in the garden. Redcurrants and blackcurrants, of course, and raspber-ries—'

'No gooseberries – they are too prickly.'

'No gooseberries ...'

The air in the tack room was freezing, the hay and horse blanket bed so cosy, she didn't leave until three o'clock, and even then Sascha had tried to hold her back. Had they both sensed they had spent their last evening together?

Morning dawned late, as cold, grey and snow-filled as the day before. The date was etched on her mind: Sunday, 14 January 1945, her last day in her childhood home. Lunch was on the kitchen table, a thin carrot and cabbage soup. Erich's face was white, pinched, his blue eyes enormous above his hollow cheeks as he looked at her over the rim of his bowl. She had been cutting bread, Martha was setting the salt and pepper on the table, and Minna was unfolding Erich's napkin for him. Then Marius had flung open the door that led in from the yard and shouted that the Wehrmacht had retreated and the Russians were in Allenstein.

He was panting, breathless. He had talked to refugees at the top of the lane who had told him that a Russian captain had toured the town in a tank equipped with loudspeakers. Speaking in German, he had ordered all the German civilians to leave their homes and run for their lives because he could not control the troops coming behind him.

Her first thoughts had been for Sascha and his men. The last thing a retreating army needed was prisoners, and she knew the new guards would have no compunction about shooting them. She hushed Marius. He had quietened immediately, looking to the lodge where the guards were resting after eating their midday dinner. The snowstorm was still raging. The prisoners were locked in their loft.

Walking past Martha and Minna, who were standing, quaking,

in front of the range, she went to the study, took her father's keys from his desk, entered the gun room and unlocked the chain that held his hunting rifles. There were sixteen of them. Some had been her father's, others her brothers' and grandfather's. Next to the gun cabinet was a cupboard that held the twins' rapiers and swords, and her father's hunting knives.

Not daring to risk Marius or Martha's life, she had carried the weapons through the study and into the tack room herself. It had taken six trips. The whole time, Martha, Minna and Marius had watched the windows but the guards never left the lodge. When all the weapons were in the tack room, she whistled to Sascha. He opened the trap-door, his eyes widening in alarm when he saw the guns and the look on her face.

'Your army is in Allenstein. It can only be a short time before they reach here.' She had pointed to the guns. 'You can have these.' Before he could offer her sympathy, she returned to the kitchen and began shouting orders: to Marius to harness the farm cart with the strongest pair of remaining horses; to Minna to pack a bag with her own, Erich's and her mother's warmest clothing; to Martha to pack her own family's valuables.

She'd run to the study, opened her father's safe, taken his keys, the deeds to the estate, lifted the land grant from the wall, and stuffed them all into a knapsack as she dashed around the room. Upstairs she tipped the contents of her jewellery chests and her mother's on top of the papers. Her brothers and father's boxes of gold studs and tiepins, Irena's jewellery ...

She was pulling the protective linen covers from her own and her mother's fur coats when she heard shots. She'd looked out of the bedroom window to see all four guards lying, broken and bloodied, face down in the snow-covered yard. Dropping the coats, she'd raced downstairs. Tearing open the door, she'd dashed outside to see the Russian prisoners crouched over the corpses. Sascha was standing behind them, rifle in hand, an expression on his face she had never seen before.

A look that transformed him from prisoner to soldier.

She had stared at him, horror-struck by the sight of death in Grunwaldsee. Sascha returned her gaze. She knew he had seen her revulsion, but he chose to ignore it. He shouldered the rifle.

'Stay with me. I'll protect you.'

Despising the soldier he had become, she'd stepped away from him and continued to stare down at the bodies. All had been shot in the back. The young guard was still holding his gun, his finger curled around the trigger even in death.

'How could you?' She had wanted to scream the question but it was barely a whisper. 'You had guns, you could have asked them to surrender.'

'They might not have dropped their weapons. I wasn't prepared to risk the lives of my men.' He moved towards her. 'What do you think war is, Charlotte?'

She didn't answer. But she continued to retreat from him while his men rifled the corpses' pockets for valuables and cigarettes.

'What do you think soldiers do?' His voice had been soft, pleading. 'Your brothers? Your husband? Me? We had to kill them, Charlotte. It was them or us. Come with me?'

She had answered him with a single word, and she had screamed it so loud that crows fluttered upwards into the air from the snow-laden branches of the skeletal trees: 'Murderer!'

Turning her back to him, she ran into the house. Minna walked towards her, leading her mother and Erich by their hands, the same panic, confusion and fear mirrored in all three faces.

The responsibilities she had shouldered on her father's death had never weighed so heavy, and she had never felt so weak, or so alone, without even the illusion of love to sustain her.

At that moment she knew with a terrible certainty that Sascha had used her to survive. And she loved him too much even to blame or despise him for it.

Chapter 15

CHARLOTTE OPENED her eyes. It was no use, she couldn't sleep. The past was so close she was back in the chaos, tragedy and terror of that final afternoon at Grunwaldsee. Her diary lay on the bed beside her. If ever there was a right time for her to relive her flight from East Prussia, it was now, after she had returned and seen her old home in its restored glory. Was it possible that she could finally lay her ghosts to rest?

JANUARY 1945

I do not know what day it is, or how much time has elapsed since I left Grunwaldsee. Days, possibly weeks ... I could even believe years. My past life seems remote, as if it was lived by someone else, in another time and another country. The present feels unreal, as though I am trapped in a nightmare.

This paper is rough and difficult to write on, but it was kind of the officer to give me the logbook. He said I could use it to write to my family. When I asked him at what address, he pretended not to hear me and walked away.

My diary is in my rucksack, although I have been too afraid to open it since Leon returned it to me in the clearing. I can feel the shape of it through the canvas. It is proof that I had a life before this.

The other girls and officers ignore me most of the time, but I know they stare at me when they think I'm not watching them. They know what happened to me and despise me for it. I don't blame them. The shame has burned into my soul but I lack the courage to kill myself.

I am only writing now so I have an excuse to sit as far from them as space allows. I know they don't want me close by.

It is so cold at the back of this open truck that the pencil has frozen to my fingers, but it is not so cold as it was that last day at Grunwaldsee.

The snow was falling — heavy, thick and silent, a horrible, dense silence that made me wonder if I had been struck deaf after hearing the shots in the yard. The bodies of the guards were soon covered. First by a thin layer that blotted out the blood, then by drifts that concealed their shapes so well the mounds could have been almost anything. But I could not forget what they were, nor forgive Sascha their murder — not then.

Martha, Minna and Marius were dashing around, collecting things and loading them into the cart. Sascha's men were packing ammunition and the remains of our food into bundles. I had my rucksack containing the family photographs, the land grant, deeds to the estate, the keys and the family jewellery. I saw that Martha had put blankets, clothes and food into the cart, and I simply couldn't think of anything else to take.

The house was crammed full, not only with our possessions but all the von Datski clutter going back centuries, but there was only one small cart, and two tired old horses. It seemed unfair to choose any one thing over the rest, so I chose nothing.

Instead I stood in the yard waiting for the others. I was aware of Sascha standing close to me, but he didn't try to make any more excuses for killing the guards and I was too numb to talk.

I looked past the lodge up the lane towards the road. The scene reminded me of a children's shadow theatre. An endless procession of black silhouettes moved across a snowy backdrop, lit by a thin, grey-white winter light, in column after column of slow-moving vehicles and people. It appeared as though not only the whole population of Allenstein but the entire country was on the move.

I remembered what Wilhelm had said about our troops killing Russian civilians and wondered if the same scenes had been played out there when our army had invaded? People abandoning their homes, farms and every-thing they had worked for to flee for their lives.

Sascha took my hand into his. I pulled it away, not wanting him to touch me.

'All the roads west will be jammed just like that one. There's more snow on the way and there'll be no food.' His voice was hoarse, but I stifled my pity. I remember wishing that the bullets that had killed the guards had also killed my love for him. Despite everything we had shared, everything we had been to one another, we were suddenly less than strangers. We were enemies.

I pointed to the mounds of snow that covered the bodies. 'You're a Russian soldier. It's your duty to kill Germans. If you shoot me now, you'll save me the effort of trying to survive and your army the bother of finding me later.'

For all the pleading in his eyes I still could not forgive him, not with the guards lying dead in the snow beneath our feet. The child growing within me chose that moment to kick. I turned away. Sascha opened his arms and hugged me. I didn't have the strength to fight him, but neither did I return his embrace.

'Come with me?' he begged.

It was then I realized that even if he and his men hadn't shot the guards, we would have had to part. He might have been able to protect me as his mistress, but not Erich, Mama and Minna. No soldier can take care of an entourage of enemy women and children. All our hopes for the future had been no more than dreams of what could never be. I wonder if he had known that all along.

We were both shivering, although I was wearing practically my whole winter wardrobe. I was so well wrapped up I could hardly move. Sascha was wearing what was left of his uniform and Paul's clothes. The cold was so intense it threatened to strip the skin from the bits that were exposed, my nose and the area around my eyes. Sascha, with bare head, face and hands, must have been really suffering.

Martha and Marius came out of the house dragging the last of the blankets and a sack of food. They had already piled the cart too high for safety. Stepping away from Sascha, I shook my head at Martha. She handed the bundles to Sascha's men, then laid her arm around Marius's shoulders and pulled him back into the shelter of the stable block.

She told me she and Marius were staying. She had prepared her argument well, insisting that she couldn't leave Grunwaldsee when her daughter was buried in the churchyard. That Brunon was bound to return soon, and what would he think when he went to the lodge and she and Marius weren't there to greet him? That the Russians held no terror for her. Sascha and his men were perfect gentlemen, every one of them, unlike the guards, who had deserved shooting. She was a Pole, born and bred, Marius was a Pole, and Brunon could speak Polish. When he returned the Russians would understand that he'd had no choice but to obey orders when he'd been conscripted into the German army.

I did all I could to persuade her. I reminded her that Brunon had asked me to take care of his family until he returned, but she remained adamant. Someone had to look after Grunwaldsee, and she and Marius were the obvious choice. Everyone knew what the Russians would do to German women and children, particularly the families of Wehrmacht officers, if they laid their hands on them. They wouldn't differentiate between good and bad Germans, but Poles would be safe.

Minna put an end to the debate by leading Mama towards the cart. Poor Mama, she started to moan and cry. Suddenly strong, she pushed Minna aside and tried to run back into the house. Sascha caught her, and I explained that we had to go to Berlin to see Papa and Mama von Letteberg. She only heard 'Papa' and I didn't disillusion her, but even then she wanted me to order the car. I explained that we had no petrol because of the war. She called for Wilhelm and Paul, saying I never knew where to get things but the boys did. In the end I promised her that we'd see them, too, but it still took Sascha and two of his men to lift her into the back of the cart.

She sat there, surrounded by blankets, sobbing into the wind, while Sascha helped Minna up next to her. Erich was clinging to my skirts. Sascha picked him up, told him to take care of his mother and put him on the front seat. He sat there, looking very small, frightened and bewildered, his white face peeping out from the layers of scarves Minna had swaddled around him.

I thought that I would never see Sascha again, but even if I'd found the words, there was no time for speeches. There was nothing I could say that hadn't already been said. Snow was still falling, thick and fast, the flakes drifting around Sascha's bare head, catching in his blond hair.

He swung me off my feet and held me close for an instant before hoisting me on to the cart, but I still refused to hug or kiss him.

Martha hissed, 'For God's sake go, while you still can.'

Sascha hit one of the horses and we began to move out of the yard. He and his men walked alongside us. It took ten minutes for us to find a gap so we could leave the lane and join the procession of refugees on the road. It was packed solid with slow-moving carts, bicycles, people on foot, and even a few cars. Women and children, wrapped against the freezing weather like water pipes lagged for winter, were trudging through the snow, pushing prams that held babies and as many of their possessions as they could cram around them.

There were young boys I recognized from the town, boys who should have been having fun sledging and skiing through the woods. Instead they were hauling sleighs weighed down with their grandparents. But for all the people, there was very little noise, only the sound of feet crunching over compacted snow and ice.

I turned my head to take a last look at Grunwaldsee — and Sascha. Leon saw me and waved. Shouldering the rifles I had given them, the men were walking back down the line against the tide of refugees, heading towards the town and the Russian army. Only Sascha remained. He stood watching us, his face blurred by falling snowflakes and my tears.

Erich tugged at my sleeve, asking if we were going to see Papa and Opa. I whispered Opa, and when I looked back, Sascha had gone.

Charlotte dropped the diary and looked around. The past was so potent in sight, sound and smell, she was startled to see the bland decor of the hotel room.

Restless, she left the bed and opened the balcony doors. The lake glistened, its surface as calm and clear as glass. The air was already uncomfortably warm; even the flowers around the balcony hung limply. There wasn't a hint of breeze. Shivering with a cold she hadn't felt in half a century, her mind remained trapped in that other time. For sixty years she had tormented herself with guilt over the way she had parted from Sascha in Grunwaldsee.

She picked up her diary and carried it on to the balcony. Ignoring the scenery, she slipped effortlessly back into the past.

I hope I never experience such cold again. The frost pierced our clothes, our bones, turning our blood to ice, making the smallest movement slow, painful torture. Mama was soon too chilled even to moan, and what little I could see of Erich and Minna's faces had turned blue.

Erich snuggled close to me on the seat, seeking warmth and reassurance I could not give him. Worried about Mama, I told Minna to heap blankets around both of them. When she finished I pulled a blanket over both their heads, and, taking another, wrapped it around Erich. I could do no more except keep the reins in my hands and the horses plodding steadily westwards.

The light was beginning to fade when an SS unit drew alongside us. A staff car overtook our cart, then trucks full of wounded barged through,

208

forcing everyone off the road into the ditches. A motorcycle stopped ahead. An officer left the sidecar. He waved his arms and shouted at me, but I was too cold and tired to listen to him.

When the horses stopped moving, I cracked the reins and looked up to see him holding their bridles. He roared, 'I requisition this cart in the name of the Reich.'

He was dressed in an SS major's uniform, but he looked too young, too short and too dark to be an officer in the Führer's new regiment. I heard him, but chose not to believe him. I thought no gentleman could turn two old ladies, a small child and a heavily pregnant woman out on the road in a snowstorm. I urged the team forward, and he pulled out his gun. I pleaded with him to let us go. Claus would have been appalled had he been with us. Firstly at the sight of his wife pleading with a junior officer, and secondly at the unkempt lout. The major's hair was long, he hadn't shaved in days, and his uniform was filthy.

He hesitated, and I offered him a ride in the cart. He replied by firing a shot in the air and hauling me down off my seat. Erich began to cry, I protested that I had a child and a sick mother, and that I was about to give birth at any moment. I told him my husband was a colonel in the Wehrmacht, my father-in-law General von Letteberg. That he could turn my belongings out of the cart to make room for himself and his troops, but I had to get my mother and child to my father-in-law's house in Berlin.

I may as well have saved my breath. Half a dozen soldiers climbed into the back of the cart. Mama and Minna were thrown to the ground. Mama landed so hard, I was sure she had broken a bone. One man, a sergeant, older than the rest with sad brown eyes, handed me Erich, still wrapped in his blanket. I barely had time to snatch my rucksack from the seat before they moved off.

I ran alongside for a while, begging for blankets for Mama. I am sure the officer and his men heard me, but they turned away. All I could do was return to Minna and Mama. Sitting in the cart in the cold had been bad enough, walking was unbearable. My winter boots were good ones, pre-war, with thick rubber soles, but they still slid on the icy road.

Minna and Mama were still sitting where they'd been thrown. I tried to tell them that the soldiers had done us a favour, that it was better to walk because the exercise would keep us warm. Taking Erich's small, woollen-gloved hand into mine and holding Mama's arm with the other, I joined the mass of refugees. We kept our heads down because the wind cut into us like knife blades. Shuffling along, I concentrated on following the heels of the woman in front; that way I didn't have to think about what I was doing, only how far it was to Berlin.

The baby chose that moment to move again, making me think of Sascha, when all I wanted was to forget him and the bodies in the snow. Then a plane flew low overhead and strafed the column.

Picking up Erich, I dragged him and Mama to the side of the road, lying on top of Erich until the bursts of gunfire moved on.

Afterwards Minna refused to get up, insisting that she couldn't move another step. Poor Minna. I was very harsh with her. I threatened her with all sorts of punishment if she didn't carry on. It wasn't her fault. Forty years as a ladies' maid in the service of the von Datski family hadn't prepared her for a trek through snow-covered countryside in the middle of freezing winter.

We had reached the forest by then. A few other women had stopped in a clearing twenty yards or so from the road. Eventually I persuaded Minna to walk as far as the small camp. Most of the women were too tired to talk, but I gathered that they had travelled much further than we had that day. They huddled together in small groups beneath the trees, sharing their blankets and eating whatever food they had brought. None of them had dared light a fire although there was plenty of wood; they were afraid of attracting the attention of another enemy plane. I left Minna to look after Mama and Erich, and returned to the side of the road, hoping to find someone I knew who would give us a ride on a cart, or at least a blanket for Mama.

On my way, I stumbled over a wounded soldier. His leg was stiff, caked with blood and frost. When I tried to help him, I realized he was dead. His eyes were blank, staring upwards at the darkening sky. When I reached out to close them, my fingers cracked a crust of ice that had already formed over his lashes.

Stepping over him, I called out to the people on the carts, begging for a ride for Mama and Erich, offering to carry their goods and walk alongside in exchange. It was useless, no one answered. Then I saw the doctor's car. I banged on the door and he stopped. He pushed back his window, lifted his hat and greeted me as though we'd just met in the café in the park in Allenstein.

His wife was sitting next to him, his three children squeezed into the back seat on top of piles of suitcases and boxes. I told him that the army had requisitioned my cart and I was looking for someone to take my mother and Erich to Berlin because they were too weak to walk.

He apologized, saying that, as I could see, he wasn't in a position to help anyone. I appealed to his wife, begging her to at least take Erich. That he was so small he would take up hardly any space. I pleaded that, as they had to travel through Berlin anyway, Erich would be no trouble. And even if my father-in-law's house was bombed, a general would be easy enough to find at the army headquarters in the Bendlerstrasse. I reminded them that if anyone could help them find safe and clean accommodation, it would be Papa von Letteberg.

The doctor's wife eventually suggested that Erich could sit on her lap. The doctor agreed. I ran back to Minna and grabbed Erich. I told him he was going in a car to see Opa and Oma. I asked him to be good, and promised I'd come for him as soon as I could. There wasn't time to say more.

He didn't cry but I wish with all my heart that I could forget the terrified expression on his face when I handed him over to people he barely knew.

There was nothing for it but to try and sleep where Mama and Minna were already lying in the snow. I took off my coat and laid it over Mama, and, with Minna on one side of her and I the other, we closed our eyes, although I spent most of the night crying over Erich.

I don't think any of us really slept, and by the time morning came, as cold and dark as the previous afternoon, all three of us were frozen to the ground. As I struggled to rise, I half-expected my legs and arms to snap and crack like icicles. Mama was in a comatose state deeper than any sleep. Minna and I picked up handfuls of snow and rubbed it over her face and hands in an effort to rouse her, but she still didn't move. Then the ground shook and we heard the tramp of marching feet.

I left Mama with Minna and went to the road with another woman. I now understand why the Wehrmacht christened the Russian army 'the steamroller'. Moving slowly up the road towards us was a tank, and behind it a solid wall of marching Russian troops.

I ran back to Minna. Mama still hadn't stirred. I picked up my knapsack and lifted Mama to her feet. She swayed there with her eyes closed. Most of the other women had already gathered their bundles and were running into the forest. I shouted at Mama to move. Minna tried to help, but Mama just *continued to stand there, rocking on her heels. The tank rumbled closer, the troops fell out, and the screaming started.*

Charlotte sat back in the chair, her mind awash with a jumble of confused images and pain – sharp, agonizing pain, – that she had never spoken of to anyone. The Russian criteria had been simple. German men and boys were robbed then killed, slowly and horribly. Women and girls were robbed, raped and, if they survived the gang rapes, killed. The fortunate were shot. Refugees who hadn't been quick enough to leave the road were knocked to the ground and run over by tanks. German soldiers in uniform were tied together, doused in petrol and set alight. No one was spared, not the old, the young, the sick nor the pregnant, and the passage of years had done nothing to lessen her sense of shame at what they had done to her.

A Russian soldier threw me to the ground. Mama's boots were on a level with my head. She was dragged away, her heels gouging twin tracks in the snow like tram lines. I can't remember if I cried out. I couldn't move because the Russian soldier was kneeling on my shoulders. Ripping the knapsack from my back, he emptied it out on the snow above my head. I could smell his sweat, and the vodka and pickled fish on his breath, as he sorted the jewellery from the papers and keys. After pocketing the valuables, he sat back on his heels and ripped open my jacket. I could hear Minna screaming. I didn't know if she was crying for what was being done to me, or herself.

I tried to fight, but another soldier came. Pushing up my skirts and petticoats, he tore off my underclothes. Others held my arms and legs. They began to laugh when the one who had lifted my skirts unbuttoned his trousers and pushed himself into me.

Once it started, it went on for ever. I closed my eyes against the men, the cold, the pain – and when it was over I tried to rise, but the grip on my arms and legs tightened, and the soldier was replaced by another and another and another, again and again and again …

The pain in my stomach became unbearable as they pressed down on me. My ears were filled with their laughter and women's screams. I felt as though I was being torn in two. I cried for myself, for Mama, for my baby, but nothing stopped them. I held my breath, wanting to die, and when that didn't work I tried to conjure an image of Sascha — his face, his gentle touch — but all I could see, all I could smell, was the stench of the men raping me.

Afterwards, when I found myself lying on the snow, too weak to cry or move, I heard a shot. Then I remembered Mama. Crawling on all fours like a dog, I followed the tracks made by her boots.

Her eyes were as cold and dead as the soldier's I had seen. But there was no wound, no mark, only blood on her naked thighs. I hope she died before they undressed her. One of the soldiers came after me. The snow was bloody around me: my legs and what remained of my stockings were soaked. I begged him not to touch me again.

Someone called my name. I looked up and Sascha was there. He ran to me and helped me to my feet. Leon followed. Stooping down, he picked up my keys, photographs, papers and diary, and stuffed them back into my knapsack before handing it to me.

The soldiers began shouting. A man who seemed to have some authority pulled Sascha away from me. Another, who spoke bad German, demanded to know what relationship existed between us. Sascha told me to tell the truth, and was kicked to the ground for speaking German.

I saw Sascha's men standing behind him surrounded by soldiers, and I feared not only for myself, but for them. I explained that they had worked as prisoners of war on the same farm as myself. That everyone had felt sorry for them, and tried to give them extra food because the rations supplied by the Reich were so poor.

The man who was acting as interpreter insisted that he hadn't seen any Russian prisoners of war who looked as healthy and well-fed as Sascha and his men, and if I didn't tell them the truth they would shoot me. His idea of truth was that Sascha and his men had been collaborators, and that they had worked willingly for the Reich.

Before I could say any more, one of the soldiers pulled out his gun. He walked over to where a group of German women were cowering half-naked on the snow. Holding his pistol close to their heads, he began to shoot them one by one, like rats in a barn. And the first one he shot was Minna.

Sascha raised his rifle and killed the man. Then he screamed, 'Run, Charlotte. Run!'

The last thing I felt was his hand on my back as he pushed me towards the forest. Clutching the knapsack, I ran clumsily, hampered by pain and the child heavy within me. As I zigzagged between the trees, Sascha's voice echoed in my ears: 'Run, Charlotte! Run!'

I didn't know whether it was real or in my head.

Bullets blasted around me, thudding into the snow. I threw myself behind a bush. Another plane flew overhead, strafing the ground. When the sound of the engine faded, I dared to look back. Soldiers as well as women lay in the snow. But Sascha's men were being rounded into a circle and stripped of their rifles.

Sascha had been pushed to his knees in the centre. An officer was standing over him, holding a revolver to his head.

Sascha looked up and, for an instant, I thought he saw me. He didn't plead for mercy for himself or his men, just shouted once more, 'Run, Charlotte!'

As I turned and ran I heard one final shot.

I haven't stopped running since.

Chapter 16

LAURA HAD to knock on the door of her grandmother's room four times before it opened.

'Why didn't you wake me, Oma? It's eleven o'clock . . .'

Laura caught Charlotte just as she fainted. She helped her to the bed and picked up the telephone.

The doctor was a small, gentle Asian, but his command of English, German and, so far as Charlotte could ascertain, Polish was excellent. He sent Laura and the hotel manager out of the room, examined Charlotte without a word, and then opened his bag and slipped his stethoscope back into it.

'You're exhausted, Madame Datski. May I ask what you have been doing to yourself?' he enquired politely.

Charlotte gave a wry smile. 'In the last week, flying from the States to London. From there I flew to Frankfurt. After taking an internal flight to Berlin, I flew to Warsaw with my granddaughter, then drove here.'

'An itinerary that would have exhausted a teenager.'

'And, very foolishly, I also made the mistake of sitting up all of last night reading.' When Charlotte saw him looking keenly at her, she added, 'I couldn't sleep.'

'What is wrong with you?' he asked quietly.

'You've just diagnosed exhaustion.'

'I am a doctor, Madame Datski,' he reminded her.

Charlotte hesitated. 'My doctor suspected pancreatic cancer. He wanted me to undergo further tests and treatment. I told him they would have to wait.'

He pursed his lips. 'I see.'

'You are not permitted to tell anyone of my condition.'

'As you must be aware, no doctor can discuss a patient's condition with anyone other than the patient, unless that patient gives their explicit consent.' He sat on the chair next to the bed. 'When do you return to the United States?'

'When I have seen all that I want to in Poland.'

'I could arrange for you to be admitted to a hospital here. You have travel insurance?'

'Yes, but my time is too precious to be wasted lying in a hospital bed. I am eighty-six years old, Doctor. I believe I am entitled to choose how to spend my days.'

He lifted his bag on to his lap and opened it again. 'As long as you realize that unless you rest there won't be too many days left to you, Madame Datski.' He rummaged in his bag and extracted a bottle of pills. 'Two of these will make you sleep for at least twelve hours. I suggest you take them and stay in bed for twenty-four, or until you feel well enough to get up again.'

Charlotte took the bottle from him. 'What will you tell my grand-daughter?'

'What would you like me to tell her?'

'The truth,' Charlotte said. 'That I am exhausted.'

He snapped his bag shut. 'As you wish. You will send for me should you have another relapse?'

'I will. Please send my granddaughter in, and,' Charlotte smiled at him, 'thank you.'

'I know the doctor said it was just exhaustion,' Laura argued, 'but I really think I should stay with you, Oma. If not in your room then next door, so you can knock on the wall if you need me.'

'How can I possibly need you or knock on the wall if I'm sleeping, Laura?' Charlotte questioned logically. 'I told you, I intend to call room service and order a sandwich. Before I eat it, I'll have a hot bath and take two of the pills the doctor left me. Then I won't wake up for hours. And, in the meantime, you have to go to Grunwaldsee to give my apologies to Marius and go riding with Brunon.'

'I couldn't possibly—'

'They would think it appalling bad manners if you didn't.'

'Not once they know that you are ill.'

'I am not ill, merely tired, as any woman my age has a right to be given the distance I've travelled in the last few days. Don't forget to give Marius my apologies. Tell him that I will accept his offer of a drive around the estate as soon as I am able. Perhaps tomorrow. I'd love to show you Grunwaldsee myself, but it is best seen from horseback, and my riding days are over. Take your digital camera and download a few snaps on to your laptop. That way I will be able to see all the old places again when we breakfast together tomorrow.'

Laura hesitated.

'I'll give you my key so you can check up on me when you come back this evening. But creep in quietly. I hate being woken.'

'You promise to eat and sleep?'

'I promise.' Charlotte smiled at her victory. 'Now go. I can't wait to see what you'll come back with.'

After Laura left, Charlotte lay back on the pillows, drained and exhausted – just as the doctor had diagnosed. She wasn't in pain, yet, for no reason that she could explain, she felt that she had very little time left.

She tipped the waiter who brought her food order, but the tray stood untouched on the table in front of the window, and, as the coffee cooled and the orange juice grew warm, she lay on her bed and once more opened her diary.

SATURDAY, 27 JANUARY 1945

My darling Sascha, knowing that you are dead hasn't stopped me from talking to you. Can you forgive me for that last afternoon, for not knowing how war changes people, or how the instinct for survival drives men to do terrible things? Even good men like you and my brothers.

Now I understand that you were right and I was wrong. The guards had sub-machine guns; you and your men only rifles. If you'd asked the guards to surrender they would have replied with a hail of bullets.

You gave your life for me, and I didn't even have time at the last to tell you how much I loved you, that I will always love you, or what a difference you made to my life. I hope you know.

As if losing you wasn't enough, Sascha, I also lost our daughter. She was

217

beautiful, tiny but perfect, and cold — as cold as the snowmen Paul and Wilhelm used to drag into our underground icehouse. She was born only a short while after I left you. All I could see, all I could think of during the birth, was you as I had last seen you, forced to your knees in the snow by the officer holding a gun to your head.

Kneeling but proud, as you refused to bow your head. I can still see the expression in your eyes, and hear the sound of the shot that followed me into the forest when I turned and fled like the coward I am. I cannot forgive myself for leaving. If I had stayed, the three of us would be together now.

I named our daughter Alexandra after you, Sascha. She was born in the forest like an animal but she never drew breath. I so wanted her to live. I tried everything I could think of. I rubbed her back, wrapped her in my scarf and held her close trying to warm her, but it was no use. I stayed hidden beneath a bush until dark, too terrified and frozen to move, and the whole time I nursed her.

She had white-blonde hair, Sascha, just like yours, only softer, and such perfect hands and feet.

While I held her I contrasted her birth with Erich's. Then, the doctor, the nurses, Mama, Mama von Letteberg and the servants had rushed around fetching boiled water, drugs, clean linen, warm baby clothes. And there I was, lying in the open, bloody, battered, bruised and used, with no one left to care whether I lived or died, least of all myself.

When darkness fell I found the courage to go and look for you. I knew you were dead, but it made no difference. I wanted us to be together. I laid Alexandra, wrapped in one of my scarves, on the ground while I scoured the blood from my legs and skirt with snow. The hooks had been torn from my fur coat, so I unwound another scarf from my neck and turned it into a belt. It was then my fingers closed around the amber necklace that you and Masha had given me in 1939.

I couldn't believe the soldiers had missed it, but knowing that I still had something you had touched gave me the strength to go on. I picked up Alexandra and started walking. I wandered for what seemed like hours, not knowing what direction the road lay in. The only light came from the snow. I tried searching for tracks, but there had been another snowfall. Then I saw a white ribbon of clear ground streaking between the trees. I couldn't even be sure it was the same road, but I reached the clearing before morning.

Someone had laid out the bodies in a neat line. I found Mama and

Minna lying next to one another, but I couldn't find you, my love. There were only women's bodies, no soldiers. I scraped away the snow with my hands and tried to dig a grave with a stick, but the ground was frozen solid, so I lay beside them and, still nursing our daughter, tried to sleep, hoping that if I did, I would never wake up.

At dawn Manfred Adolf found me.

At first I thought I had died and he had been sent to take me to wherever people go after death. But he was with a unit of German soldiers fighting alongside the Russians against the Reich for the 'Soviet National Committee for a Free Germany', or so he proudly told me. Manfred was still making political speeches but I was in no state to listen to them.

He told me that the troops at Stalingrad had not fought to the last man as Goebbels had announced. That ninety thousand of them, including him, had been marched into Soviet captivity. He had obviously used the experience to study Communism at close quarters, and he was even more committed to his Red Party than I remembered.

He gave me a blanket and some food. While we ate I told him what had happened to Irena, Wilhelm, their children and his parents. He listened grim-faced without uttering a word of sorrow or sympathy, but what could he say? There isn't a man, woman or child in Eastern Europe who hasn't suffered horribly as a result of this bloody war.

It was strange to see the earnest, idealistic boy I used to mock, along with everyone else in the orchestra, transformed into a soldier, officer and leader. Then I thought of you, Sascha, and Wilhelm and Paul, and wondered how well any of us really know the people we love.

Manfred ordered his men to prepare to move out in five minutes. They snapped to, immediately. He said the best hope I had of reaching Berlin and Erich was to join one of the retreating German platoons, and he would take me as close to one as he could.

Before I went with him and his men, I laid Alexandra on Mama's breast and kissed my mother and our daughter goodbye. I had no choice but to leave them there, lying in the open, in the hope that some kind stranger would bury them when the thaw came. There must be other good-hearted Russians besides you, my love.

Manfred risked his life to get me to this Luftwaffe unit. The commanding officer saw my dishevelled state. He made no comment, but I knew that he and everyone else knew what had happened to me. He gave me a gun (but no bullets), this logbook and the uniform of a girl who had been killed. Fortunately, it fitted, but I find it hard to ignore the bloodstains on the blouse and jacket.

I do so hope that Erich reached Mama von Letteberg safely; if he didn't, I will never forgive myself. But I also know that if I had kept him with me he would have been murdered along with all the other German women and children in the forest.

SUNDAY, 28 JANUARY 1945

We are sheltering in a bombed-out church. The roof has gone and the aisles and pews are full of rubble. We have run out of gasoline for our generator and bullets for our guns, and one of our two remaining trucks has broken down. The mechanics are trying to fix the engine. If they don't succeed some of us will have to continue our flight west on foot.

A few of the girls have lit a fire and are making acorn coffee. But I am neither hungry nor thirsty. All I can think about now is Erich.

Close by is a signpost pointing to the centre of Berlin. When our CO saw me looking at it, he ordered a roll-call and warned that anyone who tried to desert would be shot. He said no exceptions would be made, even if we had a home, friend or relative there.

I had heard about the destruction wrought by the Allied bombs, but seeing the reality brought tears to my eyes. There are still slogans painted on the walls, but of a very different kind to the Party's. Just before we stopped I saw 'One People, One State, One Rubble' chalked up on the remaining wall of a hotel, making a mockery of Goebbels' 'One People, One State, One Leader'. How Wilhelm would have laughed.

The officers have just told us that the truck cannot be repaired. Twenty of us have been ordered to gather our belongings and begin marching westwards to join any unit making a stand.

I know that none of us, officers as well as conscripts, want to fight. With death and devastation everywhere it seems such a useless exercise.

Should I risk trying to run? No. If I was seen and shot, what would happen to Erich?

THURSDAY, 29 MARCH 1945

For weeks we have continued to move westwards, but we found very few officers or soldiers who were willing to make a last stand. All the girls think the end is very close but few of us dare say it. At least it is quiet in this corner of Bavaria — for the moment.

Today I was on guard duty from four until eight in the morning. The sky in the east turned blood-red when the sun rose, reminding me of East Prussia burning in the aftermath of the Russian bombs. After duty I went to church because I was ordered to, but I couldn't pretend to pray. Not even when the officers were looking at me. If they'd asked, I think I would have told them that the Communists are right about there being no God. But perhaps I would have thought of Erich and held my tongue.

Now I know what it feels like to be a prisoner. You tried to tell me, Sascha, but I didn't really understand. It's not being locked in a cell; it's losing the freedom to go wherever you want, whenever you want.

The other girls are no longer so suspicious of me. Two of them asked me what it was like to be raped by the Russians. We have met so many other women on the road who suffered as I did, and they all had stories of friends who hadn't survived the ordeal.

The officers constantly remind us that deserters will be executed. Despite their bravado, we know that they are as terrified of defeat as we are, because the end of this war will mean the annihilation of Germany.

I was so sheltered and protected in Grunwaldsee. But now I have seen for myself the true extent of the ruin wrought by the war that we Germans allowed Hitler to start. There are terrible rumours about the British and Americans. That they eat babies, and rape and shoot women. After what happened in East Prussia I believe them, but I have told the other girls that I will kill myself rather than allow another soldier to touch me — and I mean it.

What is the point of wearing a uniform or trying to fight when every German knows the war is lost? All I want to do is look for Erich. I have written letters to Berlin, but received no answers. The only news is of terrible battles everywhere.

I have to stop writing because the corporal came to tell us that they have caught Gabrielle and Anna. They lived in a village not twenty kilometres from here and they tried to get home. Was that so criminal? I think most of us would go home, if we had homes left to go to.

TUESDAY, 10 APRIL 1945
Yesterday we were ordered to go round the local farms to look for work.

There is no more talk of stands or fighting, yet still they won't discharge us. Before we went, we had to dig Gabrielle and Anna's grave. When we finished, the officers lined us up to watch their execution. They forced both girls to kneel next to the grave before shooting them in the head and kicking their bodies into the hole. Then we were told to cover their bodies with earth. They didn't even give us a blanket to wrap the girls in. I closed their eyes: it didn't seem right to bury them while they were staring up at us.

Gabrielle was only seventeen, Anna eighteen. Shot for deserting an army that can no longer fight, only send its women soldiers to look for work on farms. To think that Hitler once said he would never allow women to fight because our place was in the home.

I felt like a beggar going from place to place pleading for work, all the while wanting to head north, but even without the risk of being killed for desertion, it would be useless to try. The refugees from there say the entire countryside is one large battlefield. A farmer's wife has given me work for the next two days. In all this mess there are potatoes to be planted and hay to be raked.

Frau Strasser doesn't know if her husband or two sons are alive. Her daughter was killed in a bombing raid on Cologne two years ago; she was eighteen. I hope that her sons and husband return, although I think even she holds out little hope of seeing her husband again. The last she heard was in December when he was defending Königsberg, and everyone knows that Königsberg was flattened by the Russians, who killed every German in the city. I think of Brunon. Was he there?

THURSDAY, 12 APRIL 1945

New refugees arrived last night. They told us there is heavy fighting in the south. Hanover has fallen and the Hartz mountains have been overrun by the Americans. It is bitterly cold.

Still they refuse to discharge us. Every day begins with a parade and a warning that deserters will be shot, not that anyone will try again after what happened to poor Gabrielle and Anna. We aren't sure who will reach us first, the Russians or the Americans. I am afraid of both. I have been hoping rather than waiting for a letter, but nothing has come.

I am so desperately worried about Erich. Some refugees say that the Russians haven't left a single building standing in the whole of Berlin, and that they burned all the survivors — soldiers, civilians, women and children

222

— while they were still alive. I hope Erich and Mama von Letteberg escaped before the worst happened and that they are safe. I know that while Papa and Mama von Letteberg still live they will take care of my son.

MONDAY, 30 APRIL 1945

All of us were sent to the Kreigs Helfer Dienst. They told us that we were urgently needed in Augsberg. We stayed in barracks last night but when we reported to the aircraft factory this morning the foreman said bitterly, 'Now, as the Tommy stands before Augsberg, you come to help?'

That was that; we had to travel back. The trains had stopped but a lorry came to pick us up. We divided what food we had left amongst ourselves; we can't even be sure of staying together. The lorry drove most of the night then stopped next to a camp. We were warned not to go near it but we could see people there. Or what were once people. They were grey, walking skeletons.

I thought of Irena, Marianna and Karoline, and threw what little food I had over the wire. The skeletons fell on it like vultures. A guard shouted at me. I shouted back that he should be ashamed to treat human beings that way. Afraid that we'd all get into trouble if the guards came after us, the girls hustled me away.

And now ... now I am truly a beggar without even a barrack roof over my head. If it wasn't for my amber necklace and the keys, papers and diary I am careful to keep hidden in my rucksack, I would begin to wonder if I had imagined Grunwaldsee and my life in East Prussia.

TUESDAY, 1 MAY 1945

All the women in my unit were finally discharged. We walked to the nearest village and I was offered a room and food in exchange for work by a farmer's wife, Frau Weser. She gave me a bedspread to make myself a civilian dress. It is not wise to wear uniform when we could be overrun at any moment, and I have no other clothes.

Everyone in the village hung white flags in their windows after our soldiers left yesterday, and there is an uncanny quiet in the street. The retreating units blew up all the bridges in the area, but at last the bombing has stopped. The first American tanks have passed through and they are not man- or baby-eaters. I am wearing my bedcover-civilian dress and they didn't give me a second glance, or, at least, no more than any other woman. The village was not touched, but no doubt the infantry soldiers will arrive soon. If they are like the Russians I will climb on to the roof of the church and throw myself off.

Frau Weser told me that I can stay with her until the trains start running and the roads open again. I am sick with worry about Erich, Papa and Mama von Letteberg, Irena and the girls – and Claus, too – but it is useless to try to get to Berlin until the fighting has stopped.

WEDNESDAY, 2 MAY 1945

It is hard to believe it is May. This time last year we were planting the fields in Grunwaldsee, but now it is cold and snowing. Everything seems to be upside-down, even the weather. The Americans came into the village yesterday afternoon and requisitioned thirty houses, but the soldiers are not so bad. They searched every building for weapons and guns, but they did not plunder, loot, rob or rape like the other foreigners who are streaming through. No one seems to know who they are or where they have come from.

I went to church on Sunday, a useless exercise, but Frau Weser expected me to go. One of her sons returned in the afternoon. I could not watch their reunion, not when I remembered Paul, Wilhelm and even Claus.

Afterwards we all went to the funeral of a communications girl who had been killed by a low-flying plane in Wegele. At least she has a grave and a place for her family to mourn her, which is more than Paul and Wilhelm. Like everyone else who does not belong in the village I live from moment to moment, trying not to think about the past or the future. It is only times like now, when everyone is sleeping, that I dare to remember.

I hated writing in the logbook; the paper was so thin and rough. Now I am in Frau Weser's house, I have dared to pull out my diary and I have fastened the pages from the logbook into it. I have changed so much since I wrote the first page. I look at it and wonder where that silly, giddy girl has gone.

Frau Weser's son insists it is true that Hitler is dead. When I think about how he executed Wilhelm and the others, and all the people who have died because of his war, like Paul, I hope that the Führer _is_ dead, and there is such a thing as hell so he can burn in it for ever.

Although I no longer believe in God and have quite given up praying, I sometimes sneak into the Catholic church when it is quiet and light a candle, just in case there is a ghostly afterlife and Papa, Mama, Wilhelm and Paul can see me. Sometimes I light an extra one in the hope that I may find Erich, Irena and the girls. But it is a hope not a prayer.

FRIDAY, 4 MAY 1945

The war is over. At nine o'clock tomorrow morning the fighting will stop in Holland, North Germany and Denmark. All weapons will be laid down. The Americans have left and de Gaulle's French troops have taken over. Frau Weser has three billeted in the farmhouse. Two are all right, the third is vile. I go everywhere with Frau Weser to make sure he doesn't get me alone.

SATURDAY, 5 MAY 1945

One of the decent French officers billeted in the farmhouse told us about a camp in Dachau for Jews and political prisoners who opposed the Reich. I had heard of Dachau even before the war. Frau Weser didn't believe his description of what went on there but I recalled the camp I had seen with the grey walking skeletons and I knew he was telling the truth.

I thought of Irena and the girls, and also Ruth and Emilia. Are they in Dachau? I cannot forget sitting uselessly in the car in Allenstein, watching while Georg herded Ruth, Emilia and all those other Jewish children on to trucks.

The officer who told us about the camp is a Jew. He offered to take Frau Weser and myself to Dachau to see the conditions there for ourselves. Frau Weser wanted to prove him wrong, so we both went. The journey did not take long, and I found myself outside the gates of the same camp I had seen when I was with my Luftwaffe unit.

How can I begin to write about the horror? Not even the little I had already seen, Wilhelm's words or Sascha's description of the prisoner of war camp had prepared me for what I saw.

The French officer showed us bloodstained torture chambers. I thought of Wilhelm and almost collapsed. I cannot imagine any man inflicting or enduring the pain of those instruments. Shocked and still shaking, I began to cry, not loud, noisy sobbing, but the quiet weeping that chokes and prevents you from talking.

He showed us shower heads that sprayed gas; baths that had been filled with boiling water; mixing machines where people had been crushed alive, and the bunker. Prisoners were locked in a two-metre wooden box for fourteen

225

days or until they died of exhaustion. I saw the crematoriums that people were pushed into, some when they were still alive.

The people were the grey walking skeletons I had thrown food to. I found it impossible to believe that anyone who had been starved to that extent could still be alive. One of them spoke to me and asked if I was the girl who tossed bread over the fence and shouted at the guard. I could not tell whether it was a man or woman, but he said his name was Samuel and that the Americans were looking after them now. There was enough food and medical supplies, but people were still dying.

I told him that I had only done what any decent person would have. He said that my shouting that the guards should be ashamed of themselves had saved his life because he realized that there were still people — and pretty young girls at that — who were prepared to treat Jews as human beings.

It was strange because, after everything that has happened, I don't feel like a young girl, let alone a pretty one.

For some the help came too late. The stench was horrendous. It hung around the skeleton figures. The American troops assured us that they will continue to look after the survivors until a better alternative can be arranged.

Neither Frau Weser nor I could speak on the journey back. The lump in my throat grew bigger and tears continued to well into my eyes. How could anyone do those dreadful things to a fellow being, even an enemy? The guards had to be animals — no, not even animals. No animal would treat one of their own kind the way those camp inmates were treated.

One American told me that the Russians have found even worse camps in Poland. Places where tens of thousands of Jews were gassed every day. Was that what Wilhelm saw in Poland and Russia? Was that the horror that lay behind his 'curtain of lies'?

Did Sascha know about them? He told me men were dying in his camp, but he talked only of starvation and dirt. Was the neglect deliberate? Was that why we were never given food for him and his men? Are the camps the truth behind the Jewish resettlement?

So many people must have known about them: the guards; the transport drivers who transferred the prisoners; bystanders like me in Allenstein who sat and watched Jews being rounded up and taken away; other soldiers who fought in the East alongside Wilhelm and Paul.

At least my brother and his colonel tried to do something to stop it. The rest of us stood by and did nothing. I had my suspicions; why didn't I ask questions? We all should have, but we remained silent, and for that I believe the entire German race will be damned by all thinking people. Wilhelm was right. What a dreadful legacy we have bequeathed to our children.

THURSDAY, 10 MAY 1945

Today we heard that Field Marshal Keitel surrendered to the Allies. It is finally over. Germany is no more, and I, along with millions of others, have lost almost everyone I love and everything I had, including my country.

So many people dead and so much gone. Tomorrow I will walk to the nearest town to find out if I can register somewhere in the hope of finding Erich, Irena, Mariana and Karoline. Surely now that it is over they can't stop me from looking for them. Someone else must have survived — they must! I am terrified of not finding my son, of discovering that every single person I knew and loved is dead.

Chapter 17

FRIDAY, 25 MAY 1945

I have just returned from the American prisoner of war camp — again. I have visited there every morning for the last two weeks, yet they still won't give me the travel warrant I need to leave Bavaria and look for Erich. I have begged and pleaded with the clerks, and told them that I sent my four-year-old son to Berlin in January.

Their reply is always the same. If I cared about my son I should have never have sent him away from me, much less to Berlin. I am too upset and angry to explain that I had no choice. That if I'd kept Erich with me, he would have been murdered by the Russians along with all the other refugee women and children.

This morning I asked if they had a list of camp survivors in the hope that I might find Irena's name on it. After what the SS said about changing the girls' names, I know it is useless to look for them. If such a list exists the Americans say they haven't a copy. Then, thinking of Papa and Mama von Letteberg and Greta, I asked if they had the names of survivors of the bombing of Berlin. Again the answer was no.

Frau Weser could see how devastated I was when I returned to the farm. She gave me a bowl of chicken broth and consoled me with the thought that tomorrow is another day. But I can't help wondering if I will ever see Erich again.

MONDAY, 28 MAY 1945

Finally I received my discharge papers from the Americans. It is official, I am no longer under suspicion as former German military personnel, and, in theory, free to go wherever I want. But, as the Americans refused to give me a warrant as well as my discharge papers, I cannot use a train.

While I was arguing with the clerks, a very thin man tapped me on the shoulder. I didn't recognize him but he recognized me. It was Samuel Goldberg, the camp inmate I had met in Dachau. He still looked ill, but better than when I had last seen him in the camp.

The American doctor at Dachau had warned him that he wasn't well enough to leave his bed, but Samuel said he couldn't wait any longer to begin the search for his family. He ran a printing shop in Hamburg before the war, and lived in the suburbs with his wife and three children. He and all his family, including his parents and brothers and sisters, were sent East in 1941. He knows that his parents and brothers are dead, but he was separated from his wife and three children in a camp in Riga in 1942 and has hopes that they may have survived.

The Americans gave him papers that entitled him to food, lodging and transport, for himself and his companions in any town or city in Germany. When I told him that I was looking for my son, parents-in-law and sister-in-law, he offered to take me with him. I couldn't believe his kindness. We are leaving early tomorrow on the first train north. Samuel intends to start looking for his wife in Hamburg. He doubts that she will have been able to make her way back so soon, but other Jews who knew them might have, and he hopes they will have news of her and his children.

And Hamburg is much nearer Berlin than Bavaria. But is Erich still there?

TUESDAY, 29 MAY 1945

I am still at Frau Weser's, wounded and angry. The horrible French soldier was very drunk when he returned to the house late last night. He and some of his comrades had spent the day looting Hitler's house at Berchtesgaden. He had a pillowcase stuffed full of women's clothes and tried to give it to me.

I knew what he wanted in return and refused, but he wouldn't leave me alone. I tried to fight him off and screamed for help, but Frau Weser and her son were in the barn looking after a sick cow and the other soldiers were out. When I smashed a vase over his head he shot me in the leg.

Frau Weser and her son came running when they heard the sound of gunfire. The bullet passed through my leg, ruining my only pair of stockings, home-knitted ones that Frau Weser had given me. My leg wouldn't stop bleeding, so Frau Weser's son went to fetch the doctor. He was out but his brother, also a doctor, had just returned from Berlin where he had been working in a military hospital. I asked him, as I ask everyone who has come from the north of Germany, if he knew Papa and Mama von Letteberg.

Miraculously, he had known and respected both of them. But he had the worst news. Papa and Mama von Letteberg are dead. They were killed when a bomb fell on their apartment block. He had heard that their grandson had been dug alive from the rubble, but he didn't know if Erich was injured or what had happened to him. I cling to the thought that at least my son was alive two months ago.

I cannot put any weight on my leg but Frau Weser's son gave me a stick to lean on. Samuel agreed to delay our departure for one day, but tomorrow we are definitely going north. I will visit the displaced persons' camps and offices in Hamburg with Samuel. If I find no trace of Erich, Irena or Greta there, I will go on to Berlin, even though it is in the hands of the Russians.

SUNDAY, 30 JUNE 1945

Yesterday, I left Hamburg. Samuel and I registered our families with the Red Cross there, and they told me that Erich had been placed in a Catholic orphanage in Celle.

I couldn't wait for a train, so, ignoring Samuel's advice, I stood at the side of the road and begged lifts from army lorries. A British corporal drove me to the door of the asylum although it was out of his way.

When I explained who I was, one of the sisters took me to Erich's bedside in the orphanage infirmary. He has diphtheria and is very ill. The sister in charge told me that he hadn't opened his eyes in two days. She could see that I wouldn't leave him, so she offered me a job as a cleaner in exchange for food and a makeshift bed on the floor of the attic dormitory where the older girls sleep.

I cannot stop thinking about Samuel and the expression on his face when I left him to climb into a lorry full of strange men. We have been as close, if not closer, than family these last few weeks.

It was heartbreaking going from displaced persons' camp to camp with him. Records of survivors are only just being made and they are not in any kind of order. I checked them as best I could for Irena and the girls, and asked every survivor we met if they had seen them but they all said the same thing. The German relatives of the conspirators were kept in separate accommodation in the prisons and camps, and no 'ordinary' prisoner or camp inmate saw them.

It was very hard to leave Samuel. We promised to keep in touch, but how will we manage it, when neither of us has a home or even an address?

Conditions in the orphanage are dreadful but the nuns work very hard to keep the place functioning. What little food there is comes from charitable donations from the British troops. Although every adult does their best to keep the place clean, it is impossible given the huge number of children here, and so many more arrive at the door every day.

Mother Superior told me that she is sure that most of the children who are brought in by Germans are their own, but she hasn't the heart to turn them away as they are all starving. Food is in such short supply that every German is hungry. At least once and sometimes twice a day, a British, French or American lorry turns up with a dozen or more small children that the troops have found in the bombed-out ruins.

The children are sleeping three and four to a bed in the dormitories, so it is little wonder that so many have caught diphtheria and measles. As if that isn't enough, one of the sisters diagnosed scarlet fever in a new arrival this morning.

If — no, <u>when</u> Erich recovers I must get him out of here. But where can we go without any money or friends to help us?

SATURDAY, 18 AUGUST 1945

At last Erich is strong enough to leave his bed for a few hours at a time. He is painfully thin and very weak, but the doctor has assured me that, given good food, rest and care, he will survive without any permanent ill effects. But where can I get good food when I haven't any money? I will take him out for a short walk this afternoon. It is warm and sunny, and perhaps the fresh air will do him some good.

SUNDAY, 19 AUGUST 1945

I am so angry I can barely hold this pencil for shaking. It was so obvious, once I was told about it. Why didn't I think to ask the Mother Superior any questions?

I simply assumed that Erich had been brought to the orphanage by strangers, but yesterday evening, when I was sitting in the orphanage kitchen, talking to the sisters about our families, I said that as soon as Erich was well enough I would begin to look for my sister and sister-in-law.

Then one of the nuns told me that I didn't have to look far for my sister if her name was Greta von Datski. That she was alive, well and working for the British as an interpreter less than twenty miles away.

The nun told me that Greta had brought Erich to the orphanage after Mama von Letteberg's maid had taken Erich to her in the last days of the war. Greta had told the Mother Superior that she couldn't look after herself, much less a child, and there was no one else left to care for Erich as the rest of the family had all been killed.

How could Greta have done it? If I had found Marianna or Karoline I would never have abandoned them in an orphanage.

Mother Superior saw how angry I was and tried to calm me. She said that life had been very hard for everyone in the weeks immediately after the war ended. She asked if Greta was my only sister and when I said yes, although I have a very good sister-in-law, she insisted that I should be grateful to Greta for taking the time and trouble to get Erich to safety, not cross with her for abandoning him.

When I reminded her about the diphtheria, she told me there was no way Greta could have foreseen that Erich would contract it. She finished by saying that life is too short to harbour bitterness or grudges and I should never forget that Greta is my sister and the only one of my immediate blood family to survive beside myself.

Although I am not sure how Greta will greet me, I have resolved to go to the address she gave the Mother Superior. Even if Greta cannot or — more likely — will not help us, it is possible that she will have some news of Irena and the girls.

This is not the first time I have written that Irena is far more my sister than Greta ever was or could be, and I have a feeling it will not be the last.

MONDAY, 27 AUGUST 1945

As I feared, Greta didn't want to know me or Erich, but she did ask a lot of questions about the family jewellery. She told me point-blank that she didn't believe my story about the Russians taking it from me, and insisted I empty my rucksack.

I refused because I was afraid that she would take the deeds, keys and copy of the land grant to Grunwaldsee. Who knows when the Russians will leave East Prussia? I hope it will be soon so we can return. When we do, the deeds and keys will belong to Irena's children, not to Greta.

I am always careful to keep the amber necklace that Masha and Sascha gave me hidden beneath my blouse, so I had no qualms about pointing out that I had lost all of my own jewellery as well as hers, Mama's and Irena's, which only made her more furious.

Greta is renting a large sunny room on the first floor of a fine house belonging to Frau Leichner, the wife of an officer who was an architect before the war. Herr Leichner disappeared at Stalingrad and Frau Leichner was very interested when I told her about Manfred. Like so many women all over Germany, she is still hoping that her husband will return. I didn't have the heart to tell her about the bodies of soldiers I had seen lying in the forest and at the sides of the roads when I fled from East Prussia.

Frau Leichner took to Erich right away, and he to her. Her own son died of whooping cough two years ago and, after hearing Greta order us out of her room, and shout that she could do nothing to help me or Erich, as she had enough problems keeping herself (I think the whole house heard Greta), she offered me a small room on the third floor in exchange for my help with the housework.

The room is very small, and only has a single bed, but there is a fireplace, and, when winter comes, I can forage in the woods for fuel. Frau Leichner offered to look after Erich for me in the afternoons so I can find work to pay for our food.

I know everyone is looking for work and there is very little about, but a room of our own means Erich and I can begin to live a sort of normal life again. Everyone was kind to us in the orphanage, but it was still an institution. I only hope I won't regret my decision to leave.

Greta was furious when Frau Leichner told her I was moving in. She accused me of having no shame, and said it was demeaning for a von Datski to scrub floors and clean up after other people. When I asked her how honest work could be demeaning she went into her own room and slammed the door.

I look on this move as a temporary measure. One day — soon, I hope — we will return to Grunwaldsee, but until that happens I will continue to look for Irena and the girls.

If she is alive she will have nothing to give me except her love, but I am certain that she will give me and Erich a better reception than the one Greta gave us.

*

I thought it would be difficult to ignore Greta as we are living in the same house, but it has been surprisingly easy. She is out at work all day, and often doesn't come in until late in the evening or early in the morning. She dresses in expensive clothes; her suits are tailored from British woollen cloth; her stockings are American nylon; her perfume, silk blouses and cosmetics French.

When Frau Leichner complained that she often wakes the household by coming in at all hours, Greta insisted she is needed to interpret at dinners and parties.

She certainly has a lot of boyfriends, and every one of them is an Allied officer, but she doesn't dare to close the door of her room when they visit her. Frau Leichner has threatened to put her out in the street if she tries, and there is such a shortage of rooms Greta knows she won't find another one as good — if she found one at all.

She works for an English major, Julian Templeton. To Greta's annoyance, he has been very kind to Erich — and me. He brings us tinned food and sweets for Erich.

He had a daughter who was the same age as Erich, but she and his wife were killed in a bombing raid on London. He offered me a job cleaning the house that his unit has requisitioned on the outskirts of the town. The money he has agreed to pay me will make a great difference. I will be able to buy good food for Erich and pay our landlady to take care of Erich when I work there in the afternoons.

I told Julian about Irena, and he promised to make enquiries about her through the Red Cross for me. I do so hope that she and the girls are alive and well. Now that Erich is safe with me, all I can think of is seeing her and Wilhem's daughters again.

'I had no idea the estate was so vast.' Laura leaned back in her saddle and looked across the lake to the woods on the other side.

Brunon offered her a roll of mints. 'Before the war it was ten times the size it is now. It bordered the town at one point. Grandfather told me that the von Datskis collected rents on forty-five farms.'

'It's more beautiful than I ever imagined. I can understand why my grandmother wanted me to see it from horseback. It would have taken us hours to walk to this point.' Laura took out her camera and snapped the vista of woods that encroached right to the water's edge. 'I also know why she wanted to come back, and why she never talked about her life here.'

'It's a pity she wasn't well enough to go for a drive with my grandfather,' Brunon said. 'He was disappointed.'

'As was my grandmother when the doctor ordered her to bed. However, if past experience is anything to go by, she will force herself to be well tomorrow. Grunwaldsee is so beautiful,' she mused. 'If it had been my home and I had lost it, I don't think I'd ever recover. It also explains where my grandmother lives now. She bought a lakefront piece of land in America and built on it, although everyone said the sensible thing to have done was buy an existing house.'

'She built a house on a lake, like Grunwaldsee?'

'Not at all like Grunwaldsee.' Laura patted her horse's neck. 'Her house is wooden, modern and very American.'

'Your grandmother is a wise woman. I doubt that Grunwaldsee could be recreated.'

Laura pulled her horse's bridle to the right, dug in her heels and followed him along the bank. 'Are we close to the summerhouse?'

'It's about a kilometre away. This lane was widened in the seventies. But the summerhouse is much older. More than two hundred years old, according to my grandfather.'

'My grandmother said it hadn't changed from the last time she had seen it, although it had obviously been recently renovated.' Shading her eyes against the glare of the sun, she looked out over the lake. 'That's a beautiful yacht.'

'Nothing with an engine has ever been allowed here, not even in Communist days. Oil pollution has killed the fish and fouled the water in half the lakes around here, but not this one.'

'And in the future?'

Brunon laughed. 'My grandfather sent the West Germans with their motor boats packing, and now that the Russian who has bought the estate is of the same mind it's probably as safe as any lake in Poland. Come on, let's see how good a rider you are when it comes to cantering through woods. I hope you know how to duck.'

Laura rode after Brunon through the trees. The warmth of the sun brought the realization that it had to be close to lunchtime. Suddenly hungry, she recalled the sandwiches and bottles of water Brunon had slung on his saddle at his grandmother's insistence.

'Is it time to eat?' she called.

'Yes, and if we walk the horses down this way, we'll come to the summerhouse. There's a bench in the garden that overlooks the lake.' He slowed his horse and, as they rode side by side, they talked of politics and everything and nothing. Laura was suddenly struck by how relaxed she felt in this young man's company. He looked about the same age as her brother Luke but was far more mature, and she wondered if it was a result of spending so much time with his elderly grandparents.

She was laughing at a comparison Brunon had made between pop music and Wagner when the lane veered sharply to the left. A car blocked her path and she found herself gazing at a tall, thin, dark-haired man with disconcertingly blue eyes. Her horse reared, she shouted at it and fought to regain control, but the stranger proved quicker than her. Dropping the fishing rod in his hands, he reached out and caught the bridle.

'Polish horses don't like to be screamed at in English.' Like Brunon, his English was American-accented.

'I don't know any Polish.' She clung on to the horse with her knees.

'As you're in the country perhaps it's time you learned,' he rebuked.

'I'll try to make a point of it,' she retorted.

'How long have you been here?' he asked, still holding on to the bridle.

'Three days.'

'In that case I'll forgive you. Aren't you going to introduce me to your friend, Brunon?'

Brunon's face had turned red, and Laura wondered if the man was a friend of the new owner. For all of Brunon's assertions that 'the owner wouldn't mind' he was clearly embarrassed at being caught riding his horses on his land. 'This is Laura von—'

'Templeton,' Laura supplied.

'Von Templeton?' The man smiled. 'Now that is an unusual name.'

'My grandmother was a "von"; my name is plain Templeton.'

'Michael Sitko.' He translated his name into name into English and offered her his hand. 'My friends call me Mischa. Are we going to be friends, Laura?'

'I doubt I'll be in Poland long enough to make friends.'

He looked at Brunon. 'You're exercising the horses?'

'And showing Laura around Grunwaldsee,' Brunon conceded.

Mischa looked at Laura. 'Apart from enjoying a ride with Brunon on a nice day, is there any particular reason why you'd want to see Grunwaldsee?'

'My grandmother grew up here.'

He grew serious. 'The lady with a "von" in her name.'

'She's a von Datski,' Brunon divulged proudly before Laura could stop him. After her grandmother's reluctance to reveal her family name to the woman in the hotel, Laura sensed that Charlotte would have preferred to keep her identity from anyone who lived near Grunwaldsee. 'She came here yesterday with Laura. My grandfather knew her at once.'

'And now you and your grandmother are staying with the Niklas family?' Mischa said.

'No, at a hotel in Allenstein; I mean, Olsztyn.'

'Which one?'

'It's on the other side of the lake.'

'I know it. The service is good and the food's not bad, either. Excuse me; I have to retrieve my fishing tackle and make a telephone call.' He opened his car and loaded his fishing rod into it.

'I'm sorry, it's my fault you dropped it,' Laura apologized.

'There's no damage done.' Mischa reached into his pocket and pulled out a cell phone.

'Are you staying tonight?' Brunon asked.

'Indefinitely,' Mischa answered. 'I'll be moving more furniture into the main house this week.'

'Then join us for supper tonight? You know my grandmother always makes enough to feed an army.'

'Thank you, I will.' Mischa sat in his car and closed the door.

'Mischa works for the new owner of Grunwaldsee?' Laura asked Brunon as they rode on.

'He *is* the new owner of Grunwaldsee.'

'*Him*! But he's so young – he looks about thirty.'

'Perhaps he is. I've never thought about his age.' Brunon stopped his horse next to a jetty and dismounted. 'You thought that an old Russian would have bought the estate? It's the young ones who have the money.'

'And run the Mafia.'

'I don't think Mischa would like being called Mafia.' He led his horse to the water's edge so it could drink.

'What does he do?'

'Something that's made him enough money to buy this place. It's not wise to ask a Russian how he makes his living, particularly if he lives well.'

'And he's moving out of the summerhouse into the main house, so he obviously intends to live there.' Laura followed suit and dismounted.

'Some people are saying that he intends to turn the main house into a hotel, but he's never discussed his plans with me or my grandfather.'

'It would be sacrilege to turn that house into a hotel.'

'Few people are rich enough to pay for the upkeep of a house the size of Grunwaldsee without an income.'

Laura recalled what her grandmother had said about the cost of renovating Bergensee. Perhaps it was just as well that the new owner didn't share her romantic notions. If Grunwaldsee were to survive into the next century with its roof and walls intact, it needed a master with his feet firmly on the ground.

FRIDAY, 26 OCTOBER 1945

The best news, Julian has found Irena. She is in a displaced person's camp near Berlin. He has promised to take Erich and me to see her on his next leave. In the meantime I have her address and I will write to her.

WEDNESDAY, 31 OCTOBER 1945

Irena arrived yesterday afternoon. Julian didn't say a word to me, but sent her travel orders, a train ticket and the telephone number of his office with a note asking her to contact him and tell his office what train she was arriving on. He met her at the station and brought her straight here.

I was cleaning the stairs when she arrived. I opened the door, but didn't recognize her. She is thin, pale and looks years older, but as soon as she sopke, Erich ran to her and hugged her.

I made us a meal of corned beef, which Julian had given me, stewed apples and boiled potatoes. After we had eaten it, we sat up half the night talking. Greta looked in briefly but she was as cold to Irena as she had been to me.

I know that Greta used Wilhelm's name to get her position as an interpreter because Julian sympathized with me about Wilhelm's death. When I asked him how he knew my brother had been hanged by the Nazis he said that Greta had told everyone how her brother had died. Anti-Nazis are given preference over Nazis as employees by the Allies. It disgusted me that Greta could bring herself to use Wilhelm's name after writing the letter of denouncement she sent to him before he was hung.

Like Erich, Irena has been seriously ill. In her case it was a bad case of typhus. She read me a part of the last letter Wilhelm wrote to her. One of the guards in Ploetzensee prison forwarded it to her in the displaced persons' camp after the war.

In it, Wilhelm begged her forgiveness, but maintained that killing Hitler and saving Germany was more important than their lives, or even the lives of their children. He finished by saying that he hoped she would understand. After she had read it to me, she told me that she didn't understand why Wilhelm had risked their lives and happiness, and never would.

She said that Wilhelm had told her about the treatment the Wehrmacht, SS and Einsatzgruppen — the killing squads — had meted out to the Jews, Russians and Poles in Eastern Europe. Even the women and children. He'd also talked to her about the camps he'd seen in Poland.

She said that all she had thought about in Ravensbruck was what Wilhelm had done, and she found it hard to accept that he had supported Colonel von Stauffenberg knowing that if the coup failed, she and the girls would be incarcerated in a similar place.

I argued that Wilhelm had been an honourable man. He knew that he was risking his own life but he couldn't possibly have foreseen what Hitler would do to his family or the families of the other conspirators. As innocents, he had every right to expect that she and the girls would be left alone, but even as I spoke I knew that Irena had stopped listening to me.

She told me that her baby, a boy, had been born in a prison cell without help from a doctor or nurse. Less than twenty-four hours later she had been taken from the prison and force-marched through a hailstorm to Ravensbruck concentration camp. She had been given only a thin sheet to wrap around the child. As a result, he had died of pneumonia two days after they arrived.

After liberation she had looked everywhere she could think of for Marianna and Karoline, but as their names had been changed she had been warned that it would be impossible to find them.

It was then she finally broke down and cried.

I had made a bed for her on the floor and joined her there. I held her tight all through the night and cried with her. Before morning I promised that I wouldn't rest until we had found the girls and they were returned to her.

Chapter 18

CHARLOTTE STARED at the bottle of pills that the doctor had left next to her bed, but made no effort to touch them. For sixty years she had been haunted by thoughts of her mother's final resting place. Time and again she had imagined the bodies of her mother, her baby and Minna shovelled hastily into a communal pit with scores of others, without dignity or ceremony. She had pictured the pit being filled in by uncaring strangers who had walked away from it without leaving a stone or memorial to mark the spot.

She had promised herself that one day she would visit and pay her respects. Why not now, when she was so close? She no longer felt as weak as she had when Laura had called the doctor, and there was no way she'd be able to sleep while she felt this restless. She swung her legs to the floor, left the bed and walked into the bathroom.

Twenty minutes later, bathed, dressed in a plain black suit, her hair caught in a lace net at the nape of her neck, Charlotte left her room. She caught sight of herself in the security monitor as she walked across the foyer, and was surprised by the old woman she had become. Reading the diary had peeled back the years, until she had even begun to think of herself as that other, younger Charlotte.

Young but shattered; tormented by grief at the loss of a lover, a longed-for baby, loving parents and brothers. She had thought she had grown accustomed to living without them and all the 'might-have-beens', but the combination of seeing Grunwaldsee and re-reading the diary entries she had made during and after the war had rekindled the pain until it had become as intense and crushing as it had been in 1945.

She had so many more things to do before she could leave – and not just Poland. She smiled wryly when she thought of David Andrews's warning that she would sleep more. Even her body appeared to recognize that time was too short and too valuable to waste in sleep.

She went into the flower shop in the hotel foyer and looked around. The holders were resplendent with long-stemmed, hot-house roses and orchids, the staples of ostentatious bouquets. She wanted something simpler.

She finally settled for three simple posies of white daisies. She paid for them, went to reception and asked the girl at the desk to order her a taxi. As they drove past the lane that led to Grunwaldsee she couldn't resist timing the journey. The miles that had taken hours to cover by horse and cart and on foot in January 1945 took only minutes by car sixty-one years later.

She searched the horizon for landmarks, but the trees and bushes had grown, changing every perspective. She couldn't even be sure the road was the same one and, just as she'd feared, no memorials had been erected to commemorate the dead she had seen lying in the snow in 1945. Sitting on the edge of her seat, she asked the driver to slow down.

'If you want the shrine, madame, it's around the next corner.' He reduced his speed and pulled up alongside a clearing that might, or might not, have been the one where she had left her mother, her daughter and Minna. Where it met the road a shrine had been erected. Built of white wood and natural stone it was no different from a hundred others she had seen between Warsaw and Olsztyn. Asking the man to wait, she picked up the flowers, left the car and walked towards it.

The sun was shining, the air warm and clear. She looked up at the sky. If this was the site of the rape and massacre, there was nothing left of that butchery to taint the atmosphere.

A garishly painted plaster Madonna gazed with downcast eyes at the offerings of flowers and candles that littered the foot of the glass case, protecting her from the elements. Charlotte hesitated, then, still clutching her flowers, entered the woods. The bushes were in full leaf, the trees taller. Had it really happened here?

'I helped build the shrine.' Marius suddenly appeared and walked towards her. 'When Laura told me you were ill, I decided to leave some flowers at the hotel desk for you. As I drove out of the lane I saw you in the taxi and followed you here.' He handed her a bunch of irises. 'These are from the bulbs your mother planted in the small garden behind the house.'

'Thank you.'

'There was so much we left unsaid yesterday.'

'It wasn't the right time.' She tried to smile. 'A homecoming, even one after all these years, should be happy.'

'And there were too many people around.' He leaned against a tree. 'I was a boy when you left and so in awe of you, and now ...'

'We're equals,' she said, when she saw him searching for the right words. 'Time and old age does that, Marius.'

'They buried some of the bodies over there.' He indicated a spot on the edge of the clearing, 'but not all of them. Russian soldiers moved into Grunwaldsee a few hours after you left. They had orders to detain every Russian soldier who'd been held prisoner by the Germans. The first ones they brought to the estate had been held in the camp outside town. They had to bring them in by cart because most were too weak to walk. They locked them in the church. The next day they brought back the Russians who'd worked for us ... My mother saw them being marched down the lane. She bribed the guards with your mother's silver candlesticks and they allowed her to talk to them. The lieutenant, Leon, told her what had happened to your mother – and you. The next morning we harnessed one of the carts and drove out here.' He hesitated. 'The captain was too grief-stricken to talk ... but he was alive.'

'Yes,' she murmured. 'Later I understood he hadn't died in that forest. But I didn't ... couldn't bear to know ...' She looked at him. 'You and Martha took a terrible risk.'

'Not really,' he said. 'The Russians were everywhere but, as my mother predicted, they didn't look twice at a middle-aged Polish woman and a young boy, and the few German soldiers left in the area were too busy trying to reach the American lines in the west to bother about civilians. We took your mother and Minna back to Grunwaldsee and interred them in the vault. My mother hoped that the family wouldn't mind the maid lying next to the mistress, but the ground was too hard to dig a grave. All the pastors and priests had fled, but we recited what we could remember of the Lutheran

243

funeral service over them. My mother only had her Catholic prayer book.'

'Thank you sounds inadequate.' Tears pricked the back of Charlotte's eyes. 'I've had nightmares about their final resting place for years. I'd imagined them tumbled into a mass grave in spring with so many others.'

'There was a baby,' he said awkwardly. 'A little girl. My mother was sure she was yours.'

Lost for words, Charlotte nodded.

'As we found her lying on your mother we put them into the same coffin. It wasn't a proper one; I made it out of wood scavenged from the stables and, unlike my father, I was never much of a carpenter. If you send the taxi away, I'll take you to them.'

Laura and Brunon had eaten the sandwiches Jadwiga had made them, remounted and ridden halfway around the lake when Mischa caught up with them. He was on a Datski grey, a stallion with a fair amount of spirit, judging by the toss of its head and the short rein Mischa was careful to keep it on. Laura was glad Brunon hadn't saddled it for her.

'Is your grandmother Greta or Charlotte von Datski?' Mischa asked in English. Like Brunon, the Russian had a direct way of talking that made no allowances for social niceties.

Laura found it disconcerting and was tempted to answer, 'And, hello again to you, Mischa,' but she was curious about his question and said, 'You've studied the family?'

'There were a few old papers in the attics.' She remembered what Marius had said the day before about every scrap of paper being burned, and decided that either the old man or Mischa was lying. Of the two she preferred to think it was Mischa.

'Really?' she said sceptically, before relenting. 'My grandmother is Charlotte von Datski.'

'The one who ran the estate during the war after her father died, and stayed right up until the invasion.'

'So I believe.' Laura looked to Brunon who nodded agreement, and once again she realized just how little she knew about her grandmother's past.

'Marius told me she was still trying to persuade his mother to leave when the Russians were practically on the doorstep.'

'She argued with her for so long, my grandfather said his mother thought she would never get away,' Brunon added.

'Marius has talked to you about her?' Laura asked Mischa, surprised to discover that he seemed to know as much about the history of Grunwaldsee as Brunon.

'It was impossible to stop him. He admired and respected your grandmother. Probably more than any woman he's met before or since, including his wife.' Mischa grinned. 'She was quite a lady when she was young.'

'She still is.' It felt odd to be sitting on a horse in the middle of the Polish countryside discussing her grandmother with a man she'd only just met.

'So, what do you think of Poland?' He reined in his horse and pushed it between hers and Brunon's.

'I haven't seen much of it, but it's not what I expected. All these woods and lakes, and this glorious weather. It's idyllic.'

'You thought a country that had been Communist for so long would be dark and cold and full of decaying tower blocks?' he teased.

'Drabber perhaps,' she agreed diplomatically.

'Ah, you were expecting to see Slavic misery, embodied in a people with long faces with a penchant for spouting tragic poetry as they stroll beneath the shadows of a chemical works.'

Brunon laughed, and the image was close enough to the truth for Laura to join him.

'Forgive me,' she apologized, 'but my grandmother told me very little about Grunwaldsee.'

Mischa breathed in deeply and looked around. 'Like Marius and Brunon who belong here, I love this place.'

'My grandfather belongs in the lodge,' Brunon interrupted in a tone that caused Laura to wonder if the Niklas family were worried that the new owner might evict them.

'And the main house. Your grandfather and great-grandparents moved in during the winter of nineteen forty-three,' Mischa revealed. 'They stayed until the Russians invaded.'

'He never told me that. How did you know?' Brunon asked suspiciously.

'Marius mentioned it when I asked him if he minded Russians buying Grunwaldsee. He said we weren't the first Russians to live here. That Soviet prisoners of war had worked on the estate during the war and the lodge was needed to house their guards.'

'Prisoner labour, here?' Laura was astonished.

'Your grandmother never told you about that, either?' Mischa was clearly taken aback.

'No. You seem to know a great deal about what went on here during the war.' Laura resented his knowledge of her family history. If anyone should be making revelations she felt it should be Charlotte, not a Russian neither she nor her grandmother knew.

'I've spent a lot of time talking to Marius. He said some grand – and on occasion wild – parties went on here when he was a child. Particularly with the twins. You did know that your grandmother had twin brothers?'

'I knew she had two brothers called Paul and Wilhelm, and that they were both killed in the war.'

'Yes,' Mischa breathed, more to himself than Laura or Brunon and as if she had not spoken, 'this place is just about perfect.'

'Then it's just as well you had the money to buy it,' Laura fished.

'I didn't.'

'You borrowed it?'

'I didn't steal it.' He winked at her. 'You Westerners need to broaden your minds. Not all Russians are Mafia, Laura von Templeton.' He dug his heels into his horse's flanks and rode back towards the summerhouse.

Marius turned the wheel of the car and drove down the lane, past Grunwaldsee, towards the small church that overlooked the lake. 'When we didn't find your body, my mother and I hoped you'd escaped. In nineteen forty-seven we heard that Greta had survived from someone who had seen her in West Germany after the war. But nothing about you, until we saw your illustrations in a book in the sixties. Mama insisted there couldn't be two Charlotte Datskis but I wasn't so sure.'

'Greta always was a survivor.' Charlotte caught a glimpse of the expression on Marius's face, and they laughed. Marius's family hadn't liked Greta either.

'Is she still alive?' Marius stopped his small car in front of Grunwaldsee church and switched off the ignition.

'Oh, yes.'

'Do you see her?'

'As little as possible.' Charlotte gathered the flowers from her lap as he walked around to open the passenger door.

'We tried to take care of the crypt in the church the way you would have if you'd been able to stay,' he consoled awkwardly.

She gripped his hand briefly and stepped outside. She hadn't known what to expect. She had caught a glimpse of the old Jewish cemetery as she had driven around the town, and seen an uneven lawn where tombstones and monuments had once stood. Buildings had been erected on the Lutheran graveyard where Irena's grandparents had been buried. But when she looked at Grunwaldsee church, like the main house and summerhouse, it stood marvellously, miraculously unchanged.

Marius stepped back respectfully as she walked inside. It was cool and dark, and smelled musty and dusty, just as she remembered. The family vault was sunk into the wall on the right in front of the altar. She kneeled before it and ran her hands over the inscriptions on the plaques.

Memorials to the first von Datski who had lived at Grunwaldsee and all his heirs, up to her great-grandparents and her grandparents. Beneath them were her father's plaque and the one she had ordered when they had received the news about Paul:

PAUL VON DATSKI
19 AUGUST 1918 – 1 JULY 1942

Her eyes filled with tears when she saw cruder carving below the fine Gothic lettering:

WILHELM VON DATSKI
19 AUGUST 1918 – 19 OCTOBER 1944

'In death they were not divided,' she murmured. 'Thank you Marius.'

A plaque with similar carving had been set alongside Wilhem's inscribed with her mother and Minna's names.

'You were allowed to erect those in the church during the Communist era?' she asked Marius.

'The large churches were closed and barricades were erected around them, but no one cared what happened in the small country churches. The stonemason didn't even charge us for adding Willhelm's name to the plaque. But then, you probably know that Wilhelm, like Claus von Stauffenberg, was regarded as an East German and Soviet hero after the war.'

She laid the flowers, one bunch below the family vault, the others below the two plaques.

'I intended one for Mama, one for my daughter, the other for Minna. I didn't expect to find a memorial to Wilhelm.'

'I know his body isn't here, but it seemed right to place his name below Paul's.'

'Very right.' She allowed Marius to help her to her feet. 'I discovered after the war that the bodies of those executed for involvement in the von Stauffenberg plot were burned and their ashes scattered to the winds.'

'I read that somewhere, too.' He led her to a pew and they sat down.

'As if the torture wasn't enough, they humiliated the conspirators at their trials. Made them wear old, civilian clothes, took away their belts, braces and shoelaces and forced them to snap to attention and salute, so their trousers fell down.'

'How do you think your brother would have felt if he'd known you'd still be tormenting yourself with thoughts of his death after all this time, Fräulein Charlotte? He was a brave young man, and so happy with his wife and family. He had purpose after he began to work for Colonel von Stauffenberg. He died doing what he knew was right. For him there was no compromise, no other way.'

'I try to remember the good times, Marius, but it's not always easy. Especially here. Seeing the house again, and these memorials, has brought everything back. I'm sorry. I didn't mean to burden you with my grief. But for these,' she looked at the plaques again, 'I thank you.'

'I know it is presumptuous of me, but I think of your brothers as my friends rather than the sons of my family's employer.'

'Had Paul lived, he would have been your brother-in-law.' She rose to her feet.

They left the cool interior of the church and walked back out into the sunlight. She paused in front of a headstone set just inside the churchyard wall, green with moss and weathered with age. 'Do you think Maria would like your irises?'

'I'm sure she would.'

She set the bunch on Maria's grave. 'She was so young.'

'You heard about my father?' He offered her his arm and she took it.

'I saw his name on a list of the soldiers who died defending Königsberg.'

'As you see, we put his name on Maria's headstone.' He shook his head sadly. 'There's so much death here. I think it's time to go to the house. You will stay for afternoon coffee?'

'I should get back to the hotel. Laura doesn't know where I am.'

She's riding with Brunon. They will have to return to the stables, and Jadwiga won't let her leave without eating or drinking something.'

She hesitated and looked back at the church, preoccupied with the one question she hadn't found the strength to ask – yet.

'Thank you, Marius, coffee would be lovely.'

Charlotte watched Marius's wife walk away from them across the lawn with an empty tray. 'I feel as though I've driven Jadwiga away.'

'More of the new owner's furniture is about to be delivered to the main house. He's left explicit instructions with the firm transporting it as to where it is to go – and I don't doubt he'll be on hand to oversee it himself – but you know women, especially Polish ones.' Marius shrugged. 'Anything domestic and they have to check and double-check for dirt beforehand, especially in the places where heavy pieces will be placed.'

'So she's not just being tactful in leaving us alone.'

'That, too.' Marius refilled their coffee cups without asking Charlotte if she wanted any more.

Charlotte sat back in the wooden chair that had replaced the antique ironwork garden furniture her family had used. 'I never thought I'd sit here again.' She glanced up at the arbour that had been planned and planted when the house had been built. The wooden stems of the wisteria and clematis that climbed the pergola were thicker than she remembered, the flowers less abundant. She wondered if the changes were the result of the plants' age or her memory playing tricks.

'I've had to cut a few pieces of wood into the framework here and there. But it is still fairly sound, considering it's probably close to three hundred years old.'

'You've done a good job, Marius,' she complimented. 'I can't see any joins.'

'Because I hid them by training the plants around them.' He offered her a small tray and a plate. 'You must eat one of Jadwiga's strawberry tarts. If you don't, she'll take it as an insult to her baking.'

'Thank you.' Charlotte dutifully laid one of the tiny cakes on the ugly brown and white earthenware plate Marius had handed her.

'Not quite Grunwaldsee porcelain,' he apologized.

'Somewhere in Russia there must be a house that holds many familiar things.'

'Given the way the troops who were stationed here behaved when it was the area headquarters, I'd say many houses. There was gambling and fighting in the courtyard every night over your family's possessions.'

Charlotte cut the tart with a fork but made no attempt to eat it. 'Things are just things, Marius. At my time of life the only possessions I value are my family, my photographs and my memories.'

'Still my mother had time to hide one or two of your family's belongings. I unearthed these for you yesterday.' He unzipped an old sports bag he had carried out of the lodge when they had decided to sit outside, and removed an ancient leather-bound Bible and three photograph albums. Charlotte recognized them as part of a handsome Victorian set her grandfather had bought on his honeymoon in London. Half of them had been empty when his only son, her father, had married. One of her earliest memories was sitting on the floor of her father's study, watching her parents cut down photographs to fit the slots in their pages.

'All the photographs are still in them,' he divulged proudly.

Charlotte took one into her hands and ran her fingers over the heavily embossed leather cover. 'Wherever did your mother hide them?' she asked huskily.

'The same place she hid the Bibles, prayer books and hymnals from the church. Wrapped in tarpaulin under the manure heap in the stables. After the Russian army left for good and the house became a riding school and hotel, we kept them under a false floor I built at the bottom of the linen cupboard in the lodge.'

'They are in beautiful condition.' She opened it. On the first page was a studio photograph of her father as a young man. She turned the page to a portrait of a young woman holding a newborn baby. The date was inscribed beneath it: 16 October 1913. 'My mother with Greta.'

'You haven't told me how your sister managed to survive the war.'

'It's typical of Greta. She left the War Office in Berlin as soon as she heard that the Russians had crossed the border into East Prussia. Hildegarde, who worked in the same building, told me years later that Greta went to their superior and asked for leave so she could go to Grunwaldsee. She used Mama and me as her excuse. She said she was worried about us, particularly in view of my advanced state of pregnancy. Her supervisor tried to persuade her not to go because of the danger and lack of transport. Greta told him that her fiancé had given her his car and she had enough petrol because he had saved his ration for months against just such an emergency. And, the biggest lie of all, when it came to her family, danger was of no consequence.'

'But she never reached Grunwaldsee,' Marius protested in bewilderment.

'Because she drove west not east. She always did have a good sense of timing, and an even better one of self-preservation. She left Berlin before the serious fighting began. And, being Greta, she enlisted the help of Helmut's father in converting all the marks in her bank account into gold. When she reached striking distance of the British and American lines, she rented a room in a house in a small town between Hanover and Braunschweig. Her landlady's husband was missing presumed dead in Russia and, having no money, she was taking in refugees.'

'At that time Hitler was conscripting everyone to make a last-ditch stand. Surely Greta didn't escape that.' Marius spooned sugar into his coffee.

'She did. She'd kept enough marks to pay her landlady two months' rent in advance, and abandoned her uniform when she left Berlin. Dressed in civilian clothes, she pretended to be a war widow who hadn't been conscripted because she'd had a child to look after, who'd unfortunately recently died. And there she sat in comparative comfort until the British took the town. They ignored women who were out of uniform.'

Marius pulled out a battered pack of cigarettes and offered it to Charlotte. She shook her head.

'Even before Germany surrendered, Greta applied for a job in a British army unit as a typist and interpreter, using Wilhelm's name as an anti-Hitlerite to get the job.'

'My mother always said that one had no shame when it came to looking after herself. Was Helmut with her?'

'No. Not even his father could save him from being posted to a fighting unit during the last days of the war.' Charlotte sipped her coffee. 'Helmut's platoon surrendered to the Americans and he was put in one of their prisoner of war camps in the Rhineland. When the Americans discharged him early in nineteen forty-seven, he looked for Greta. I was lodging in the same house as her at the time. We'd heard that Helmut had been taken prisoner, but it hadn't occurred to Greta to register her name and address, or Helmut's name, with the Red Cross, and, assuming she had, I didn't bother. By the time he found us Greta was engaged to a British major.'

'Really?' Marius asked in surprise.

'As soon as the anti-fraternization laws were lifted she went to Britain on the first German bride boat. She married in England. Her in-laws refused to receive her but that didn't bother Greta. She made sure that her husband had his own bank account and house before marrying him. They settled outside London and still live there.'

'Did she have children?'

'No. She never made any secret of the fact that she didn't want any, even when she was engaged to Helmut and they were both active members of the Nazi Party. Which I found strange, as the Party insisted

252

a woman's first duty was to produce children for the Fatherland.'

'What happened to Helmut?' Marius asked curiously. 'I remember him as weak-willed when it came to Greta but he wasn't a bad sort. He used to slip me marks and my mother tins of meat when Greta wasn't watching, and always with the whisper, "Don't tell Greta".'

Charlotte smiled. 'I remember him slipping Erich money for his piggybank, too, with the same warning. It was awful, Marius. Helmut arrived at our lodging house one evening in early February. Erich and I were sitting at a table by the window of the room that did service as kitchen, living room, bedroom and bathroom for both of us. I saw Helmut walking up and down the street checking house numbers. He was filthy, unshaven and dressed in the rags of his uniform. He saw me, waved and ran to the front door. I left the table and went down to let him in. He hugged me, all the while asking about Greta. Then he looked up and saw her standing on the stairs above us.

'He dropped me and ran to her. I can even remember his first words: "We may have lost everything, Greta darling, but we still have one another. We can build a life together."

'She stepped away from him and said, "Not with me you can't. Germany is finished and I'm getting out. I have a new fiancé, an Englishman, and a place on a boat that's leaving for England soon. He's taking me to London. He has a house there, a fine house, and his father owns a business." Greta even flashed her engagement ring, an enormous, dazzling emerald and diamond cluster. Then she said, "I'm sorry I can't give you yours back, Helmut, but I had to sell it to get food. If you'll excuse me, I'm late."'

'That's Greta,' Marius said philosophically. 'Did you really expect her to stay in a country everyone thought was finished and remain poor?'

'I expected her to be kinder to Helmut. When I asked her later about the way she'd treated him, she told me it was better to be realistic than offer a pretence of kindness.'

There was more that Charlotte couldn't begin to describe to Marius. He had lived all his life at Grunwaldsee, and she doubted he had an inkling of the type of woman Greta had become at the end of the war.

The expression on Helmut's face had told her he'd missed nothing

– Greta's fashionable suit, expensive hair-do, new shoes and nylons. There had been no need for her to explain to Helmut what had happened to her sister. More than half the German girls in the country, married and unmarried, were fraternizing with any and every one of the conquerors who had food, cigarettes or black market goods to spare. French, American, English – it made no difference. But Greta had set her sights higher than the common herd. She only socialized and, when the acquisition of essential luxuries demanded, slept with officers, and well-to-do ones at that; and, unlike most of her countrywomen, she succeeded in catching one.

'And you? We heard that the SS requisitioned the cart and that you were forced to hand Erich over to the doctor. The doctor and his wife told us about it when they returned to visit Allenstein a few years ago.'

'After the doctor took Erich, and Mama and Minna were killed, I hid in the forest. My daughter was stillborn there. And afterwards ... afterwards, Manfred Adolf found me.'

'He came here once with General Paulus. Mama was surprised to see German troops fighting for the Russians.'

'Manfred had always been a Communist. He hated Hitler even before the war. In changing sides he succeeded in fighting for what he had believed in all along. How many soldiers could say that at the end of the war? Not many Germans I know,' Charlotte said sadly. 'He became quite famous on the post-war East German political scene, but then you'd know that better than me. I wonder if he remained faithful to the Communist Party after the wall came down.'

'He died a month afterwards. Some say of a broken heart.'

'Manfred risked his life, and those of his men, by taking me within sight of a retreating Luftwaffe unit. The officer in charge conscripted me. I was forced to stay with them until I was demobbed in Bavaria in May nineteen forty-five.'

'So far from home.'

'The worst was not knowing where Erich was, or even if he had survived. I don't have to tell you about the chaos at the end of the war. It was weeks before I found him in an orphanage.'

'Didn't Greta look for him?'

'It was Greta who put him in there.' Despite what the Mother

Superior had said about Greta taking Erich to safety, Charlotte had never been able to forgive her sister for abandoning her son.

'Your father would have horsewhipped her,' Marius said in disgust.

'Probably.' Charlotte couldn't bring herself to talk about it. 'After I found Erich, and Greta – not that she was glad to see us – I discovered Irena had survived.'

'And her baby?' Marius asked.

'Died soon after he was born.'

'A boy.' Marius's face fell. 'How Wilhelm would have loved him.'

Charlotte didn't trust herself to make a comment.

'So you, Greta and Irena all ended up in the north of Germany at the end of the war.'

'Not that Greta wanted to see Irena any more than she wanted to see me and Erich, for all that she had bandied Wilhelm's name around her new friends.'

'The conspirators were brave men. If they had succeeded things would have been very different.'

'Perhaps, but Irena would disagree with you about the bravery, Marius. Ravensbruck had changed her,' Charlotte said sadly. 'She wasn't the Irena we knew. She had suffered a great deal, not only physically, but mentally from not knowing where her daughters were, or what was happening to them. She was very bitter.'

'She was entitled to be.'

'I helped her search for Marianna and Karoline. Marianna was almost too easy; we located her in an orphanage within a week of my finding Irena, but we didn't find Karoline. That was the hardest, not knowing whether she had been killed, died from disease, or been adopted. When our last attempts to track her down failed, Irena took Marianna and moved to the south of Germany. She changed her name and went to a town where no one knew her. She said she didn't want any reminders of her life with Wilhelm, including me.'

'She never wrote to you afterwards?'

'No, and I couldn't write to her because I didn't have her address. I wrote to Manfred to thank him for saving my life and asked after Irena, but if he received my letter he never replied. I would have liked to have known what happened to Marianna, but I never heard any more.'

'And your husband?'

Charlotte looked at Marius and saw that he knew at least some of the story. 'Greta wasn't the only one who married a British officer. While I was helping Irena to look for Marianna I received a parcel containing Claus's gold watch, identity card, the contents of his pockets and a note: "*Regret to inform you, Colonel Claus Graf von Letteberg was killed in the defence of Berlin, thirtieth of April nineteen forty-five.*" It had taken over a year to reach me.'

'So that is why you married an Englishman?'

'You and your mother worked for the Russians. I married an Englishman. Was there any difference, Marius?'

'I didn't mean that as a criticism, Fräulein Charlotte ...'

'There was nothing to keep me and Erich in Germany.'

'Not even the Russian captain,' he said quietly. He saw her looking at him. 'My mother and father guessed that there was something going on between you almost from the time you arranged for them to move into Grunwaldsee, Fräulein Charlotte.'

She fell silent. There was no point in denying the obvious. After the war, when Russia had become 'the Cold War enemy' and she had Erich and later Jeremy to worry about, it was different. But what did it matter to either of the boys now, what she had done when they were children? Or in Jeremy's case, before he was born. 'I never was any good at lying, or hiding my emotions, Marius.'

'They kept all the Russian POWs in the church for a week before sending them back to Russia. The Communist regarded prisoners of war as traitors who had betrayed the Motherland. Imprisoned first by one side then the other, and treated abominably by both. But the captain and the others weren't treated badly while they were here. My mother and I smuggled food to them when we could.'

'The captain saved my life, Marius. He risked his own life and the lives of all his men for me.'

'Leon told my mother that the captain had killed a man who was trying to kill you. After he told her where we could find your mother and Minna, we expected to find you, too. When we didn't, the captain begged us to look for you and, if you were alive, to hide you somewhere where he could find you if he escaped. He talked about escape right up until the time they marched all the POWs east. Of escaping, finding you and building a new life somewhere away from Russia and Germany.'

She smiled. 'It was a hopeless dream, Marius. We both knew it.'

'When my mother was forced to accept that my father would never come back to her, she used to say, "The best of life lies in our dreams and memories."'

The jacket Charlotte had draped loosely around her shoulders fell on to the lawn. Marius picked it up and replaced it, but Charlotte was so lost in the past she hardly noticed.

Chapter 19

CHARLOTTE AND Marius were still sitting beneath the shade of the pergola half an hour later when a young man walked across the lawns towards them.

'Mischa, I didn't know you were back.' Marius rose to his feet and shook his hand.

They spoke urgently for a few minutes in Polish, then Marius led him to where Charlotte was sitting, a cold cup of coffee and mangled strawberry tart still set on the table in front of her.

'Fräulein Charlotte, may I present Mischa Sitko, the present owner of Grunwaldsee. Mischa, this is—'

'Charlotte Datski.' Charlotte rose from her chair and offered the young man her hand. Like Marius, he kissed it.

'May I?' Without waiting for permission, he pulled up a third chair and sat with them. 'I saw your granddaughter riding down by the lake with Brunon.'

'The horses need exercising,' Marius murmured defensively.

Mischa laughed and slapped Marius lightly across the shoulders. 'I wasn't complaining, Marius. I am glad to see Brunon working on my account. Your granddaughter – Laura – told me you lived here, Fräulein Datski. I took the liberty of telephoning my grandfather who was going to come to Grunwaldsee at the end of the week. He has decided to come sooner so he can meet you. You do want to meet him?'

'Your grandfather intends to live here with you?' Charlotte bristled at the thought of being at the beck and call of the new owners of her family home.

'With me?' Mischa repeated. 'You misunderstand the situation. I bought and renovated Grunwaldsee with funds my grandfather allowed me to access. But then, he knew that even if I made a balls-up of rebuilding this place the investors would be able to sell it again for what he had paid out.'

'That isn't fit language to use in front of a lady, Mischa,' Marius reprimanded.

Marius's attitude took Charlotte back to the gentler days before the war had changed her life. She couldn't remember the last time a man had rebuked another for swearing in front of her. 'Why does your grandfather want to meet me?'

'Because you're a famous artist and he has some of your original works waiting to be hung on the walls of the main house.'

'Really?' Charlotte asked in surprise.

'He enjoys collecting art.'

'Should I have heard of him?'

'No. And, although he helped me to buy Grunwaldsee, we don't own it.' Mischa turned to Marius. 'We wanted to keep it as a surprise, because there will be an official announcement in the press soon. The house, the gardens and the land all belong to a charitable trust. I am to take care of the estate, with your and Brunon's help, Marius. That's if Brunon wants to live and work here.'

'What kind of charitable trust?' Charlotte asked suspiciously.

'That is for my grandfather to say. He doesn't want to give away too many of his plans, just yet. He had a hard task persuading my father to let me come here. My father wanted me to work for him after I graduated, but now he's grooming one of my younger brothers to take over his business interests when the time comes. He has enough sons to choose from. I had seven half-brothers when I last counted.'

'Large family,' Charlotte commented.

'Families. I have had five — or is it six? — stepmothers. It was useful; they were always too busy watching my father to notice what I was doing, and my father was too busy chasing women to pay any attention to me. He wanted me to become a doctor or lawyer, but by the time he found out what I was studying it was too late.'

'What did you study?' Charlotte asked.

'Nothing useful,' Mischa answered evasively. 'But does anyone learn anything worth knowing in university?'

Marius asked the question uppermost in Charlotte's mind. 'Are you going to turn Grunwaldsee into a hotel?'

'Let's just say that a house this size has to be put to some practical use. It's the only way to preserve the place. Few people these days have the money to run a mansion without using it as a base for a business. You were lucky to have been brought up here, Fräulein Datski.'

'And unlucky to have lost it, Mr Sitko,' Charlotte commented without rancour.

'Mischa,' he corrected. 'No one calls me by my surname, except my grandfather when he's angry with me, which fortunately isn't often. So what can I tell my grandfather? Will you meet him when he arrives?'

Charlotte looked across to the house and saw Laura and Brunon riding into the yard. 'Yes, I see no reason why we shouldn't stay for another few days.'

'Good. I'll telephone him to tell him the good news. Good afternoon, Fräulein Charlotte Datski.' He kissed her hand again and sped off.

'Incredible young man,' Charlotte observed to Marius.

'Direct, or, as some people are fond of saying, you know exactly where you are with him.'

Charlotte saw Laura walking towards her, and braced herself for a scolding for not spending the day in bed. 'I will see you the day after tomorrow, Marius.'

'I can fetch you in the car. But won't you come again tomorrow?'

'I have no idea what plans Laura has made with Brunon, but I think I really will follow doctor's orders and rest tomorrow.' Ignoring his proffered hand, she hugged and kissed him. 'Thank Jadwiga for the strawberry tarts and coffee, Marius.'

'Do you think modern architects deliberately design the public areas of hotels to look like the interior of cruise liners?' Laura asked Charlotte as they walked down an endless windowless corridor on their way from the dining room to their rooms.

'I believe they simply cram the maximum number of rooms into the smallest possible space.' Charlotte unlocked her door and switched on the light; Laura followed her inside. The maid had been in, and Charlotte's towels had been twisted into swan shapes on her bed, her reading glasses perched on the beak of one, a red geranium balanced on the head of the other.

'It's stuffy in here. I can understand the cleaning staff closing the French doors against burglars but not drawing the blinds. Open them and the window for me, please, darling?' Charlotte stooped down and unlocked the mini-bar.

Laura did as her grandmother asked, then stepped outside and looked out at the lake. Twilight had fallen, greying the woods that encircled the bank and casting purple shadows across the waters. A yacht dipped towards the jetty at Grunwaldsee. She wondered if Mischa sailed and, if so, if he had bought a boat and berthed it on the lake. She glanced back into the room and noticed that the bottle of pills the doctor had left for Charlotte lay untouched on the bedside cabinet.

Charlotte saw her looking at them. 'If I can't sleep tonight I will take two. I intend to take it easy tomorrow and have a lie-in.'

'Then you admit, even after everything the doctor said about you needing to rest, that you didn't take them today?'

'Guilty as charged.'

'You look . . .'

Charlotte caught sight of herself in the mirror. 'I know what I look like, darling, but, as the doctor said, I'm exhausted. Emotionally from seeing Grunwaldsee, and physically from travelling and now that enormous dinner. It's years since I've eaten two let alone three courses. But I never could resist sour herrings, and they were good, weren't they?'

'I'm not sorry I ordered them. Everyone should try everything at least once in their life,' Laura replied.

'You ate them.'

'The jury is still out on whether I liked them.'

'But the duck in black cherry sauce and the cherry blinis smothered in cream that we had for dessert were delicious, weren't they?'

'They were. I only wish you had eaten everything on your plate.' Laura had been increasingly concerned about her grandmother's lack of appetite during the few days they had spent together.

'Eat little, often and healthily, or so my doctor keeps telling me. But I might make an exception for those cherry pancakes and have them again for breakfast. I'd almost forgotten what they tasted like.'

'Did you used to eat like that every day at Grunwaldsee?' Laura pulled a chair close to the edge of the balcony and sat down.

'I don't know about that, but we certainly had cherries every day in season. And, at harvest time, our cook – Marius's grandmother, Martha – and our housekeeper would set up trestle tables in the ballroom to feed all the workers. They would cover them with food from one end to the other. But to start we always had sour herrings.' Charlotte opened a bottle of mineral water she had taken from the fridge and carried it, together with two chilled glasses and a bottle of vodka, on to the balcony table. 'Like a nightcap?'

'Russian style?' Laura smiled.

'Polish.' Charlotte set the bottles down.

'Thank you.' Laura took the glass of water Charlotte gave her and added a measure of vodka. 'So, we both met the new owner of Grunwaldsee today.' It was a subject that, conscious of the other diners around them, they'd skirted over dinner.

'He's extraordinary, isn't he?' Charlotte moved her chair so she could look at the section of lake that fronted Grunwaldsee, although she could see very little except the light on the jetty and a faint glow that might, or might not, have been a light in the summerhouse window.

'He is,' Laura agreed. 'He also said that he wasn't the first Russian to live on the estate. Russian prisoners of war worked there during the war.'

'They did.' Charlotte's heart beat erratically.

Laura sipped her drink. 'And that Paul and Wilhelm were twins . . . I would have rather heard it from you, Oma,' she reproached.

'I'm sorry. Somehow there never seemed to be a right time to talk about the past.'

'To me?'

'To you, to Claus, to young Erich and Luke. I tried to discuss it with your father and Uncle Erich before I met you in Berlin, but they didn't want to know. Both believe it has no relevance to their lives now. Perhaps they are right.' Charlotte glanced back into the room.

Her diary and the book she had brought were lying neatly stacked on her bedside cabinet. She rose from her chair, crossed the room and picked them up. 'This is my diary. I started it on my eighteenth birthday in nineteen thirty-nine and have kept it, on and off, ever since. To be truthful, more off than on. I started reading it the day before I left America for England and it was amazing how much I had forgotten. Not events, but emotions. I only have a few more pages to read, but, if you really want to know about the past, I will give it to you tomorrow.'

'To read?'

'As a gift.' She held up the diary, pristine no longer as it had been when Hildegarde and Nina had given it to her on the train out of Russia at the end of that fateful Hitler Youth tour, but battered and stained by use and the passage of years. 'When I began it, I was a very silly young girl who dreamed of a fairy tale wedding and life in a castle.'

'Bergensee?' Laura ventured.

Charlotte smiled and shook her head. 'I dreamed of a wedding, but my imagination never reached as far as marriage. And, I was so bored by politics I refused to think about, or discuss, anything serious until politics destroyed my way of life and so many people who were very dear to me.' She hesitated for a moment. 'It also holds the story of a love that changed my life.'

'To Claus's grandfather?' Laura asked.

Charlotte looked her in the eye. 'No.'

'That's what my father used to tell us. That Uncle Erich's father was the love of your life.'

'He was wrong.'

'Did you ever care for grandfather?' Laura questioned.

'Did he tell you that I didn't?' Charlotte countered. When Laura didn't answer her, she murmured, 'Yes, of course, Julian must have believed that I used him.' She carried the books out on to the balcony and sat opposite Laura again. 'After the war, Germany was in chaos. I had nothing until I started working for the British army. I didn't even have enough money to buy food for Erich. Then I met your grandfather. We had both lost people we loved. He was kind to me and I desperately needed kindness. In return I tried to be kind to him.

'I think we both mistook mutual respect and pity for love, which it most certainly was not.'

'Grandfather lost someone?' Laura asked.

'His first wife and baby daughter in the London Blitz. Has he never told you?'

'Secrets seem to run in the family.' Laura took another sip of her vodka and water. 'I must have been twelve years old before I made the connection between you and grandfather, and even then I couldn't believe that you'd once been married. Shared the same house and produced my father. Grandfather is so ...' Laura searched for words that wouldn't sound either derogatory or patronizing. 'Middle-class English,' she said finally. 'And you're so European, cosmopolitan and artistic. Why did you marry him, Oma?'

'Middle-class and English meant security for me and, more importantly, for Erich. After living through the war, I'd had enough excitement for ten lifetimes. I'd also been seriously ill and I wasn't sure that I could carry on looking after Erich. Your grandfather might not have been the best stepfather in the world, but he meant well and he wanted to give Erich every advantage of upbringing and education. It's a pity his idea of advantage included a public school education and a separation that neither Erich nor I appreciated at the time.'

'So you never loved him?' Laura asked bluntly.

'Not in the way a woman should love her husband, no,' Charlotte confessed.

'And Uncle Erich's father?'

'Claus von Letteberg was a German aristocrat, career soldier and gentleman who subscribed to the accepted philosophy of his country and the time; that a woman's place was in the home. Not that I was ever immersed in drudgery. No von Letteberg wife had to cook, clean or scrub, but she was expected to bear children and oversee the housekeeper and maids. I realized on our wedding night that I'd made a huge mistake. I'd fallen in love with love, not the man. But we were only together a few days before he had to rejoin his regiment. And during the war I hardly saw him. He took his duties as an officer seriously, although he was neither a Nazi nor an ardent supporter of Hitler. And,' she gave Laura a small smile, 'he had his mistresses.'

'You accepted that he had other women?' Laura was aghast at

the thought that any wife, let alone her beloved grandmother, could accept her husband's infidelity so calmly.

'Our private life was so bad I was glad of any diversion that took Claus away from me. And I can't blame him or his women for the failure of our marriage. He dazzled me when I was too young and naive to realize what being a wife meant. Later, I fell in love. Deeply in love. That affair gave me the happiest days of my life and left me with memories that, in my blackest moments, gave me my only reason for living. Because I thought, quite wrongly as it turned out, that if I ended my life, no one would remember my lover or mourn him. The only question – and it's one that has tormented me most of my adult life – is whether or not he really loved me.'

'What happened to him?'

Charlotte didn't answer. Instead she picked up the diary and the book beneath it. 'If I am going to finish reading my diary tonight, it's only fair that I give you something to read.'

'After we talked about *One Last Summer* the other day, I bought a copy in the hotel bookshop. And this time I promise I'll finish it.' Laura poured herself another glass of water, without the vodka.

'If you do, think of me when you read it.' Charlotte rose to her feet. 'Thank you for being here with me, darling.'

Laura sensed her grandmother wouldn't explain any more, even if she pressed her, but she remained seated.

'You want to see me swallow the pills?' Charlotte asked.

'Yes,' Laura replied frankly.

'They're quick-acting, so, if you don't mind, I'll have my bath first. But I promise that I will take them tonight if I can't sleep. And, if you use the extra key the manager gave you to check up on me, steal in quietly in the morning. I really do intend to have that lie-in.'

MONDAY, 7 MAY 1947

I can't believe that the trees I see through my window are in full leaf. The last thing I remember is pulling Erich through the snow on the little sledge Frau Leichner loaned us. Her brother, Albert, made it before the war for her son. Albert, like Peter, was killed in France in 1940.

I left my bed this morning for the first time in over three months. The doctors tell me that I have suffered a complete mental and physical breakdown. I only know that suddenly, without warning, there was no reason for me to live. The last thing I remember is Erich's face, white and fearful.

I wanted to comfort him but I couldn't stop myself from closing my eyes and shutting him out. I was thinking of Sascha and I know now – although I can't say why I know – that I will never see him again.

For the last two weeks the doctors and nurses have been injecting me with something to keep me awake. Julian visits. He brings flowers and chocolate and the drawings Erich makes for me. I feel guilty when I look at them because Erich draws himself with tears in his eyes. If only someone else had survived the war who could look after him, like Papa and Mama von Letteberg.

Julian keeps telling me that I must make an effort for Erich and his sake. I know that if I don't, the doctors will keep me in hospital indefinitely. I am very grateful for everything that Julian has done for me and Erich. He has taken care of the hospital bills, and is paying Frau Leichner to look after Erich. If it wasn't for him, Erich would be back in the orphanage because Frau Leichner could not afford to keep my son. It would never occur to Greta to look after him.

I have never felt as ill as I do now. Greta visited me yesterday with Julian. She spoke to the doctor outside my ward and I heard her say that I was never strong, even as a child. I told Julian she was lying, but I'm not sure he believes me. Greta also insists that I am too unstable to take care of Erich by myself.

Julian has offered to marry me and adopt Erich. Greta told me that I should consider myself fortunate that Julian asked, because no other man would consider a sick, penniless woman with a child a good marriage prospect. She said I would be mad to turn him down and, as we have no one else to turn to except one another and she is going to England, we should remain together.

Julian told me that I only have to say the word and he will get tickets for me and Erich on the first German bride boat, which leaves Hamburg for Tilbury next month. Greta already has her ticket. Should I leave Germany?

I can't understand why Greta wants me to live close to her when she has never loved me the way a sister should, the way Irena did before she and Wilhelm were taken away in July 1944.

I cannot bear to write some of the things Irena said to me when she left for the south of Germany with Marianna, over a year ago. They were cruel. I will never forget the expression on her face when she said she wished she'd never set eyes on Wilhelm. From that moment on, she said, I would be as dead to her and Marianna as my brother.

We were both desperately unhappy because we hadn't found Karoline. Everyone in authority told us that as her name had been changed it would be impossible to find her. Irena kept insisting that, like Marianna, Karoline had been old enough to remember her real name when they took her away. Now, I think Irena knew otherwise all along, but simply wouldn't admit it.

If only Karoline had been kept with Marianna ... But she wasn't, and, as a result, is undoubtedly lost to us for ever. And neither Irena nor I can come to terms with the deaths of our babies. While we remained together, we constantly reminded one another of our pain, incapable of comforting or helping one another, but that doesn't stop me from missing her dreadfully − my sister of the heart, who loved me once. So unlike Greta, who has always made it plain that she doesn't even like me.

I feel weak and tired. It would be so easy to allow Julian to make all my decisions for me.

Much as I dislike Greta, I think she is right. I have no choice but to ask the doctors to discharge me into Julian's care and try to make a new life for Erich and myself in England with him.

FRIDAY, 30 NOVEMBER 1948

It has been a long time since I opened this diary. I had hoped that I could build a life for Erich and myself in England with Julian but, after almost a year and a half of trying, I realize now that life without love is a life not worth living. And England is so very, very dark and dismal. Unlike East Prussia, it rains her all the time; spring, summer, autumn, winter − it makes no difference. The sky is always grey and the air wet.

Erich and I suffer from endless cold and chills; we are miserable the whole time and afraid to try and make friends or talk to anyone lest they call us terrible names like 'Jew murderers'.

The women, children and men who didn't fight in the war are the worst. I have only been shopping once since I arrived. The assistant refused to serve me. Since then, Julian has dropped off the lists of groceries we need. The delivery is always full of dented and damaged tins and rotten vegetables, but I dare not complain again. When I tried, the following week's delivery was even worse.

Erich was badly beaten when we sent him to the local school so, after only a week, Julian arranged for him to be transferred to his old boarding school. As he promised, he formally adopted Erich and changed his name to Eric Templeton, but Julian can't make Eric Templeton learn English any faster than Erich von Letteberg, or soften his accent.

Poor Erich was only seven when Julian sent him away. I dread opening the weekly letter he sends me. They never change. He writes that he hates England, hates his school and misses being with me.

I have succeeded in making Erich's life as miserable as my own, and it is no one's fault but mine. Julian tries to be kind to both of us. I think he even believes that he loves me, but all I can offer him is respect. I cannot stop thinking about you, Sascha. My first thoughts when I wake in the morning and my last at night are of you. I even dream we are together.

It is hard to block out the horrible events of the last two days that I saw you but I try to concentrate on the happy times. The winter evenings we spent together in the tack room. That summer evening we risked our lives to go swimming in the lake. We were insane but it was a madness I am grateful for now, when all I have of you are memories and the thought that even if you used me to ensure your own and your men's survival, you had to love me a little to save my life at the cost of yours.

And then, inevitably, my thoughts turn to the last word I screamed at you: 'Murderer!' That look you gave me when you shouted to me to run from that clearing.

Sascha, I cannot forgive myself for misunderstanding you. For not realizing that you had no choice but to kill the guards. I must have been mad when I gave you the guns to think that you would only use them to protect yourselves.

In the evenings when Julian is out, or if he's home, listening to the radio and completing his Times crossword, I practise my drawing. Sketching the way you taught me. The first two pictures I completed were of you and Grunwaldsee. They are not very good but I have only to look at them to hear the sound of your voice and see your lips curving into a smile as you swing down through the trap-door in the tack room.

I close my eyes and picture you in the fields, pitchfork in hand, helping with the haymaking. Do you remember how many arguments Brunon and I had with the guards before they would allow us to give you and your men pitchforks and other tools that they said you would use as weapons?

I see you and your men lining up in the yard at twilight before the guards marched you up to the stable loft and locked you in for the night. But most of all I like to remember you curled close to me in the tack room, your eyes glittering in the flickering reflection of the flame in the old oil lamp as we talked, read and dreamed of a life together, a life that could never be.

Julian knows something is wrong. He thinks I miss Grunwaldsee, which I do, but he sees only the big house, the servants, the money – all the benefits of wealth that Greta talks endlessly about. Whatever the conversation or whoever she is talking to, Greta always manages to manoeuvre the discussion on to the subject of our aristocratic heritage. I wish she wouldn't. She doesn't impress anyone with her stories about the past. In fact, she annoys people. That is, the ones who are forced to listen to her. The cook and cleaner her husband employs, and the vicar when he calls on her.

I keep telling Julian that I am not Greta, and money, beyond having enough for food and the necessities, doesn't mean anything to me, but he doesn't believe me. He constantly contrasts our modest house and standard of living with Greta and her husband's. No matter how many times I tell him that they live courtesy of inherited wealth, he feels that he should be able to provide Erich and me with a larger house and more money. Not that there is much to spend money on after so many years of war. Greta tells me that the shops are almost empty. If that is right, then, in that one respect, England is not so very different from Germany.

In some ways Julian is similar to Claus. Both wanted a wife and family, and both wanted their wives to manage their households, provide sex and bear children without interfering too much in their 'man's world'. Not that Julian's life is anything like Claus's. I am certain that Julian doesn't have a mistress, but he does enjoy the company of other men, and spends most of his evenings in his retired servicemen's and political clubs, which means that I spend most of my time alone.

No one besides Greta and her husband visits us, and, after Grunwaldsee, where farm workers, servants and tenants were in and out of the house at all hours, I find my present existence lonely. I can't help wondering if Julian's friends and their wives won't visit him at home because of his German wife.

But I have nothing to complain about. Julian never comes home drunk, or behaves badly, like some of our neighbours, who wake everyone in the street when they return singing and shouting from the pub late at night. I know, from what little he says, that he spends more time talking in his clubs than drinking. I asked him what he talks about, but all he ever says is 'men's things'. He thinks he can't talk to me – or any woman – about important things because we aren't intelligent enough to understand anything that happens outside of the house.

When I was a child I didn't mind Papa patting me on the head and saying, 'It's nothing for you to bother your pretty little head about,' because I adored Papa and never questioned anything he did. But after everything that I have been through I resent Julian treating me that way.

Before I met you, Sascha, I accepted the pet-dog life of a rich, pampered married woman that Claus offered because I thought that was what married life was like. I didn't realize, not even after seeing Wilhelm's relationship with Irena, that there could be so much more between a man and a woman.

I have made a mess of my life as well as Julian's and Erich's, and, before I married Julian, Claus's. Hundreds of girls would have regarded marriage to a von Letteberg an honour, and made a far better job of it than me. And many women would be content with Julian, and make him happier than I can. I should never have married him. I had hoped to give Erich a father, but Erich has one he does not want and I suspect, does not even respect.

On the surface I have everything a woman could want. We live in a nice, fairly modern house. Julian travels to London every day on the train to work while I do the housework with the help of a charwoman. Erich is benefiting from an expensive education, and we both live more comfortably than we would have done if we'd stayed in Germany, but I have discovered that it is not enough just to live well.

Erich is working hard to make his English as perfect as possible, but the other boys in his school still bully him because he is German by birth. They haven't attacked him as savagely as the children in the local school did, but every time we visit him, his face and arms are black and blue where he has been beaten by his house- and classmates.

Julian says they will accept him in time – how much time he never says – but that is no consolation when I know Erich cries alone in his bed at the school and I cry alone here. When I asked Julian if we could try the local school again, he reminded me of the nervous breakdown I had after we met, and said that, even now, I am not strong enough to make decisions on my son's behalf.

If only I could find the courage to ask Julian for a divorce, but I have no money other than what he gives me. Where would I go? What would I do? How could I take care of and educate Erich?

I know that Julian has talked to Greta and her husband about me. She warned me that if I don't pull myself together, Julian would have every right to put me away. Presumably in an asylum for the insane.

Perhaps things would be better if we didn't live so close to Greta. Because her husband and Julian are friends, they insist on us having dinner together at least once a week. I hate it, but Julian simply refuses to see how much Greta upsets me.

Just like Claus, Julian was very much an army man. He didn't want to resign his commission, but he maintained he had no choice, because an officer with a German wife could expect no promotion or advancement. I suspect that he blames me for the loss of his career and for having to work in that dark, dingy accountant's office. Probably rightly so.

Greta has enough money to buy all the clothes, cosmetics and perfumes she wants. She has also thrown herself into charity work in the hope of making friends, but from what she says about the women she meets at the organizations set up to help refugees and war orphans, they are more interested in gossip and showing off their clothes and jewellery than in the people they are supposed to be raising money for.

Greta wanted me to join the groups but Julian wouldn't allow it. He said I wasn't strong enough to organize coffee mornings, bring and buy sales, and bazaars, but the real reason is he wants me to have a child.

I am already pregnant. The baby will be born next May, but I haven't told Julian yet, because I am afraid he will treat Erich differently once he finds out that I am about to have his son or daughter.

Greta keeps telling me that I should make more of an effort. That marriage out of Germany was the only option open to us and I should be grateful to Julian for asking me to be his wife. She constantly reminds me that I couldn't care for my son the way I was, and without Julian, Erich would have been returned to the orphanage.

If he had, would it be so much worse than the school he is in now? At least he could have continued to speak his own language, and been brought up with children who would not have bullied him and blamed him for the war.

The worst is the knowledge that I have failed Claus and Papa and Mama von Letteberg. They would have been devastated at the thought of a Graf von Letteberg growing up in an English boarding school.

Married life with Julian is not at all like married life with Claus. He goes out every Monday, Wednesday, Friday and Saturday evenings, and, as we go to church on Sundays, that gives us very little time together. He is so tired most nights when he comes to bed that he only wants me once or twice a week, and it is soon over. For that I am grateful. It is hard to bear another's man's touch after you, Sascha.

But for the sake of the child I am carrying, and Julian and Erich, I must make more of an effort, which means no more self-pity, writing in this diary, or thinking and writing in German. Which also means saying goodbye to you on this page, Sascha.

I could no more stop breathing than thinking of you. But from this moment on I will work hard to become everything Julian wants me to be: an English wife and mother.

Chapter 20

CHARLOTTE TURNED the page of her diary. The words had conjured up all the dreary, cold, damp darkness of those first years in England, and she saw herself back again in Julian's dismal brown-brick, three-bedroomed, semi-detached house in the London suburb, its windows curtained with blackout material that shut out most of the light. They'd never saved enough coupons to replace them.

She recalled Erich's misery whenever they visited him in school, and the fracturing and eventual severing of the close relationship they had shared when they had lived at Grunwaldsee. His heartbreaking withdrawal from her when he did come home at half-term and holidays. The silent meals she had shared with Julian, no longer the dashing captain who had brought her flowers and chocolates, but a careworn man, with a perpetual frown on his face, who rushed between work and ex-servicemen's and political party meetings.

SUNDAY, 29 MAY 1955

Julian has taken Jeremy and Erich, who are home for the weekend, from school to church, and I am alone in the house. I have lost yet another child. My fourth miscarriage since Jeremy was born. The doctors have warned me that it must be my last. The lack of medical care after Alexandra's birth damaged my womb. I was lucky to have Jeremy.

Poor Julian is disappointed. He would have liked more children, especially a daughter to replace the one he lost, but he will not consider adoption.

Jeremy is sickly, always ill with coughs and colds, which I put down to this damp climate. I wish he were in better health. I worry about him. Julian adores him. But much as I love Jeremy, every time I look at him I can't help thinking of Alexandra, our daughter who never drew breath, Sascha. She would have been ten years old now, and every year I remember

273

her birthday. I cannot celebrate the day when I lost both of you, but I think of you and hope that wherever you are, you are together.

I wouldn't have believed it possible to miss anyone as much as I still miss you, Sascha. I am busy all day long, cleaning the silver and dusting the ornaments that Julian doesn't allow the daily to touch, making the stolid English meals he insists we eat, washing and starching his shirts because he doesn't trust the laundry. My mind is never on what I am doing. Instead, I spend hours imagining how our lives might have been if I had fled east with you and your men instead of west.

Would we have met a less suspicious Russian officer? Or would I have still lost Alexandra? Would you and Mama and Minna have been killed anyway?

I realize that, in spite of my determination to become a good English wife and mother, I spend far too much time living in the past, which is not fair on Erich, Jeremy and Julian. Whenever life goes badly and I am unhappy – as I am now – I turn to this diary, if not to write in it then to read it. So I have promised myself for the second and final time that this will be the last entry. When I have finished writing I will lock it away in my old suitcase in the attic and not look at it again until I am an old, old woman.

I must live in the present and think of Julian, Jeremy, and Eric, who is Erich Graf von Letteberg no longer, but Eric Templeton, a very English fifteen-year-old boy, who has ambitions to study international law at Oxford. I like to think that his father and grandparents would be proud of his accomplishments, if not his nationality.

So, Sascha, this has to be our final goodbye.

For all of her determination that would be her last entry, there were seven more.

SATURDAY, 30 JULY 1955

So much has happened and, like every other crisis in my life, I have only this diary to turn to. Erich and I are on a boat going to West Germany. I cannot bring myself to think of it as my homeland. That was and always will be East Prussia, but now that the Russians, Americans and British have divided the country between Belorussia and Poland I am resigned to never seeing Grunwaldsee again. However, the unbelievable has happened. I will see Claus.

274

Two weeks ago I received a letter in the afternoon post from the Red Cross, informing me that Standartenführer Claus Graf von Letteberg was not dead, but newly released from Soviet custody and the Siberian prison camp where he has been held since 1945. He is not the only one. Hundreds if not thousands of women all over Germany have received the same news about their husbands, sons and brothers, and I can't help wondering how many wives, like me, have remarried and made new lives for themselves and their children.

When I read the letter I broke down and cried, and that was how Julian found me when he came home that evening from work, crying in the kitchen with no dinner cooked.

He telephoned Greta, who came round at once. She urged me to contact the Red Cross so they could inform Claus that I had married again and wanted nothing more to do with him. But all I could think of were the vows I had made to Claus in Grunwaldsee church and the lectures Mama had given me on the sanctity of marriage.

I know that I never made Julian – or Claus – happy, but if Claus needs and wants me, he has prior claim and it would be my duty to go to him. So, I told Julian and Greta that I had made up my mind to go back to Germany and meet Claus and talk to him.

Poor Julian, he looked dreadfully confused. He arranged to take the following day off from work, and we drove to Erich and Jeremy's school. Fortunately, Erich's summer examinations had finished, and when we told his housemaster that we had serious family business to discuss with him, he arranged for us to see Erich in private. Erich says he can only just remember Claus, which is not surprising given how few times Claus was able to visit Grunwaldsee during the war.

I sensed that, after eight years of trying to conform and be accepted as English, it was hard for Erich to grasp that he has a German father who wishes to see him. But he agreed to meet Claus, although he has reserved the right to finish his education in England; at Oxford if he is offered a place there.

Telling Jeremy that I was leaving the country with Eric was much, much worse. Jeremy cried, he screamed and then begged me to stay with him. He even said Erich should go to Germany by himself. Jeremy has never liked Erich and Erich has never liked or accepted Jeremy.

I knew that Erich was jealous of Jeremy when he was a baby because

Jeremy stayed at home with me. By the time Jeremy joined Erich at boarding school, the seven-year gap between them was an insurmountable barrier. I had hoped that if they couldn't be friends as children, they might be as young men, but it looks now as if that will never happen.

Being a gentleman, Julian told me that he will wait for me to write to him after I have seen Claus. I promised I would do so. Then he surprised me by asking me to sign a paper giving him full custody of Jeremy should I decide to remain with Claus.

I pleaded that it was far too soon for me to make any decisions about my own future, let alone Jeremy's, but he was most insistent. I think I even half-promised him that I would return to him as soon as I had seen Claus, but all he said was if that happened, he would tear up the paper.

The only time I had ever seen Julian so adamant before was when he refused to discuss taking Erich out of boarding school. The last thing I wanted to do was quarrel with Julian or part from him on bad terms, so I signed his paper. After he had locked it into his desk drawer he asked me if I knew what I would be giving up if I decided to stay with Claus.

It was then I realized that Julian has never loved me or Erich, or even considered us as people in our own right. We are nothing more than pets to him. Pets he treats kindly enough, but only when we do what he wants us to, while conforming to his idea of what a wife and stepson should be.

I couldn't believe that he was trying to keep me with him by threatening to take away my child and I told him so. He said he couldn't believe that I was prepared to walk out on him after all he had done for Erich and me: caring for us when we had nothing; buying our food; paying my hospital bills when I had a breakdown; marrying me when most Englishmen would have walked away from a German widow.

Like the time Irena said dreadful things to me, I knew that Julian wanted to hurt me because I had caused him pain, but I couldn't listen to any more of his ranting, so I went upstairs and packed my bag.

He was very cool when he saw Erich and I on to the boat train at Victoria station.

Now I have to face Claus. What will he think of me and my marriage to an Allied soldier? Will he see it as a betrayal of him and my country? Will he hate me for allowing Erich to be educated in an English public school? How can we ever pick up the pieces of what little life we had together, even if we want to?

276

TUESDAY, 2 AUGUST 1955

Before I saw Claus, a major came to speak to me. He told me that conditions in the Russian prison camps were harsh, and tens of thousands of German soldiers died in Siberia. All things I already knew. Didn't he think I read the papers?

Some say that the suffering the Russians inflicted on our soldiers is just retribution for what the Germans did to the Jews in the concentration camps. I think it is just one more example of the sickness that stems from war.

After the major left, Claus's doctor came to see me. He warned me that Claus's health was completely broken in Russia and he will be an invalid for the rest of his life. He will never be strong enough to do any physical work again and, because of the lack of any kind of medical care, he is susceptible to infections and illness. He finished by bluntly informing me that Claus needed a nurse more than a wife.

He was right. When I went into the ward and saw Claus and his fellow patients, I felt as though I was looking at Sascha and his men back in the barn at Grunwaldsee.

Claus's eyes reminded me of those of the stags my father and brothers used to corner in the woods before they shot them. He has aged thirty years in the ten since I last saw him. His skin is yellow, like parchment, his hair white, and his hand shakes like that of an old man.

Among other things, the doctor is treating Claus for exhaustion, malnutrition and stomach ulcers. Claus's right arm was amputated in the field by a medic at the end of the war and the stump has never healed properly, so the doctor is trying skin grafts.

When the medic removed the arm, he took off Claus's jacket; all his personal possessions, including his watch, were in it. Claus thinks it must have been left behind when the Russians captured him and his men, and that is why I received the contents of his pockets together with a letter saying that he had been killed.

It doesn't take much imagination to picture just how many soldiers' bodies were left lying unattended, so it was an understandable mistake.

The first question Claus asked me was how long I intended to stay in Germany. I told him as long as he needed me and I meant it. He looked so lost and broken I felt I couldn't say anything else.

Claus did not say anything for ten minutes, and when he finally spoke his voice was hoarse. If I hadn't known him better I would have thought that he was crying. He said that I was his wife and he would always need me. Claus didn't mention my marriage to Julian – or Jeremy – although I know the Red Cross told him about both of them.

After we spent half an hour together I went to the waiting room and fetched Erich. Claus couldn't believe how tall he has grown. He was so proud of him, and I was happy when I saw that he was prepared to love Erich just as a father should. I am glad I insisted that Erich keep up with his German.

Once the initial awkwardness was over they couldn't stop talking to one another. Claus has agreed that Erich can return to England to finish his education and, if he is accepted at Oxford, study law there.

So, father and son are happy in their reunion. I have a new role as a nursemaid and I am content. Both Claus and I have received some compensation from the West German government for the loss of our pre-war bank accounts. It is not much, but, together with Claus's back pay, we hope it will be enough to buy a small apartment in West Germany, Claus favours the south of the country. As we cannot return to Allenstein it doesn't matter to me where we go.

Claus's pension won't support us, but, as he is sick, it will be up to me to go out and somehow earn money. I am looking forward to working. It will give me something to do other than housework.

Now that I have finished writing this, I will write to Julian and ask him to arrange to annul our marriage. I will also write to Jeremy and try to explain why I have to stay with Claus in Germany. He is very young, but in time I hope that he will understand that, much as I love him and need to be with him, Claus is very sick and needs me more.

WEDNESDAY, 21 SEPTEMBER 1955

I have been applying for positions as a translator. While I was waiting in a publisher's office for an interview I looked at some children's books. The illustrations were very poor so I went out and bought some art materials. Once the paintings I am doing are finished I will return to the publisher, who has agreed to look at them. The von Letteberg name is still good for something.

Claus died at two o'clock this morning. It was a release from a long and painful illness. Or rather, his body died. I think his soul died somewhere in Siberia in 1945.

The stomach cancer that killed him was slow-growing, dehumanizing and agonizing. He pleaded with his doctor more than once to give him something that would kill both the pain and him, but the end when it came was calm and mercifully peaceful.

I nursed him and I was sorry for him, but there was nothing left between us at the end except my sense of duty, Claus's gratitude for my presence – and Erich.

Claus never touched me or shared my bed after he returned. Sometimes I think he saw me as a reminder of a past he regretted so much he could never move on.

As there is nothing left to keep me here, I am making arrangements to leave Europe for America. My publishers say they will continue to commission me no matter where I live, and dear Samuel Goldberg, who persuaded so many publishers to put work my way after he saw my illustrations in an English copy of Hansel and Gretel, *has agreed to act as my European agent.*

Sascha, who would have thought those drawing lessons you gave me in the tack room all those years ago would have led to a career and the means of supporting Claus, myself and Erich, until Erich left Oxford to take up a position in a West German law firm.

I am looking forward to making a new start in a country that holds no memories. Erich is married and successful in his chosen career, but there is no love left between us. He never forgave me for allowing Julian to put him in an English boarding school, or, once Claus returned, for remarrying when there was a possibility that his father was alive. I showed him the official notification that I received of Claus's death together with his gold watch and other effects, but he still insisted that a wife 'should have remained faithful and hoped'.

I saw Jeremy last month. He was in Germany on a walking holiday with friends. He still condemns me for leaving him when he was so young. He has decided on a career in the army and has already gained a place at Sandhurst. Both fathers have every right to be proud of their sons. They are carbon copies of the officers and gentlemen Claus and Julian were. And, if there should be another war between England and Germany, I am sure that they would be only too happy to shoot one another in the name of patriotism.

Erich and Jeremy were acutely embarrassed to see my photograph in the newspapers when I joined the anti-apartheid and anti-nuclear demonstrations. They cannot understand why I have become actively involved with so many organizations that are working towards a free and peaceful society, or how I see blind compliance with authority and political apathy the route to allowing another Hitler free rein to dictate to the world and wreak tragedy and destruction all over again.

Who would have thought that Wilhelm and Paul's nephews could turn out to be such stuffed shirts?

Connecticut, America
WEDNESDAY, 28 MAY 1969

I never thought it would happen, but in this book I can be truthful. There is another man in my life, an editor. He is not like you, Sascha, but no one could ever measure up to you. Anthony is kind and thoughtful. I met him at a publishing party in New York a year ago. His wife is in a psychiatric hospital in New Hampshire, but I would not marry him even if he were free. Two failed and unhappy marriages are enough for one lifetime and, in truth, I now like living alone.

You taught me what true love is, Sascha. Even if you didn't love me and only used me to survive, you made me love you, and I now know that loving someone means wanting the best for them and forgiving them no matter what.

Anthony still loves his wife, although she doesn't know who he is any more. In the absence of anything better we have settled for friendship, companionship and, for the sake of our respective children, discretion. So this is how my life is to end. In a new country, with work and new friends to fill my days, although I will never forget or replace the people I have lost.

Connecticut,
MONDAY, 13 OCTOBER 1969

A book has been smuggled out of Russia. Written by a prisoner in a camp in Siberia, it is called **One Last Summer**. It is our story, Sascha, I am sure of it. There are too many coincidences for it to be otherwise. The author is Peter Borodin. Is it you, Sascha? Is it possible that you are still alive?

New York

Today I went to a book signing in New York. Peter Borodin has been par-doned by Gorbachev and been allowed out of Russia to give a series of lectures and talks on his life and the events that led to the writing of his great novel, One Last Summer, *which has won him such acclaim in the West.*

When I saw him, tears came to my eyes. I picked up two copies of the book, and placed them in front of him. He looked at me and I saw that he knew me. When he signed them I noticed that his eyes were as full of tears as my own. Neither of us was able to speak.

Afraid of making a fool of myself in front of so many people I walked away, resolving to go back and talk to him when the signing was over.

I waited an hour, then returned. He was still sitting at the table in the bookshop talking to people, but I was careful to stand behind a display so he could not see me.

I stayed for a while before I realized that there was nothing we could say to one another that we didn't already know. If I spoke to him I would only succeed in opening old wounds and making new ones that would pain both of us.

I watched him sign a few more books, then I walked away.

I did not look back at him again.

Charlotte finally closed her diary. On her bedside table was the copy of *One Last Summer* that she had brought from America with her. She picked it up.

'Sascha.' She whispered his name. And the tears she had held back for more than sixty years finally fell from her eyes.

Chapter 21

SHOWERED, STRETCHED out on the bed in a pair of Mickey Mouse pyjamas Ahmed had hated, which she'd packed on principle, Laura poured herself a vodka and took it and the book she'd bought in the hotel shop to the bed. She placed her drink within easy reach on the bedside cabinet and settled back on the pillows.

Considering she hadn't opened *One Last Summer* in years, she was surprised to discover that she could recall the opening paragraph almost word for word.

When sleep fades and I stir into consciousness, the first emotion I feel is fear. What am I? Where am I? With recollection comes knowledge – and wonder. There is such a miracle as life. I am part of it and I touch the woman lying beside me, intensely thankful I am not alone.

I embrace her body as I embrace her soul. But the caress brings new fears. They linger like a hidden cancer that consumes the body below the outwardly healthy skin; silent, contaminating, defiling every moment that might have brought perfect happiness.

They corrupt every loving touch and smile. Fears that go beyond the dark primeval one of death that has spawned so many religions and mercenary priests.

She and I have accepted the inevitable slow process of decay and disintegration that comes to all living things. When that happens, as it must in the course of time, we will even welcome it, if we can share the same earth. We dream of a tall and beautiful tree, its roots reaching down into both our bodies, the only regeneration and resurrection I can bring myself to believe in. And, although she has her God, the dream is now hers as much as mine.

The fears are of something far worse: of losing one another. But for now, I am grateful that we have been given another morning, another day. I try not to think beyond it.

Our bed is soft, clean and warm. The linen crisp, bleached by the sun and scented with forest air. Our cover light, stuffed with down and feathers. A clean bed is the ultimate luxury.

I kiss her lips. She returns my caress without breaking the rhythm of her sleep. Leaving the bed, I slip on my old green and white towelling robe and creep to the door. Treading softly over the gnarled floorboards, I look in on our children. The baby, lying in the cot I carved while he was still in his mother's womb; his arms raised above his head, his fists curled loosely alongside his sleep-flushed face, his white-blond hair, the same shade as my own, plastered damply around his face. Close by, his two-year-old sister, a perfect miniature of her mother, is coiled like a cat beneath the covers on her tiny bed. Only her blonde curls can be seen above her eiderdown.

My flesh and blood, so small, so vulnerable. Fear returns. How can I protect them if I am no longer with them? Then I remember, I have been given this morning. For the moment they are safe. I am able to watch over and care for my family.

I walk to the head of the narrow wooden staircase, avoiding the most rickety and warped floorboards. All the woodwork in the cottage is dry, old and creaking. I stop to gaze at my wife's paintings on the white-washed walls. Watercolours of the children and the countryside, painted with love and care. My favourite is an ink wash of a *dacha*. The building is small, little more than a summerhouse, yet it is exquisitely proportioned, Eastern European in style and architecture. I trace the lines of the single gable above the door with my finger. It is a simple rustic cottage and our home.

Laura sipped her drink, turned the page, and continued to read the author's description of his house. It was either the lakeside summerhouse at Grunwaldsee or one exactly like it. Wondering, she followed the author's progress as he walked up the lane that led to the stables of the 'big house' and harnessed a grey stallion. Was it a Datski grey? She read on.

I may not have been born to this, but the old proverb 'scratch a Russian and find a peasant' is true. It is good to ride in the fresh air early in the day, to look out over fields and see the work that has been done and note what needs doing. To smell the dew and pine needles in the forest. To run my hands through tilled earth and see the crops I planted grow and ripen for harvesting.

I linger by the lake, watching the mist rise through the trees that encircle the water. A pair of swans and a train of cygnets glide out from the bank. Boris whinnies. He knows it is time to return to the stable. But I continue to watch the rays of the rising sun play on the water, and the herons searching for fish.

Storks swoop low overhead, before landing on their nests on the roof of the big house. Boris stamps his hooves, and I finally turn back. After leaving Boris with his stable-mates I return home.

The cottage is half-hidden by the fruit bushes that hedge the garden. I hear my daughter's chatter above the sound of clattering pans in the kitchen. The doors and windows have been flung wide and I see my wife, moving around the table in her faded blue cotton frock.

The table is covered with the everyday red and green embroidered tablecloth. The bread plate is full of steaming white milk rolls that have just been lifted from the oven. The scent of coffee, cheese and spicy sausage is strong in the air, and I realize I am hungry.

My daughter runs to greet me. My wife smiles. I kiss her as I pass her on my way to my chair at the head of the table.

Breakfast is my favourite meal of the day. I eat slowly, my daughter on my lap. Her blonde curls brush against my chin as I watch my wife feed our son. He falls asleep at her breast, and as she puts him in his basket I pour us third cups of coffee. We linger at the table, talking and laughing until it is time for work ...

Laura followed the hero's progress through a day in the fields. Not the lonely day of the modern farmer, working in isolation with his tractor, but a day spent wielding hand tools and harvesting in the company of scores of farmhands, women as well as men. A day when his wife worked alongside him, and his children slept and played at the edge of the fields within their sight.

At sunset all the workers and their families headed for the ballroom of the big house and the harvest supper that had been laid out there. Afterwards, there was music, dancing and drinking, but the author and his wife returned to the cottage with their children.

I lift my sleepy daughter on to my shoulders. My wife carries the baby in his basket. When we reach the lake, the little one insists on climbing from my shoulders, taking off her shoes and stockings, and jumping in the shallows. It is her last burst of energy before sleep. We go into the house, fill the tub and bathe the children.

While my wife dresses the children for bed, I go from room to room lighting the lamps. My wife carries our son to his cot and I chase our daughter up the stairs. The last ritual of our children's day is story time. I sit at the foot of my daughter's bed and tell them the tales that my father told me; tales passed on down through generations.

We stay with the children until their eyes close. Later, I wander into the garden while my wife plays the piano. The piece she has chosen is one I introduced her to. It mirrors our peaceful life here – the lake, the countryside, the fields, the woods. The sun inches slowly downwards and disappears into the lake, drizzling a red-gold path in its wake. The last glints of gold and red fade to purple, and darkness closes in.

The music has stopped. My wife is at my side. I embrace her, and for the first time I notice the swelling in her body – our third child ...

Laura set the book aside and poured herself another drink. She walked to the window and looked out, but instead of seeing the lake as it was, splattered with modern yachts, she allowed her imagination free rein and recreated the unspoiled lake of *One Last Summer*.

The impersonal hotel room faded as the author's description of the peace and beauty of his simple and quiet life transported her into that other time. *Was* it Grunwaldsee?

She envied the author's perfect marriage and, for the first time, she realized that the problems that had plagued her own disastrous, fleeting affairs might well be her fault. Unlike the author and his wife, she had never even tried to understand any of her partners. For her, work had always come first. The men she had allowed, albeit temporarily, into her life had been diversions. Someone to spend time with, when she had nothing better to do; people to be left behind when a job took her hundreds of miles away to other countries and occasionally even other continents.

Was it impossible to build a perfect loving relationship with someone in the modern world? Could the kind of marriage of mind, body and soul depicted in *One Last Summer* exist only in the slow-moving world of rural life as it had been lived for centuries by peasants the world over?

Mechanization and speed had replaced horse-drawn ploughs and scythes, and infiltrated every aspect of people's lives. How would the author have felt if his wife had woken up alongside him that morning, and said, 'Your turn to have the kids today, sweetheart. I have to fly to Australia to make a documentary on the exploitation of crocodiles in National Parks.'

She smiled, then opened the book again.

She is everything to me, this woman I love. The air I breathe, the earth beneath my feet, food, drink – all pale into insignificance when set beside my need for her. She clings to me for a moment, we kiss silently. Everything that needs to be said between us has long been said. Arm in arm, we wander back through the garden into the house. She walks up the stairs. I blow out the lamps in the downstairs rooms, close the doors, then follow her. I step into the children's room and look at them sleeping peacefully in their beds before going into our bedroom.

The windows are open and the white cotton drapes flutter in the breeze. She sits at her dressing table. I stand behind her chair. Taking the brush from her hand, I loosen the braid in her hair and run my fingers through it before combing it out.

In bed I reacquaint myself with her body, which I know as well as my own. Our flesh fuses into one and later, much later, we lie happy and exhausted in one another's arms. I watch her face intently as she drifts into sleep. I try to fight, but it is impossible.

Holding her, terrified that she will dissolve into the shadows, my eyelids grow heavy. I cannot stop them from closing. The pain begins.

Knowing what was to come, and having read a little of what followed, Laura closed her eyes for a moment. When she opened them, she went out on to the balcony. The night was warm, the air soft. She switched on the outside light, sat at the table and continued reading.

My body is pierced by insufferable cold; it penetrates my bones, paralyses my limbs and freezes my blood. The last thing I want to do is move. But the clang of a hammer striking metal jerks me into the nightmare world. And I know that if I don't stir myself I will be killed. Nothingness is a seductive prospect but a selfish one. If I succumb to temptation, I will never be able to return to my wife and children again.

I lift my hands. The stench of them makes me retch. But a man with an empty stomach cannot vomit. My knuckles are stiff, the stink emanates from the sores that weep pus every time I raise my fingers. The stinging is worse than mosquito bites. Tears start in my eyes, burning behind my glued eyelids. I rub at the crusts that bind my lashes with my thumbs. It is hard to open them. When I succeed I stare at my hands. Despite the pain I feel as though I am looking at a part of someone else's body. Then I glance past my fingers.

The log-built shelter is rotted with damp and age, but in winter the damp turns to ice, gilding the walls with a sheet of silver that might look pretty somewhere else. The hut cannot protect us from heat in summer or cold in winter. My work party cuts logs in the forest and every day we scrounge wood for the stove, but the stove is make-shift, and without constant care it soon goes out.

The only heat we can rely on is generated by the packed layers of reeking bodies around us. The shelf I am lying on is hard, the straw that lines it scant, and what little there is moves, alive with lice and bugs that fight with those that have already laid claim to a space within my rotting clothes and body. Can they think, these lice and bugs? Are they aware that if they don't fight for an unoccupied nook or cranny in my flesh they will freeze to death?

I swing my legs down and icy air cuts through my rags like a blade. I am wrapped in all the clothes I possess: a pullover more hole than wool; a jacket; a cap; and what is left of my army uniform. I have lost count of the years that have passed since I first put the trousers on. The shredded cloth is stiff with dirt, the holes rub my skin raw, opening old sores and creating new ones, but I dare not remove a layer, not between the onset of winter and the spring thaw. It would be stolen in seconds and I would never find another to replace it.

The air is foul with something worse than the usual excrement and unwashed bodies. I hear a cry.

'Nikolai is dead.'

His team leader growls, 'Hide him.'

No one objects to keeping Nikolai's body in the hut. We are ac-customed to living with corpses. The way we look and smell, none of us is far from death and it holds no terror for us.

Those who can move the quickest, flock around Nikolai. A piece of bread, black from age and the dirt in Nikolai's pocket, disappears down someone's gullet. I see Nikolai's hat bobbing on one man's head, his coat on another's back. I don't join the scavengers. Not because I have any scruples, but because sickness has slowed me. Even if I grabbed something, in my present weakened state it would soon be taken from me.

Nikolai's body is pushed beneath a bunk and logs heaped in front of it. That way, his team leader can continue to claim his rations until the guards eventually discover what is left of his corpse. In winter, that can take a week, sometimes two.

My team Leader shouts the roll-call command. I pull the blanket from my bunk and wrap it around my shoulders. Only idiots and newcomers leave them to be stolen. The floor is compacted earth, ice-encrusted and bitterly cold to bare feet. I join the men who swarm on the heap of felt boots behind the door. Most are split and don't keep out the snow, but there is always the chance of exchanging your pair for something better. But pick carefully. The size must be the same, but the owner weaker than you. Disregard those rules and you may not live to wear them.

My fingers are too stiff to search, so I settle for the ones I wore yesterday and the day before, and I think even the week before that. They are safe because they are the thinnest and most worn in the pile. No one else wants them.

The team leader drives us out of the barracks. I notice that I am

288

leaving bloody prints. My boot soles have worn through. Too cold to shiver I join the queue at the well. The bucket has come up empty. Paul, the strongest man in our team, because he has no qualms about stealing food from the sick as well as those weaker than him, sends the bucket down again, dropping it with all the force he can muster on to the ice that caps the water. It still comes up empty. Today, like most winter days, there will be no water for washing. Making tea means finding fuel for a fire, and a can to melt snow.

The rich who possess that rare luxury are envied. I have a can but I will have to give it up soon. I am too weak to hold on to it. There are only enough in the camp for one man in ten. The possession of a can means getting one of the first portions of tea from the pot and an early helping of soup at midday.

I look around for someone stronger than me who will protect it for both of us. Someone I can trust who will give it to me straight after he has used it so I can drink my soup and tea rations before the pot is emptied.

There is never sufficient for everyone, which is why Nikolai died last night. He has been at the bottom of the pile since I've been here, and no one in his team would help him, not even by lending him a can. He was too weak to help them fulfil their work quota, and unfilled work quotas mean half-rations for the whole team.

There are men here that I have, and would, trust with my life but they, like me, have been sentenced to hard labour and are in the same weakened state. Perhaps I should simply lie in the snow and wait for death. If I could be sure of closing my eyes and waking in that other real and perfect world with my wife, I would do so. But it doesn't happen when I try to sleep in the day. It never works unless I am in my bunk.

A cart drives in through the gates; our team leader joins the other leaders who crowd around it. He returns with a sack of bread. He hands it out. In winter it arrives frozen, too hard to eat. No one can swallow it until it is soaked in warm water, and we will not be able to build fires to melt snow until we reach our workplace in the forest.

The guards arrive to march us out; their dogs growl at us as they approach. I hear Nikolai's team leader tell them that Nikolai is going to report sick. They shrug in indifference, and we head off to the workplace.

We pass a mound of corpses stacked one on top of the other in neat layers, like logs, next to the entrance gate. The feet of those on the bottom layer point towards the road into the camp. The feet on the layer above rest on their heads. I wonder if it is easier to place them that way. Does it reduce the risk of the pile toppling over? All are frozen solid, their faces bleached white and, like their hair, coated with frost. No cart has been to pick them up for months, but there is no point because graves cannot be dug while the ground remains frozen. They will be buried in the spring and by then there will be many more.

We reach the work place. I see the trees waiting to be cut down. The team leader hands me a saw. My head is full of fog and mist and cold. I cannot think clearly. All I know is that, somehow, I must survive until the night, when I will take in that other world . . .

Laura snapped the book shut. Just as before, the contrast between the slow-moving, sun-drenched, perfect dream life and the nightmare winter world of the Siberian gulag was too harrowing for her to contemplate. Who was this man?

Had he been one of the Russian prisoners who had worked at Grunwaldsee during the war?

Then she recalled her grandmother's words: '*Think of me when you read it.*'

Was Oma the wife in the author's dream world?

Chapter 22

CHARLOTTE WAS still asleep when the telephone rang. She checked the clock when she picked up the receiver. Seven o'clock. Her first thoughts were of Claus, Carolyn and the baby, but her sister's heavily accented English grated down the line.

'Is that you, Charlotte?'

'Greta?' Charlotte struggled to sit up. 'What's wrong?'

'Why should something be wrong?'

'It's seven in the morning.'

'It's eight here. But I've been up since six. I've had to be an early riser with a house to run and a husband to look after. But, since you ask, I'm not so well. My stomach is playing up and my arthritis is extremely painful. It's this damp weather. I suppose the sun is shining over there. East Prussia was always so much warmer and drier than England.'

'The weather is fine, Greta. Thank you for asking.' Greta had never telephoned her without wanting something, and Charlotte wished that her sister would get to the point of the call.

'Charlotte, this telephone call is too expensive to waste on your sarcasm. Jeremy and Marilyn told me where you were staying. Have you been to Grunwaldsee yet?' A hard note crept into Greta's voice.

'Yes.' Charlotte answered shortly. 'The house is exactly as it was. The new owner has renovated it beautifully.'

'My God. You've actually spoken to the man!' Greta's voice rose in indignation.

'His grandson but I've arranged to meet him.'

'How *could* you . . .'

Charlotte interrupted Greta mid flow. 'Marius is still here and living in the lodge.'

'Then he must have saved some of our things,' Greta said eagerly. 'The jewellery, the silver ...'

'I've told you, the jewellery was stolen from me after I left the house, Greta,' Charlotte snapped.

'So you say.'

If Greta had been in the room, Charlotte would have slapped her. She took a moment to calm down. 'Marius told me the Russian army set up their headquarters in the house. They stripped it. Literally. The soldiers even used the wooden floor as firewood. But he did manage to save some of our things.'

'Ah! And would you have told me about them if I hadn't telephoned?'

'Of course.' Charlotte struggled to keep her voice on an even keel. 'He saved three of the leather-bound photograph albums from the set Opa bought in London when he was on his honeymoon. And our family Bible.'

'That's all?'

'That's all,' Charlotte reiterated firmly.

'There has to be more. The house was full, and then there were the attics. All the antiques ... Papa's family never threw out a thing. There has to be something ...'

'Papa's cupboard, Greta. If you're so keen to have a memento, I suggest you come and retrieve it.' Charlotte slammed down the receiver.

She heard the key turn in the lock and Laura peeped around the door.

'I'm sorry to disturb you but ...'

'You heard the telephone?' Charlotte's anger with her sister dissipated at the sight of her granddaughter.

'Yes.'

'It was Aunt Greta after the family heirlooms she's convinced I've stolen and hidden from her.'

'Poor you.' Laura walked over and hugged Charlotte. 'Are you hungry?'

'Yes,' Charlotte answered, determined that Greta's call wasn't going to ruin her or Laura's day. 'Let's be extravagant and have it on my balcony instead of the dining room. I'll order it be delivered at,' she glanced at the clock, 'eight. That will give me time to count to a hundred and forget Greta while I luxuriate in a long, lazy bath.'

'I finished *One Last Summer* last night,' Laura confided after they had finished eating.

'And?' Charlotte reached for the coffee pot and refilled both their cups.

'I haven't changed my mind about the misery in the Siberian Gulag. It was still unbearable.' Laura steeled herself and looked into her grandmother's eyes. 'Were you the wife in the author's dream world?'

'I'm not sure,' Charlotte said quietly.

'Did you know the author?' Laura pressed.

'Yes, I knew him.'

'And you were in love with him?'

Charlotte hesitated, just as a voice interrupted them.

'Good morning, Fräulein Charlotte von Datski. Good morning, Laura.'

Charlotte turned and looked behind her. A boat had sailed up and berthed practically beneath her balcony. Mischa dropped down the sails, tossed an anchor overboard, rose to his feet and steadied himself on the balcony railings.

'And good morning to you, Mischa,' Laura replied.

'It's a beautiful day. Come for a sail, both of you? We'll go back to Grunwaldsee, eat one of Jadwiga's lunches and ride around the lake afterwards. What do you say?'

Charlotte shook her head. 'My sailing days in anything smaller than a cruise ship are over. But Laura would love to go.'

'Oma!' Laura protested.

'What? You'd prefer to sit around here with me?'

'We were talking ...'

'And we can pick up the conversation later. Go on, off with you. Here, take my diary with you. I finished it last night.' Charlotte went to her bedside table, picked up the book and thrust it at her grand-daughter. 'It's not every day you get an invitation from a good-looking young Russian to spend time with him. If I were your age, I would jump at it.'

'You're grandmother's right, Laura. I am a very good-looking Russian and if you keep me waiting I might change my mind,' Mischa teased.

'Ever had the feeling you're being got at?' Laura left her chair. 'I'll fetch my jacket.'

Charlotte leaned over the edge of the balcony. 'She'll be with you shortly, Mischa. Would you please tell Marius that I've changed my mind about resting today? I'll drive up to see him this afternoon.'

'One of us could fetch you, Fräulein von Datski,' Mischa offered.

'No need. I'm not so decrepit, that I can't drive myself.'

Charlotte stayed on the balcony until Laura joined Mischa. She watched him raise the anchor and sails of the yacht, then head out to the centre of the lake.

The waiter knocked on the door and cleared away the remains of their breakfast. She was debating whether or not to rest for the remainder of the morning when the telephone rang. She crossed the room, steeling herself for another fight with Greta.

'Frau Datski?'

'Yes.'

'It's reception. There is a man at the desk who said he heard someone call your name outside the hotel. He was most insistent I telephone you and ask if you would be prepared to meet him, that's if you are the Charlotte von Datski who lived at Grunwaldsee.'

'I haven't used the "von" in many years,' Charlotte replied.

'What would you like me to tell him, Frau Datski?'

'What is his name?' Charlotte listened to a hurried whispered conversation but she couldn't make out a word.

'He says he knew you when you were a girl and would like to surprise you.'

Curious, Charlotte asked, 'What does he look like?'

There was suppressed laughter in the receptionist's voice. 'Distinguished, mature, grey-haired.'

Charlotte recalled the average age of the staff manning reception, and realised that 'mature' could mean anything from forty to eighty. She glanced at her watch. Ten o'clock. What could be the harm in meeting a strange man in a public area of a hotel at this time of the morning?

'Tell him I'll be in the bar in fifteen minutes.'

Charlotte took more care over her appearance in the ensuing ten minutes than she had done in years. She slipped on her favourite black skirt and copper silk blouse, applied her make-up carefully, took down and brushed out her hair before twisting it back into a knot, pushed in the amber earrings she had bought years ago to match the necklace she always wore, and freshened her perfume. Checking the time and her reflection in the mirror, she locked her balcony doors and stepped out into the corridor.

'Distinguished; mature; grey haired' was a description that could be applied to almost any man from her past, even, heaven-forbid, Georg. In her eagerness to see an old friend who remembered the Allenstein she had known and loved instead of the Olsztyn of the present, she hadn't considered the people she would have preferred not to become reacquainted with.

Wondering if there was any possibility of seeing whoever it was before he saw her, she walked cautiously into the bar.

'Charlotte, I'd know you anywhere. You haven't changed from the elegant woman who ran Grunwaldsee all through the war.' The receptionist had been right. He was distinguished with thinning grey hair.

'Don't you remember me?'

Like Marius, Charlotte recognized the voice before the features. 'Helmut?' She looked for a trace of the young man who had spent so many holidays at Grunwaldsee with her sister during the war. 'What are you doing here?'

'The same as all the other East Prussians who return. Taking a last look at the old country before I die. I couldn't believe my ears when I heard that young man call out Fräulein Charlotte von Datski by the lake. Are you here by yourself?'

'No, with my granddaughter.'

'You and Claus had grandchildren? How marvellous.'

'Not Claus's granddaughter. Laura is English.'

His face fell slightly, but he soon recovered. 'I should have remembered the English.'

'The peace treaties were signed a long time ago, Helmut.' Charlotte spoke gently. She felt he had a right to be bitter after the way Greta had jilted him.

'I'm with my wife. She's on the terrace waiting for us. You heard I married?'

'No. I'm afraid I lost touch with everyone.'

'We never saw you at any of the reunions. You did know about the Allensteiner reunions?'

'I heard, but unfortunately never had time to attend any of them.' It wasn't the truth, and Charlotte sensed Helmut knew it. No time in over half a century? She could have made the journey if she'd wanted to. It was the memories that held her back. Memories of Ruth and Emilia being herded on to a truck at gunpoint by Georg. Of her brothers dead years before their time. Of the immorality of every principle she had been taught to believe in by school, state, Hitler Youth and even her parents.

'We knew you were doing well. Your book illustrations are famous.' Helmut led her to a table. A woman turned to face them, an apprehensive look on her lined face.

Unlike Helmut, Charlotte recognized her at once. She'd lost weight, and most of her beauty, but her eyes were just as blue, if less open and trusting. She rose to her feet as they approached, drawing close to Charlotte, but holding back from an embrace.

'We've followed your career, Charlotte.'

'We even managed to stretch our budget to buy two of your paintings,' Helmut added.

'How kind,' Charlotte stammered in shock.

'Kind had nothing to do with it,' Helmut assured her, feeling the need to say something to fill the silence that had fallen between the two women. 'I know a good investment when I see one. I had no idea that you were such a talented artist. A musician, yes, but not an artist. You never played professionally after the war?'

She finally turned away from Irena and looked at him. 'I didn't have the time or the money to continue my studies, even if I had wanted to.'

'And you had a family to care for. How is young Erich?'

'Not so young any more.'

'I've often wondered if he is the Erich von Letteberg who made such a name for himself in the law courts in the sixties.'

'He is,' she answered briefly.

296

'He never used Claus's title.'

'The days of kings, princes and counts are long gone, Helmut. But Claus was proud of Erich's choice of career. Erich's younger son, also an Erich, will be going to Berlin to study law later this year,' she volunteered, happier to talk of her grandchildren than her children.

Helmut pulled out a chair for Charlotte. 'Please, sit with us. I think this calls for champagne, not coffee.'

'Please.' Irena kissed Charlotte's cheek.

Charlotte returned the pressure of Irena's hand on her arm, before taking the chair Helmut offered her. 'Erich has an older son, too, named after Claus. He has built a successful business designing and making furniture. He lives close to me in America.'

'A carpenter.' Irena smiled. 'Your father would have approved of that.'

'Yes, he would have,' Charlotte agreed, thinking of the practical side of her father's nature. 'But what about you two? How did you meet? You must tell me everything that's happened to you since the war.'

'That's a long story,' Irena said. 'I've wanted to get in touch with you for years, Charlotte, but I wasn't sure you'd want to see me after the terrible things I said to you after the war.'

'It was understandable you felt that way, after being imprisoned in a camp, separated from the children, and losing the baby and Karoline.'

'We never found her,' Helmut broke in quickly, and Charlotte knew that even after sixty years Irena hadn't entirely given up hope of finding her daughter.

'I've often thought about you, Irena.' Charlotte laid her hand over Irena's on the table.

'What a lot of wasted time. If it hadn't been for my stupidity we could have remained such good friends.' Irena leaned forward and hugged Charlotte.

'Perhaps not, Irena,' Charlotte said soberly. 'We would have constantly reminded one another of things best forgotten.'

'I could never forget ...' Irena began.

'Every German had to,' Helmut interposed. 'At least to the point where they could look forward instead of back.'

'But we've a lot to catch up on now.' Irena took a tissue from her pocket. 'I went to my father's house yesterday, stood in the street outside the synagogue and thought back to that afternoon.'

'I've never been able to forget it,' Charlotte said quietly.

'I've often wondered what would have happened if I hadn't stopped you from leaving the car.' Irena crumpled the tissue in her hand.

'We would probably have been loaded on to the truck along with the children. Babies and all.'

'We still should have done something,' Irena murmured. 'You wanted to ...'

'Who was it said, "For evil to flourish all it takes is good men to be silent."' Charlotte looked at Helmut. 'You know what happened?'

'Irena told me. She also told me that a boy you two knew, Georg Mendel, was involved in the round-up. Did you know that he went to Chile after the war? He and some of his former SS comrades proved very useful to Pinochet and his henchmen. They were expert torturers.'

'That day was the first time I had seen something for myself,' Irena confessed. 'I had never questioned the official line. That the Jews were being resettled in the East – or Africa, or Madagascar. Then Wilhelm returned from the East. You saw how changed he was.'

'He told you the truth?' Charlotte asked.

'Some of it,' Irena qualified. 'He said some things were too horrible to describe.'

'Be realistic, both of you. What could two young girls have done to stop the SS?' Helmut asked.

'Emilia survived the war,' Irena revealed. 'Nina met her in nineteen forty-six. She was on her way to Palestine.'

'And Ruth?'

Irena looked down, unable to meet Charlotte's gaze. 'We should have done something that day.'

'If you had, you wouldn't be here now to talk about it.' Helmut commented.

'Some things are worth dying for,' Irena said quietly. So quietly Charlotte wasn't sure she had heard her correctly.

'I'm not sure that all the forty-one million people who died in the war would agree with you,' Helmut interposed.

'No.' Charlotte said. 'I'm sure not all of them would, but some might, Helmut.'

'It took me years to forgive Wilhelm. But in my heart I always knew he was right,' Irena confessed. 'I just hated having to live on without him and the children we lost.'

'He would have been proud of you for building a new life for yourself and Marianna,' Charlotte sympathized.

Helmut braved the silence that had fallen over the table. 'I saw Claus in the sixties. Did he tell you?' Helmut glanced at the label on the champagne bottle the waiter had brought and nodded approval.

'He mentioned he'd met you at one of the army reunions,' Charlotte concurred.

'Would you believe we were in the same regiment, Claus for the duration and me for the last six months? But the Claus von Letteberg I met after the war wasn't the man I remembered from my trips to Grunwaldsee. It must have been hard on you, Charlotte, having to nurse him. I'd heard that the conditions in the Russian prisoner of war camps were worse than the conditions in the American camps, and I thought *they* were hell. But we didn't know the full truth about the Soviet camps until men like Claus came back. He didn't want to talk about it to me, of course.'

'Or to anyone, Helmut. But surely you of all people can understand why?'

'There is a great deal of difference between eighteen months in an American camp in the Rhineland and ten years in Siberia. Even so, all I remember from my eighteen months is wanting to die. Waking, sleeping, living in filth in the open. I had never known such cold and hunger, such a feeling of being forgotten and abandoned by the rest of the world.'

'So what did you and Claus talk about when you saw one another?' Charlotte prompted, not wanting to discuss Soviet or American prisoner of war camps.

'What every old soldier talks about at reunions: the poor decisions made by High Command. What about Greta?' Helmut took Irena's hand and patted it as though he needed to reassure her that he had no feelings left for his old fiancée. 'How did she like England?'

Charlotte tried not to sound bitter. 'You knew Greta. Like a cat she has a talent for landing on her feet.'

'Her husband really was wealthy and had a big house?'

'He didn't lie about that. It was big all right, and cold, draughty and dilapidated. He sold that, and some farm land he'd rented out, to buy a modern and luxurious house that Greta approved of. Also, he was rich enough to employ a cook and a maid, which suited Greta very well. She still places herself and her own concerns before everyone else's.'

'She didn't have children?' Helmut asked.

Charlotte shook her head. 'She always said, even as a girl, that she never wanted any.'

Helmut looked at Irena. 'I wouldn't be without our two girls.'

'Tell me about them?' Charlotte asked eagerly.

'Our daughter or Wilhelm's?' Helmut asked.

'You told Marianna who her father was?' Charlotte fought back tears.

'I didn't have to. She remembers him and our last day in Grunwaldsee,' Irena tightened her grip on Helmut's hand. 'She often says it was the end of her childhood. When I went to Bavaria after the war we both used my maiden name. Then, when Helmut and I married, we changed our names to his. You know how difficult it was for relatives of the conspirators after the war. So many people regarded us as traitors. But now she uses the name von Datski, and proudly.'

Charlotte looked away. The scars of strain and suffering were evident on Irena's face.

'I tried to get in touch with you when Helmut and I married in Munich in nineteen fifty-three but Frau Leichner had sold her house and moved on, and the new owners knew nothing about any of her lodgers,' Irena explained. 'I said so many stupid things to you after the war, Charlotte. Cruel things that I didn't mean and soon regretted. Looking back, I think I had a breakdown, but that isn't an excuse. I wanted to blame someone for all that I had endured and all that I had lost. It wasn't enough to lay the guilt on Wilhelm. He was dead. I couldn't hurt him, or make him see how much pain he had caused me and his children. But you were there. And your heart was as broken as mine. I knew that from the way you cried over Karoline. Afterwards – for a long while afterwards – I wanted to write to you. Later, when

I knew that I could contact you through your publishers, I thought about it but I wasn't sure you'd want to know me again after all the things that I'd said.'

'You should have known that I would, Irena. We were closer than most sisters,' Charlotte said feelingly.

'Marianna is an architect,' Helmut announced proudly.

'Wilhelm and Paul would have been pleased.'

'That's what we told her when she graduated.'

'And we called our daughter, Wilhelmina after one of the bravest men I have ever met.' Helmut handed Irena and Charlotte two of the glasses of champagne the waiter had poured.

'She is a doctor. Both of them are married and both have children. Mina has a girl, and Marianna twin boys.'

'Twins?' Overcome with emotion, Charlotte reached into her pocket for a tissue.

'Wilhelm and Paul. And they are just as I remember their grandfather and great-uncle. You must come and stay with us, Charlotte, and meet them.' Irena rummaged in her handbag and handed Charlotte a photograph.

Two blond smiling young men looked back at her. Irena was right; there was a strong resemblance.

'You can keep it if you like,' Irena offered. 'I have another.'

Charlotte laid it on the table in front of her. 'I am so glad that you two found happiness together,' she murmured, unable to tear her attention away from the snap.

'A toast.' Helmut lifted his glass. 'To both Wilhelms and Pauls.' After they'd lifted their glasses and drank, he said, 'You must come and see us in Frankfurt, and that isn't one of those polite, meaningless invitations people are always giving one another.'

Irena delved into her handbag and produced another tissue and a card case. Extracting a card, she gave it to Charlotte. 'Soon, perhaps on your way back from here?'

Charlotte turned it over in her hand, and read the business address on the other side. 'You own your company, Helmut?'

'After Greta told me she didn't want to know me, I went to live with my one of aunts for a while. I borrowed some jewellery from her, pawned it and bought an American truck. It probably wasn't the soldier's to sell, but a lot of people wanted things taken from one end of the country to the other. It was a way of making a living, and I was able to redeem my aunt's jewellery within a month.'

'Four years after that he had a fleet. Ten years later his company was placed in the top fifty German businesses,' Irena said.

'*Our* company,' Helmut corrected.

'Greta would be green,' Charlotte smiled.

'I'd forgotten how much you two quarrelled.'

'We've never stopped, Helmut.'

'Do you still live in America, or have you returned to Europe to look for a new home?' Irena asked.

'This trip has convinced me there's nothing to come back for.' Charlotte sipped her champagne.

'We saw the article on you in *Life* magazine.'

'I hope you didn't believe everything it said, Irena. I'm just a jobbing painter lucky to be in work.'

'Have you been to Grunwaldsee?' Irena asked.

'Yes, and Marius is still there.'

'One of the reasons we came back was to take photographs of my father's house and yours, for Marianna and Mina.' Irena set her champagne glass on the table.

'Marius would love to see you, Irena. You, too, Helmut,' Charlotte added. 'In fact, only yesterday, we talked about you and your habit of slipping people presents with the whisper, "Don't tell Greta".'

He laughed. 'Greta had a mean streak. She hated to see me giving anything away, even if it was something she didn't want.'

'Marius has worked hard to look after Grunwaldsee. He even put memorial plaques in the church for Paul, Wilhelm, Mama and Minna. And the new owner has done a first-class job of restoring the house. Be prepared to see it just the way it was. Tomorrow I'm going to meet him.' Charlotte gripped Irena's hand. 'Come with me?'

She looked at her husband. 'Could we?'

'If Charlotte is sure that we will be welcome.'

'I am.' Charlotte left the table. 'If you'll excuse me, I have some things to do.'

'Of course, but you'll have dinner with us here tonight?' Irena asked.

'Yes, I'd like that.'

'We'll meet you in the dining room at eight.'

'I'll be there.' Charlotte kissed Irena and then Helmut. 'It's so good to see you again. Both of you.'

Charlotte paused as she crossed the foyer. The kiosk that sold gold, silver and amber jewellery glittered and sparkled seductively beneath the reflected light of a crystal chandelier. She studied the displays of earrings, necklaces, brooches and bracelets, then stepped inside. Further inspection revealed the pieces to be finely crafted, of good quality but expensive, as was almost every artefact manufactured in Poland with the German market in mind.

She looked around until she found a tray of more traditionally wrought pieces. Attracting the attention of the assistant, she began to buy. The final bill made the assistant blanch, but Charlotte handed over her credit card with equanimity. Asking the girl to parcel all the purchases in one box, she took a slip of paper from the notepad used to total the bills and wrote: '*To Greta, in recompense for the jewellery the Russians stole from me at the end of the war*'.

She hesitated. To write '*Love Charlotte*' would be hypocritical. Instead she settled *for*: '*With all good wishes, Charlotte*'.

Chapter 23

BACK IN her room, Charlotte glanced at her reflection in the mirror. Her face was pale, accentuating the shadows beneath her eyes. Was it lack of sleep? Or was the cancer winning the battle raging within her body? She suddenly felt bone-weary, too exhausted to face routine living, let alone any more trauma or heartbreaking memories. It would be so easy to buy a novel, lie on the bed and wait for death, no longer the bogeyman of childhood, but, at best, a welcome friend that would take her to the people she loved and, at worst bring a longed for, and much needed rest.

Again, she sensed her body was telling her she had very little time left. There was no mistaking the message or its urgency, but there was no sense or logic behind it. She wasn't even in any real pain.

One thing she was certain of, after meeting Helmut and Irena, was that she wasn't quite as prepared as she thought she was. She had organized the settlement of her estate and the disposal of her most personal and precious belongings, but there were still letters to be written. To Wilhelm's grandsons, his and Paul's namesakes, whom she would never meet. An apology to Claus and Carolyn for returning to her homeland without them and deceiving them about a second trip they'd never make — at least, not together. To the executor of her will, Samuel Goldberg, to change the funeral arrangements she had made for cremation and the scattering of her ashes in Connecticut. And, to her immediate heirs, her sons and grandchildren, that they allow her to be buried without ceremony in the place she had always belonged — Grunwaldsee.

And Greta? Should she add something to the cryptic note she had put in with the jewellery? Perhaps not. Maybe some things were best left, because she didn't doubt that if she did offer Greta the olive branch of forgiveness from beyond the grave, her sister wouldn't understand what she had done to offend her in the first place.

She picked up the telephone and dialled the number Marius had given her for the main house. It rang for a few minutes before a strange man picked it up. Fortunately, he spoke German and, after asking her to repeat her name twice, fetched Marius. Judging by the amount of background noise – banging, thumping and masculine swearing, in Polish and Russian – she assumed the new owner's furniture was being moved in.

'Fräulein Charlotte, is anything wrong?' Marius gasped breathlessly down the line.

'Not at all, Marius, I'm sorry to disturb you. Please accept my apologies. Something has come up this afternoon and I am unable to visit you ... yes, thank you, I will be with you tomorrow morning ... I am quite well, it's just that business has caught up with me, and I have letters to write ... Laura? ... Yes, if she's there, I'd love to speak to her. Thank you.'

Charlotte carried the telephone over to the table she'd moved in front of the open window. It was close enough to breathe in the air from the lake and feel the warmth of the sun, and out of the breeze that would have ruffled her papers.

'Oma?' Laura was even more breathless than Marius had been, and Charlotte realized he must have called her in from outside. 'Mischa is going to drive me back to the hotel. I'll be with you shortly ...'

'No, darling. Please don't interrupt your day. I'm terribly busy.'

'Busy?' Laura repeated. 'Aren't you resting?'

'Some friends heard Mischa calling to me this morning and recognized my name. They made enquiries with reception and asked the staff to contact me. I haven't seen them since shortly after the war, so we have a lot of catching-up to do.' Charlotte felt it wasn't entirely a lie.

'Oma ...'

'I really am fine, Laura. I've arranged to have dinner with them in the hotel restaurant at eight. You can join us if you like,' she added as an afterthought. 'But if you'd prefer to stay with Brunon and Mischa, that's fine, too. I like to think of you enjoying yourself with young people.'

'Brunon's girlfriend is here from Warsaw. Mischa is organizing a barbecue for tonight ...'

'Then you must go.' Charlotte was relieved that Laura wouldn't be there to put any constraints on a conversation that was bound to be centred on events that had happened long before she had been born.

'These people, can I meet them tomorrow?' Laura asked.

'They're going to visit Grunwaldsee. Tell Marius ... tell him Irena von Datski is coming home and looking forward to seeing him again.'

'A cousin?'

'Sister-in-law.'

'One of your brother's wives ...'

'There's far too much to tell you on the telephone, darling. We'll talk later. Enjoy yourself with Brunon and Mischa this evening, and give Marius and Jadwiga my love.'

Charlotte finished writing her last letter at six o'clock that evening. She folded the paper neatly into three, opened an envelope, pushed it in and sealed it. She placed it on top of the pile on the table in front of her, leaned forward and flicked through them.

They were in no particular order, and she glanced at the names she'd written on the outside, trying to think if there was anything that she had forgotten to say to any of them, or if there was anyone she had left out.

Laura – to tell her that she had left her all her jewellery, which she was free to sell or wear as she chose, but she would prefer her to keep the amber necklace, wear it occasionally and remember not only her, but Sascha. Also she entrusted her diary and all the paintings and furniture in her house to her, as well as the sketches of Grunwaldsee and Sascha. And one of the three photograph albums that Marius had kept for her.

Claus – to tell him that she had left him one of the albums as well as all her land in Connecticut and her house; but not her furniture, paintings and jewellery, which she had left to Laura.

Samuel – to inform him of the new arrangements she had made for the disposal of her body. And, along with her gratitude for his

306

sixty-year friendship, all the paintings she had loaned to London galleries to do with as he wished.

Irena — she smiled when she saw her sister-in-law's name. If there was such a thing as fate, surely it had brought Helmut and Irena to Olsztyn and this particular hotel at the same time as her; the third photograph album that Marius had saved, together with the family Bible so Marianna's sons' names could be written below hers, their missing Aunt Karoline's, and Irena and Wilhelm's baby son, who had died in Ravensbruck.

To her sons, Erich and Jeremy, and her youngest grandsons, Luke and Erich, simple goodbyes.

Marius — she hadn't expected to find Marius, but there was over fifty thousand dollars in her personal account, and she asked Samuel to see that he, Jadwiga and Brunon received it.

Greta — the jewellery she had bought in the hotel gift shop.

To the trust fund set up in the name of Peter Borodin — the residue of her estate, all her paintings that remained ungifted and unsold, and all her future worldwide royalties which the IRS had estimated as a little over six million dollars.

She placed all the envelopes on top of the parcels she had wrapped inside her empty suitcase, which stood on the luggage rack next to the wardrobe.

She opened the wardrobe, lifted out a plain black evening dress and jacket she had bought for a dinner held in Claus's honour the year he had been released from Russia, and hooked it on to the door before going into the bathroom to run her bath.

Laura leaned over the side of the yacht and trailed her fingers in the lake. The sun had set hours before, yet the water was warm, the sky above them pierced with what looked like a million glittering stars. She felt light-headed from too much wine, song and even enjoyment. It had been a long time since she had taken time out for a holiday, and even longer since she had gone through an entire day without sparing a single thought for work.

'It's been fun and it was a lovely barbecue, thank you,' she said to Mischa, who was crouched in the stern, moving the tiller in an attempt to catch what little breeze there was.

'It was a good day,' he agreed, 'and when my grandfather comes tomorrow it will be an even better one. He's a one-man party.'

'I look forward to meeting him. Isn't Brunon's girlfriend sweet?'

'Very,' he agreed dryly. 'They make a lovely young couple.'

'That sounds patronizing and sarcastic.'

'Does it?' He filched a cigar from his pocket, pushed it into his mouth and, holding and striking his lighter in his free hand, lit it. 'Don't they make you feel a hundred years old?'

Laura looked up. His eyes were dark in the moonlight and it was difficult to make out his expression. 'At least a hundred and ten,' she answered flippantly. 'But then I've felt that old since I turned thirty.'

'The third decade is the cynical one. I should know, I'm thirty-three. But as you said, the girl is sweet and they do make a nice young couple. I have no doubt that in a year, or maybe even less, the Catholic priest will be marrying them. She'll be in a white dress with a wreath of rosebuds on her head and a bouquet in her hand, and he'll be dressed in a dark suit and a white shirt with a stiff collar, looking very grand and very uncomfortable.'

'There are worse fates in life.'

'Definitely. I've nothing against marriage, especially in this day and age of easy divorce.'

'You *are* cynical.' She watched him exhale, and the cigar smoke hung, blue and thick in the air between them. 'Smoking is very bad for your health.'

'But sometimes, like now, at the end of a long, sunny and pleasant day, it's fun.' The end of his cigar glowed in an arc as he lifted his hand to his mouth again. 'Marius is very excited about seeing your great-aunt again. What is she like?'

'I've never met her,' Laura confessed.

'I thought I didn't know much about my family, you seem to know even less about yours. Weren't you ever curious enough to ask your grandmother about her family and her life here before the war?'

'One of the reasons I came here was to find out about my grandmother's past. We haven't done much talking as yet, but, as you saw, she gave me her diary to read this morning. I intend to start tonight.'

'Are you pleased or disappointed with Grunwaldsee?'

'It's not what I expected. From what little my grandmother had said, I assumed it was a small farm, and newspaper reports led me to believe Poland would be poverty-stricken.'

'Don't let appearances fool you, it is. But it won't be for long the way everyone is working.'

'So how *did* your grandfather make enough money to buy and renovate Grunwaldsee?' she probed.

'How do you think?'

'I have no idea.'

'He didn't ask my father to give him any Mafia money.'

'Are you never serious?' she countered irritably.

'How do you know I'm not being serious? But, on the other hand, my grandfather did take many, many bribes when he worked for the KGB.' He laughed when she frowned. 'You English, you're so naive when it comes to the Russian way of doing things. It's easy to tease you.'

'You must admit: one minute you were all Communists with no personal possessions, the next there's a glut of millionaires.'

'My grandfather mined gold. In Siberia.'

'Do you never speak the truth?'

'Only about trivial things. But unlike you stiff-upper-lip British, we do talk about our families and the dead all the time in Russia. Especially to those in mourning. We think it comforts them to know that the people they loved are not forgotten. After all, death is a natural state and we'll all be in it one day.'

'Spoken like a true melancholy Slav.'

'And what would you know about melancholy Slavs?'

'I've read some of *One Last Summer*.'

'That was the gold my grandfather mined in Siberia. He wrote it.'

'*Really?*' Mischa was such a strange mixture of sarcasm and flip-pancy, Laura wasn't certain whether or not to believe him.

'He says that every life should be spiced with a little gloom, if only to provide a counter-measure for happiness. However, he curses the fates for tipping the whole spice pot into his. But he still insists it's impossible to fully enjoy the good times when you have nothing to contrast them with. And if you haven't experienced tragedy and misery you can't identify with the poor, and if you can't do that you won't give to charity, which is why he bought Grunwaldsee and put it into a trust.'

'Who is going to benefit from this trust?'

'Me, for a start,' Mischa smiled. 'I'm moving into a self-contained apartment in the main house.'

'That doesn't sound very charitable to me.'

'I lost my mother when I was six, so I am half a deserving orphan. But the trust is going to need a great deal of money if it is to continue. Grunwaldsee is expensive to run. That's why my grandfather and I are still talking to my father. He has more money than he knows what to do with. Occasionally he siphons a little away from his gambling dens, drug rings and brothels to donate to charity.'

'Now you're laughing at me.'

'Not at all.'

'You're a fine one to talk about charity. Between your sailing boat, sports car, horses, summerhouse and renovations of Grunwaldsee, what are you doing to alleviate poverty?'

'Not enough.' He inhaled on his cigar for the last time, jabbed it into the lake, then carefully dropped the stub into his pocket. 'But you see what a caring soul I am; I don't want to poison the fish. And here is the jetty of your hotel.' He dropped the sail and tossed the anchor overboard.

'Thank you for bringing me back. I enjoyed the journey. Would you like to come in for a drink?'

'At this hour everything will be closed.'

'Not the mini-bar in my room.'

'I've heard about you English girls. How you seduce and discard men. I don't intend to become your toy, not even for one night, Fräulein Laura.' He held out his hand, she took it and he helped her on to the jetty. When she was standing on it, he pulled up the anchor and the sail. The dinghy was already edging into the centre of the lake when he called out, 'Goodnight, Fräulein Laura. See you in the morning.'

SATURDAY, 28 MAY 1988

I stayed for a while before I realized that there was nothing we could say to one another that we didn't already know. If I spoke to him I would only succeed in opening old wounds and making new ones that would pain both of us.

I watched him sign a few more books, then I walked away.

I did not look back at him again.

Laura jumped, startled when the alarm clock on the bedside table rang. She realized that she had spent the whole night reading her grandmother's diary, and she had told Marius that she and her grandmother would be ready at ten so he could drive them to Grunwaldsee for lunch.

She pulled back the drapes, opened the door and walked out on to the balcony. The sun was strong, the concrete warm beneath her bare feet. She looked over the wall. Charlotte was sitting close to the wall in a narrow strip of shade, a smile on her face, a cup of coffee in front of her.

'Good morning, Oma.' Laura sat on the wall and swung her legs over to Charlotte's side. 'Did you have a good dinner last night?'

'Very good,' Charlotte smiled.

'Marius was very excited when I told him that Irena von Datski would be visiting Grunwaldsee today. He said she was your brother's wife.'

'She was, and she is looking forward to meeting you and telling you all about your second cousins. She and her husband Helmut will be joining us at the house after lunch.'

'Have you been awake for long?'

'Not long. Isn't it a beautiful morning?'

Laura looked at the lake. 'It is.' She turned back to Charlotte. 'I read your diary.'

'All of it?'

'All of it,' Laura confirmed.

'Then you couldn't have slept.'

'I didn't.'

'You must be exhausted.'

'No, I'm not. And now I understand why you made the decisions you did. Especially why you left grandfather and my father.'

'That decision wasn't easy, Laura. But Claus needed me more than they did.'

'Mischa told me last night that his grandfather wrote *One Last Summer*.' Uneasy when Charlotte remained silent, Laura added, 'He's always making jokes, I wasn't sure whether or not to believe him.'

'I've suspected it.'

'Then Mischa's grandfather is your Sascha?'

'No. That much I do know.' Charlotte trembled as she rose from her chair.

'We don't have to go to Grunwaldsee this morning.'

'Yes, we do,' Charlotte contradicted. 'I want to meet Mischa's grandfather again, yet I am terrified of facing the truth: that the one great love of my life was a one-sided pretence. That Sascha saw I was vulnerable and naive, and used me to save his life and those of his men. And despite everything he did for me, including saving my life in the forest, I never meant as much to him as he did to me.'

'The diary ...'

'Was written by a lonely, unhappily-married young woman, who saw only what she wanted to.'

Unable to offer comfort, or comment on Charlotte's fear, Laura said, 'I also understand now why Aunt Greta hates all Russians. Uncle Erich told me once what they did when they invaded East Prussia. The rape, the murder, the brutality ...'

'What I wrote in my diary was the truth, Laura.' Charlotte broke in. 'But the Russians behaved no differently from the Germans who invaded Russia in nineteen forty-one. And, unfortunately, no differently from the way armies are behaving in half a dozen countries in the world right now.' She looked her granddaughter in the eye. 'Given the choice, all most people want to do is live quietly and peacefully, surrounded by their families and loved ones. Preferably out of poverty and want, in order to bring up their children decently so they can look forward to a future worth living.'

'If only everyone could do that.'

'Wouldn't it be wonderful? But that's enough philosophising for one morning.'

'I am so dreadfully sorry, Oma.'

'You can't be sorry, not for things that happened before you were born. And, on the whole, I have had a very good life. Much longer and better than most people on this earth. Now, go and get changed out of those Mickey Mouse pyjamas, or Marius will think you're a refugee from Disneyland.'

An old man ran down the steps of the main house the minute Marius drove past the main gates of Grunwaldsee. Tall and slim, his age was only apparent when he walked into the direct sunlight that streamed into the yard. Walking a few steps behind him was Mischa.

He opened the front passenger door as soon as Marius stopped the car.

Charlotte stepped out, stood in front of him and stared, before hugging him.

Sensing that neither of them was wanted, Mischa escorted Laura into the main house.

'You have quite a grandson, Leon.' Charlotte laid her hand on top of the car in an effort to steady herself. 'I should have known at once. Tall, thin, black hair ...'

'It's been a long time since I had a full head of hair.' He ran his fingers over his thinning grey scalp. 'I keep warning Mischa that this is what he has to look forward to in old age.' He held out his arm. 'Would it demean you to walk with an old man who first came to Grunwaldsee as a subhuman Russian prisoner of war, Gräfin von Letteberg?'

'I never thought of you or any of your fellow soldiers as subhuman, Leon.'

'Sorry, bad joke,' he apologized. 'I owe you my life.'

'What little I did was the least one fellow human being could do for another.'

'You gave us food, soap, clothes and saw that we were kept warm in winter, and you risked your life and the lives of your family to do so. People were shot for less.'

She faltered when they reached the first step. Suddenly faint and breathless, she leaned heavily on his arm.

'I think you need to sit down.'

313

'It's the heat.'

'Or the shock of seeing Russians moving their furniture into Grunwaldsee,' he commented, as a man walked past them carrying a stack of chairs.

'I've seen the downstairs rooms. I don't think many von Datskis would disapprove of your renovations.'

'When I was finally released from the camps and given a general amnesty, I found myself an extremely wealthy man. My London and American agents had opened bank accounts for me. I looked at all that money and knew that I could never take it for myself. I talked it over with Mischa, and it was his idea to use it to set up the Peter Borodin foundation to fund an academy for young musicians. A place where pupils could come with their teachers and play with others, with a view to making a truly international orchestra. It seemed like a good idea. Music is an international language. And it was music that first brought you and Sascha together in Russia.'

'I read the interview you gave *Time* Magazine when you set up the foundation, but I had no idea that Grunwaldsee was to be the site of the academy.'

'Neither did I – then. But I knew you approved of the idea of the academy because of the generous donation you made to the trust fund. And I've seen the details of the bequest you've made to the trust in your will.'

'You saw my will?'

'I'm treasurer of the trust.'

'It's a wonderful idea, especially the scholarships for refugee children who don't have a country. I can't think of a better way to combat the kind of prejudices that flourished during the war or a better use for Grunwaldsee.'

'When I made a pilgrimage here shortly after my release and discovered it was for sale, it seemed like fate. But there is still a lot of work to do.' He waved his hand in the direction of the old cottages that she, Laura and even Marius had assumed were being turned into hotel rooms. 'We won't be operational until we have a place for the children to sleep. Has Mischa told you that he is a gifted musician?'

'No.'

'We have appointed a director to run the academy, but Mischa will be one of his assistants, and as soon as the dormitory block is finished the first classes will arrive. Hopefully, by the end of the month. Also, we have asked UNICEF to nominate suitable candidates for the refugee places.'

'It would be wonderful if there could be a day when the world no longer has any refugees.'

'I doubt if it will dawn until you and I are long gone.' He led her into the drawing room, empty no longer, but filled with comfortably upholstered chairs and small tables. 'Would you like coffee or a glass of wine? Mischa has a couple of bottles here that he has been saving for a special occasion, and I can't think of anything more special than this.'

'Wine would be lovely, thank you.' She sat in a chair and looked around. Understandably, the furniture had been chosen more for its strength and durability than its appearance, but nothing could destroy the peaceful atmosphere of the beautiful room. For the first time she looked to the future of her old home instead of the past, seeing the room crowded with students, discussing music, art, politics, poetry – setting the world to rights, just as every generation did in its turn, and hopefully making a better job of it than their predecessors.

'We were only given permission to house the academy here eight weeks ago.'

'And if it had been refused?' she asked.

'We would have had to grease more pockets.'

'Sascha used to say you'd joke with Satan at the gates of hell.'

'Who's joking?' He opened the bottle. 'Now that most of the details have been finalized, I confidently predict that every bed in this place will be filled as soon as it is ready. At the last count, Mischa has managed to offer places to two hundred children from fifteen countries during the coming year. Not a bad start.' He filled her glass and laid it on the table beside her. 'What do you think of our Mischa?'

'He has very familiar blue eyes.'

'You noticed.' He lifted his glass. 'To your very good health and happiness, Grafin von Letteberg.'

Charlotte held back. 'I'd rather toast Sascha, Leon.'

He touched his glass to hers. 'To Sascha.'

'Can we talk about him?' she asked quietly after they both drank.

He took the chair next to hers. 'Where would you like me to begin?'

'The clearing in the woods. I don't understand why they didn't shoot you all then and there.'

'None of us did at the time. Later we heard that Stalin's son had been a POW in Germany. Hoping to use him as barter for high-ranking German prisoners, the Germans had given him whatever he wanted: food, drink, women. As a result when he was liberated, he told his father that no Russian soldier who had been in German hands could be trusted. So they sent us to Siberia for "political re-education" and hard labour.'

'I heard a shot as I was running away,' Charlotte said.

'The officer who was holding a gun to Sascha's head saw one of the German women move. He fired at her.'

'Marius said they marched you back to Grunwaldsee?'

'Yes, at the time we were simply glad that we weren't lying in the snow alongside your mother and her maid.' Leon's eyes clouded with the pain of remembering.

'You were all sent to prison camps?'

'Yes. They didn't bother with trials. We'd been caught behind enemy lines, it was obvious we'd been prisoners, and, thanks to you, we didn't look as though we'd been ill-treated or starved.'

'How long were your sentences?'

'Don't you know the old joke about the prisoner who complained he'd been sentenced to five years in Siberia for nothing, only to be told that he had to be mistaken? The sentence for "nothing" was ten years. Sascha and I were given a lot longer.'

Charlotte covered her mouth with her hand.

'All we wanted to do was to go home and see our families, but every one of us was given a one-way ticket east.'

'After all you suffered ...'

'There was nothing to do but accept the inevitable. Summon the legendary streak of fatalism in the Russian soul. But you have read *One Last Summer*, Charlotte. You know what happened.'

Chapter 24

CHARLOTTE FORCED herself to return to that snow-filled day in January 1945. Once again Sascha's shouts rang in her ears as she ran for her life, away from the corpse-strewn, blood-stained clearing in the woods.

'I've never forgotten the last time I saw Sascha.' She looked inward and conjured the final image she had of her lover. 'He was kneeling in the snow, an officer was holding a gun to his head, but he never stopped shouting for me to run ... and I ran because it was what Sascha wanted me to do ... but I've regretted it ever since, Leon.' She turned to him. 'If I had stayed in that clearing we could have been shot together.'

'Sascha wouldn't have been shot, but you would have been and you were carrying his child,' Leon reminded her. 'That would have been one hell of a burden for Sascha to carry into Siberia.'

'He died anyway.'

'Not until nineteen forty-seven and his nights, when he was in his dream world with you, were good nights.'

'I heard that shot when I was out of sight of the clearing and I was so sure that the officer had killed Sascha. I believed he had died there, until I heard about a book called *One Last Summer* that had been smuggled out of the Russian gulag into the West. I bought a copy as soon as it was published, years before you came to New York on that publicity tour. And, when I read it, I began to hope.'

'Sascha and I never spoke of the journey to Siberia once we reached the camp. It was simply something to be endured, which was why I didn't mention it in the forward to the book.'

'It must have been horrific.'

'A journey to the worst Catholic hell could not be as terrible, although it might have been warmer. There were hardly any trains because they were needed elsewhere, so we spent days and sometimes weeks in transit camps. There were never any buildings to house us. On good days we had only one meal of watery soup; on the bad days, nothing. There were more bad days than good and without shelter it is hard to survive a Russian winter. By the time we reached the logging camp which was our final destination, only four of us were alive out of the twelve who'd left Grunwaldsee.'

'I'm so sorry, Leon.'

'There were times in the camp when I thought the ones who had died had been lucky. As punishment for shooting a superior officer and helping an enemy to escape, Sascha was sentenced to political re-education and hard labour for life. As his lieutenant I was given forty years.'

'It was my fault,' Charlotte cried out.

'Nothing our countrymen did to Sascha after we last saw you was your fault, Charlotte. I expected you to ask me about him that day you bought *One Last Summer* in New York. Why didn't you?'

'Because neither of us could talk for crying at the time, and I didn't want to make a scene. I had nursed a small slim hope that Sascha still lived since the day I first heard about *One Last Summer*. After I read it, I was sure that he had written it. When I heard that Peter Borodin was touring the States I decided to contact him through the publisher. But before I posted the letter I wrote, I saw an interview you gave on television, and I knew that Sascha was dead and that you, not he, had written the book ...'

'Charlotte—'

'Please, Leon, let me finish. When I saw you sitting in that book-store I knew I wasn't strong enough to hear how Sascha had died. Just the idea of his suffering ...'

Leon reached out and took her hand in his.

She looked up into his eyes. 'In my heart I knew that Sascha had died a long time before then. I had a breakdown in February nineteen forty-seven. I had Erich to care for but I didn't want to live, not even for him. And, looking back, I think it was connected in some way to Sascha. I couldn't stop thinking about him, and I knew even then that I would never see him again.'

'February ...' Leon fell quiet for moment. 'Sascha went to sleep as usual on the night of Saturday, the twenty-third of February nineteen forty-seven, and never woke up. I like to think he simply stayed in that other life he dreamed of every night and spoke to me about in such detail. He would have written the book himself if he'd been allowed pencil and paper. Instead we spoke of it every night and he made me commit it to memory. Even when I said I was too tired to listen he talked. It was almost as though he knew that I would survive and he wouldn't.'

'Then *One Last Summer*—'

'I've just told you, Sascha wrote every single word,' Leon said firmly. 'It was his story, his and yours. I simply held the pen that put his words on paper. And I swear that, wherever he is, he looked over my shoulder when I wrote that book. If I deviated by as much as one word, he'd snap at me, forcing me to remember those long Siberian winter nights when he made me listen to him and repeat his words, over and over again, although all I wanted to do was sleep. That is why I couldn't keep any of the royalties. They weren't mine. They were his – and yours.'

'The book really was his?'

'I swear it. Not on a Bible because, like Sascha, I am an old Communist and atheist, but I'll swear on *Das Kapital* if you like.'

'I believe you, Leon,' she smiled.

'When I was pardoned I wanted to tell the world that Sascha had written it, but my publishers wouldn't let me. A live author can talk, excite interest and media attention. A dead one will warrant one article at best. The book was a success in the West, it was about to be published in Russia. Everyone wanted to meet a survivor of the infamous gulags. Mischa had seen the royalty statements and persuaded me to keep up the pretence for the sake of the Peter Borodin foundation. The name on the book was neither mine nor Sascha's, but, as Mischa said, the story belonged to every Russian soldier who had been held prisoner first by the Germans then their own countrymen. What mattered was the use the royalties were put to. He was most persuasive.'

'I think Sascha would have approved of what you did with the money.'

'Your donation meant a great deal to me. Not because of the money but because I knew that you had given the idea behind the foundation your blessing. Did you know that I went looking for you before you came to that signing?'

'No.'

'I saw you.'

'Where? When?' Her hand began to shake.

'In New York.' He took the wine glass gently from her and set it on the table in front of them. 'It was at an art exhibition; you were with a young man. He looked so like your husband, I wondered if he had been frozen in time.'

'You saw my grandson Claus. He looks exactly like my husband, but he is nothing like him in character. He is a carpenter.'

'A carpenter is a better occupation than a soldier,' Leon observed.

'You should have spoken to me.'

'You looked so busy, so happy with your friends, I didn't like to interrupt.'

'You haven't said anything about your wife. Did you go back to her after you left the camp?'

'Ludmilla?' Leon laughed. 'She would sooner move in with the devil than me. Did Sascha tell you that he and I had been friends since we were three years old?'

'Yes.' Memories came flooding back of sitting in the tack room, listening as Sascha talked about his life before the war.

'Sascha and I did everything together – school, music college, even marrying our girlfriends on the day we received our call-up papers; one or the other of us thought we should have someone to come back to when we returned as heroes. Not a bright idea, but war is the cause of many mistakes big and small. Sascha and I both enjoyed a week's honeymoon and marched away. I didn't see Ludmilla again for forty years. Sascha never saw Zoya again.'

'If you never went back to your wife, was there someone else?'

'Dozens,' Leon laughed again. 'But there was never one special person. Not like you and Sascha. And Ludmilla wasn't the sort to sit around and wait. She wasted no time in making a life for herself even before the war ended, and believe me, that one knows how to live. But after *One Last Summer* was published legally in the Soviet Union, she looked after the royalties, and well. She also looked after our son and, after Zoya died of starvation during the war, Sascha's daughter. Zoya called her Alexandra after Sascha, and she and my son Alexei grew up

320

together. In Russia children who had been born during the war, and grew up during the Cold War, learned to live for the moment. The memory of what the Germans had done to Russia and the Russians in the war hung over the whole country. We all expected to be turned into clumps of radioactive dust any moment by an atomic bomb lobbed at us from America. Perhaps it was different for Westerners.'

'Not different at all,' Charlotte said seriously. 'We were just as afraid of you as you were of us.'

'Sascha's daughter started drinking. Ludmilla tried to stop her but it proved impossible. My worthless son Alexei didn't help. Even before Alexandra drank he saw no reason why he shouldn't go from one woman to another. He has had so many wives and lovers I have lost count. But one good thing did come out of the short time they spent together. Mischa is Sascha's grandson as well as mine. But you knew that from his eyes. It's quite extraordinary how some things can skip a generation. Alexandra didn't look at all like Sascha and her eyes were grey.'

'Ludmilla brought up Mischa?'

'We may not get on and she may not want me around, but she is a good woman. She saw the way Alexandra lived – endless men, drinking parties, sometimes disappearing for days at a time – and took Mischa to live with her when he was two years old. Sometimes Alexandra came and took him away, but Mischa always found his way back to Ludmilla. It was no wonder; she was the only one who fed and clothed him and kept him clean. Alexandra died when Mischa was six, Ludmilla sent him to school and, when his teachers discovered he was musical, she badgered them until they sent him to a conservatory. We both went to his graduation. At twenty-five he became the youngest professor ever appointed to the conservatory. They will be sorry to lose him, but, as I said, the idea to turn Grunwaldsee into an international academy was his, and I would have been tempted to ask him to work here even if he wasn't my grandson. He really is gifted, not just as a musician but a teacher.'

'Does he know about Sascha and me?'

'Yes. I told him the story behind *One Last Summer*.'

Charlotte's eyes darkened in pain. 'Was Sascha buried in a common grave in Siberia?'

'The winters are long and hard in Siberia, and, as I said, he died in

February. We had to wait for the spring thaw to bury him. I managed to get assigned to the burial detail and dug a separate grave for him away from the common pit. I marked the spot so I would be able to find it again.'

Picking up her glass, she left her chair and walked to the window that overlooked the woods around the lake. 'Thank you, Leon.'

'For buying your old home?'

'For saving it from dereliction,' she contradicted.

'And for telling you how Sascha died when you had already guessed?'

'For telling me what I wanted to hear. That the only man I ever loved truly loved me. And that our love was as unselfish as I always believed it was.'

'I find it difficult to believe that you could ever doubt it, Charlotte. You and Sascha had something few people ever find in life. I envied you every time I saw you together. One look across the yard at Grunwaldsee between you two was like ten hours of conversation between most people. And it was memories of you that kept him alive through all the horror and misery of the gulag.'

'Until he gave up.'

'No, until he was able to go into that other world he dreamed of every night.' He left his chair and joined her at the window. 'I'll drive you down to the summerhouse.'

'Why?'

'You'll see when you reach there. I'll bring the other bottle of wine. Then we can sit there and toast his memory – and you. I fell a little in love with you, too, you know.'

'Leon—'

'But don't flatter yourself. You were the only presentable woman of my own age I came close to in almost forty years.'

Leon stopped the car in the lane outside the summerhouse. He opened the door for Charlotte and offered her his arm, but didn't lead her inside. Instead they walked down to the bank of the lake, to a spot screened by trees and bushes, where you couldn't be seen except by someone swimming or boating or standing on the opposite bank. A concrete bench had been set there and Charlotte sank down on it. It was only then that she saw the stone at her feet:

ALEXANDER (SASCHA) BELETSKY
1921–47
WHO WILL FOR EVER BE PYTOR BORODIN TO ALL WHO READ
ONE LAST SUMMER.
AND NOW THESE THREE REMAIN, FAITH, HOPE AND LOVE,
BUT THE GREATEST OF THESE IS LOVE.

'After the amnesty I applied for permission to return to Siberia,' Leon said. 'I didn't ask for permission to bring him here. I was afraid that I wouldn't get it. I'd made his coffin myself so I knew it would stand the test of a few years. I unearthed it late at night, put it in a packing case, and bribed the guard to take it as freight on a train back to Moscow and from Moscow to here. Mischa, Marius and I buried him here at night. We didn't ask permission from the authorities to bury him here either, in case it was refused. The stone came from the mason who worked on the von Datski tomb. I know the text is biblical, from Corinthians—'

'Communists now read the Bible?' Charlotte smiled.

'It was the only book available in the camp. The Christians who had been sent for re-education always managed to smuggle in copies. Sascha and I were both ardent Communists before the war, but we both stopped believing in man-made creeds long before we reached the camp. It's hard to believe in an ideology that's destroyed your life. And we were both too cynical to believe in an omnipotent, all-caring Christian God after living through the war. But no other words seemed as appropriate as these for Sascha. I know that for him the greatest thing *was* love. And there is his symbol of regeneration and life after death.' He pointed to a sapling planted next to the grave.

'A weeping willow.' Charlotte gazed at the branches that brushed the surface of the lake.

'I thought it appropriate.'

Charlotte turned back to the stone.

'As I said, I like to think that, like the hero of his book, he went to sleep and stayed in that other world. And it was real to him, Charlotte. Much more real than the camp. He watched your daughter grow and change day by day, celebrated her birthdays with you, sat up with you the night your son was born ...'

She still had one question to ask. 'You don't think he was haunted by the memory of a young pregnant woman standing in the snow-covered yard of Grunwaldsee screaming, "Murderer?"'

'No, Charlotte, I don't. I know every memory that he carried of you, and that wasn't one of them.'

Silence fell, and they were both content simply to sit – and remember.

'We have been here for over an hour, Charlotte.' Leon rose to his feet. 'You'd like to stay here a little longer, alone?'

'Please, Leon.'

He reached out and touched her hand. 'You're cold.'

She looked up at him. 'Leon ...'

'I know.' He looked down at the grave. 'There is space to put another name there someday, but I hope it won't be chiselled there for many years.'

'Thank you, Leon. There was never a need for many words be-tween us either.'

'I'll be back later with Mischa and Laura. You would like Laura to see this?'

'Yes.'

'She knows ...'

'Everything, Leon.'

Charlotte heard music drifting down from the small drawing room in the house. Ghostly music played on the piano by her other younger self. The Shostakovich Sascha had loved and written out for her on a piece of feed wrapper.

A shadow blocked the sun from view. Blue eyes looked down into hers. She saw the slow, familiar smile she loved, and took the hand that was offered to her.

She is everything to me, this woman I love. The air I breathe, the earth beneath my feet, food, drink – all pale into insignificance when set beside my need for her. She clings to me for a moment, we kiss silently. Everything that needs to be said between us has long been said. Arm in arm, we wander back through the garden into the house. She walks up the stairs. I blow out the lamps in the downstairs rooms, close the doors, then follow her.

324